An Iraqi woman must either trust the Americans or support the insurgency.

Crossing the Tigress

A story of desperation, betrayal and survival.

To my father...

I dedicate this book to my late father, George B. Olson. He shaped me more than any other person, and therefore, part of him and who he was is intertwined in the thoughts, philosophy and style reflected in my writing.

PREFACE

We survived the Kuwait War
tip toes barely reaching ground
dangling from a rope
wounded, but neck unbroken—
kicked by the convicted man

Why didn't the hangman
have mercy and snap our necks?
Why prolong despair?
–Sahar

Every person associated with war has a unique perspective. This story is from a point of view you may have yet to hear. While in Iraq in 2003-2004, as part of the Coalition Provisional Authority's Ministry of Health team, I worked with a staff of forty Iraqi architects, engineers and healthcare providers. I attempted to write this story from their perspective.

Being a part of the effort to establish the reconstruction program for the Iraqi healthcare system, I saw how the effort was shaped, executed and portrayed. But more importantly, I saw how the impact of the war on the Iraqi people was usually either under-emphasized or outright ignored.

I witnessed that history tends to be tainted by heavy doses of fiction and I learned that fiction is often heavily influenced by actual events. This, my first novel, is both. It is fiction—but I strived to ensure that the events portrayed were plausible.

Please note, that I repeatedly refer to the coalition as "Americans." This was not intended to slight the many great contributions and sacrifices of other coalition members, it was an attempt to simplify the situation to draw focus on the emotions on the events and the Iraqis—not on the coalition members.

*As you are reading, please refer to the **Glossary**, located at the end of the book, for definitions of Arabic and military terms.*

-jMike Olson

PART I: UNDER SADDAM HUSSEIN
CHAPTER 1
Baghdad: November 1980

"The slogan of the Arabic Socialist Ba'ath Party: One Arabic Nation with eternal purpose," the two hundred high school kids arranged in untidy rows chanted in unison, the taller among them squinting as the sun crested above the roof of the school building beyond the fluttering flag.

"The objectives of the Arabic Socialist Ba'ath Party: One—Unity. Two—Freedom. Three—Socialism…"

When the kids finished the *Estifaf*, the lone teacher on the playground blew his whistle, and a low-lying cloud of dust arose from the mostly dirt field as the lines of teenagers filed from the schoolyard and into the building.   Girls and boys headed to different classrooms, chatting to one another under the disapproving eye of the physical education instructor who took his position just inside the school's entrance.

"Hurry now, it's time for class," he said in his booming voice.

The twelfth-grade girls filed down the hallway and through the door nearest the entry. At the front of the classroom their teacher awaited them. Once they all silently stood next to their assigned seats she nodded and they all sat down at once. As soon as it was quiet, the teacher looked at Sahar and said, "Recite the *Bayan*."

Sahar was prepared. She had watched the *Bayan*, the twice nightly TV broadcast that provided the news from *Qadisya Saddam*, the war against Iran. Every night the newscaster told the Iraqi public of the battlefield victories against the Persians. Always victories—never defeats.

Sahar bowed gently as she began, "*Siit*, yesterday the brave soldiers of the Martyrs Brigade of the Third Corps attacked the Iranian positions at Abadan. They met stiff resistance but in a second effort, they smashed through the defenses. The Brigade lost forty heroic soldiers, but killed over three hundred of the enemy. Under Saddam's leadership, they captured eighteen tanks and hundreds of small weapons, forcing the enemy to run away and carry their shame towards Qum and Tehran."

The thirty students, were all dressed in the school's *sadrya*—a grey skirt and an armless white blouse. Some were also wearing a blue sweater, and a few of them, like Sahar, also wore a *hijab* covering her hair. Sahar and her classmates sat in pairs with their forearms resting on the uncluttered surfaces of the three rows of small tables in the sparsely decorated classroom. Large windows, stacked three high, dominated the wall to their left. The top and bottom windows were cranked open, passively cooling the high ceilinged-space.

Above and behind the teacher's head, a small red, white and black flag with three green stars, was pinned on the painted plaster wall. Next to the Iraqi flag a cheaply framed photo of a dignified-looking Saddam Hussein wearing a black beret, his mustache perfectly trimmed, watched over the classroom with a stern expression on his face.

The teacher nodded, but she didn't smile. She rarely did, at least not in front of her students. The teacher was about thirty. Tall and thin with a narrow face, her eyes constantly darted every which way as though she was always looking for something— something that if it existed, was invisible. She habitually paced back and forth, and when she spoke her voice seemed to race to complete the words in quick bursts, as rapidly as she could.

10

Sitting nearly arm to arm with her tablemate, Sahar exhaled quietly and sank a bit in her seat. The teacher, still standing at the front of the classroom began, "Yesterday, if any of you remember, we were discussing the importance of petroleum production in the development of the region."

Sahar stole a quick glance at her table partner who responded with a barely audible sigh.

Looking at another girl across the room, the teacher said, "Explain the importance of the port of Um Qasr."

As the other girl began, Sahar's lips curled up a tiny bit.

"Um Qasr, and the surrounding region between Kuwait and Iran is important to our country's economy because the port is vital in exporting the region's oil."

The neighborhood public announcement system, the one that sounded the call to prayer several times a day, crackled, then began to build up its whistle until it reached its high-pitched crescendo. Sahar immediately sat straight up in her seat. The girl stopped talking as everyone looked towards the windows. The teacher held up her hands and motioned for silence. Her chin up, her lips opened slightly and her eyes focused forward as she listened. An annoying, rather high-pitched buzzing, the sound of a flying motor grew louder and louder until they could easily hear it above the warning whistle. The girls glanced towards one another, some got out of their chairs and crouched, seemingly unsure as to whether they should stand or remain seated. Many of them clasped the hand of the girl next to them, their mouths open, but nobody spoke. The engine sputtered, once, twice, then it went silent.

Sahar's hands tensed, and her eyes widened as the teacher in front of the classroom stood as though poised to flee, but afraid to move.

"Get to the floor," the teacher yelled, as she brought her arms down in front of her, "Now!"

As the girls fell out of their chairs and dropped to the floor, all the windows instantaneously shattered. Sahar shut her eyes tightly to protect them from the bright flash that simultaneously came and went. At the same time, she brought her chin as far down as she could and moved her hands to cover her ears to protect them from the incredible blast—the loudest sound she had ever heard. A hail of gravel, debris and broken glass pelted the walls and the furniture inside of the room, thrashing everything about, like a furious tornado—all in less than a couple of seconds. Then a hot wind blew back towards the source of the explosion. Sahar involuntarily gasped for breath but had trouble inhaling.

Surrounded by her stunned classmates, Sahar lay heavily on the tile, now covered with dust, gravel, and shards of jagged metal and glass. She lay there motionlessly, not even willing to look around. The pale skin on her face was wet with sweat, tears and blood. Lying there, Sahar breathed heavily, grimacing with each slow movement, staring at a spot directly in front of her. She didn't move until she raised herself to her knees and elbows to retch. Then, she shut her eyes and collapsed back down again, her hands covering her ringing ears. The fabric of her sweater darkened as her arm slid through her vomit.

As an ambulance crew rushed into the torn-up classroom, some of the girls were screaming, others crying—a few were stunned. The vehicles' sirens wailed right outside the damaged wall. The rescuers shouted to one another as they quickly assessed and triaged. They placed bandages to stop bleeding, and quick splints to prevent broken bones from breaking worse. Then they hurriedly slid some of the girls onto stretchers and carried them out as another group of responders arrived to help others sit up and stand. Until they came for her, Sahar dared not move. When they talked to her, she couldn't focus her eyes and she didn't seem to understand, at least that is what she was later told. Sahar did not remember any of it.

CHAPTER 2
Baghdad: December 1980

A month later, after alternating restlessness with moments when she would hold her breath to listen intently to every noise—real and imagined—Sahar got out of bed. She pulled her night robe over her extra-large, extra-loose tee shirt that she slept in, slid into her house slippers and quietly crept down the short hallway to the kitchen.

Pulling the chain on a lamp, she sat down next to her schoolbooks that she had left strewn about the table. It was approaching 11:00. She picked up an old homework assignment and wrote out the thoughts that had been hindering her sleep.

Buzzing overhead, robotic hornets
fall to earth when their tanks run dry.
Dumb and blind
they know not who they kill—
Any life will do.

Buzzing hornets know not whose house they burn.
This old man's or that infant girl's?
Let God decide.
Tehran burns also.
As do Basra and Qum.

I hate the sound, coming or going.
Going... going like the soldiers.
Gone. I see their mothers and fathers,
their sisters and brothers.
They don't want their men to die.
Yet die they do.

When leaders scream, that war is freedom,
death and freedom become one.
"Allah Ahkbar" "God is great"
fighters claim God's love.
But if God thinks this great
then I think God is not.

Iraq is Saddam and Saddam our father?
My real father is afraid.
Mother is terrified.
We cannot endure father's embrace,
Insha'Allah, one day we will all be free.

While she was refining her poem, she became aware of the disciplined rhythm of the passing seconds precisely marked by the clock in the darkened family room. The sound made her think of marching soldiers goose-stepping in unison.

It was happening again. She quickly folded the poem and stuck it into her robe's pocket as the boots marching in her mind seemed to grow louder and louder. Thousands of boots marching on the street... on the walk... boots stomping on the porch...

The familiar room began to look foreign, and the rhythm sped up, louder and faster. Her breathing quickened, but each inhale was shallower than the last. Her face reddened. Sahar took a breath and held it as she put her forearms and hands on the table to steady herself. For a moment, she did not move, then she exhaled and pushed herself up and away from her seat. She immediately gasped and grabbed her left arm. She glanced down at her leg and cringed. Her lips were grimacing, the room was spinning, Sahar turned around and moved towards the back yard where the reflection of her scars across her face and her frightened eyes seemed to jump towards her off the door's window. Rushing, she stumbled into the door jamb. Not pausing to steady herself, she barely kept her balance as she staggered outside.

The cool air and the erratic sound of insects welcomed her into her private domain that extended as far as the nearby windowless wall of the neighbor's house. Sahar had to catch her breath. The openness to the sky replaced the denseness of the crowded room, and her crowded mind. The sound of the marching soldiers retreated. Sahar breathed deeply and made her way over to rest her hand against the gnarled trunk that rose from a shallow tree well. She leaned there slightly stooped under the canopy of tightly packed olive leaves until she stopped shaking.

Feeling better, she stepped out into the open, it was a typical cloudless, beautiful Baghdad night. She timidly approached the concrete bench with the wood backrest on the opposite side of the olive tree and gently sat down. Ignoring the aches and pains from her mostly-healed wounds, she took pleasure in knowing that no one knew she was there. She let her shoulders drop as she took a moment to listen to the faint rustling of the narrow, dense leaves and the serene chirping of crickets scattered about in the manicured vegetation that encircled her as she sat alone. Above her, the crescent-shaped moon shimmered; but the concrete bench pushed against a bruise prompting her to shift her meager body weight. When she did, her robe pulled against one of her remaining moist scabs on one of her knees. Seeking relief, she slid her hands under her thighs and then slowly leaned back against the backrest.

As she did almost every night, Sahar inhaled the sweet scent of the localized humidity in the otherwise dry air. Then she reached down and fished around for and picked up the candle and matchbook that she kept hidden behind a rock under the bench. She lit the candle; its flame added a soft, yellow glow and elongated the shadows on the walls surrounding her nocturnal paradise. Above her, clouds of uncountable stars shared the sky with the moon. When all around her was perfect, Sahar lightly bit her lower lip and ceremoniously unfolded the poem that she pulled from her pocket.

She held up her candle and allowed the fire to kiss the paper she had just written. For a moment, the poem flourished illuminating her young but somber face. For that moment, both glowed as if the tribute were a requiem for her hopes and dreams. She held on until the flames stabbed her fingers with a painful sting, then she let it go. Her eyes followed her fading thoughts as they slowly spiraled to the dirt that had been swept so many times it looked as clean as a sidewalk. The glow dimmed as the flames turned to embers. When they landed, she frowned.

She stared as the ash disintegrated as it delicately danced in an imperceptible breeze towards the corner of the garden. Watching them disappear, she sadly muttered, "It is better this way. I hope you understand."

When the sun rose, Sahar would boastfully tell her classmates that sacrifice and suffering were an honor; "My life for *Arrais* Saddam…" but looking at the last few ashes laying lifeless in the dirt, she lamented, "My meaningless life for Saddam."

She touched a tear as it rolled down the smooth skin of her scratched, delicate cheek. She whispered what she and her classmates said as a common response to the good news that accompanied most of his actions: "Saddam is Iraq; Iraq is Saddam."

As she stood up a streak of light flashed across the sky above Sahar. She ducked and her pulse raced. She held her breath as she waited for the rumble of a distant explosion. None came. "A falling star," she exhaled as she stood upright again. "May God save us from our enemy—"

Looking over the roofline at the electric glow of the horizon she continued to whisper her wish, "—and may He guide an Iranian buzz bomb into Father Saddam's bedroom window."

CHAPTER *3*
Baghdad: December 2002

Standing unnaturally straight in front of the full-length mirror among the lavish decorations and finishes of the Al Rashid Hotel's special reception desk, Zaid flexed as he checked his posture. In the lobby, the sound of muffled voices reverberated off the hard surfaces. The scents of *chai,* the popular local tea, and roasting lamb, accentuated by cumin and other spices, floated in from one of the hotel's restaurants. His neatly-combed black hair framed his dark, commanding eyes that peered out from above his well-trimmed mustache. Tanned and weathered, deep wrinkles added a sinister appearance to the perpetual frown on his face. He smiled, but only long enough to check his teeth. Looking at the reflection of himself he waited for the serious-faced, tuxedo-wearing man carrying an AK-47, to inspect his exclusive invitation. He adjusted his tie and brushed a speck of dust off his navy-blue business coat and he nodded approvingly as he admired the polished gleam reflect off his fingernails.

"*Sayid* Zaid, here is your room key, would you like to freshen up or head down to the event?" the man who also sported a Saddam-style mustache asked as he respectfully returned Zaid's invitation and extended an envelope to him.

After receiving the items, Zaid glanced at his watch, "The event."

"This way, *sayid.*"

Zaid gazed into the mirror for a moment longer before sliding the items into his pocket and pivoting, taking another moment to assess the extravagantly adorned, colorful, thick Persian rugs that partially covered the marble floors, and walls that were richly highlighted with detailed, wood moldings and elaborate tapestries.

This night was special for Zaid. The two stepped into an elevator, which was as excessively ornamented as the spacious lobby. Zaid had been to each of the restaurants and clubs on the main level, but this was the first time he was allowed access to the private club that also served as a bomb shelter. As they descended the thirty feet to the basement below, Zaid beamed to himself—he was moving up.

Another guard snapped to attention as Zaid wordlessly emerged into a narrow hallway. He then silently stepped along the heavily padded, tightly-woven carpet down the corridor towards the sounds of music, talking and laughing.

His legs spread slightly, his hands above his head, two more straight-faced men patted him down. As they searched, Zaid peered through the final doorway and saw an elegantly finished bar, a space for congregating, and a curved wall that formed the outside shell of what appeared to be a much larger room. The shiny marble surfaces and the rococo-like details screamed power and wealth, but the imperfect joints and ripples showing in the thin façade revealed the crude structure and poor quality construction lying beneath it. Colorful lights danced over the heavily-patterned carpet marking two entrances to the discotheque portion of the club.

Allowed to proceed, Zaid lit a cigarette as he approached the bartender who formally bowed from behind a counter made of marble and polished wood.

"Whiskey," Zaid ordered as he dropped a few hundred dinars onto the bar before he strolled into the disco carrying both a small bottle and a glass. The room was circular and being three stories underground, windowless. Massive columns and deep exposed beams provided visual comfort but hindered the view across the crowded space.

Like Zaid, all the men were dressed in dark colored tailored suits, though some had removed their jackets. The women wore delicate, expensive dresses and were adorned with generous amounts of makeup and fancy jewelry.

There was a group of about eight men dancing on one side of the shiny wood floor and a smaller group of women who danced in a tight circle nearby. Couples holding one another as they swayed to the music filled the rest of the hardwood space. Surrounding them, well-dressed patrons, many with obligatory smiles and darting eyes, moved from pose to pose alternating between talking, listening and watching themselves in one of the many mirrors that covered the walls. Zaid made no attempt to mingle, instead he stood by himself with his back against the wall near the main entrance. His bottle sat on one of the crowded tables in front of him, as he held his glass in one hand and a cigarette in the other. When the song ended and some of the dancers were returning to their seats, Zaid spotted an isolated table in the far side of the room. There, at that table, sat *Aeusteth* Uday.

The hair on Zaid's neck leapt to attention and a shiver ran down his spine. To disguise his glances at his Excellency's elder son, Zaid hid behind his drink and pretended to be looking at a young woman at the table in front of him. After a couple of sips his breathing returned to normal. Across the room, Uday looked more bored than happy. *Maybe we have something in common, you and I*, Zaid thought as the bass from the sound system speakers rumbled through his body.

Uday's gold watchband reflected the light just below the sleeve of his perfectly-fitted Italian suit as he sat looking to Zaid's left. Zaid followed Uday's gaze towards the far entrance beyond the dance floor where the great leader's son's attendant was bending forward as he spoke into the ear of a rather attractive, curvy woman. He was touching her shoulder with one hand and waving the other invitingly in the air as he nodded his head towards the notorious playboy. She tilted her head and pointed at herself with all ten fingers lightly touching her pearl necklace as she looked up at him and then across the room at Uday. Though still outwardly smiling, she shook her head back and forth as her female tablemates squealed and blushed as though their friend had just won the lottery.

The man sitting beside her held his hands flat on the table in front of him as he silently looked up at the suit-wearing servant pulling the lady's chair out for her and then persuasively and physically helping her rise to her feet.

Zaid watched her simultaneously wave to her table mates and look back at the man whose features visibly darkened across his tight face as he stared down at his impotent hands. Anxiety replaced her smile as she was led across the floor.

Zaid took a few steps towards the center of the room and propped himself against a column. He noted that most patrons glimpsed frequently towards Uday, yet no one dared to meet his eyes. Most of the men in the room sat or stood relatively quietly, most smiling, some laughing, a few frowning. But the women talked and laughed loudly, constantly smiling; their large eyes constantly shifted from one friend to the next, all talking at the same time. Upon noticing that the laughter's volume, duration and frequency seemed strategic; and the faces adorned with pasted-on smiles seemed to continuously seek reaffirmation from one of the many mirrors; Zaid exhaled heavily, refilled his glass and looked back towards the isolated table.

Uday's legs were casually crossed, but he was facing away from his new tablemate—his chin up as he scanned the room above everyone's head. Across from him, she shifted her arms back and forth while her legs were rapidly shaking under the table. Frequently glancing away, but then back towards Uday, the light reflected off her sparkling, dark red dress as it draped over her slender shoulders.

Zaid relaxed and slowly expelled a deep breath. He reached over and put his cigarette into an ashtray that sat on the table next to his half-empty whiskey bottle. As he stretched and tightened his muscles, he noted that some of the other smoldering butts bore bright lipstick stains. Looking at the faces around the table he sought to match each cigarette to each woman. Soon he was checking-out all the nearby women in-turn as though he were inspecting horses or soldiers—seeking the one most flawless. He grinned and flexed as his eyes journeyed around the room's female occupants another time.

Zaid froze when his glance returned to Uday. A playful look of mischief had replaced Uday's dull stare. One hundred people sat, stood, or danced less than fifteen meters from Saddam's heir, yet only a few saw that he was now holding, with more affection than respect, an AK-47 Soviet style assault rifle. The woman's painted face silently pleaded as she mindlessly played with her fingers at arms-length as Uday balanced the rifle in his left hand while he reached out with his right to take a 30-round, banana clip magazine from his attendant who dangled it between his thumb and forefinger as though it were a mouse.

Uday's date, if that would be an acceptable way to describe her, tried not to watch. Her head high, her big, shiny smile dominated her face. She tossed her hair from side to side, her movements more mechanical than seductive. She looked like she was begging for help, but in this crowded club, she looked as though she were completely alone.

Zaid laughed to himself, *such power, Saddam is Iraq; Iraq is Saddam.* He put his glass down and craned his head forward as Uday slapped the magazine into place and slammed a round into the chamber. As casually as if he were sipping his drink Uday inserted earplugs, neglecting to offer a pair to the distraught young woman across from him. Then he pointed the rifle toward the ceiling and pulled the trigger.

20

The loud bark and its echoes made everyone jump. Ladies screamed and ducked. Uday's companion scampered across the dance floor, staying as low as her tight dress allowed. Knocked off tables by startled partygoers, drink and wine glasses fell to the floor. Uday pulled the trigger again, and a mirror on the wall behind Zaid shattered.

Besides a high-pitched ringing, the blare of the music was the only sound for a moment. As the smell of sulfur disseminated, relieved but anxious voices quickly chimed-in, laughing and loudly complimenting the son of their great leader for his cleverness. His finger still on the trigger he held the rifle muzzle upright, Uday sat in his chair grinning. He slowly turned his head, his beaming face on display for everyone in the room to see as he surveyed the reaction of the crowd. Everyone clapped and cheered. Sitting up straighter, Uday extended the rifle to the servant who stepped forward to retrieve it as he ceremoniously removed his earplugs and sat back, a smirk across his contented face.

Like every other man in the room, Zaid grinned as all the beautiful women laughed, sang, and clapped along with the current song as if it had always been their favorite. The women shook their heads to the rhythm, their moving hair charging the atmosphere with euphoria, a façade, concealing the fear that their make-up, eye shadow and lip stick smiles could not completely hide.

He continued to watch how the singing and dancing and loud compliments to their great leader and his sons had brought the party to life. And so, the women smiled, laughed and sang. They raised their arms above their heads, very much aware of the men, who grinned, sipped their drinks and hungrily watched them. The only reason for the vibrant atmosphere, Zaid knew, was that Uday wanted it that way.

There were certainly worse ways to stay on the good side of a Hussein, Zaid thought as he winked at the beautiful woman standing nearest him. She stepped closer and let her arm brush up against his. Soon she was gently caressing his thick, black hair as she rubbed her hands up his sleeves towards his forearm.

Zaid left the party with the enthusiastic young woman who was all but begging to be freed from her tight black dress. In the hallway outside his room, she pressed herself up against him and playfully tugged on his tie. With the woman nibbling on his ear he cracked a sincere smile as he unlocked the hotel room door. With his free hand, he swept the wall for the light switch. After he kicked the door shut behind them, he dropped the key. He did not bother to pick it up preferring to toss his giggling plaything onto the bed and closely follow her to continue his celebration for advancing another level up the *Ba'ath* party hierarchy.

CHAPTER *4*
Baghdad: Mid December 2002

After dinner, the cassette tape recorder in Dalia's and Hadeel's bedroom played Euro disco music. Dalia was on the lower of the bunk beds. A light blanket over her legs, she lay on her side, one hand supporting her head, the other keeping the page of the science book she was reading from flipping closed. Across the room, a poster of Haitham Yousif looking out from his seat behind a polished grand piano was tacked up next to a shelf that held a plastic horse, an old purse full of small toys, and a stack of books and papers. She smiled as she glanced above the top of her open book at her mother and sister who were on the rug in the center of the room.

Crayons scattered around her, Hadeel lay on her stomach with her feet swaying back and forth in the air drawing a picture of a woman with long, flowing hair and three camels encamped near a group of palm trees. Lying down, her chin in her hand, Sahar reached past her daughter's arm and drew eyelashes on one of the camels. Giggling, Hadeel rolled over onto her back and looked up at her mother's face. She played with Sahar's long hair as it hung down towards the floor. Dee Dee, as her mother called her, then slipped back onto her side and grabbed a crayon. Glancing back and forth between her mother, who was making silly faces, and her drawing, Hadeel drew a big brown mustache on the camel standing next to the one with the eyelashes.

"Mom, mom," Hadeel grabbed at Sahar's arm. "This is the father and that one is the mother," she explained between giggles.

"Oh, you are so silly, Dee Dee," Sahar said pushing up Hadeel's t-shirt to expose her tummy. She tickled her younger daughter and blubbered her belly making a big fart sound.

"You are so silly; Camels don't have brown mustaches," she said as Hadeel flopped around, turning red as she laughed and thrashed on the floor.

"They have black mustaches," Sahar exclaimed, letting go of Hadeel to draw one on the third camel.

Dalia smiled and again let her eyes drift away from her reading.

Sahar lifted her eyebrows as the current song wound down and a new song began.

"Listen," Sahar ordered followed by a long pause, "Dancing Queen."

She jumped up and began to dance around the room with Hadeel only a half-step behind. Dalia stuck a piece of paper into her book, and a moment later all three of them were singing along, dancing, and laughing. At the end of the song, Dalia sat back down on the bed and Sahar and Hadeel returned to their rug, panting.

"Mommy, when I get married, I want to live with you and daddy," Hadeel said taking a crayon and sketching out the tall, thin trunk of a date palm.

"I'm sure we'd like that dear, but you really should go live with your husband."

"You mean like we live with daddy?"

Sahar answered slowly. "Yes dear, just like that."

Just like that, she thought to herself, as she sighed. As Hadeel drew; Sahar sat upright with her eyes unfocused ahead of her as in her mind, unspectacular, disorganized memories replaced her surroundings. She hugged her legs with her chin resting on her knees as she rocked forward and back for a few moments, then she shook her head a bit as she reengaged with the present. She looked to see if Hadeel had been watching. She hadn't.

Dalia coughed as she read. Sahar looked up and watched her concentrate, her eyes eager to feed her mind its nourishment. The fifteen-year-old looked a lot like Sahar did when she was in high school, but Dalia wasn't quite as skinny and her features were more beautiful than her mother's. *Dalia is becoming a young woman.* Sahar smiled a moment, then looked back towards her baby.

"Dee Dee, whatever happens, I really hope you have a wonderful life, my dear," she said as she pulled her in for a hug. "I love you, my little Dee Dee."

"I love you too, Mommy."

Sahar hugged her younger daughter tightly and then quickly turned her head away to hide a tear that appeared in her eye. Sahar stood up and stepped to the door. She didn't open it, instead she turned her back to it and leaned against it.

Lying on her stomach, Hadeel continued to draw, talking to herself, her feet swinging above her. Dalia continued to read.

Sahar slowly turned the knob on the bedroom door and said, "Dalia, you are becoming a beautiful woman."

Dalia looked up and then at her sister who was also looking up from her masterpiece. Dalia smiled softly, "Thanks mom. Good night."

Sahar stepped out of the room. As she pulled the door shut behind her she heard the girls giggle.

CHAPTER 5
Baghdad: Mid December 2002

Crying she told me,
"Three days ago, they vanished."
Taken. How? and why?
Details we shall never know
lie hidden in unmarked graves.

24

Condemned to fade away, weak pleas echoed through the dark hallways of the labyrinth under the city. Standing nearly two-meters tall and weighing 100 kilos, overpowering the prisoners before him was never physically challenging: instead, overcoming their meager defiance energized him. Broken or merely terrified of greater retribution, they all begged for mercy like women as they tried haplessly to shield themselves with their arms or legs. But they never fought back.

The air smelled of mildew mixed with sweat and excrement, and of a damp, dirty mop. The rancid dust clogging his nostrils made the *amin* breathe through his mouth; either way, the rot settled heavily in his lungs. He firmly pulled against the resistance offered by the limited natural range of motion of the man's arms. The *amin's* eyebrows diverted the beads of sweat on his forehead away from his already irritated eyes that twitched and itched. His nose ran. These were the occupational hazards of working in the stale, moist air of the underground chamber.

The *amin* clenched his teeth and snarled as his ripped biceps, forearms, hands and neck bulged as he worked. He coughed lightly as he grunted. The *amin* was a teacher. He taught men how to behave. His job was to remind the errant of their proper place in Saddam's society. Torture was often a lesson. Usually, if his victims learned their lessons, the *amin* wouldn't have to kill them later. If not, well, then he'd kill them—there was nothing wrong with killing—some people deserved to die. It was up to the prisoners. But this time, the case file contained a note from the director, Qusay Hussein, himself. This session was not a lesson; this session was punishment.

Perhaps this anonymous slab of living meat made the mistake of believing he was a man; but he was wrong, because men understand power. Saddam was powerful. Without power, there would be no respect. Without respect, there would be no discipline. Without discipline, there would only be weakness. God does not like weak men. Therefore, this man was wrong to speak against Saddam or his family. It did not matter if Uday raped and killed his wife, or whether he pushed her out of his penthouse window on the top floor of the Al Rashid Hotel, like the man he was beating allegedly stated. By accusing Uday, he had insulted a Hussein. Saddam Hussein was their leader. *Saddam is Iraq; Iraq is Saddam.* No one insults a Hussein. Any other truth was irrelevant.

When the *amin* felt that the living carcass ceased all effort to stand, plea or cry, he let him fall. He fell, not like a sack of potatoes, but less dramatically—slower and more gracefully. The man hit the concrete slab hard making a single thump, and then other than his shallow breathing lay motionless in a shapeless heap.

He fell a like bag of rice.

Squinting to better see the details on his victim's face, the taste in his mouth reminded the *amin* of his bleak surroundings. Standing upright, he towered over his conquest. The *amin* turned his head and nodded to his assistant, his posture perfect he said, "Send him to Section Five, Khadimiah."

The skinny young man with short brown curly hair, who until that moment quietly stood at a respectable distance, responded immediately and with a bow, "Yes, *seidi.*"

Then the *amin* pivoted and stepped towards the unpainted door at the end of the room. He walked past a cane-like whip and a crowbar that were leaning against the wall casting their shadows from the single naked bulb that was barely bright enough to reveal the stains and the mold that irritated the *amin* so much. Other equipment of the trade—an automobile battery, some bare wires and connectors, a few sticks and staffs of various sizes, rope—sat neatly on an old bookcase leaning against the wall next to the doorway.

The assistant noticed that the *amin* had made no effort to interrogate his prisoner. That would have normally meant that the intent was merely to scare. Prisoners receiving such treatment were often citizens who said something they shouldn't have in front of a government plant posing as a friend or coworker. Those lessons were a quick and efficient way for Saddam to remind the public that the Regime was watching. Had that been the case with this prisoner, all he would have to do now would be to release him back into the streets. But, unfortunately for this man, now he must arrange transport to the Security and Intelligence Agency in Khadimiah, across the river then a few kilometers to the north. There the treatment he would receive would be much worse.

"Poor bastard," whispered the smooth faced youth as he began to gather the load off the floor, "I hope you are on good terms with *Allah*."

Chest out and head held high the *amin* strutted down the center of the hallway. Though technically, having been recruited from the Republican Guard into Qusay Hussein's Internal Security Force, he was no longer a soldier; he chose to wear an army uniform as he worked, but he did not put his blouse on as he headed for the fresh air. Skipping every other stair, he effortlessly ascended three flights to reach the exit door. Pushing it open to the flutter of scattering pigeons he stepped out into the bright sunlight. He smoothly withdrew a pack from his right cargo pants pocket and stuck a cigarette into his mouth. His short, pitch-black hair was barely long enough to blow in the wind. Again, he squinted, but this time only because the sun's glare reflected brightly off the surrounding buildings. Inhaling the fresh air, he took a deep, leisurely drag on his cigarette. He strolled through a small puddle of water over to a nearby wall and casually leaned his body into it, his boots digging into the shallow mud. Sparing himself the effort, he let the wall catch his weight.

Another puff.

He looked up at the twelve-story building across the broad boulevard letting his clean-shaven face absorb the midday sun. He let his gaze rest on the yellow-brown, dusty looking concrete panels. It was a handsome building, perfectly adequate to mark the power behind a ministry of one of the Middle East's regional powers. The rhythm of solids and voids created by closely placed windows clearly defined each floor level where lazy bureaucrats sat protected from the sun and the requirement to do the physical work of real men. Women worked there also.

The cigarette gone, he flicked the butt much farther away than necessary. He cleaned his boots by wiping them gently over the puddle before stomping them authoritatively on the concrete slab near the door. Then without looking around again, he reentered the darkness. The clanking of his boots echoing down the metal staircase announced his return to the depths of the ISF's chambers, this bureau housed with the Officer Personnel Management Office of the Ministry of Defense.

CHAPTER 6

Standing in the sunshine next to an open window, Sahar shivered as the thin fabric of the wool sweater she wore over her western-style business blouse warmed her chilled skin. Her light green *hijab*, decorated with a grid of yellow and white flowers, was pulled tightly over her head completely covering her hair. Having lived her entire life in Baghdad, twenty degrees Celsius was cold. Standing between two of the narrow tables that formed a "U" along the three door-less walls of the office, she touched her jaw and lightly traced its prominent angle. Her neck was skinny but well-proportioned because her head, her shoulders and her entire body were lean as well. Sahar's tendency to push her slender shoulders forward gave her the appearance of a small bird: a thirty-nine-year-old bird with black circles accenting the worry of her eyes.

Behind her the voices of two of her office mates, one of which was her good friend, Reem, continued talking without her as they sat at a table exchanging gossip and sipping tea. Sahar leaned forward, her thin nose—a bit longer than she wished— stood out even more because of the slenderness of her cheeks. Absorbing the heat, her eyelids struggled to stay open in the bright sunlight. She let her fingers brush over the tabletop, feeling the invisible, chalky grit that perpetually covered the standard dull-grey metal furniture until it found its new home blocking the pores of her skin. Standing up straight again, she patted her hands on her skirt, and then crossed her arms in front of her.

Cleansed by an earlier rain shower, the skies of Baghdad were clear. Taller buildings, both modern and old, jutted out of the urban monotony of rooftops compressed together in erratic patterns between an irregular grid of major boulevards. Below her lay one of the broad avenues that met at traffic circles adorned with sculptural tributes to Saddam and the heroes of wars dating back to ancient triumphs. The hectic roadways of the capital city, clogged with hundreds of thousands of neglected cars, looked serene when distance rendered them silent and the spacious sky diluted the potent exhaust.

To the right, the dark swath of the Tigris River provided the region with lush greenery that hugged the banks and scattered out in clumps among the surrounding brownness. In every direction cranes towered above the forms of half-built palaces and mosques giving the illusion of vibrant progress. In truth, many of the cranes had stood silent for years. Construction sites that had turned into salvage yards served as testimony of the effectiveness of the United Nation's post-Kuwait War sanctions as they tightened over time.

The Ministry of Health marked the entrance to Baghdad's Medical City: a regionally known collection of a large general hospital and several small specialty hospitals. Though it was only a noontime shadow of what it had been before Saddam Hussein brought neglect, it was still considered Iraq's center of medicine. The storerooms in the once prestigious hospitals were now lined with empty shelves. A lack of supplies, equipment, and skilled assistants frustrated the doctors as they tried to care for their desperate patients, but far too often, their once life-saving treatments had deteriorated to little more than hollow gestures.

Below Sahar's south facing perch, the offices of the Officer Personnel Management of the Ministry of Defense spread out on the other side of the four-lane road. A scattering of pigeons pulled her eyes to the man wearing the army trousers and a sweaty green t-shirt as he pushed his way through a door and into a courtyard. Sahar shook her head as he flexed his chest and massive arms and slowly lumbered across the small yard confidently sticking a cigarette between his lips. She had never seen him close enough to see his features well, but she had become familiar with his arrogant swagger and disciplined strength along with the way he always leaned against the wall in the sun when he smoked his cigarettes, alone.

Behind Sahar, the other office mate departed leaving her and Reem alone.

"There he is again," Sahar said, "I wonder if he has a family, how he treats his children."

Reem rose and stepped forward, "Who?"

Sahar nodded with her head toward the man puffing on his cigarette nine stories below. Reem leaned forward, "Ahh, wow. Who's he?"

"He's an *amin*."

"Really? How do you know?"

"Just look at him, calmly standing there, he probably just strangled someone and didn't even bother to wash his hands before he came out to smoke."

Reem bobbed her head a little side to side and stood on her toes leaning so far forward she almost touched the glass with her nose. But she did not answer, instead she bit her lower lip.

Reem's youthful and perfectly symmetrical face, over a decade younger than Sahar's, encouraged a second look. Her skin was smooth and flawless and Reem's soft round cheeks made her look even younger than she was. A tiny mole between her cheek and lips accentuated her constant, convincing smile that accompanied talk of love or treachery equally well. Her eyes glowed softly as they habitually darted around avoiding eye-to-eye contact except for very short periods.

Sahar spun briskly away from the window toward the middle of the room. The nearly naked walls of the office held little of even mild interest to help erase the image of such a frightening man. The fluorescent lights buzzed from the acoustic

30

tile ceiling above her, the stale smell of burning cigarettes floated freely throughout the building. Outside the office, she could hear men and women as they walked across the corridor's dull, light-grey speckled floor tiles, some quickly, but most leisurely, as the day panned out in normal fashion.

Sahar sat down and picked up her teacup of *chai*. She added a couple tiny spoons-full of sugar.

Reem glanced back at the courtyard and then slid over and sat down next to Sahar. Sahar leaned back on one of the grey metal chairs grasping the small cup with both hands, slowly raising her elbows to keep the steaming *chai* close to her body. She sipped gingerly, though a bit boisterously to avoid scalding her lips or throat.

"You drink as noisily as a horse," Reem said, smiling.

"You're calling me a horse?" Sahar responded.

"I like horses, especially how loudly they drink."

Sahar laughed. "Well how do you drink? Everyone drinks *chai* like this."

"Sure," Reem replied, moving her head in a quick upward circle as though she were trying to shake a fly away with her mane. "Everyone does."

Sahar shook her head. "Reem, you are my *chalawi*, but what am I going to do with you?"

After a few sips, Sahar and Reem went to stand in front of the window again. Both glanced down to see whether the *amin* was still there. He was. They watched him flick his cigarette and stamp his feet on the concrete walk just before he disappeared back through the unmarked doorway. Sahar let off a long exhale and her muscles loosened a bit. Reem sighed.

Hanging loosely around her wrist Sahar's gold colored watch indicated that it was a few minutes later. The *chai* and chat were working; time was passing. The women had been dutifully present at the Ministry of Health since 9:00. It was now after noon. At 2:00 it would be time for Sahar to dash off to her dental clinic. The effortless Ministry of Health job provided the house to her and her family, the clinic job earned most of her income.

"Everyday looks the same," Reem complained as she peered out towards the cross of a Christian church that stood in the middle of the sea of roofs and across the street from one of the countless mosques.

"I worked here since I graduated from Dental College," Sahar proposed a new subject as she sat back down.

"Back when it was the Ministry of Sumerians, you would go home to work the first crop of wheat, right over there near where that bridge now stands," Reem added pointing down the road towards the Tigris to their west.

"It was right before I got married, too," said Sahar.

Reem looked down. Reem was married—kind of. Two years earlier, only three months after she became his wife, her husband disappeared. No one knew whether he ran away from their arranged marriage, a match which neither of them wanted, or whether he was arrested and possibly killed. Some considered her a widow, but her new family insisted that one day he would return. And so, she lived life as a married woman, but she existed without a husband.

"Sorry."

"It's okay," Reem replied.

"I wasn't happy when I was graduating," Sahar mused.

"Why not? Graduating, getting married, starting a new job, all are exciting, how could anyone not be happy?"

"Well, if it were my life I was living, then it would have been perfect."

Reem looked at her, "What do you mean?"

"You know, there was the mother in law…"

Reem laughed a little and stepped closer to Sahar.

"You know, I didn't do any of those things because I wanted to," expanded Sahar, "I did them because I was supposed to."

Reem cocked her head a bit.

"When I look up on a clear night, the stars and galaxies we see are just like memories, they are all from the past. Some of that light began its journey thousands of years ago. Perhaps when your 'Sumerian woman' looked up from outside her hut she saw a similar sight, just as distant, just as old, though she wouldn't have known it. I suppose she didn't get to do whatever she wanted to either, but maybe it is such knowledge of other things that makes it more painful to not live your own life than it had been in the past."

Sahar sat upright, arms on the table, looking at her hands as they surrounded her cup. "And when I look at this starlight, I realize, that it has been traveling much longer than even those distant times, only to enter my eyes—and perish."

"Ugh, so depressing. What's your point?" asked Reem as she sat on the table next to her.

"Exactly, that is the point. Why does it come so far? The stars we see may no longer even exist. Their light may be all that's left. But light neither knows nor cares. Its journey is a one-way trip. My eyes absorb it and my mind extinguishes it. The light ends with me, yet I know not what to do with it."

Sahar, looked at Reem, who looked back at her as a child would look at a professor demonstrating the mathematical proofs regarding the Theory of Relativity. But Sahar continued anyway.

"I was worried about everything. Would I be able to please my new mother—a woman who could not be pleased? I would never be good enough for her, yet, I would live my life trying. What if my fiancé didn't love me? My father told me not to worry. But what's the point of marrying a man without romance? What if we lived without love? Was my future predestined? Was it my duty to live how I was told and not how I desired? Was I to support a man and his family? What would I become? A slave? A star? Would my purpose be to shine for the enjoyment of others before I faded away into nothingness?"

Reem looked at her, then after a pause that lasted a bit too long, she reached her hands out and placed them on Sahar's. She looked in to her older friend's eyes and said, "My friend, you need help."

"I mean really, when I looked back up towards the stars, the harder I squinted, I would see yet another, slightly dimmer light between two of the fainter, dimmer stars. I realized that it never ended. I wondered if the stars would be grateful that I recognized them for what they were. I thanked them for sending me their light, that I recognized and appreciated their sacrifice. And I wondered if anyone would ever recognize or appreciate mine."

Reem just stared at Sahar for a few moments. "Really. And you worry about me," she replied as she stood up and began to wander about.

Sahar laughed. "You are the only one I talk like this with."

"Why? Don't you like me? Why don't you just slap me?"

Sahar laughed harder and gave Reem a light tap on the arm. "You know, I spend a lot of time thinking and writing about these things."

"You do? Why? You mean you write this stuff down?"

Sahar looked straight ahead and nodded.

"Well, bring it in, let me see it."

Sahar looked up at her shaking her head.

"Why not? I won't tell," pleaded Reem.

"I can't."

"Oh, come on, you can trust me."

"I don't have it anymore."

"What did you do with it?"

"I burned it."

"Burned it?"

"Yes."

"Why?"

"So no one would ever know what I really think."

Reem placed her cup of *chai* onto the table where she had been sitting and began to walk around. "Well, I can understand why you don't want anyone to read it," Reem said in a sing-song voice.

Sahar could not help but smile as Reem fluttered around the room. Sahar may have looked like a bird, but Reem actually behaved like one.

"I never visit my mother-in-law," Reem said while walking the short distance toward the door.

Dressed livelier than Sahar, Reem wore a light green skirt that flowed with her body, a matching blouse hung from around her shoulders. The mid-section of the outfit hugged her shapely waist just above her flaring hips.

"It must be tough," said Sahar.

"It is, I guess, but I'm not sure her son was the right man for me to spend my whole life with anyway."

Sahar nodded, "I think about my marriage sometimes."

"What do you think?"

"Well the other day Hadeel said she wants to live with us after she gets married. That made me think. Do I love Muraad? Maybe. But now I don't necessarily think that love is a prerequisite to living with a husband. He is good to me—most of the time anyway. But certainly, there should be more to it than that."

Reem nodded.

Sahar sighed. "Maybe he feels the same way about me. I remember the brief couple of years where I felt the excitement of mutual and often urgent physical attraction, but not anymore."

Reem touched her cheek, "You mean sex. Why can't you just say it?"

Sahar continued, "Now, he just seems, remote—distant. This doesn't make him a bad man, but it doesn't make him a good man either. Now, I have my role, and he has his."

"Wow. That's so serious."

"Gradually, I guess I just stopped thinking about our marriage. Things are the way they are."

Reem continued to pace around. "Well, really that's nothing. Last night I saw a squirrel water skiing on the internet."

Sahar laughed.

"It was a small squirrel with a white stripe on it. The skis were custom made for him."

Once momentum gained, Reem's mouth would move continuously. Her voice chirped, unaware that she often changed subjects every few words, racing to move on to the next, more interesting topic.

"Do you like squirrels?" Reem asked as she looked toward the door, hopped a few steps in that direction and intently watched a man walk down the hall.

Sahar smiled as Reem bounced around as if determined to look for food under every leaf, but never actually looking under one before she excitedly spotted and approached the next. Reem turned her head in small sharp movements, interested by every detail in the room, yet distracted by all the others.

Not giving Sahar an opportunity to respond, Reem answered herself. "I think they are like rats with tails. Same with bats—rats with wings."

Her delicate white neck exposed, she cocked her head forward as though she saw a small but interesting object on the wall decorated by nothing but marks left by furniture that had banged against it long ago, sometime since its last forgotten paint job.

"Squirrels are living, breathing, walking, water skiing, cobra food. That's what they are."

Sahar smiled warmly as she listened to her friend chirp.

When Zaid stepped in from the hallway Reem immediately stopped talking. Sahar stood up and stepped back away from the door and towards a wall, turning slightly to face the window. Reem turned towards him, put on a sweet smile and bowed her head a little and said, "Good afternoon *seidi*."

Zaid stood close to Reem and paid no more attention to Sahar than he did the unoccupied chairs in the room.

"The contractors will bring their bids by tomorrow," Zaid told Reem. "When you gather them, I would like to review them before you bring them to the committee."

UN Regulations required all bids to remain sealed until the Compliance Committee opened and reviewed each one for completeness. But in *Kimadia*, the State-run Medical Logistics Company, Zaid always reviewed them beforehand, sometimes modifying them and occasionally losing some of them, so his reminder to her was not necessary.

Because of the UN bureaucracy and the *Kimadia* method of countering its intent, the Ministry of Health had a Compliance Committee, an Evaluation Committee and a Selection Committee as part of a complicated contracting process. The process neither protected the government from fraud nor awarded the contracts to the most qualified or least expensive contractors. It certainly did not guarantee that the Oil for Food money was spent on what it was supposed to be spent. Its multi-committee review process merely complicated everything so much that in the end, nobody could discern why any contractor was ever awarded any individual contract. This gave *Kimadia* the authority to award every contract to whomever they wanted.

"Yes, as you like," Reem answered so softly Sahar could hardly hear her from scarcely two meters away. Sahar shifted so she could watch and hear better. Reem giggled and batted her eyelashes when standing in front of Zaid. After she spoke, Reem filled an awkward moment of silence by poking her chin and her round cheeks with her thumb and index finger. Sahar rolled her eyes.

Zaid strode past Sahar and looked out over the city. "The Americans tried to destroy Iraq," he said, addressing Reem as he looked out across the skyline at the dozen or more easily visible cranes and the bustling streets below. "But even with the obstacles the Americans and the UN throw at us, we continue to prosper."

Sahar's eyebrows rose a bit, but her lips didn't move. Reem followed Zaid towards the window.

"Invasions, embargos, no-fly zones, meddling with the Kurds, America and Europe can't stop us. They can't keep us down."

"No, *seidi*, they can't," said Reem quickly enough to not interrupt.

"Each day we prosper, we show the world that Iraq, and Saddam personally, cannot be controlled from Washington or New York, Brussels or Geneva."

Zaid turned and began to walk towards the door, "Saddam is Iraq; Iraq is Saddam. And don't forget, I want to see the bids."

"Yes, *seidi*," responded Reem as he strode out the door.

As soon as he was gone Reem looked at Sahar who was staring back at her.

"What?" Reem asked.

"You know how he looks at you, like you are dessert."

"He does not."

"Oh yes, he does, and you practically dribble honey on yourself for him."

Reem shook her head, "Oh, come on. I don't."

"What if he were to touch you, are you ready for that?"

"He won't."

"Don't be so sure. He's a snake. He's thinking about touching you every time he sees you. Don't you see him sticking out his chest and flexing for you. He's like a, you both act like a pair of peacocks when he's around."

"Peacocks?" Reem exclaimed half laughing, "Just because you're an old mother hen. You act like you're not even here, like you're hiding."

"I am hiding. He's dangerous. The closer you get to him, the closer you get to an *amin*—or worse—to being a prisoner in *Abu Ghraib*. One mistake in front of him, and you could be there."

Sahar paused for a moment, then added, "Look Reem you probably have no intention of ever actually getting physical with or emotionally attached to Zaid, but if you want to remind yourself that you're a woman, find someone else to pose for. If you just want to have a little fun while at the office, there are safer ways."

"He's married anyway."

"Yeah? You think that matters to a man like him? He's probably trying to figure out the best way to… to gain access to your treasures, just biding his time. He's eagerly anticipating the day he'll see exactly what kind of girl you really are, and if you disappoint him, he could really make it hard for you."

38

Reem looked away, "'Treasures.' It's amazing I even know what you're talking about."

"You have to be more careful Reem. Sometimes you are just way too naïve. You have to be very careful who you trust."

CHAPTER 7
Early January 2003

"*Habibati*, meet our daughter, meet Amel," Mohamad Jawad said holding their new daughter next to the bed occupied by his smiling—though perspiring—wife. Smiling, tear tracks on her face, her hair in disarray, moisture returned to Bushra's eyes. Reaching out his hands Mohammad held the blanket-wrapped newborn out to her. Her face still discolored from birth, the baby Amel cried in the heart-piercing voice only a newborn can wail.

"*Habibti*, she is so beautiful, so beautiful," his wife replied taking her in her arms.

"*Amel*, Hope, a beautiful name for a little girl," he whispered, watching his wife cuddle their newborn.

A lady shrieked with pain on the other side of the curtain as a nurse paid attention to the interval between her contractions. Attendants scurried in and out bringing water and pillows to the soon-to-be grandmother who used them to help comfort her daughter.

In the hallway people rushed by; the maternity ward in the public hospital was always a busy place.

Mohammad sat down next to his wife. The three of them shared the narrow bed. Soon Amel drifted asleep for her first nap, her little ear rested right over her mother's heart. Tightly wrapped in a clean blanket, she looked like a little boat rising and falling, gently rocked by her mother's breathing.

Smiling at her husband, Bushra's eyes closed and she too drifted off to sleep. Mohammad sat quietly though awkwardly, one leg off the bed, holding Bushra's hand with one hand and gently patting Amel's chest with the other.

"Thank you, God, I am not worthy," he said as his face glowed with joy and pride.

CHAPTER 8
Baghdad: Early January 2003

The news bulletin interrupted the TV broadcast in Baghdad, but this was not uncommon on the state-run television networks, which in Iraq in January of 2003, were both primary channels. Clad in a wide assortment of clothing ranging from western business suits to the white *dishdasha* with the *keffiyeh*, the headscarf men wore, few of the men in the small, crowded café looked up at the screen. Many of the them were smoking hookahs, the tall and ornate water pipes that dispensed colored and flavored tobacco as they talked or read the newspaper. The thin trails of sweet-smelling smoke hung in the air before being sent into a frenzy by the ceiling fans, as the patrons also drank scalding *chai* from ceramic cups the size of shot glasses.

There were only three women in the open-air café, but they represented well the diversity of Iraq under Saddam. Sahar, on her way home from her dental clinic, was still in the long, brown skirt, white blouse, tan sweater and *hijab* she wore to work; Dalia, her hair flowing freely down to her shoulders, was still in her school's blue skirt, white blouse and dark blue sweater; and a *chador*-clad elderly woman. All anyone could see of her was her hands and the part of her face around her eyes, though the male customers did not indicate that they could see her at all, as she skirted around them bent forward at the waist busily sweeping the floor with a short-handled broom called a *muknasa*.

Sahar stopped by to see if her husband was there, perhaps to walk home together. Not seeing him, she quietly stood at the cashier end of the counter watching the TV that sat atop a recently added, homemade shelf. Dalia stood next to her mom curiously observing the men's activities.

Saddam Hussein came on the screen and began a routine America-bashing tirade. In the café, only the young nationalists and those who still mourned the deaths of their loved ones during the Kuwait War listened closely. Some men at a nearby table began talking about the news. "The United States is like a lion: powerful, unpredictable and menacing," one man said. "You don't know what they will do."

"Yeah, like why did they invade us before? I thought they liked us," said a second man.

"That's why you should never be a friend with a lion," answered another, as the table broke out in laughter.

"Mom, why did America attack us?" Dalia asked quietly.

Sahar just shook her head, "I don't know dear, probably because they wanted our oil. But that is over. We cannot change the past."

Sahar greeted the man behind the counter as he worked his way over to her, "*Salam Alekum.*"

"*Alekum Salam,*" the old man answered.

"I'm looking for my husband, have you seen *Abu* Dalia today?" she asked.

"Not today *Um* Dalia. Perhaps he is at home with his wife." He offered with a slanted eye and a crooked smile.

Sahar grinned suppressing a laugh, "Your jokes are as tired as your *chai* is stale."

The old man behind the counter mocked insult, "It's fresh, made as it's ordered."

"Yes, as it always is," she added.

The man nodded, beaming, "Yes, as it always is."

"Well then, I'll go be with my husband who is already at home with me."

"Yes," replied the old man in a very gravelly voice that could easily be misinterpreted as wise, "But be sure to knock first."

She shook her head and smiled as she turned away, "Of course. *Ma'salama.*"

"*Ma'salama,*" he laughed as he grabbed a small towel from behind the counter, his grin lingering a bit longer than his attention as he walked toward a customer part way down the counter.

Stepping toward the street, Sahar glanced up to the TV screen. Saddam Hussein was telling the Iraqi people to "Prepare to defend the walls of Baghdad, prevent them from falling into the hands of Mongols."

She froze. All adult Iraqis knew these words. The reference went back to Genghis Kahn's grandson, Hulaghu Khan, who, in 1258 put an end to the *Abbasiin* Muslim Empire, which was commonly referred to as the Golden Age of Baghdad. The Mongol invaders mercilessly butchered many of the city's residents and decimated the symbols of Iraqi culture. With these words, Saddam Hussein implied that Iraq would soon be attacked, and that if they were to lose the upcoming war, the merciless invaders, the Americans, would indiscriminately kill the people and the culture would disappear for ages.

Looking out into the street, Dalia tugged on her mother's arm. "Come on, mom."

She stopped pulling and stood still when she noticed the intensity of her mother's eyes as she watched the American president whose face covered the television screen. Saddam's press secretary now spoke, "The American president is sending troops to the region to attack the peaceful people of Iraq. Father Saddam will again save us from the insatiable greed and injustice of the evil American Empire and keep Iraq free and prosperous."

Sahar gripped her daughter's hand and dashed through the streets towing Dalia behind her. They stopped by a cousin's house only long enough to pick up Hadeel and then they rushed on in silence. As they made their way along one of the dirt and gravel walks that lined the street, they occasionally tripped on shallow roots that were hard to see in the early twilight's darkness. They passed the equally spaced trees and irregularly parked cars on their left side and the alternating stucco and bare masonry walls—interrupted by rectangular metal gates—on their right. The houses not obstructed by a front wall, such as their own, were set back from the otherwise well-defined property lines. Their flat roofs and strong horizontal porches and floors

42

hugged the earth, though tall, thin palms and steel telephone poles hosting shining lights pulled the eyes upward toward the wide-open sky. The intermittent amber tint and hue shadows guided the three as they rushed along their route toward their home.

When they arrived onto the porch, for the first time since they picked up Hadeel, Sahar looked at Dalia's face. Standing next to one of two large, steel drums that held water that had dripped from the roof over the winter, Dalia stood staring back, a quizzical look on her youthful face. Sahar forced herself to smile. Dalia had been a toddler during the Kuwait war; she didn't understand.

Sahar looked at Hadeel. Her younger daughter was looking at her hands as she waved them back and forth, her mouth moving as she whispered to herself, engrossed in the personal world of a five-year-old. Sahar retrieved the key from her purse and while her trembling hands searched for and unlocked the door, she was praying her husband was at home. The door swung open into the dark living room. The TV was on, Muraad snored on the couch.

CHAPTER 9
Baghdad: 05:00 20 March 2003

The high-pitched warning whistles blared, interrupting the pre-dawn silence and rudely awaking Baghdad's five million inhabitants. They rose just in time to witness the air defense guns shoot so rapidly that the roar sounded like an uninterrupted ghoulish groan, yet the tracers were spaced out by so many rounds that from a distance, the streams of burning hot, steel-shrouded, lead looked more like lazy fireworks arcing as they gained altitude. But each of the hundreds of thousands, if not millions, of lethal projectiles that were shot into the air, would also fall back to the earth—at dangerous velocity.

Next came a series of massive explosions. Eruptions turned masonry and concrete buildings into blindingly hot infernos that sizzled like tremendous, blazing torches scattered about the city. Shock waves rumbled outward through the ground while hungry fireballs sucked in howling winds of oxygen just above it. The impacts sounded—and felt—like out-of-control freight trains rushing down every avenue in all directions.

Clouds of smoke and dust above the city glowed orange as the light from the fires reflected off floating debris. The next salvo of frantic, outgoing tracers was partially obscured by the haze. But the haze was unable to conceal the evidence that the threat was real.

At the sound of the first whistle, Sahar leapt out of bed, draped her robe over herself and ran into the girls' room to rush them into the kitchen. Sahar grabbed blankets, matches, candles and a jug of water, as Muraad ran from window to window in the family room and kitchen quickly making a masking tape "X" across the glass to help minimize the risk of shattering. Then they all huddled against a concrete wall under their kitchen table and began to cover themselves with thick blankets in the candle-lit room. Sahar's chest moved rapidly but her shallow breaths moved little air.

Muraad's face was covered with whiskers from a couple days without using his razor. He was wearing long undershorts and a white t-shirt which he quickly covered with his favorite green sweater that he grabbed on his way out of the bedroom. After he pulled a corner of the blanket over himself, Muraad quietly sat looking at his girls, his neck bent up against the underside of the tabletop. Wearing the oversized t-shirts that they slept in, Hadeel silently leaned against her mom as closely as she could, shivering as she nervously reacted to every sound. Dalia sat near their feet.

"Dalia, put that blanket over you," Sahar instructed, her pulse visible in her neck.

"But I'm not cold."

"It isn't for the cold, it's so you don't get cut in case broken glass flies. Now put it over you."

"We aren't going to get hit."

"We'll take no chances. Put the blanket over you and get closer to the wall."

Sahar held Hadeel tightly as the city absorbed another sortie of American air strikes.

The conversation silenced as the tortured wailing of failing steel and the ominous rumble of crushing concrete bellowed out from the deafening blast.

"Wow, I can feel it in my legs," Dalia said, "it feels like finger nails scraping against a chalkboard."

Hadeel stuck her face into her mother's shoulder and Sahar put her arm over her.

"And it smells like your dentist's drill, as if you were grinding someone's teeth into shards, like it's spinning and burning against the roots of someone's teeth."

"That's enough Dalia," said her father.

Sahar and her family listened to the sirens during the lulls. A girl's voice rang out. "Is that Iman? She must be on their roof watching," said Dalia.

Hadeel was in her mother's arms, her eyes wide, tears smeared across her face, but she was as silent as a mouse caught on the open floor staring into the eyes of a cat.

"Mom, let me go out, I can hear Iman is on their roof. She is even younger than me, how come she gets to watch while I'm stuck here watching you scare Dee Dee?"

Sahar slowly shook her head, "No, Dalia, stay here."

"This is history. And I'm missing it," she argued. "My children will ask me, 'Mom, where were you when the Americans attacked?' I'll have to answer that I was hiding on the floor like an animal."

She crawled out from under the table but her dad intervened, "Dalia, get back under here."

She turned her head to continue to argue with her parents, "The Americans aren't going to harm us. They'll free us."

Sahar looked to Muraad then back at her older daughter, "Stop acting and talking like a fool. Only God knows our fate."

Dalia stood up. Her father got up and blocked her exit with his tall frame and his slightly protruding waistline, he reached out and grabbed her arm, "Dalia, get under the table with your mother and stop speaking like a fool. We'll take no chances."

An explosion shook the house. The windows rattled violently for a couple seconds.

"Maybe they just hit the air defense battery in that vacant lot up the street," Muraad said. "That's close. That's why you must obey your parents."

Dalia looked at her father's stern face, he let go of her arm and she reluctantly crawled back under the table.

A young boy shouted from the neighbor's roof.

"God help us all," Sahar said.

The family hushed as they listened to the chaos outside their door. Though they could not hear what the neighbor's children were saying, the four of them could easily hear their excited voices.

"Mom, listen," Dalia yelped after hearing more amazed shrieks from the nearby rooftop. "I want to go and see."

"Dalia. No." Her father replied.

In the wavering movement of the candlelight, Sahar could see tears in Dalia's eyes as her daughter clenched her teeth to keep her mouth closed.

Sahar frowned and shook her head. "One stray round and they all could be killed. What are their parents thinking?"

Dalia turned away. The bombing continued.

When the warning sirens went silent and it had been mostly explosion-free for about fifteen minutes, they heard the neighborhood kids go back inside.

"Okay Dalia, now we can get up," Muraad said.

Dalia leading the way, they emerged from under the table. Her dad opened the front door, then he and Dalia walked out past the water drums and looked around from the center of their yard. Sahar stood in the doorway looking out as she held Hadeel. No one was in the street and although they could not see any damage from where they stood, they couldn't avoid the acrid smell of the clouds of smoke that darkened portions of the dawn sky. They could also easily hear the shrill sounds of various types of sirens increase around them.

As the two approached the porch, Sahar, with Hadeel still gripping her around her neck, looked at her husband and older daughter, "*Habibti*, we decided to stay in the city this time. I hope that was the right decision. We should consider ourselves fortunate. I don't want any foolishness. Do you hear me Dalia?"

"Yes, Mom."

"Good, we don't know what is going to happen. We should thank God for sparing us, but one thing is for sure—this is real and this is deadly." Sahar struggled to keep her voice from trembling. "We should show God our appreciation by not doing anything foolish," she said firmly as she hugged her reluctant teenage daughter with her free arm, still holding Hadeel up with the other.

CHAPTER *10*

Every night I see them,
tall, powerful American soldiers.
Eyes crazed
expressions brutal—hardly human,
compassionless killing machines.
Blood in their eyes,
their uniforms dirtied with the remains
of those they had already slain
wiped across their pant legs.
Every night, the rumble of explosions
jolt me from the nightmares of my sleep
tossing me into the terrors of my awake.

Sahar jumped. Her heart pounding, she shot upright in her bed. Her eyes wide open in the dark room she heard Hadeel scream in her sleep. Muraad rolled over as Sahar hastened across the short hallway. Sahar picked up her sniffling, little angel and sat down on the lower bunk next to Dalia's legs. She rocked her little girl, gently rubbing and patting her soft skin as Hadeel clutched her around her neck, her eyes wide open.

"It'll be alright, Dee Dee," Sahar reassured her.

Dalia just lay there silently watching with a blank expression on her face.

"Shhhh, don't cry my little sweetie, everything will be alright."

After she closed the bedroom door for the second time for the evening, her two girls asleep on the lower bed underneath the shelter of the reinforced top bunk, Sahar silently unlocked and pulled the front door open. Stepping out into the darkness of the porch, she sat in the corner hidden from the street by one of the water barrels. Leaning back against the house her shoulders began shaking as she silently prayed, "Dear God, I'm not lying. Protect my girls. Please make sure they are safe."

She peered out into the night. There was no movement. The relatively cool air felt good on her face as she sat listening to the crickets and the silence.

CHAPTER *11*
Baghdad: 3 April 2003

Sahar and Reem stared out from their ninth-floor office window at the plumes of black smoke marking the prior night's destruction. Below them, the Ministry of Defense buildings no longer existed. Every building in the complex was damaged; the wall the *amin* used to lean against was now impossible to locate among the immense piles of rubble. The Ministry of Health, on the other hand, was hardly touched. A few broken windows and some scattered impact marks made by wayward shrapnel were the only visible collateral damage.

Sahar and Reem, along with two of their women coworkers, watched as soldiers combed through the rubble and pulled another body from the dusty, ashen debris. The soldiers sorted their findings into three categories: bodies, weapons, and documents. The bodies and the weapons were loaded onto trucks and periodically carted away. Two officers and a civilian wearing a suit supervised a squad as they busily tossed boxes and stacks of documents into a bonfire that roared in a cleared corner of a parking lot.

No one spoke as faces of stone hid whatever thoughts were behind them. All four of the women turned around as unfamiliar voices in the hall preceded the entrance of three well-dressed men into the office. The women scattered to the side walls away from the window.

"Things are happening as planned," the most elderly party member of the group said as he and his colleagues approached the window. Overlooking the wounded city, the newcomers spoke as though they were alone in their own office, completely ignoring the women they had just displaced.

"The trap is set. American blood will fertilize the soil. They will never step foot in Baghdad," a serious looking man with a deep, vertical wrinkle in his forehead stated.

The other two nodded thoughtfully as he continued. "I believe our Republican Guard will ambush the Americans over there as they come north from Hillah," he said pointing to the southern horizon." Then pointing to the southeast, "That is where the US Marines are rumored to be massing. We will smash them hard and mercilessly before they can cross the Sirwan River."

As the man spoke, Reem looked at Sahar and rolled her eyes. Sahar's eyes opened as widely as possible and she shook her head in short, frantic movements trying to get Reem to stop.

"Great leader's plan is ingenious. Father Saddam is Iraq; Iraq is Saddam," said the third as the trio turned and marched out, never acknowledging the women who had remained in the room. Immediately after the men were in the hallway, Reem laughed. Sahar cut her off. "Shhhh," she commanded.

But Reem didn't stop. The other two women glanced at Reem and quickly filed out.

As soon as they were alone, Sahar turned on Reem. "Are you crazy? You want them to kill you?"

"It's okay. They were just putting on a show. In a couple days, they'll be pretending they never even heard of Saddam."

"Reem, Be careful. This is a very dangerous time. You don't know what's going to happen. You don't know who you can trust."

"Oh, all right. But you can't believe them. The Americans are almost here. They are coming this time."

Sahar turned away again facing the window. "Reem, you are too young. You must be careful," Sahar said watching two men across the road add another body to the growing row. "Have you thought about what will happen when the Americans do get here?"

Reem looked out the window, "I don't know. What would you do if you were them?"

Sahar, stood still and answered mechanically, "I don't know. It doesn't matter what I would do. That's why you must be careful."

"Do you think they will capture Saddam Hussein?"

"Well, I certainly don't think they'll let Saddam capture them." Sahar touched her chin and cocked her head, "Where is Saddam, anyway? He hasn't been on TV for about a week now," Sahar responded.

Reem shook her head before she looked away and out the window.

Sahar stared across the city pondering it all, then she wiped her forehead. As she watched the men walk back to retrieve yet another exhumed body, she said, "All this death… You know, if the *amin* is dead, I feel no sorrow for him. But most soldiers only fight because they must. And so many have died."

She raised her head and looked south, "So many more are there, waiting for the Americans. They know they will die. They're waiting for death."

Reem moved to stand next to her.

Sahar continued, "I don't know what the Americans want, but I know we can't trust them. Whatever it is, what they want, they'll take."

Reem took Sahar's hand. Sahar squeezed it a bit and held on to it. Then Sahar continued speaking, "Ever since I was in

50

high school, I've wondered, hoped for, but now, now that it may happen, I'm too afraid to consider that in only a few more days, we may be freed from the nightmare that has become our lives."

Reem gently said, "Sahar, it'll be alright."

Sahar did not look at her, instead, she stared out the window, "God forgive me for my hatred. But what will happen now?"

CHAPTER *12*
Baghdad: 4 April 2003

As Zaid stood on one of the gravel roads that subdivided *Kimadia's* warehouse complex at Al Dabbash he could clearly hear the battle—the sound of the Iraqi Army disintegrating near the Airport, about ten kilometers to the southwest. He looked up and down at a row of yellow-brown painted steel buildings. Saddam was missing; the night before Baghdad lost electrical power; soon the Americans would control the airport. The time had come to prepare for the enemy's imminent arrival.

Zaid directed a team of men as they were finishing their task of unloading pre-designated items that were collected from offices and other warehouses around the complex off two trucks and carrying them into the warehouse. When they reemerged, they were carrying other pre-designated items and loading them on onto a third truck.

A large explosion shook the horizon. Zaid turned to study the black cloud that spiraled upward marking the destruction of something large. He looked at the position of the sun in the sky and then his watch before he walked over to the truck being loaded. He handed a sheet of paper bearing his stamp to the driver just in case someone from the Ministry of Interior were to inquire as to his cargo or its destination. As the driver sat down behind the wheel and reviewed his instructions, Zaid inspected a crate that was marked with the UN seal, *Oil for Food*. The red tag next to the United Nations seal reassured him the air handling unit the label suggested was no longer inside.

He looked up as a couple of the workers placed a crate labeled, "Air compressor" onto the truck, "Is that everything?"

"Yes, *seidi*," the closer man answered, holding his hat in his hand in front of this chest.

"Cover all of this with a tarp," Zaid instructed.

The man nodded and the two workers withdrew to the warehouse. They returned a moment later with a tarp and a rope and began to cover everything in the cargo bed.

When they finished, Zaid walked back over to the driver and asked, "Do you have any questions?"

The driver shook his head rapidly, "No, *seidi*."

Zaid handed the driver a handful of dinar, "See that this is stored as directed and my instructions are burned. Before dark."

"*Shukren seidi*, I will move it with my own two hands, *Insha'Allah*."

"Good, because I know your family," Zaid said frowning.

The driver's forced smile vanished, and he started the engine. "*Seidi*, I will do exactly as you instruct and then I will forget."

"Good, because I won't," Zaid said as he tapped the side of the truck with a firm downward stroke. Leaving more exhaust than dust, the truck drove past the warehouse at the end of the row. Zaid watched it round the corner then he turned and ensured the cargo beds of the two other trucks were empty as he walked past them on his way into the warehouse. He walked the full length of each aisle, using a flash light when necessary, to ensure that all the documents and computers that he had dispersed among the medicines, supplies and equipment were where he wanted them. Satisfied that they were, he walked back to the entrance. At the entrance to the building, two men each stood beside an acetylene torch and a five-gallon can of gasoline. Zaid nodded. The two men each picked up one of the gas cans and walked into the warehouse. Five minutes later they returned to his side, the gas cans empty. They picked up their acetylene torches and Zaid stood by as the two men parted, one going left, the other going right, lighting the base of the wood columns and boxes that had been splashed with gasoline amongst the palette racks. As the flames began to grow, Zaid walked away. By the time the two men met at the large doors on the other side of the warehouse the flames were already through the roof and Zaid had already departed *Kimadia* 13 in his 2002 silver Toyota Avalon. He headed back to the ministry, where more items that had best not fall into the hands of the Americans awaited him.

CHAPTER *13*
Baghdad: 14 April 2003

Late in the afternoon, as the buildings cast long shadows across the street, an American Army patrol, supported by a tank and an armored personnel carrier, passed by the neighborhood water distribution point that the community set up after the public water system ceased to function. Their approach was announced by the excited shouts of the kids, barely heard over the imposing rumbling engines and squealing tracks of the two heavy vehicles. Young kids and teenagers, who were dressed not-unlike many of the soldiers when they were off duty shouted, "George Bush number one," and "USA," as they gave the thumbs up sign and ran alongside the heavily armed foreigners. Two lines of serious faced soldiers, one on each side of the road walked ahead, some scanning the roof tops and the upper floor windows, while others skimmed the faces of the people lining the sidewalks. Most of the soldiers maintained a stoic face, though some made eye contact and marginally smiled.

Dalia and Sahar watched the American patrol as they stood in line to fill their buckets with water at the truck-mounted faucet next to the open-air café where Sahar had first heard that the war was inevitable. Sahar leaned over to talk directly into Dalia's ear, "The walls of Baghdad had been scaled. The 'Mongols' have arrived."

Mother and daughter watched the closest soldier as he passed within three meters of them. He, like all of them, wore brown boots. Across the chest of his camouflage uniform of numerous shades of tans and browns, was an armored-plate covered with light brown cloth, which was partially concealed by a webbed cargo-carrying vest. His dusty brown kneepads looked practically worn out, and goggles were strapped atop his helmet. The black automatic rifle he carried with an ammunition magazine sticking in it pointed toward the ground in front of him, his gloved finger next to the trigger. He had smoke grenades, fragmentation grenades and additional magazines in his cargo vest, and a big, sheathed knife hung on his belt. He wore a water bladder on his back that connected to a flexible rubber hose that hung near his mouth just above a loose fitting greenish-tan bandana. His face was sweaty with remnants of camo and dirt stuck to his jaw and cheeks mostly hidden behind the chin strap that secured his kevlar helmet. As he passed he momentarily locked eyes with Dalia and when he did, he nodded slightly in her direction as he continued to march.

Sahar glanced away from him to look at her daughter. Dalia stood motionless staring at the soldier. Neither Sahar nor Dalia had ever seen an American soldier in person, and neither could say a word. They could feel and hear the tank approaching. The tank's gun tube appeared first, a light brown muzzle emerging from beyond the sidewall of the next building over. Sahar moved closer and put her hand around Dalia's shoulder and left it there. Dalia leaned towards her mother and reached over to hold her free hand.

A few soldiers poked their heads out of the tank. One appeared to be the driver with two others manning big machine guns. The two women stared and braced their stances, as a very heavy smell of diesel exhaust washed over them in a hot dusty wind as the metal monster rumbled past. A Humvee and more soldiers passed, then the personnel carrier, with filthy duffle bags covering its shell, roared by slowly. Several soldiers were standing or sitting in it attending large machine guns that were pointing up towards the roof lines, ahead and behind the column.

Behind the two big vehicles more dismounted soldiers passed. Two more Humvees rolled by, each with a machine gun and gunner who pivoted from side to side as if to demonstrate to the onlookers that they could immediately shoot lots of bullets in any direction.

Two soldiers, one an Arab American, walked beside one of the Humvees, next to an officer who sat in the passenger seat talking on a radio. The officer pointed at the café and shouted something to the soldiers, who, immediately ran over to the entrance.

"Salaam Alekum," the American announced in perfect Arabic to a table of older gentlemen who were watching the patrol pass. "*Alekum Salam*" answered the eldest as they all stood up.

"*Shukren*, but please sit back down, I do not mean to disturb you," the Arab American sergeant responded. The other soldier stood just inside the entrance, his rifle pointed down as he surveyed the occupants of the café.

The oldest man nodded, and took his seat followed by the others.

"We hope we are not disturbing you too much. We are sorry for the circumstances of our arrival. We want you to know that we are not here to harm you."

The men didn't respond.

"Please understand that we are concerned for your safety, and that means we must establish security as quickly as we can. We vow to damage as little as possible," he said putting his right hand over his heart.

The eldest man nodded, but said nothing.

"I thank you for your time," the sergeant said, "*Ma'salama*,"

As he turned to go, the eldest of the group spoke up, "Do you have any instructions for us?"

The soldier turned back around and bowed, "*Hajji*, please know that we are working to restore services, and we are looking for some government and army officials."

"Officials?"

"Yes, for example, do you know where Saddam is?" the American asked the group of men grinning.

"We do not know," the elder man firmly responded.

"Of course, Saddam isn't here," another man sternly added.

The American looked at the man who just spoke, then looked around the room. He then stepped over to an unoccupied table and cocked his head. The group tensely cringed when he got down on a knee and looked under the table as if he saw something. He stood up and with a serious expression on his face and looked back towards the group he had been speaking to and announced, "He's not under this table."

For a moment, there was silence, then the sergeant smiled and bowed as he turned to depart. Some of the men laughed, including the owner from behind the counter, who wiped his brow with a small towel as the Americans departed the café.

Sahar stood with a straight face as she observed from just outside on the sidewalk.

The last of the American patrol streamed past in the street as the translator ran to catch up to the officer.

As the streets quieted again, lively discussions broke out among the Iraqis in the café.

The eldest man, whom the Arab American soldier had addressed, sat quietly for a moment and then started to speak, "Our army could not defeat the Americans. The Americans will control Iraq for as-long-as they choose."

The younger man who had also spoken to the American spoke up again, "No, the Americans can beat armies, but they cannot beat people. America does not have the patience for insurrection."

A third man leaned forward and while running his fingers through his dark beard said, "The Americans are not the greatest threat. If the Americans were to leave now, Iran would surely invade. What do the Americans want? Saddam? Oil? Either way, they are not as dangerous as the Iranians."

"But the Americans are infidels. At least the Iranians are Muslim."

"It all depends on Saddam. What if the Americans capture him?"

"What if they don't? What can Saddam do now that the Americans are here?"

"Yes, what can Saddam do? Our army is defeated. You just saw the Americans. Their weapons are too strong."

"But the Americans are weak-minded. They cannot handle the taste of blood. Remember the Kuwait war? How can we trust them to do what they say they will? They have failed us many times."

"Yes, but they are here now. And they have never been here before," said the oldest man.

After filling their water containers, Sahar and Dalia began their hike back home. As they walked a block down the major street that the Americans had passed, they arrived at another open-air café near the turn off to their home. Sahar stopped Dalia and they stood silently next to a concrete column to listen. Inside this café, a group of about a dozen men in their twenties and thirties shouted at each other.

"The Americans are killers, butchers, violating God's will by coming into our lands as invaders. We must avenge the insults and injury cast upon us, our families, and God. They have no reason to be in Iraq. We cannot stand for this and still be men."

"But you saw their weapons, and this was only about forty soldiers. They have many thousands. We cannot stand up to them and survive."

"Then we shall die, but die with honor."

"And what good does honor do for my wife and my children? They need food, not the honor of a dead husband."

"But wait. Remember that we don't have to defeat them, we only need to fight them. We must restore our honor. We cannot do nothing."

"But if we fight them, we will lose. The Americans destroyed our army. If our army couldn't beat them, how can we?"

"But why are they here? What do they want?"

"Maybe they want Saddam."

"Why would they want Saddam? It must be oil."

"It doesn't matter what they want. They are here, infidels on our soil, uninvited and they must be expelled."

"But we cannot expel them, how could we?"

"What honor has Saddam brought? Where is he? What is he doing?"

"Saddam is waiting for the right moment, and then he will fight."

"What will he do? He has no army. With what will he fight the Americans?"

"Saddam is a great man. He will not abandon his country."

"He is probably already dead."

"Just wait. He will strike back when the time is right, *Insha'Allah*."

"Look, if Saddam calls for us, we will join him, that is honor."

"But what if he doesn't return? What will we do then?"

"We will survive."

"No, we will strike at the Americans. We could ambush them, all of us, together."

"Did you see those guns? How could we ambush them and not be killed?"

"We don't have to fight them. We hit them, then we run or hide before they can strike back."

"We could trick them to stop, and then blow them up."

"We could plant mines. We don't even have to be there when they come."

"But how would we stop children or women from triggering the mines? There's no honor in killing our own families."

"Remember, we don't need to kill an American, we just need to try to kill one."

"Perhaps we could take a quick shot. If we are fast enough, we could be gone before they can shoot back."

Sahar looked to the ground and frowned. Dalia was quiet—she looked pale. "Come on child, let's get this water home."

The two walked home in silence.

CHAPTER *14*
Baghdad: Mid May 2003

"They are supposed to come today. Do you think they will?" asked Reem.

An American engineer from ORHA, the Office of Reconstruction and Humanitarian Assistance, had met with the minister numerous times over the last few weeks. The day they scheduled for the ORHA advisory team to come had arrived. Sahar answered, "That's what the minister said."

From their office, standing where tables used to stand, their faces against the glass of the ninth-floor window, Sahar and Reem peered as far to the right as they could, hoping to see the approaching convoy.

"Sahar, do you think Saddam will come back?" Reem asked.

"Come back from where? I think that if he could, he would have already come back."

"The Americans said they'll install a democracy, that we'll be free."

"Well, when have the Americans ever done what they said they will?" responded Sahar.

"No, really. Do you think it could be true? Do you think Saddam is gone forever?"

"Look Reem, I'm afraid to think about that. For so long... I just can't be so disappointed."

Reem looked at her and nodded a little. "I'm just asking, what if the Americans are here to help? What if they do help us become free?"

"Reem, after the Kuwait War, the Americans encouraged the Shi'ite to rebel and then stood back as Saddam killed them.

Time and time again, they said they were going to help and then when people committed, the Americans didn't help them, and they were killed. How can we trust the Americans when they have let us down so many times in the past?"

"So, I guess it doesn't matter whether they catch Saddam or not..." Reem summarized.

"Maybe not. But what matters most right now is how long the Americans stay and what they do when they're here," added Sahar.

"There they are," said Reem.

The two could see the convoy approaching from the other side of the bridge spanning the Tigris.

"Look at them. They come across the bridge as though they are heroes," said Sahar.

"I don't see any tanks. Do you think they have guns?" Reem asked.

"Of course, they are not here to die. Americans are afraid of death," Sahar answered.

"Aren't we all?" Reem said. "What do you think they'll do? Will they fire all of us?"

"I heard that they'll fire the *Ba'athists*," Sahar responded.

"Well, that's all of us."

"No. They'll probably only fire the real ones, those who actually supported Saddam."

"Everyone supported Saddam. That's why we have jobs. That's why we're alive," Reem added.

"They can't fire all of us. If they did, what could they do?"

After a short pause Reem asked, "What can they do anyway?"

With that they both looked around them. Although the structure itself was sturdy, the Ministry of Health was a terrible mess. Immediately upon the news that the Americans took the airport, the ministry employees along with many people from the street rampaged through the building taking everything that they could carry and destroying much of what they couldn't. But this was not a spontaneous reaction by a mob. This looting was planned and supervised by the *Mukhabarat*, the Iraqi Intelligence Agency.

The mob had sanitized the ministry in the span of a couple hours. On Doctor Jassem's order—who in addition to being the director general of *Kimadia* was also a *Mukhabarat* agent—Zaid led the group that burned thousands of files in two rooms on the fifth and sixth floors. After the rampage had become self-perpetuating, hat-in-hand and escorted by his bodyguards, Doctor Jassem calmly walked through the turmoil and went down *Kimadia's* private elevator to a waiting Mercedes limousine. Where he went, no one knew or said.

Among the sensitive data destroyed were *Kimadia*'s record books. As Zaid was burning the paper records and floppy disks in the MOH, all the recently erased computer hard drives that had held this knowledge were either being carried out the doors on the shoulders of looters or were being thrown out of windows by vandals.

Zaid entered the room and displaced Sahar and Reem at the window as the convoy of white SUVs sandwiched between a couple Humvees passed on the street directly below them.

Zaid put his palms on the glass and peered down. His eyes were sharp and moisture clouded the window near his nose and mouth. "You women talk too much," he sneered.

Sahar and Reem watched Zaid as he observed the column of eight vehicles circle the statue commemorating a battle of the *Qadisiyat Saddam*. The creases in his forehead burrowed deeply. He frowned as he quietly turned away from the window and departed looking at the floor, his mind clearly elsewhere.

There were no telephones in the MOH. There were no computers, no functioning network infrastructure, no remaining office supplies, and in some locations, many doors and windows were broken or missing, no light switches, no light bulbs, and no electrical outlets—electrical power itself was only on for a few hours a day. Only half of the elevators and a few of the toilets worked. Remnants of furniture, glass from windows and lights, and trash were everywhere. In the rooms that served as burn pits powdery ash still covered the floors and clung to nearby walls.

"So, what will they do?" Sahar whispered staring out the window after the last of the vehicles turned the corner to enter the ministry parking lot. "What can anyone do to change this?"

"God help us all," was Reem's response. As soon as the convoy disappeared below them, Sahar and Reem joined the crowd and headed down the stairs to watch their new bosses enter the building.

PART II: THE CPA
CHAPTER *15*
Baghdad: 16 May 2003

The minister and most of the ministry employees crowded into the entrance lobby. They hushed as one of the leafs on the decorative, over-sized doors was pulled open from the outside. A tall American army officer with short, black hair and an eagle on his desert tan uniform entered first. The colonel removed his hat and took a few steps into the room before he stood there straight and unflinching. He scanned the hundred faces looking at him. He did not smile but he did nod his head before he looked back towards the door and waved his left hand, in which he held both his sunglasses and his hat. His entourage tentatively streamed in through the entrance behind him.

An older, distinguished looking, grey-haired man stepped forward and moved past and in front of the colonel. He stood about half a head shorter than the army officer as he turned slightly towards the exterior wall adjusting his tie. His pale skin highlighted his cheeks and nose, which glowed red, as he wiped his face and neck with a handkerchief that he pulled out of the back pocket of his pleated slacks. An Iraqi man, who was obviously a translator, closely followed the older man as a group of nearly twenty others worked their way in to the reception lobby and spread out in a semi-circle behind the two leaders. Six were women, three of whom wore US Army uniforms, their weapons slung over their shoulder or secured in holsters. There were five other soldiers and another tall man with a dark mustache in a US Navy uniform. The styles of the civilian clothes on the remaining people, and how they wore them, indicated that the other men and women were either from the United States or Europe.

The minister was facing the grey-haired man from his position along the wall perpendicular to the entrance doors. Standing amongst his own entourage of several of his key directors general on the steps leading to the minister's hallway, above the sunken lobby he looked for the ORHA engineer. Not seeing him, he looked away from the visitors and scanned the crowd who quietly stood looking up at the visitors who had now filled the raised entrance platform.

"This place is an unbelievable mess." Looking beyond the people at the broken fixtures hanging from the ceiling and the damaged railing directly in front of him, Mister Banks quietly asked Colonel Newborne, "How can anyone fix this?"

Colonel Newborne glanced from right to left systematically evaluating the building, the people and the trash. Then he answered, "By taking charge."

Seeing the puzzled look in Banks's eyes he muttered for only Mister Banks to hear, "Be careful what you ask for."

Mister Daniel Simmons Banks had asked to come to Iraq. He had served in numerous mid-level political appointments since the year he married his college sweetheart during the turbulent year of 1968. Along the way, he had developed a reputation for being smart, distinguished-looking and reliable.

Banks had no doubt that God was behind the US effort, and he believed that the president was on the right path for America. He suspected that Secretary Rumsfeld would rely heavily on fiercely loyal, though untested, interns and political appointees—neocons—who would call in all favors to obtain one of the career-accelerating positions that controlling the Coalition's activities in Iraq was sure to offer. So, he prayed.

"I believe I can provide some of the seasoned leadership that will be necessary to turn this energy into results," he told his wife as they pulled into the driveway of their suburban home in a gated community months before. "I think God wants me to go."

By the time the American army approached the outskirts of Baghdad, Mister Banks had been informed that he was selected to be ORHA's senior advisor to the minister of health. And by the time the TV displayed American soldiers working with the enthusiastic crowd to pull a statue of Saddam Hussein to the ground, Mister Banks was at Fort Bliss, Texas, learning a few military skills that could help him survive in an active Theater of Operations. That was the first time in his life that he had ever been on an army post. He never understood soldiers, but at that moment he felt great pride in knowing that he would soon be in Iraq with the troops, helping to rebuild that tattered nation into a great democracy.

While at Fort Bliss he was paired with Colonel Newborne. Newborne had been an enlisted infantryman in Vietnam, then left the Army only to come back in after college as a Medical Service Corps lieutenant. If he could learn to deal with the colonel's idiosyncrasies he figured Newborne would be a good ally to have.

As broadcasts of the air raids on Baghdad filled the TV screen at Colonel Newborne's Northern Virginia apartment, he remembered watching the vapor trails—left by the bombers— add a brilliant contrast to the clear and beautiful desert nights during the Gulf War. He remembered hearing the distant rumble of the B-52 strikes even at thirty or more miles distant—still ominous. Now being much older, he gave more thought of how terrifying such explosions must be for those poor souls at the receiving end.

When most Americans saw the TV screen momentarily white out, they saw an explosion. Newborne saw death.

Someone's action or inaction killed him. Whoever it was or whoever they were, for them the war was over.

Donald Edward Newborne had mixed feelings about the practice of embedded reporters. Though he thought it would be good for the public to see this more personal perspective on war, he didn't like the practice because he thought the reporters being there could be an unnecessary distraction, or worse yet, could encourage foolish actions.

Nevertheless, while he watched, the colonel remembered what it was like to be a grunt. Combat soldiers don't know the grand plan and they usually don't see the big picture. In fact, he knew what most soldiers usually saw: everyday things like buildings, roads, trees, people, trucks, made different by the surreal situation of combat. Soldiers would be very aware of their own heartbeats, their own footsteps and those of their fire teams; they'd hear whispers of their squad mates and the shouts of the rest of their platoon. At times, they heard nothing but high-pitched ringing—triggered by outbound gunfire, or inbound artillery.

Newborne knew first-hand how soldiers feel: tired, scared, sweaty, thirsty, hungry. The bruises and the cramps, and the knife handles digging into their hips. Grunts knows the smell of burning rubber, sulfur, flesh, and the oily stink of insect repellent they call 'bug juice,' which would chemically react leaving sticky finger prints on the muzzle guards of their M-16s. Newborne remembered how the white salty powder made of dried sweat three or four times over, would plaster his t-shirt and underwear and stick to and inflame the rashes that covered his unexposed skin; while dirt, insect bites, sunburn and windburn would cover the rest of him.

And god-damned blisters.

In Vietnam, there were times Private "Fast Eddie" Newborne was so exhausted he could hardly see. He remembered the hoarseness in his voice as his already dry throat was rubbed raw by his own yelling and heavy breathing. He remembered laughing at stupid-ass shit, and times when everything fucking sucked. The nightmares after killing someone—wondering if there had been another way—or realizing that he could have been the one with blood pumping out of his head as he fell to the ground.

At night, he frequently still remembered, more than thirty years later, the screams of his burned and mangled buddy who outlived the mine he stepped on by about five minutes. Newborne still suddenly jolted awake sweating—still holding him—now as then, long after his screaming stopped.

Newborne was proud that he understood these things, and he loved every single *swinging-Richard* who had also earned the right to truly understand. Because of what they were willing to do, because of what they have done, in his mind, soldiers were the best damned people in the world. And he knew there was no way these experiences could be transmitted via airwaves, not by embedded reporters and not by the traditional press conferences. It was his combat experiences in Vietnam that made him part of the exclusive club among soldiers—those who have *truly* served. This was what made Newborne love the Army.

His combat experiences also taught him compassion, but for the good of all, the colonel kept his compassion hidden deep inside his rugged demeanor of unbending respect for discipline and authority. During the build-up, the media thoroughly reported the Bush Administration's search for a justification to invade Iraq, one that the American public and Congress would support. Colonel Newborne understood that the military was a tool to achieve objectives defined by the politicians. To the colonel, *"When?"* was an important question. *"Why?"* was irrelevant.

"Theirs not to question why, theirs but to do and die." Alfred Lord Tennyson's poem was a testament to incompetent leadership. The colonel hoped that he would be able to help keep the dying part to a minimum. And that was why he went to Iraq. He wanted to be part of this team because he was determined to do everything he could for the US to win a quick victory with as few lives lost as possible.

Now, face to face with what they had asked for, Mister Banks and the colonel stood in front of the attentive crowd of Iraqis. Mister Banks began addressing his curious audience, "On behalf of Ambassador Bremmer, Secretary Rumsfeld and President Bush, I want to express our gratitude to each of the Ministry of Health employees for coming to work and for dealing with such hardship. I am acting minister of health, Daniel Banks. With me is Colonel Don Newborne and a team of physicians, healthcare administrators and allied fields specialists. We are here to help you get your healthcare system back up to the lofty standards that it enjoyed decades ago."

The Iraqi minister of health stepped back as Bank's translator stepped up and read his transcript in Arabic to the crowd. Murmuring rose from the audience.

Mister Banks continued, "Now that you are free from Saddam Hussein's regime, it is time to rebuild. You may have heard that for this next step, ORHA, excuse me, the Office for Reconstruction and Humanitarian Assistance, has recently been replaced by the Coalition Provisional Authority. The new envoy, Ambassador Bremmer, has replaced General Gardner as head of the CPA."

Mister Banks pulled a neatly folded sheet of paper out of the breast pocket of his jacket. He unfolded it while scanning his audience, "I am certain, you will be thrilled to know that as his first official action, Ambassador Bremmer is freeing you from the grips of the *Ba'ath* party."

Alternating lines with his translator, he began to read Bremmer's order, "People in the top three levels of the *Ba'ath* party holding ranks of *Udw Qutriyya, Udw Far'a, Udw Shu'bah,* and *Udw Firqah* are hereby removed from their positions and banned from future employment in the public sector. Also, to protect the common Iraqi from the threat of intimidation, human rights abuses and depravations, 'Individuals holding position in the top three layers of management in every national government ministry, shall be interviewed for possible affiliation with the *Ba'ath* Party, and be subject to investigation for criminal conduct and risk to security. Any such persons determined to be full members of the *Ba'ath* Party shall be removed from their employment. This includes those holding more junior ranks of *Udw* and *Udw 'Amil.*"

As his translator finished reading the statement in Arabic, Mister Banks looked up from the sheet he had been reading from and cleared his throat.

"For the rest of you, here in the Ministry of Health, we are not going to punish you for actions you may have taken in the past if they were dictated by the regime. Regardless of our cultural differences or religious beliefs we are here to help you, but you must help us to do that."

Many in the audience silently stood with their mouths open, their eyes darting back and forth. Some covered their faces with their hands and looked downward.

Sahar looked toward Reem who glanced back at her, her eyes wide. "They are disbanding the *Ba'ath* party. They're really doing it," Sahar's voice was barely audible above the sudden buzz in the room.

The Iraqi minister of health gasped. He looked at his assistants at his side and saw from the shock on their faces that they too heard and understood what Banks had stated. All of them down to director general, and then a sizable number beyond, were at least *Udw* and *Udw 'Amil* level *Ba'ath* party members.

Mister Banks continued, oblivious to the commotion that his statement had created. "Tomorrow morning, let's meet in the conference room on the second floor at 10:00 o'clock. And please, everyone, understand that I am sincere," he said as he placed his right hand over his heart in the Iraqi gesture of sincerity.

The minister of health's entourage looked at each other and began asking one another whether they had been fired or invited to a staff meeting. The minister just shook his head as Banks continued, "You are free now. You will be treated with respect."

Banks put his hand over his heart again as he bowed his head toward the crowd. Then the coalition team retreated out the door they had entered to begin the tour of the ministry with the surrounding grounds.

As the CPA team exited the building, Sahar overheard an exuberant Facility Protection Services guard who sounded as though he were almost giddy.

"I told you they were here to help, and they clearly mean action," he said.

His companion, an older looking, less cheerful man replied, "This doesn't prove anything. Actions will speak louder than words."

Sahar looked for the source of the optimistic voice, it was the bright-faced, slightly curly-haired guard, Mohammad Jawad. "The Americans bombed when most people were at home sleeping. They intentionally did not target the MOH, or any apartment buildings. Their air strikes and the invasion force were very careful because they are not trying to kill us. They are taking power away from the *Ba'athists*, they are here to help us, *Insha'Allah.*"

Sahar watched Mohammad smile as he continued to try to convince his friends that this was legitimate. Sahar had not seen Mohammad frown since before the birth of his youngest child. Reem was smiling also, as were many of the employees. The room buzzed in mini conversations, but Sahar maintained her stoic, emotionless, public-face.

From a few stairs up the wide, office tower stairwell that opened-up into the lobby, Zaid watched. He shook his head and bit his inner cheek. He surveyed the crowd, taking note of people's reactions. He saw Reem and Sahar in the middle of the crowded lobby. When he saw Sahar, he studied the hollowness in her eyes and the quiet tenseness of her lips.

Good, he noted to himself, *at least she isn't a fool.*

After the assembly thinned, Zaid turned and began his assent to the sixth floor to his MOH office. He went

immediately to his desk and prepared a message for Doctor
Jassem:

> *Hatherat Al-Aeusteth,*
> *I humbly report that an old man named Banks will*
> *represent the Americans. Today he introduced himself as*
> *the 'acting minister.' They fired the leaders and kept the*
> *work force; making enemies of the most powerful men*
> *here. With the leaders all gone, no one will remain who*
> *knows of my recent promotion. Therefore, I am confident*
> *that I will be able continue to safeguard Kimadia until*
> *your anxiously awaited and well-timed return.*
> *Your servant, with great respect,*
> *–Zaid*

After Zaid reread his message he sat silently and
reflected, *the Americans are fools. Fear is how one gets respect*
and power in Iraq. Decisive action is strength; leniency and
kindness are characteristics of the weak—and of the oppressed.

CHAPTER *16*

"Wow. This morning was certainly eye-opening," Mister
Banks said to his team assembled around the large table in Room
S-200, a second-floor conference room located at the northwest
end of the south wing that jutted ninety degrees out from the
main rectangular building of the Republican Palace. The room
had a high ceiling with several large, gold-tinted chandeliers
hanging well out of reach, and fans twirling warm air between
them, along the space's center line. White paint and marble trim
surrounded large bulletin boards attached to the long-
dimensioned walls; the wall running from the southern corner to
the eastern corner of the room also comprised of the dark-
varnished wood double-doors, which opened-up to the corridor's
terminus towards the room's eastern end. Three layers of
curtains, one decorative, one functional, and the third translucent,
covered the large windows on both ends of the room. Gold-
edged Victorian reproduction furniture with floral-patterned

padding on the seats and backrests—furniture that seemed designed to scream for attention yet lacked the quality of keeping it—filled the room. Mercifully, the table and chairs covered most of the ornate terrazzo floor that with its circles and spirals, and multiple color schemes, seemed determined to avoid providing any visual respite to the room's occupants.

To be sure, the design of the room perfectly matched the décor of the rest of the palace, which sat facing away from the bend in the river, in an oasis-like neighborhood of amply-irrigated, lush vegetation that included beautiful palm trees soaring high into the deep, blue skies. The palace grounds hugged the bank of the Tigris River in the area which the Americans had recently dubbed, the *Green Zone*. Though the grounds were green, the area wasn't named for its color. It was named the Green Zone because in army talk, *green* is synonymous with *go, passable,* or *safe.* This area was secured from the surrounding, lesser-controlled areas of Baghdad by the river on two sides, by tall, pre-manufactured concrete barriers that had begun to appear throughout the city, and by soldiers of the 3rd Infantry Division.

"We need to clean up that mess. Can you believe it?" Banks asked the eighteen men and women who occupied the chairs around the large table and against the walls surrounding it as they settled in after the nerve-racking drive back from the Ministry of Health through the disorganized Baghdad traffic.

Mister Banks sat at one end of the table, a retired Marine Corps Vietnam veteran now serving as a medical finance specialist who had worked with Mister Banks for years back in the states, sat to Banks' left next to Major Eileen Chong, a well-organized, precise officer who served as an admin officer. Colonel Newborne, retitled the chief of operations, sat with his back to the door in the middle of the long table next to a quick-witted black haired logistician who loved to break every challenge into its most minor details, Lieutenant Colonel Tony Weeks, and a suavely dressed surgeon from Holland who had made responding to humanitarian crisis his life's calling, to Tony's left.

At the opposite end of the long table from Banks, sat the rear admiral public health officer wearing a navy uniform, who when not in Iraq served as the director for the Indian Health Service. To his left sat a lieutenant colonel public health officer who was borrowed by the CPA from one of the US Army preventive medicine units that provided coverage to the Baghdad area. To her left was Major Thomas D. Cross, a solidly built, serious looking operations officer with very short blond hair and a Master Sergeant operations NCO, Sergeant Marty, who seemed to find himself dragged everywhere Newborne went. Finally, a captain medical logistics officer sat between him and Carson Prance, a twenty-eight-year-old election campaign veteran, who was newly appointed by Secretary of Defense Rumsfeld to be the chief of staff. To Mister Banks's right, Carson sat, his dark brown hair nicely combed, his sunglasses tucked in along the two undone buttons below the front of his neck near an orange alligator logo on his dark green pull-over shirt.

In chairs against the walls of the room sat a civilian accountant from London, another couple physicians, one from the UK and one from Serbia, an Italian pharmacist, a pharmacy tech from Spain, all civilians, and two army E-5 sergeants, one, an operations NCO, and the other, a log tech.

"We need to show change," said Mister Banks as he looked around the room.

"Let's do some high-visibility, fast projects first, to demonstrate that we are here and we mean business," added Carson, his chief of staff.

The acting minister of health nodded before he continued, "We need to go in there and show them that we are here to work with them. So, tomorrow, go in and introduce yourself to your counterparts and do all you can to get to know them. Until we know differently, this is how we'll organize: I'll run the front office which includes finance and accounting from Room S-214, down the hall then make a left, then on the left, above the dining facility. Admiral, you run the clinical and public health team out of Room S-206, which is just past the stairwell on the right, and colonel, you run the operations team from here."

He paused and looked around, "Does anyone have any questions?"

Half of the people replied, "No sir." The others remained quiet.

"Carson, please go over our list of personnel requirements."

The chief of staff read his notes, "A contracting expert, a lab manager, a LAN expert, and information technology people."

"Colonel Newborne, we also need an engineer here on our team. Why don't you see if the Army has one laying around?"

"Yes sir."

"Gentlemen, think it over tonight. Let me know tomorrow if you need anything else. And everyone keep in mind, we must be very frugal with our funds. We will be held accountable." Banks looked around the room. "Anything else?"

Then he looked over at Lieutenant Colonel Tony Weeks, the logistician, and added, "We need to find some furniture, for here and the ministry."

"Yes, Sir," replied Weeks writing it down.

After a moment of silence, "Oh, one more thing Colonel Newborne,"

"Yes sir?"

"No more uniforms. I don't want the Iraqis intimidated by soldiers. We are their peers, not their conquerors. Go get yourselves some civilian clothes. But right now, everyone, go get yourselves some dinner."

As the front office group and the public health team began to migrate out the door, Mister Banks smiled. With a lightness in his step, he walked down the marble corridor toward the office that had been set up for the CPA MOH front office group.

When they had gone, Newborne stood up and walked around to the end of the table to his left, just past where the admiral had been sitting, about midway to the far wall. In front of him extra chairs and a few small tables were randomly scattered about. He turned towards the other military who quietly remained in their seats watching him. "Go eat. Then get your asses back here."

As his team filed out, Newborne turned around and walked towards the window. Just before he got there he stopped and looked down at his camouflage-patterned, desert tan uniform, magnificently illuminated above his knees by the late afternoon sun flooding into that end of the room. It contrasted sharply against his brown boots, which his pant legs were neatly tucked into, and the floor, which remained in shadow. "Civilian clothes? What the fuck?"

CHAPTER *17*

At 10:00, four Iraqi Ministry of Health workers took seats in the folding chairs around the folding table that the CPA team had brought with them from the palace.

"Where is everyone else?" Mister Banks asked. "There are at least a dozen directorates in the building, aren't there?"

The four Iraqis looked at each other, then towards the table. "Sir," one of them finally responded in labored English. "The others will not be here. Sir, with your permission, they were *Ba'athist* party members, sir."

"All of them?" Mister Banks looked at Carson, the admiral and Colonel Newborne. Then he extended his glance to the blank stares of the other six coalition members who stood behind them.

Hesitatingly, the spokesman by default answered, "Yes, Sir. All of them."

"Where did they go?"

The Iraqi spokesman shrugged his shoulders and then looked down.

Mister Banks quickly interrupted the pause, "Okay, who is left? Please introduce yourselves."

CHAPTER *18*

He was late and it was already dark when newly promoted Lieutenant Colonel Joseph Brown arrived home from work. His wife was cooking dinner in their eleventh-floor Silver Spring apartment. After a bit of small talk about what mom and the baby did that day; Joe flipped the channel from Barney the Dinosaur to CNN. His baby daughter—sucking on her turquoise colored pacifier—sat in his lap as they watched the news. Looking at his daughter's round cheeks Joe was considering the best way to break the news to his wife.

In the spring of 1987 during the Cold War, with very few exceptions, combat veterans still in the Army were senior NCOs and warrants, field grade or flag officers who stayed on or came back in after Vietnam. At Fort Sam Houston, one of Joe's Officer Basic Course instructors had asked his platoon, "Who thinks that sometime in your career, you will be on a real battlefield?"

That was when the term battlefield referred to an all-out confrontation with the big mean Soviet bear. Joe did not raise his hand. He had a hard time envisioning such a war. He joined ROTC after President Reagan explained that the "surest path to peace was a strong deterrence." This made sense to Joe, so he became part of that deterrence. Deterrence was not war. Therefore, just having an all-out war with the Soviet Union would have been a failure, and Joe didn't expect that to happen.

In the sixteen years since that day, however, Joe had deployed twice, first to Operation Desert Shield and Desert Storm—the two major phases of the Gulf War—and the second time to Haiti. Now when he smelled diesel, or when he heard the downshifting of a five-ton truck, his mind was transported back to a serene desert night northwest of Haffir Al Batin, Saudi Arabia, when he and the rest of second platoon, 145th Medical Clearing Company, drove under black-out conditions across the seemingly-unending, flat desert toward their perimeter a couple clicks off Tap-line Road.

Now he was working for the US Army's Health Facility Planning Agency (HFPA) running a project office managing medical design and construction in the North Atlantic Region. Over the last month, more and more of his buddies from Walter Reed Army Medical Center and other army hospitals were receiving orders to fill vacancies in field units, bringing them up to strength before they deployed.

A few hours earlier, Joe received a phone call from Colonel Rick, the HFPA Commander. Orders assigning him to the CPA were on their way. The conversation he and his wife were about to have would be the second hardest part of the deployment. Leaving his baby girl would be the hardest.

CHAPTER *19*

His car parked two blocks away, Zaid stood inside the walled yard, surrounding Doctor Jassem's luxurious house in the Khadamia district of Baghdad. A couple of large men carrying AK-47s and wearing suits and sunglasses stood at predesignated positions around him.

"*Aeusteth* Jassem," announced Zaid, quietly, with utmost respect, "Thank you for seeing me."

"Zaid, do you have news for me?" Doctor Jassem said, holding a foreign newspaper and a cigarette.

"Yes, *aeusteth*. Yesterday, the first group of Americans arrived to the MOH," he said as he handed him his handwritten message. "It appears that ORHA has been replaced by a new organization called the Coalition Provisional Authority."

Doctor Jassem opened the message and read it.

"As the first organization led by an army general was intending to work with the ministry leadership, the first thing the new group did was fire them—the top four levels of *Ba'athists*," stated Zaid.

As Doctor Jassem read, Zaid continued, "They kept all the workers. In fact, the number of workers has grown. Today many family members and friends reported to work as though they have always worked there. The Americans have no way of knowing who is who."

Doctor Jassem looked up from his reading and motioned his hand for Zaid to continue.

Zaid checked his posture and added, "Incredible that Ambassador Bremmer made deba'athification his first-priority, *aeusteth*. Wasn't General Garner going to work with the top leaders in each ministry? Not fire all the managers?" he asked.

Doctor Jassem looked at Zaid a moment before answering, "Yes. Perhaps General Garner was not meeting the expectations of his government."

"There must be a reason," Zaid said, "But what would be worth insulting the most connected, most experienced, most capable people in Iraq? Many of them would have been willing partners with them, and the Americans turned them into shamed, desperate men."

Jassem silently looked at Zaid then nodded slowly.

Zaid continued, "Their honor alone, much less their anger, will demand that each one of them vow to take vengeance on the Americans."

Zaid dropped his eyes and stood silently until Doctor Jassem handed Zaid's message to the man who was standing nearest him.

"What are your orders, *aeusteth*?" Zaid asked as humbly as he could, again standing stiffly.

"For now, you are my eyes and ears at the ministry. Be aware of actions and make a list of whom we can rely on. When it is time to act, I will send you word."

"Yes *aeusteth, ma'salama*."

CHAPTER *20*
Baghdad: 24 May 2003

A week after the newly formed Coalition Provisional Authority issued their first directive, the CPA issued its second: to disband the Iraqi Army.

After carefully reading a copy of the Coalition Provisional Authority Order Number Two, twice, Zaid leaned back in his office in the ministry, the windows behind him, he put his feet up on his desk and his hands behind his head.

After a moment of silently staring upward, a smile crossing his face, he quickly dropped his feet to the floor. Hastily grabbing a pencil and a yellow pad out of his desk drawer, he centered the paper in front of him and wrote:

40,000 party leaders
+ 400,000 soldiers

He underlined and then circled the numbers. *40,000 rejected and insulted leaders, plus 400,000 trained, recently unemployed, disillusioned, dishonored, and desperate men.*

He stood up and turned, looking north over the parking lot and the cemetery six floors below he grinned and spoke aloud to no one. "What are they trying to do?"

CHAPTER *21*

"Time to go to the ninth-floor," Lieutenant Colonel Tony Weeks told Lieutenant Colonel Joe Brown after their two-vehicle convoy drove into the parking garage at the MOH. Joe had accompanied Tony to BIAP, Baghdad International Airport, on his first full day in Baghdad. The official temperature was 54.4 Celsius, about 130 degrees Fahrenheit. On the tarmac, out in the sun, it was even hotter. They and some of *Kimadia's* warehousemen spent most the morning receiving, unloading and processing a cargo plane containing a gift from the Republic of Pakistan—blankets. Palettes of blankets.

Tony stood about average height, but was stocky. He looked like he used to wrestle in high school. Topped with thick black hair his facial features were large, and he was cursed with fast growing whiskers that showed as a perpetual afternoon shadow. While in Iraq he always wore a hunting vest over a golf shirt and body armor, the many pockets full of small notepads, writing utensils, an apple or an orange and extra ammo for his 9mm pistol, which he wore in a shoulder holster, and his MP-5, which he slung over his other shoulder. Joe mounted his 9mm Beretta in a holster and two fifteen-round ammo clips in a pouch attached to his belt.

"Colonel wants me to introduce you to the director general of engineering," he said.

"Sounds good," replied Joe. Above his brown army boots and his khaki pants Joe wore a maroon shirt that he stretched over his body armor. His black backpack held his computer, some note books and the other odd items he thought might be useful.

"Yeah, the DG, that's what the head of each directorate is called, is a man named Sattar. He seems to be a really good guy."

Joe nodded as they started up the stairs.

As they passed the sixth-floor landing, Tony told Joe, "My office is right in there, second door on the left. The floor is different than all the rest because *Kimadia*, the medical logistics company, kind of controlled the ministry under Saddam."

Joe nodded as they passed, continuing to go up the stairs.

"You alright?" Tony asked him as they approached the last landing before entering the ninth floor.

"Sure, I'm just a little hot, I'm sweating like a damn pig."

Coming out of the stairwell, Tony stopped to take a quick look at Joe, being about the same height Tony looked directly at his eyes, "You got any water in there?" he asked tapping his backpack.

Joe nodded.

"Well, they say you get used to the heat, but I haven't seemed to yet. You may want to loosen your body armor a little bit too, it looks like you may have it on too tight."

Trying to control his breathing, Joe nodded, "Okay."

Many curious eyes managed to catch a glimpse of them as the two walked down the hall, Tony seemed not to notice, Joe nodded and smiled whenever he made eye contact. Joe was surprised by the wide diversity of clothing style, skin color, and hair color. Seeing the women and how they dressed, Joe had to remind himself that under Saddam, Iraq was mostly secular, not a fundamentalist Islamic country like Saudi Arabia.

The two stepped into one of the many identical, narrow offices that lined the corridor, "*Sayid* Sattar, this is Lieutenant Colonel Brown, he is being assigned here as an advisor."

Sattar smiled and stood up. The several people in the office moved towards the walls and out of the way as the two Americans approached Sattar's desk that was positioned with his chair backed against the window.

"I am glad meeting you Brown," said the light skinned man with a Kurdish accent. He held his hand out to shake as the smile on his round face beamed below the few brown hairs that jutted out from his mostly bald head.

Joe, also smiling, reached out and shook his hand. Sattar was one of the few DGs who continued to work at the MOH. Joe didn't know why and he didn't ask. Joe bowed, Sattar returned the bow, and as he did, one side of his dark blue pull-over shirt collar comically flopped out of place. Sattar continued beaming as he said, "Welcome Brown."

Then Sattar looked over to Sahar who was one of three women in the room. He said something to her in Arabic.

Sahar nodded to the chief engineer, then she stepped away from the wall, "We are happy to have you here, Sattar has asked me to speak for him as he is embarrassed by his English."

"Oh no, his English is far better than my Arabic," replied Joe smiling at Sattar.

Sattar nodded his head to a young woman who stood nearby, he whispered something and she looked at Joe, then she quickly scurried past him and out the door. Sattar looked over towards Sahar.

"May I introduce you to the staff?" Sahar asked as she began to present the second eldest man to Joe.

"This is Hamid," she said.

Hamid stepped forward and shook his hand. His clean-shaven face remained stern, "Hamid is an engineer, he is our master planner."

Hamid was tall and thin with a rectangular face that seemed attentive to every detail. His white, short sleeve shirt had a simple grid pattern of grey and black stripes below the collar, buttons ran down the front. His voice was calm and soothing, "I am happy to meet you, Brown."

"This is Wasan, she is our chief architect."

Except for her face and her hands, Wasan was covered from head to toe with a plain black *abaia*. Joe reached out his hand, but Wasan pressed her hands tightly against her *abaia*. Then she smiled broadly and said, "I am sorry, but no touching."

Joe smiled and nodded. "I'm sorry. I understand."

Then Sahar said, her accent swinging high and low, and back and forth with each syllable, "And I am Sahar, I am a dentist, my job is to represent the healthcare providers to ensure that the buildings can support their services."

Sahar put her hand forward to shake.

Joe didn't move.

Tony laughed as he put his hand on Joe's shoulder pushing towards Sahar, "You can shake her hand."

Joe quickly glanced around and reached out his hand, "Of course, I'm sorry."

"You're on your own now, call me if you need something."

"Thanks Tony, I'll come down in a few hours."

"Be at the security office at 14:30. See you then." Tony nodded at the group. As he departed, he held the door open so the young woman carrying a silver platter with a pot of tea, several small ceramic cups, a sugar bowl and tiny spoons on it could re-enter the room.

Sattar waved his hand to the group to sit down and for the young lady to serve the tea.

"Mister Joe Brown, it is time for some *chai*, please sit down," said Sahar.

After Joe sat down, everyone else took one of the simple metal folding chairs that were scattered in the space in front of Sattar's desk.

"I am honored to be here, thank you," Joe said looking at each of his new acquaintances one at a time, "and please, please call me Joe."

CHAPTER *22*

Sahar, along with Joe and Captain David Maxwell were working their way through the piles of hospital and clinic assessments that had been collected from Non-Governmental Organizations, the World Health Organization, military units, and the ministry's own people.

Colonel Rick sent Captain Maxwell on the deployment with Joe in response to Colonel Newborne's request for an engineer. Like some others on the CPA MOH team, the thin, baby-faced captain sported a scruffy goatee.

"Are you growing a beard?" Sahar asked him as they began their third day going over assessments.

Max blushed as he stroked his chin with his hand, "Well, since we are wearing civilian clothes and often driving around Baghdad without any real firepower, we are kind of a soft target. We don't want to attract attention to ourselves by looking like soldiers."

"Oh," responded Sahar as she looked across the table that was covered with stacks of hundreds of the crinkled papers. Some of the assessments of the Iraqi healthcare system's hospitals and clinics were written in Arabic; others were written in English, French, German, Spanish, Japanese and even a few in a Slavic language that none of them recognized. Some of the assessments included sketches, others were narratives written by architects or engineers, quite a few were by physicians, and nurses, while others were written by equipment vendors, soldiers, or by MOH employees. Some were in pencil, others ink. Unfortunately, at some point, some of the papers had been wet—probably by either dripping sweat or spilled sips of water––rendering them nearly illegible. Spelling inconsistencies, such as 'Al-Yarmouk' or 'El Yarmook,' were typical, as not all Arabic sounds translate well into other languages.

There were numerous assessments for various Saddam Hussein Hospitals, as each governorate, which is the word used for a province or a state, had at least one hospital named after the now deposed dictator. These hospitals were usually the largest hospital in each governorate. Interestingly, but adding to the confusion, they were often also called the Japanese Hospitals, in recognition of the Asian country's role in building them.

In many cases, there were multiple assessments of the same facility, but often they were not of much value because the assessments were frequently radically different or even completely contradictory from one another. While the nurse assessor from the US Army may have used one scaling system and evaluated the facility to be *red* or unusable, a Dutch physician from Doctors Without Borders may have determined that it was, *a bit neglected, but fully functional.*

"How do you say this hospital's name again?" asked Joe, for the third time.

"Al Hamza General Hospital." Responded Sahar, "*Al Ham-za,*" she repeated herself emphasizing her mouth movements. "It specializes in surgery. In *Qadissiya.*"

"*Al Ham-za,*" repeated Joe. "Didn't we review an assessment from there already?"

"No, that was Al Amirya, in Falluja, in Anbar Governorate," responded Sahar.

"Also surgical?" asked Joe.

"Yes, all general hospitals have surgery."

"Okay. And what condition did the assessment sheet say *Al Ham-za* was in?"

"Functional, but they don't have any physicians, and their radiology equipment is broken," she responded.

"Okay," he answered Sahar, then Joe looked over at Captain Maxwell, "Did we capture all of that in our spreadsheet correctly?"

"Yes, sir. Right here," answered Max highlighting a line in his spreadsheet on his screen.

"Great. Thanks."

It took more than a week to go through the entire stack, then a few more days to sort and study their data looking at it by governorate, by city, by hospital and by condition, capacity and capabilities. Finally, they had sorted and filed the assessments into four notebooks and loaded the data into one spreadsheet. They had a picture of what they thought was out there, though they didn't know how accurate their picture was. Joe asked Sahar, "Well, that's all we can do with the assessments. Time to show the bosses. What time can we get in to see them?"

"They're waiting for us now," answered Sahar.

Hamid, Sattar, and Wasan were in Sattar's office when Sahar, Max and Joe entered.

They crowded around Max's laptop so they could see the screen; Joe and Sahar sat across from them. Max began to walk them through the spreadsheet.

"That's not right," said Hameed, after about ten minutes when the discussion was about one of Bagdad's largest facilities.

"Okay," said Joe, "*Sayid* Hamid, what do you and your staff know about Al Yarmouk Hospital?"

In his trademark calm voice, Hamid answered, "Its condition is very bad. They need everything new."

"But we had an assessment that said it is fully functional," countered Joe, opening one of the notebooks and placing his finger on the page he was referencing.

"Yes, it is open. It is very bad, but they are operating that facility. They have no choice," the master planner responded.

"Does their water supply system work? In other words, do they have enough clean water?" asked the American.

"Yes."

Joe nodded, as he made a mark in his notebook, "And they have electricity?"

"Yes, except for the brownouts."

"They have generators?"

"Yes."

"Do the generators work?"

"Yes."

"And they have supplies? Medical equipment? The sewer works?"

"Yes, all three yes."

"So, this assessment that declares that Al Yarmouk can see patients, is correct?" Joe asked.

"No, it is not right. It needs a lot of work," replied Hamid.

Joe paused a moment to look around. Then he continued, "To meet minimal levels to function?"

"Yes, it needs much work before it can function."

"Specifically, what work does it need to function?"

"It needs water."

"You just said it has enough clean water."

"Yes, but sometimes they don't have enough. The faucets on the second floor don't work."

"A water pressure problem?"

"Yes."

"Okay. Anything else?"

"Electricity."

"What about the electricity?"

"The neighbors take the electricity."

"What?" Joe asked recoiling slightly.

"The neighbors tap into the feed and that is how they have power at their houses."

"Well, un-tap them."

"But then what will the people do? They won't have power."

Joe pressed the button-end of his mechanical pencil into his chin and thought a minute. Without looking up, he asked,

"Do the neighbors take so much that the hospital cannot function?"

"No. It is not that much."

"So, what's the problem?"

"The generators are the problem."

"You told me that the generators work."

"Yes. But they don't have fuel and they are in bad condition. Sometimes they don't start."

Joe lifted his head and glanced over at Captain Maxwell who was sitting in the middle of the group manning the keyboard doing his best to keep a straight face as the discussion bounced around him. "No fuel, and they are not reliable. I see."

"So, *Al Yarmouk* is not functional?"

"No, *Al Yarmouk* is one of our better hospitals. If you spend money there you must spend money everywhere else first."

"Right. I know it will eventually come down to where we spend money, but right now let's just define what we must do to make all the hospitals functional. So, *Al Yarmouk* is functional then?"

"Yes."

"So, *Al Yarmouk* is not functional then?"

"Yes."

Sahar watched Joe look at his Iraqi counterparts and then speak carefully. "To develop a program, we must identify what is not working. Our priority is to fix the buildings that are stopping the critical healthcare delivery from being performed. To prioritize, we need a rough assessment of all the hospitals in the country so we know where there are people without coverage so we can focus our initial efforts there. Once we know where the services are not available, we can develop scopes of work to provide the infrastructure to enable the services and attach funding to efforts that will do the most good for the most people, the quickest. So, is Al Yarmouk functional or not?"

"Joe, Al Yarmouk's condition is good and bad, as you like."

"Okay, Hamid. But that gets us nowhere."

Joe looked over at Hamid's boss, the DG of engineering. Sattar was genuinely a kind and considerate person. Joe spoke to him as he would speak to his own grandfather.

"*Sayid* Sattar, we need to better identify our criteria so we know what we're talking about. Let's talk about our goals."

Sattar nodded and smiled.

Then Joe looked at Sahar who was sitting next to Hamid. "Sahar, please get with the engineer staff, and write down the main problems that they think the facilities have. Not any hospital particularly, just common problems across the inventory. We will worry about individual facilities after we have something to rate them by."

"I will do it." Sahar answered immediately.

Joe smiled. "Thank you. Maybe you all can work in the conference room down the hall, and if Sattar agrees, maybe you can pull in a representative familiar with each discipline and governorate."

Sahar relayed the suggestion in Arabic, Sattar nodded his head and authorized the action.

"Captain Maxwell, you go with them," Joe directed.

"Yes sir."

"How detailed?" Sahar asked looking at Joe leaning forward.

"Not. I don't want us to get lost in the details. Let's get the concepts first. We'll have to figure out how detailed we need to be after we agree on the main issues."

Sahar stood up, she and Max departed together.

When Sahar and Max had interviewed and documented input from some of the staff they returned to Sattar's office. They quietly entered and stood out of the way along one of the walls and listened.

As she entered, Joe was asking, "*Sayid* Hamid, how are we going to do this?"

"Joe, our process is that first we receive our instructions from the minister of planning, and then we develop the scope of work and bill of materials."

"Okay. But the minister of planning is not going to give us anything. We have to come up with a program on our own."

"Oh no, Joe. This is how it's done."

"But Hamid, we are trying to determine what we must do to reestablish the healthcare system. We are not going to get this information from the Ministry of Planning."

"As you like."

"Right. As I like."

Then Hamid stated, "We should add beds to most of our hospitals."

"Why?"

"Because they are old."

"But Hamid, old may mean outdated capabilities or poor condition, but it does not necessarily require additional capacity."

"But we know these things Joe. We have a program."

"You have a program?" asked Joe incredulously.

"Of course," responded Hamid, in the same calm tone of voice he almost always spoke.

"Why didn't you tell me this before?"

"I didn't know you wanted to see it."

"But we have been discussing this for a couple weeks now. Please show it to me," Joe said, trying to imitate Hamid's calm demeanor.

Hamid spoke with Sattar in Arabic for a couple minutes. Sattar then spoke to Wasan who had been sitting silently. The senior architect's roundish face glowed with enthusiasm as she discussed something with Hamid for a moment before she scurried out of the room. While she was gone the three discussed what was needed to develop the MOH program.

"Oh, no, Joe, that is not the process. We provide our program back to the Ministry of Planning," protested Hamid.

Wasan ran back in carrying a single standard size piece of paper. Joe braced himself.

"*Shukren*," thank you, "*Sayida* Wasan," Joe said to her as he took the paper. Wasan rapidly withdrew her hands as soon as Joe touched it.

The list was in Arabic, but because of the numbers, it was obvious that the entire program consisted of eight projects. Joe nodded looking up at Hamid, "Please explain this to me."

As Hamid was going over it, Joe took notes and made some calculations. Sahar continued to stand quietly off to the side but Max returned to his chair at the table signing back into his laptop and opening the spreadsheet. When Hamid was through, Joe asked a couple questions.

"*Sayid* Hamid, the total cost for this list equates to about $40 million US. Right?"

"Yes."

"And you are telling me that this list represents what the Iraqi MOH needs to build so its healthcare system will be functional, right?"

"Yes, Joe."

"So, if you were to get $40 million you could do everything you need to do to fix all of your buildings so they would all be functional."

"Yes."

"So, if something is not on this list, it does not need to be done. Right?"

"Yes Joe."

"Okay. *Al Yarmouk* is not on this list. So, we don't have to do anything at *Al Yarmouk* to make it functional."

"But Joe we already discussed this, we need money to fix *Al Yarmouk*."

"Yes, I know, but it is not on this list."

"No, this is the list from the Ministry of Planning. This is our program."

Joe took a deep breath while glancing at all the faces in the room, ending up at Sattar's. Sattar sat back in his chair grinning, glancing between Hamid and Joe.

"Okay." Joe spoke slowly, "Then I need to do a better job explaining what we need to do. We need to figure out what critical work we need to do immediately that will have a significant positive impact on the healthcare system's ability to serve the population's healthcare needs. Then we must identify what critical projects are needed to execute this work and estimate how much it will cost. Then while we are executing these critical projects we must build a program on how we can make the entire healthcare system more functional, safer, more effective and more efficient. Do you understand?"

"Yes," replied Hamid.

"Okay then," said Joe shifting his eyes to Sattar.

"Yes. Good," replied the DG.

Joe sat there next to Max for a moment. Then he smiled and started chuckling. Soon all the Iraqis realized that Joe was laughing. Though they may not have known why, soon everyone in the room laughed along.

"We don't even know what we are saying to each other, do we?" inquired Joe in between breathes.

"Yes. *Insha'Allah*," Sattar answered seriously, while pleasantly beaming at Joe.

Everyone laughed harder. Sahar nodded at Max and stepped forward to address the group. "Joe, we have the list you asked for," she said.

Joe glanced at Max, who kept his eyes on his computer screen.

Joe shifted his gaze over to Sahar

"Okay, let's see it."

She handed him a single sheet of paper. On it were six words: *Sanitation, mechanical, electrical, nursing, size, and architectural.*

Joe put his free hand up against his mouth as he continued to look at the paper. Sahar was surprised and amused when he then pushed air through his puckered lips making a "phtpthpth phtpthpth" sound.

"Well, that about covers it. What about furniture and equipment?" Joe asked.

"Yes, that too," answered Sahar.

"Of course," Joe said, adding them to the list with his mechanical pencil that he pulled from a pocket. Joe grinned broadly and then looked at Max sitting in front of his computer.

"Now we are getting somewhere," Joe said smiling.

"Yes," said Sattar.

Sahar and everyone in the room laughed again.

CHAPTER *23*

The ceiling fans in the South Wing of the palace whirled, pushing warm air around the room as Carson, his face glistened with sweat, told the rest of the CPA MOH staff about the great things his colleagues at the United States Agency for International Development, USAID, were doing. Although the challenges they overcame to get the public schools ready for the 2003-2004 school year and their efforts to renovate clinics by painting them battleship grey—the only paint available at the time—were certainly noteworthy; Joe thought calling them *great successes* may be a bit exaggerated.

Wrapping up his summary, Carson added indifferently, "The CPA put out this afternoon that they need the reconstruction project lists on 13 September. They need to send the program to Congress."

Joe straightened up in his seat and looked at his watch, it was just after 4:20 Tuesday afternoon, 19 August. Joe shook his head. Carson was looking at him, "Lieutenant Colonel Brown, anything you would like to say?"

Joe stiffened and said, "September 13? That's less than a month from now. What exactly does the CPA want by then?"

"The project list, everything Congress needs to appropriate funding."

Joe sat still a moment, his mouth closed, then he said, "There is a huge difference between a project list and an appropriations program."

Carson nodded, "Whatever is needed for Congress to fund the projects."

Joe sighed heavily, "So, they want a multi-year program to fix the condition, and align capability and capacity of a healthcare system that has been neglected for twenty years with the twenty-five million people it needs to serve, in a country the size of Texas, in three weeks? If it weren't for the World Health Organization giving us a list of the 240 hospitals and 1,200 clinics we wouldn't even know where they all are."

"Not just healthcare, all types of construction, from power plants, to airports, roads, everything."

"And you don't see a problem with that?"

Carson didn't respond. Joe just shook his head.

"That timeline isn't realistic. We don't have the data on the population or the facilities. It will take us much longer than that just to assess the current situation," Joe said.

"It has to be complete and correct. Congress needs to know exactly what the CPA needs and how much it will cost."

Joe didn't smile, "What they are asking for is ridiculous. Whoever is pushing this deadline has no idea what it takes to develop a good program. And if you start construction without a good program, the very best you can hope for is to do the wrong things well. It's not possible."

Joe was going to continue but Mister Banks intervened, "Let's pull it together guys, we are one team here."

Joe looked over at Mister Banks, "Sir, we are already working on an emergency program of obvious needs that we can turn in to fix specific problems, that we could start designing while we continue to develop a more comprehensive program. But we should not kid ourselves that we, or any other ministry, can do anything more than that in the next several weeks."

Then Joe looked back towards Carson, "Is Congress demanding this, or is this a self-imposed time-line?"

"No one else seems to have a problem with the deadline," repeated Carson.

The windows shook as a large boom resonated across the city.

"Damn. That was a big one," Banks understated in a calm voice. The red-faced gentleman turned toward his young and eager protégé. "Go find out what that was."

Carson ran out of the room. The Public Health Services Rear Admiral began talking about how investing in public health labs and blood banks would enhance the Iraqis' ability to perform preventive medicine. Carson returned and all eyes turned toward him as he entered. The doctor stopped talking.

"It was a car bomb at the Canal Hotel. The UN is hosting a conference there right now. They say it was a big one."

Looking at Newborne, Mister Banks said, "Colonel, I need security to go and take a look. Get a team together, we leave in fifteen minutes."

CHAPTER *24*

Baghdad: 19 August 2003

Mister Banks' intent was to see the Iraqi healthcare system's response to this crisis, but when he arrived at the bombing site he discovered that the building adjacent to the Canal Hotel was a hospital that was badly damaged by the blast. No walls remained standing in the one-story hospital wing closest to the bomb crater. With no electricity, the water shut off, all the patients of Iraq's only spinal cord injury hospital were already being relocated to other facilities. Mister Banks, Carson, Major Chong and Max entered a gaping hole in the sidewall, just a few rooms away from the front door.

"Colonel Newborne," Mister Banks said into his cell phone, "We need a security team to guard the Spinal Cord Hospital tonight to protect it from looters."

As Newborne hung up his phone he looked out the window he had parked his desk in front of, and noted that the sun had already begun to make its final descent. He turned around and looked at the three officers who were in the office with him, "We're going to the ministry to pick up some guards, then we are going to the Canal Hotel. Thom, you're with me. Tony and Joe, you'll be the tail car."

The four shut down their computers, put on their body armor, and hurried out to the parking lot. Less than ten minutes after they were notified they departed the Green Zone through Assassin's Gate, the checkpoint along the most direct route to the ministry named after the Alpha Company *Assassins*, an armor regiment in the 3rd Infantry Division. Their goal was to get to the Canal Hotel before dark. The blue Suburban and the white SUV skidded into the parking lot at the ministry, and Mohammad Jawad, the security guard in charge of the shift ran to greet the unexpected Americans.

"How many men do you have on duty here right now?" greeted Newborne.

"I have eight men on duty here right now sir," answered Mohammad, standing with his feet together and chin held high.

"How many do you have on call?" the colonel asked.

"All eight of them are here. They are not on call."

"No, what I mean is how many more men do you have on call?"

"We have forty more men, eight of them are here."

"Can you get six more men to come in tonight?"

"Yes, but we already have eight here."

"I need you and five of your men who are here right now to come with us to the Spinal Cord Hospital."

"But then there will only be two men at the ministry. Two is not enough."

"I know. How long will it take to get five or six new men to come here?"

"Eight new men will come in at midnight."

"I need them here now."

Mohammad cocked his head, "When do you want us to go to the Spinal Cord Hospital?"

"Now. One minute ago," Newborne responded.

Mohammad's eyes widened, he formed the Iraqi gesture for "wait a moment" or "patience" by turning his wrist inward and extending his middle finger and his index finger together, and touching his thumb to the two. As he did this, he let his pinky and ring finger curl in pointing back in to the palm of his hand. Then holding his wrist up, he flipped his hand up and down a few times as if his hand were a woodpecker pecking the air in slow motion. As he did this he turned to another guard who was standing nearby. He spoke rapidly in Arabic. The other guard ran off shouting, as he and the other security guards ran to collect their gear and gather near the front entrance.

Mohammad looked back at the colonel, "Okay, six of us will go. One will go get more guards, and one will stay here."

"That isn't enough."

Newborne got on the phone with his Operations NCO who was back at the palace.

"Sergeant Marty, I need you to get a four-gun detail together, six if you can, and get here to the ministry asap. Until you get here there will only be two guards. Once you get here one of the Iraqis will go get more guards, once the new guards arrive, you head back to the palace." He folded his phone and put it back into his vest pocket. "Tell the two who are here to stay here until Sergeant Marty arrives. He should be here in about twenty minutes. Then your guy will go get your additional guards."

"Yes sir," replied Mohammad. He then ran over to the assembled men and gave his instructions. Six of the security force members climbed into the two crowded SUVs. Kicking up dust, they took off through the streets of Baghdad.

Although few cars were on the road, many people were outside as the merciless sun receded leaving relative coolness in its wake. The SUVs zoomed past men that stood about appearing as though they had nothing to do and all the time in the world to do it. Children made games out of everything and nothing. Destroyed buildings and garbage heaps served as playgrounds. The women cooked over fires fueled by whatever wood or trash they could gather.

Joe, who shared the back seat with two of the well-armed Iraqis puckered his nose and lips at the foul smell of the smoke.

Mohammad smiled at Joe. "If you are hungry, they will share," he said in his labored English.

Joe smiled back, "Perhaps on the way home."

Mohammad translated, the other guards in the vehicle laughed, the tallest man, whose legs were tightly packed into the leg space of the SUV, gave Joe a huge smile and a thumbs-up.

The dust and smoke in the air added color to an already spectacular orange and red sunset. But as the sun went down, each passing moment added difficulty to the already challenging task of peering into the deepening contrast of shadows and glaring glass windows as they scanned for potential threats. The vehicles were easily identifiable targets on the nearly empty Baghdad streets just before dark, so they drove fast.

Darkness arrived at about the same time they approached a make-shift check point. It seemed as if every type of military vehicle that the U.S. Army had in Iraq was congesting the last eight hundred meters to the hotel site. Driving was slower than walking, but since a team of AK-47 wielding Iraqis were among them, none of whom spoke English fluently, everyone remained in the vehicles. They slowly made their way through the traffic jam to pass into the American perimeter established around the Canal Hotel itself.

Four hours after the car bomb exploded, the spillover from floodlights of the rescue effort cast distorted shadows across scraggly trees and damaged walls, transforming the surreal into a haunting scene. The urgent sounds of digging and shouting echoed over the loud drone of generators and vehicle motors. Scraping metal on metal, the earthmover blades squealed, sounding like the ghosts of the day making their sorrowful departure.

Fifty meters from where an engineer unit sifted through the rubble of the bomb site, it was hard to imagine how everyone in the destroyed wing of the spinal cord hospital had survived the blast.

Mohammad began assigning positions. Joe frowned as he watched the MOH security team form their own perimeter inside the US Army's much larger perimeter. At the open tailgate of the SUV, Major Thom Cross, the assistant operations officer who was responsible for security said, "Shit, we didn't bring enough water or food."

"No problem," Mohammad responded. "Everything that is in that building now will be there tomorrow morning."

"No problem at all," Thom mimicked. "Just another day in Baghdad."

After Mohammad distributed the security force, Newborne walked up from the damaged hospital's front entrance, "Thom, you and Mohammad go coordinate with the Infantry Battalion Commander. Joe and Tony, you go find some water and food."

While walking towards the line of Humvees parked along the road, Joe asked Tony, "Why are we doing this?"

"Doing what?"

Joe motioned all around them, "You know, inserting six armed Iraqis who barely speak English, to form a perimeter inside a perimeter made up of half the US Army in Baghdad, uninvited and at night, to guard a blown-up building."

"I guess Mister Banks either doesn't trust the Army or wants to display the self-reliance of the MOH," rationalized Tony.

"Yeah, either of those could be it, but although I can't think of anything good that could come of this, I certainly can think of some bad things. I mean think about it, Tony. What are our Iraqis supposed to do if a US soldier accidentally stumbles into the hospital at 02:00? Shoot him?"

Tony frowned, "You know, it's funny that no one asked us for our opinion."

"Yeah, hilarious," Joe sighed as they walked up to a soldier standing next to the first Humvee they came to parked on the side of the road near the hotel.

"How's it going sergeant? Can you spare a few pork-less MREs or a box of water?"

CHAPTER 25

That night, in the Al Rashid Hotel, Mister Banks stared toward the ceiling above his bed. In the darkness, his mind kept staring at the hand on the remnants of a second-floor balcony. A wedding ring was wrapped around one of the fingers as it lay there on the dusty ledge casually, as though it were patiently waiting to be reunited with its owner, and his wife.

Banks sat up and switched on the light. His mind could not slow down. He got up and started pacing as much as his hotel room permitted, three steps turn around, three steps, pause, turn around. Logically, he could tell himself that the hand was on the ledge because the force of the bomb blast severed it, picked it up and threw it higher and in a different direction than the arm it had once been attached. Mister Banks looked at himself in the mirror on his closet door; an old and worn man with pillow-fuzzed hair looked back at him. Peering into his own eyes he knew that the laws of physics would not help him find the answer he desperately sought.

He rubbed his hands over his face. Then with determined movement he looked back at himself and inhaled, holding the air in his chest. He nodded slightly and then silently recounted some of the many times in his past, where he and politicians he worked with had so bravely, with complete conviction, arrogantly, and ignorantly stated that the use of force was necessary.

"I never knew," he whispered.

Before now, never in his life had he seen, much less felt, the consequences of such resolutions. He and his fellows had always been isolated, and sheltered from the actions and their effects. He never had had a clue how much suffering—misery and pain—were caused by his faux-principled decrees. To them they were just soundbites, designed to associate themselves with an image of strength and determination in the minds of the gullible electorate. Mister Banks, after decades of regarding it as nothing more than a political tool, was finally on the cusp of truly understanding why violence was such a powerful weapon.

The skin around his eyes sagged.

Again, he searched into his own depths. He realized that his past bold talk had never been courageous—just pompous. Not liking what he was seeing, he looked away from the mirror and resumed his pacing. After a few more minutes, he turned the lights off, again.

CHAPTER *26*

All morning as Mister Banks sat alone in his office tears streamed down his face. His heart was in his mind, thinking about the power that the sword can have when it sliced into flesh. In front of him a stack of papers awaited his attention, but after his sleepless night his focus was elsewhere.

A quick knock on the door caused him to stir. He inhaled, patted his face below his eyes and dabbed his nose with a tissue before he opened his mouth to invite his guest to enter. But he found it very difficult to find the words, "Come in," he said weakly. He cleared his throat, "Come in," he said again this time loud enough to be heard.

Newborne stepped in and as soon as he saw Mister Banks, he stopped. He looked at him a few moments then looked around the room. Instead of his normal brusque style of busting in and getting straight to business, the colonel quietly shut the door behind him and approached Banks's desk slowly, then without invitation he lowered himself into one of the two chairs in front of the desk. By the time the drawn-out creak of the padded wooden chair stopped, Newborne was sitting silently watching his boss's face. Banks just looked at him without moving.

After half a minute, Newborne broke eye contact and looked around the room again. The drapes were drawn, as they often were. The muffled colors of blue and gold smothered the room's walls, floor, and occupant with depressing weight. He glanced back at Mister Banks. The older man tried to smile.

The colonel slowly handed a note to Mister Banks, that once signed and stamped, would allow Mohammad and his wife to bring their baby, Amel, to the pediatrics hospital in Medical City. The baby girl had diarrhea and the parents feared that dehydration would kill her if they could not get her to eat or drink. Without words, the minister read the paper, pulled his stamp out of his top right drawer, firmly pressed it into the ink, and transferred it onto the request transforming it into an order. He took a moment to place the stamp back in the drawer, then with a flash of his pen, he signed his name, restoring hope to a desperate family.

As the colonel's hand reached across the desk, he took the simple piece of paper with the stamp of power on it.

"You're a good man. Thank you."

Newborne stood up but instead of moving toward the door, he advanced toward the window. He pulled the curtain all the way to the side in one graceful swoop, allowing a flood of the sun's yellow shine to wash into the office. A second later, the left curtain was also open revealing the full force of the bright day. The triumphant feelings of promise and purpose suddenly overtook the gloom and despair. Without a word, and without looking over at Mister Banks, Newborne walked out of the office as though adventure and promise awaited him. Mister Banks watched him go.

"No, thank you," Mister Banks mumbled as the colonel disappeared through the doorway.

Blinking his eyes as they adjusted to the strong light, Mister Banks straightened his back and with the palms of his hands began to chase the wrinkles from his shirt.

CHAPTER 27

Joe held his cell phone up to his ear and listened to the reply as he looked out across the Baghdad skyline from the office he now shared with Max, Sahar, and two others on the ninth-floor. Sitting at the table next to him, Max could hear the voice on the other side of the phone, but not what was being said.

"Exactly, until we know what the requirements of the healthcare system are, it's kind of difficult to know where we need to invest the construction dollars," Joe said. "Especially in environments such as this. Even the low bar of doing the wrong thing well would be difficult to achieve. The most likely outcome would probably be to do the wrong thing poorly, which would waste years, hundreds of millions of dollars, and fail."

Joe held up his finger and mouthed "Just a minute" to the captain as he listened to Carson's reply on his phone.

"I recognize that politics is important, and I realize that we have to show progress. I do. I really, truly do. But what good are headlines screaming success today if the goals are never achieved? Maybe that's what the ambassador needs to do, establish achievable expectations, not feed into unrealistic fantasies."

Response.

"It isn't just about headlines. It is about figuring out what needs to be done before we commit to doing it. And regardless of what Congress or the president say they need, if they don't allow us the time to figure it out, we have very little if any chance of doing it right. Maybe that's what you need to pass up to Bremmer and maybe that's what he needs to tell Congress.

"What I do know, Carson, is that you are a smart and dedicated person, but in this case, you don't know what you're doing. This entire venture is becoming a lost opportunity to have a positive impact. The hard truth is that even with you and the hundreds of other fanatically devoted, hard-working people who found their way into the CPA, if they set unrealistic expectations and if most of their effort is focused on creating the illusion of progress in the minds of stateside Americans instead of actually making real progress on the ground, this whole thing will be a catastrophic failure."

As the chief of staff responded, Joe frowned and turned to look out the window.

"The president is not going to look good regardless of how cleverly the truth is misrepresented because the claims will never be realized."

After a long pause, Joe glanced back at Maxwell and changed his tone, "Look, we will do what we can. But don't ever go around and say that our list is our program."

Pause.

"Fine. Look, I got to go now... Thanks. Bye."

Shaking his head, Brown touched the hang up button, folded his phone and slid it into his pocket.

Looking up at Max he exhaled heavily and then said, "You know, nothing good is going to happen here very quickly, regardless of how badly we want it or even need it. Much of this healthcare system needs attention. We aren't going to be able to assess, program, design, build and outfit scores of construction projects faster than we could in a perfect environment at any price—and this environment is far from perfect. Spending our time and money on ill-conceived and counterproductive activities isn't going to speed up the reconstruction effort, it will kill it."

The captain nodded.

"Okay, you know our situation. They want the lists before we can develop them. Our challenge will be to meet their needs without derailing the train. Any ideas?"

Max sat upright and then shook his head, "Sir, we need to give them a list."

Joe clenched his teeth. "You are probably right. I've got an idea or two, not good ones, but let's get with our Iraqi friends and see if we can come up with a plan."

"Yes sir," Max said as he got up and prepared to depart.

"But hold on a minute, so how are you today? You looked a little queasy at the Canal Hotel last night."

Max was on Banks's security detail. He looked down when he was asked, shaking his head he replied, "Sir, I don't know what to say. It was the most horrible thing I'd ever seen."

Sahar entered as Max continued. She stood next to one of the tables that ran the length of the bare and dirty office wall.

"Well, the van carrying the bomb left a crater maybe twenty feet deep, and completely destroyed the closest parts of the hotel."

Max sat back down at the table, "An engineering unit was already there helping dig people out when we got there, and it seems like there were a hundred medics and docs taking care of the victims. They were gathering and triaging the victims."

Reem entered the room and quietly joined the audience next to Sahar.

"They had an LZ established, helicopters and ground ambulances coming and going, non-stop. It was awful, along a wall were the expectants, they were expected to die so they moved them out of the way and didn't expend many resources on them." He slowed his delivery as the pitch in his voice rose. "An army medic was providing water and morphine, a man had a pole through his head. I can't imagine how it must be to be waiting to die like that." Max looked up and glanced at Doctor Sahar and Reem. He was fighting back tears.

Sahar looked away. Reem shuffled her papers until Sahar looked at her. Then Reem whispered, "I'm sorry but I have to interrupt. I need a bill of materials; can you help me find it?"

Sahar stepped towards Max and in a tender voice told him, "I'm sorry." Then she and Reem left the room. Joe and Max stood up, "David, let's talk more about this later. If you are up for it, let's go see the DG."

"I'm good," replied Max as they too departed, leaving the room empty.

Sahar and Reem found the paperwork they were looking for in a filing cabinet in another office and brought it back to the shared office to review. Hurried footsteps announced Zaid's arrival. His usually groomed hair was ruffled and his breathing was heavy and rapid. His face held its usual glare of dissatisfaction.

"What's taking so long? I need to get back to Al Dabbash."

"I'm sorry, we're almost done." Reem tentatively replied.

"What could possibly be taking so long? It still needs to go to the fourth floor for funding."

"Yes, I'm sorry."

Sahar offered a defense for her friend, "It is my fault *Sayid* Zaid. I was not available until only a couple minutes ago."

"And what were you doing that was so distracting from your duties?"

Sahar did not answer, instead she looked towards Zaid's feet.

Zaid said talking to himself, "*Naqiset aqil wa deen.*" Women, deficient in mind and faith.

Sahar looked up and started to open her mouth, but caught herself. Zaid raised his eyebrow and tilted his head towards her.

"What? Do you wish to say something?" asked Zaid as he stepped toward her.

"No, *seidi*, I'm sorry," Sahar said quietly, her heart beating rapidly.

He shook his head, "You should remember your place."

Then he stood between Sahar and Reem and said loudly for both to hear, "Don't let the Americans give you any false ideas. Soon life will return to how it should be. Yesterday was just the beginning of the end for the Americans and their puppets. Another bloody nose and they will flee like Iranians, and run home crying. Then we shall be honored by the return of our great leader."

He glared at Sahar, took a step toward her, and then towered over her so closely that she could smell his warm breath. He whispered very slowly exaggerating each word, "Things will return to how they should be."

She stepped back. He laughed as he crouched down a little to look directly into her eyes. Sahar turned away to hide her face.

Turning towards Reem, Zaid said, "The cowards will flee like dogs and Iraq will once again be home for true Iraqis. So be sure that you don't find yourselves among the fools, the traitors––"

He let his sentence trail off, unfinished. Reem was writing as fast as she could. Zaid stood waiting standing with his feet apart and his hands on his hips. Copying the last of the required numbers, her scribbling was barely legible. Sahar dropped her head and slumped her shoulders forward.

"Finished," said Reem raising the paper up into the air.

Zaid grabbed it while he shifted a glance back toward Sahar, *"Ent'ethree wa shufee."* Wait and see. He beamed a broad exaggerated smile, nodded his head very slightly toward Reem, then he left.

"What was that all about?" asked Reem after the two found themselves alone in the room.

"I hate that man." Sahar replied. "I think he's more snake than human."

Reem's eyes met Sahar's and fixed themselves there. "What was he talking about?"

"I don't know."

"And you, you almost talked back to him."

"I don't know, I suppose he was just boasting, trying to make us think he's such a big important man, but I know the cloth he's made of. He's not as tough as he pretends, but his arrogance, the way he was standing, he reminded me of the *amin*," proposed Sahar.

"Who're the fools and the traitors?" asked Reem in the same tone of wonderment a child would ask her mother.

Sahar weakly raised her shoulders and shook her head from side to side, "I guess he means anyone who works with the Americans."

CHAPTER *28*
Baghdad: Late August 2003

"Did you hear? Last night the UN announced they are going to relocate its Iraq Reconstruction office to Amman, Jordan," said Joe as he and Max entered the narrow office on the ninth-floor.

"That will be one more hurdle in this perfect environment for the construction program."

Sahar cringed and quietly left the room to find Reem who was in her work area on the sixth-floor. When she got there, Reem looked up to greet her, "What are you doing here? You almost never come to *Kimadia*."

Sahar sat down at the table beside her and leaned forward until almost touching Reem. "Yesterday the UN announced they are leaving Baghdad," she whispered.

"So?"

"Don't you remember what Zaid said?"

"When?"

"He predicted this. He said that the Americans and puppets would flee."

Reem looked at her, her expression blank.

"The invaders are now on the run. That's what Zaid told us would happen. And then he said that Saddam would come back after this happens."

Reem inhaled and held it, then she put her hand on Sahar's, which was lying flat on the table.

Sahar added, "This could this be the start of an insurgency against the Americans. If it is, a war between Saddam loyalists and everyone else is sure to follow," said Sahar her voice still very low.

Sahar sat back and deflated in front of her friend, "Reem, I don't know exactly what I want, but I know that I don't want more war and I don't want Iraq to return to the way it was."

CHAPTER 29

"You're excused," Sahar told her daughters.

Dee Dee watched Dalia push her chair away from the kitchen table before she leapt from her own chair laughing. The five-year-old darted the short distance past the front door to their room at the start of the short hallway with Dalia walking behind her looking down at her giggling sister. Music started just after the light clicked on and the door shut closed.

At the table, the remnants of the evening meal still in place, Sahar turned to her husband.

"*Habibti*, what do you think will happen when the Americans leave?"

"What makes you think they'll leave?" he asked.

"Well, the UN is heading out already, because of the bombing. Maybe they won't be able to stand the insurgency."

He swallowed a big spoonful of his half-eaten soup, slurping while looking at Sahar.

"The Americans must have expected it. They couldn't have thought they could invade, fire the *Ba'athists* and the Army with no push-back. They wouldn't have come if they didn't plan to stay here a long, long time."

She watched Muraad tear a piece of bread off the loaf and dunk it into his bowl of broth. He stuffed it in his mouth as if he wanted to eat it in as few bites possible.

"I don't know. The Americans at the MOH seem to be different. I don't think they have any idea of what's going on. They just come in and try to get us to do things their way."

"Do they know what they're doing? They don't hurt you, do they?" he asked.

Sahar shook her head. Elbows on the table, she toyed with the curls hanging down from her forehead.

"If they don't hurt you and they pay us, what difference does it make how long they stay? They have money, we have food."

Sahar watched him as he chewed. He took a big gulp of water from his plastic cup.

"What about the girls, what kind of country will this be when Dalia gets married?" she asked.

He looked at her and put his spoon down. He reached out and took her hand and gently held it as he rested his on the table top.

"*Habibati*, we can't change these things, why worry about them? Look around you, we have what we need. Dalia and Dee Dee are healthy. We have food, and we have a house. Don't ask God for any more than we are already fortunate to have."

"Yes, we're very fortunate. But what will it be like for Dalia?"

"There's no way for us to know. And even if we knew, what could we do about it? We don't know who will win. Just don't make any enemies and don't pick sides. We'll be alright, *Insha'Allah.*"

Sahar sat quietly while Muraad finished eating. When his bowl was empty, he looked at his wife for a moment. He patted her hand before he brushed the crumbs off his shirt and wiped his mouth with a napkin. Then he put the napkin on the table as he pushed himself away.

"*Shukren,*" he said, touching her shoulder as he passed her on the way to the couch, a few steps away. Clicking on the lamp he scooped up a newspaper from the coffee table and sat down.

The girls' muffled voices and their music floated in from their room as Sahar sat looking at the pictures, mostly portraits, that were hanging on the two corner walls behind Muraad: the two of them when they were a young couple, the girls, pictures of both pairs of their late parents, and a family portrait with her brother in it. When she noticed the ticking sound of the of the passing seconds on the clock, she sat upright. Then she turned and glanced across the empty dishes on the table and pushed herself up to clean the kitchen.

CHAPTER *30*

"*Sayid* Zaid."

Zaid sat up in his desk chair in his utilitarian, windowless office in the *Kimadia* 13 Warehouse complex, the fluorescent bulbs' ballasts buzzed overhead. The man standing in front of him looked ferocious and strong. Zaid puffed himself up and frowned as he listened.

"I've been sent by a mutual acquaintance. He wishes me to convey his greetings. He also wishes for you to direct my services to targets that would best destroy the morale of the Americans and send a message to those of our countrymen who are considering treason."

The man's pants and his plain, grey, pull-over shirt, were clean and though not new, showed no sign of wear or tear. His face was partially hidden by a thick black beard but his hard, merciless eyes bore holes through Zaid. His posture and his false willingness to be subordinate expressed arrogance.

Zaid nodded, trying to maintain an aura of authority.

"Oh, one other thing, *Sayid* Zaid, the grey haired one is to remain unharmed."

"Yes," Zaid nodded and leaned back in his chair, "I understand."

He sat there a moment before he realized that the humorless face opposite his desk was waiting for something. Zaid leaned forward and reached into his top center drawer retrieving a sheet of paper and a pen. He wrote a name and description identifying an American working for the CPA who was beginning to inspire Iraqis to stray. Forcing himself to look back into the penetrating eyes of the powerful man in front of him, he slid the paper forward.

The man nodded a deep respectful half bow, and smoothly reached forward to retrieve the document. "*Allah wiyaak*," May God be with you, the mysterious man said with complete confidence.

"Yes. *Ma'salama*," stumbled Zaid.

Without leaving even the sound of a footstep in his wake he left Zaid sitting at his empty desk in his nearly empty office. Zaid didn't smile and he didn't frown. Letting his hands lie cupped on the surface in front of him, Zaid stared at the doorway. Then he forced a smile. "Finally. Finally, it is time to act."

CHAPTER *31*

"The program will include: re-establish a maintenance capability, re-establish a distribution program, obtain replacement medical equipment, build and equip as many neighborhood clinics as we can, fix the critical systems that are damaged in each of the hospitals, and renovate hospitals that cater to the most vulnerable and underserved population groups," said Joe looking up from his seat facing Sattar who sat at his desk, his back to the window.

Sahar, who was standing near Max leaning against the wall looked over at the door when it opened. She pushed away from the wall and stood up straight, and Hamid and Wasan shifted in their seats as Zaid approached Sattar's desk.

Joe continued talking, "We will give them an estimate based on the most common problems hindering the facilities to claim some money. For example, we will assess the sanitation, mechanical and electrical systems in ten hospitals in Baghdad and assign each of these systems on a proportional scale. For a facility needing total replacement of their HVAC system we will estimate 100% of the mechanical costs, if they need a major renovation of the system, we will estimate 80% of total costs of a mechanical system, if it needs medium renovation 60%, minor renovation, 40%, and minor fixes, 20%. Then once we have these percentages we extrapolate what we find against the total inventory. Then we calculate costs based on the ministry's historical costs for new construction per square meter. We derive the size of the hospitals by the MOH planning formula of 100 square meters of gross hospital space per bed in general hospitals, 150 in specialty hospitals."

Zaid looked down at Joe as he came to a stop directly in front of Sattar's desk. In Arabic, Zaid said to Sattar, "Don't listen to these Americans. They cannot be trusted. The planning is my responsibility. When I need a bill of materials, I will ask for one."

Sattar stood up from behind his desk, and looked Zaid eye to eye as Zaid's lips curled in a snarl.

Sattar replied, also in Arabic, "No. This isn't Oil for Food money."

"It is money from the outside. This planning is the responsibility of *Kimadia*."

"No. Engineering manages construction, *Kimadia* is only involved with Oil for Food funded projects."

Sahar shifted and looked around. She and the others grew nervous as they watched the two influential men face off.

Joe sat upright in his chair and asked, "Sahar what are they saying?"

Sahar answered, "They are talking about who controls the money that will build these projects. They each claim it."

"All outside money goes through *Kimadia*, not engineering," shouted Zaid.

Joe stood up, "What's the problem here?"

Zaid turned to glare at Joe, then in English he said, "Go run home to your mom; this is not your concern." Then he looked back at Sattar.

"If you have a problem with the role of engineering, go discuss it with the minister," Joe responded.

Zaid stepped back from Sattar and stepped toward Joe. Standing near the wall next to Sahar, Max's hand touched his pistol. Glaring at Zaid, Hamid moved to stand next to Joe.

Glancing at Hamid, Zaid said, "Oh, I see how this is working now. The great Engineer Sattar, DG of Engineering, and his puppies take orders from an American," he said in English. Then he mumbled something in Arabic.

The Iraqis in the room gasped.

"What's going on?" Joe asked Sahar, not taking his eyes off Zaid.

"Joe, I can't tell you," said Sahar.

"Damn it, tell me what he said."

Hamid shook his head, "It isn't good, Joe."

Joe glanced around. Everyone in the room was standing but no one made a sound. "I need to know what he just said."

"Joe," said Hamid, "He threatened to hurt you."

Joe stared at Zaid who was standing tall, flexed from toe to head, arms back from the shoulders, and his hands in fists. Joe shifted his weight forward, his face glowing red.

"You need to leave," Joe said very deliberately.

Max took his pistol out of his holster and pointed it down, his finger on the safety switch.

Zaid stood perfectly still, not even breathing. His cold, hard eyes stared right into and through Joe until finally, Zaid whispered something. Then moving his threatening stare from

Joe to Sattar he addressed the room in Arabic, "The Americans are nothing. They will be dead or gone by spring. Traitors will be remembered and punished."

Then Zaid took a breath and relaxed his body, then he took two steps backward and turned around. Without looking at anyone he walked toward the door. A moment later he was gone. Everyone let out a sigh of relief.

Max went to the door and watched Zaid walk down the hall. Then he turned back, "Sir, are you alright?"

Joe exhaled noisily, then after a pause said, "Sure. I'm okay. Everyone else?"

"Yes, we are fine. But what can we do? He is a dangerous man," answered Hamid.

"Sir, we better report this to Major Cross," Max suggested.

"Yeah, good idea. You saw the whole thing; why don't you go? But be careful, bring a witness."

"I'll go with you," volunteered Hamid. "We'll take the other stairway."

The two departed.

Joe sat down. Sattar did not take his eyes off Joe.

Sahar told him, "You know, he is a very bad man."

"I guess I'm forming that opinion of him too," replied Joe.

Sahar exhaled and watched Joe. Then she turned and hurried out of the room. She caught up with Max and Hamid near the stairwell. "I want to come with you," she told Max.

Max glanced at Hamid then nodded. The three started the trek down the stairwell.

On the second floor, Captain Maxwell knocked on Major Cross's office. There was no answer. They heard Thom's voice next door in the colonel's office. The door was open and from in the hallway the three saw the colonel standing at a chalkboard showing Major Cross and the MOH security chief, Chief Thamer, where he wanted guards posted.

Max stood waiting for an appropriate moment to gain the major's attention. Colonel Newborne looked up, "What do you need, David?"

"Sir, I need to talk to Major Cross."

Cross looked up from his notepad, "Shoot."

Standing in the doorway, Max began to tell the story, "Sir, the man from Kimadia, uhhh..."

"Zaid," said Hamid.

"Zaid, interrupted a meeting on the ninth-floor and threatened Lieutenant Colonel Brown. He also..."

Colonel Newborne asked Hamid, "Exactly what did that prick say?"

Max glanced at Hamid and opened his mouth but Hamid said it in Arabic first, and then in English, "Sir, Zaid said to Joe, that you'll be the next name on my list."

Colonel Newborne looked at Max and said, "You fucking interrupt my meeting to tell me that Zaid told Joe that he'll write his name down, and you get your panties in an uproar?"

Sahar backed up a step. Still looking at Major Cross, Captain Maxwell hesitated.

Hamid spoke up. "Sir, it is much worse than that. It was a threat, he also threatened all of the Iraqis in the room, calling them traitors, and said that all the Americans will be dead or gone by spring."

Max nodded.

Shifting his body away from the chalkboard Newborne looked over to his Iraqi security chief, "Okay Thamer, what do you think?"

"Sir, *Kimadia* is very dangerous. I think we should investigate what he means by 'his list.' I think he was threatening your man."

"A list? A list for what? Kill him? Hurt him? Buy him a Christmas present? Look, if we are going to have an impact on this place we cannot overreact to every little incident. If Brown feels that his life was threatened, then he should come down here and say so himself. This is a fucking war. Everybody and their brother are getting or giving death threats. If we responded to every one of them we wouldn't get a damn thing done, and the fucking Saddam lovers would still be in control. We need to take control away from these guys by not giving them power. 'Add him to a list,' or whatever the fuck he said doesn't sound like a credible threat to me. It sounds like he is trying to derail something by being intimidating. If Joe can't handle that he shouldn't fucking be here. Tell him to get to work and not back down. If he does, he's a pussy."

Max and Hamid looked at each other.

"Yes sir," Max said.

The colonel and major returned to the chalkboard. In the hallway, Sahar touched the captain on his sleeve, "Max, Joe needs to be careful. He has probably never met a man like Zaid before."

"Doctor Sahar, I think you're right."

CHAPTER *32*

Bushra cradled Amel and Mohammad put his arm around Bushra's shoulders. Stepping out of the hospital's main entrance, Mohammad, still dressed in his Facilities Security Force uniform, told her, "If not for Colonel Newborne, we would never have been able to come here. The Americans saved her."

Bushra gazed into Mohammad's eyes, "God saved our daughter, the Americans were only his tool."

"Even so, I will never forget this. The Americans are here to help. We must help them."

She looked at him, "You're a good man. I'm lucky you're mine."

"No, *Habibati*, I'm the lucky one. I am not worthy. God is smiling on me."

CHAPTER *33*

The war is not yet finished,
but the nature of it has changed.
The fighting has diminished,
but the peace remains estranged.
The champ has yet victory to embrace
the people and the place
trapped in an unnatural zone
insurgents have no reason to the victors to atone.

Americans run our cities,
some Iraqis are like Vichy French,
like the ones sitting on committees
and the ones sitting on the bench.
Who will hold the power?
When the war reaches its final hour?
That is when the victor will emerge
to determine who dies or lives during the coming purge.

Americans, powerful but unreliable,
they triumph, they boast, they quit.
Their resolve seems somewhat pliable,
their ideals seem somewhat split.
The loyalists bide their time in shadows
tending to their pain and woes,
strike hard to make their enemy bleed
some for honor, some vengeance, and some for greed.

"Thank you for coming," Mohammad said standing on his front porch holding his hand over his heart, "It's such an honor, please come into our home."

"Mohammed, it is my honor, thank you for your invitation," replied the colonel.

Colonel Newborne, Major Cross, their translator Firas, and Chief Thamer, the MOH security chief shuffled in off the porch and closed the door. Two security guards stood outside and watched the vehicles parked in the circular driveway just off the road.

"Here is our daughter, Amel," Bushra said as she held their baby girl in her arms. "And our sons, Marwan and Heider." The two kids, with matching crew cuts smiled broadly as they bowed but remained silent.

"We cannot tell you how happy we are that you were able to get Amel into the hospital."

Letting Amel grip his finger, Mohammad said to Newborne, "We owe you her life."

"We did nothing. I'm so glad she's doing well. I'm sorry but Mister Banks must send you his regrets that he can't come today."

"We are happy to have you, please sit down."

"We have *maskoof*, so I hope you like fish, and we have vegetables, olives, a plate of *biryani*, and some *kababs*," explained the hostess.

Looking down from the second-floor window in the house adjacent to Mohammad's, the shooter waited. Since arriving at his position thirty minutes before the American contingent, the man had made little movement and no sound. He was too disciplined to smoke while on a hit, and he did not allow his mind to wander too far from the task at hand. He knew that the moment he must strike was not his to choose, so he remained ready for whatever moment his targets decided to expose themselves.

Like a great cat, he leaned forward motionless and attentive. His rifle sat effortlessly balanced on his hand supported by his elbow that rested on the table that upon his arrival, he had pushed against the window. The rifle had been modified to hold a sniper's scope, but for this job, he removed it. A round was chambered and twenty-nine more were in the magazine. Two more loaded magazines lay on the table near his right hand. All he had left to do was lean forward a bit more, lower his head, and kill.

The muzzle of his AK-47, just inside the open window was invisible from the outside. Below him on the same side of the street, he had earlier watched the Americans arrive in the two parked cars. "Soon," he told himself, "soon I will spring forward, *Insha'Allah*, with all the strength of God's fury and bring down the beasts that are defiling the *Wadi Al-Rafidain*," the cradle of civilization.

He could have picked off the Iraqi guards who stood outside the front door at any time during the last one hundred and twenty-eight minutes. But what good would the deaths of two Iraqi guards be, traitors that they were, if doing so came at the expense of missing out on killing the Americans? He had determined the order in which he would eliminate his targets: First, the senior American, second, the junior American and then the Iraqis in the order they looked capable of fighting back.

His primary target was last to leave the house. Following the colonel in his sites from the moment he emerged from the front door, the shooter could have taken him out at any moment. The colonel hugged his host and they kissed each other on the cheek. Then the two men stepped back and pressed their right hands over their hearts. A moment later, his target turned and strode swiftly toward the Suburban with his MP-5 swinging from his side as he unnecessarily told his subordinate to get into the car. Although he was confident he could have shot each of the targets in a firefight, he decided to wait until his targets were in their vehicles and would have most difficulty shooting back.

The shooter patiently leaned forward and set his sights on the driver's seat, where the tall, loud American would sit, he rehearsed the coming moments in his mind and thanked God that he had this perfect perch from which to do His work.

The younger American was shutting the passenger door as the colonel slid in behind the steering wheel. The security chief and translator were already in the backseat adjusting themselves for another commute into the city's unruly traffic. The two Iraqi security guards were in the trail car with the engine running.

As his primary target started the car, the shooter aimed at his head. Controlling his breathing he steadily squeezed the trigger.

Before anyone in either car realized what had happened, the colonel was slumped over the steering wheel, the blood from his head wound sprayed throughout the cabin, and all over Major Cross in the seat next to him. A second shot and Cross felt the slam of a sledgehammer into his left arm. The translator Firas, sitting directly behind Newborne, ducked down and held his hands tightly over his head, screaming in Arabic. Next to him, Thamer, pistol in hand, awkwardly peered over the back seat frantically searching the surrounding buildings for the shooter.

The driver of the tail car did not want to remain in place waiting for another shot to be fired. "Get out of the Kill Zone!" He yelled in Arabic to the colonel in the Suburban.

The security guard riding shotgun attempted to charge his rifle, but instead, he mistakenly ejected his magazine and emptied the round from the chamber. When there was no response from Newborne, the driver rammed his white SUV against the back of the Suburban. As they banged the Suburban, the 30-round clip the guard was trying to reach bounced off his boot heel and slid under the front seat. Ahead of them the Suburban began to spin clockwise.

At the sound of the shot, Mohammad, who had been standing in the doorway with Bushra, pushed her inside and across the room. She caught her balance as she collided with a chair. She immediately reached for the boys who were standing behind them holding on to each other, and crawling, pulled them towards the hallway and the safety of being behind a second wall. Bushra stood up and ran into the first bedroom to grab their baby girl before bringing the three children into the room furthest from the front door. Once Mohammad saw that they were behind cover, he ran down the hallway to retrieve his rifle. As Bushra pulled the door closed in their bedroom, he loaded a magazine and slapped the charging handle forward and ran back to the entrance to help fight off the attack.

As the Suburban stopped spinning, Firas, the translator, clawed his way over Thamer and dove out the open backseat window rolling when he hit the ground hands first. He immediately sprang up and took off down the street, screaming. He weaved to hide behind every parked car, tree, and bush that he encountered as he ran as quickly as he could away from the ambush.

Newborne was slumped over the steering wheel, more blood escaping with each beat of his heart—repulsive streams and small pools forming in the front seat. Cross struggled with his good arm to unbuckle his seat belt, but before he succeeded, Newborne's body shook beside him and he made a gurgling sound. Then Newborne moved his arm. Cross abandoned his attempt to get out of the vehicle. He reached over with his right and with an awkward, painful movement he shifted the vehicle into neutral and grabbed the bloody steering wheel.

In the tail car, the two security guards were shouting as the driver was still trying to push the Suburban out of the kill zone and the other was still groping for his magazine that was out of reach under his seat. Dust from the vehicles' spinning wheels created a welcome cloud providing some concealment.

Thamer slid over behind Newborne and looked upwards for the shooter's gun, but he couldn't locate it. Both vehicles lurched forward, and in a spray of exhaust, dust and gravel the Suburban rammed a car that was parked five meters in front of it.

The tail car continued to push and Cross grunted as he pulled hard on the top of the steering wheel as the Suburban scraped past the parked car and out into the middle of the road.

Seeing the vehicles work their way to freedom the shooter realized that the major was not going to exit the vehicle. He shifted his aim, and took another quick shot towards the steering wheel. He squeezed off another few rounds and took out the back window of the Suburban and the left-rear window of the tail car. The sound of metal on metal added an eerie screech to the melee as the two escaping vehicles banged their way out of the kill zone.

Out of primary targets, the shooter took a shot at the translator as he ducked around a car parked in the street two houses down—but missed him. "Shit."

Behind the cover of the doorjamb, Mohammad scanned the surroundings for the shooter. He began to push himself out of his prone position to run out the door but stopped. The shooter could still be ready to fire and to run down the street chasing the cars would do nothing but leave himself and his family exposed. So, he settled back into his firing position and waited, ready to fire if necessary. He peered out of his doorway searching, but he saw nothing but the dust settle and onlookers tentatively begin to investigate the violent scene.

The shooter realized the cars were out of his range and the translator was out of his line of fire. He took a long breath and pressed his lips together tightly, then silently packed up his rifle and picked up his spent shells. He left the window open and the table in its new location—no need to draw attention to his position. He closed the back door on his way out and retraced the path down the alley he had used to access the house. As he departed he prayed, "God I will be more competent the next time I am given a gift as valuable as this opportunity had been. Please forgive me for my failure."

After ramming their way a couple of blocks down the road, the tail vehicle pushing as Cross steered the Suburban with his right arm as well as he could over his wounded limb while fighting his seat belt harness from the passenger seat; Thamer shouted and gestured to the tail car to stop. The Suburban coasted to a halt as it glided into yet another parked car.

The security guard riding shot gun ran forward from the tail car and he and Thamer pulled the colonel out from the driver's seat and into the backseat. Thamer hopped into the blood-saturated seat and took the wheel and the guard jumped in back to hold the tall American and try to slow his bleeding as they, with the lone driver in pursuit, raced to the nearest hospital.

Firas ran for several blocks before arriving to a crowded market where he slowed down. Sweat stained and gasping for air, he turned and ran some more, bumping into people and booths as he repeatedly looked back to see if he was being followed. Seeing his distress, an old woman approached him, but he waved her off. He crept into a corner formed by two vender stalls and dropped to the ground. An elderly man, sitting on an old metal drum next to the socks he was selling, stared at him. His squint exposed the gaps between his remaining teeth. He looked at Firas but asked no questions.

Offering no explanation, the translator hugged his knees with his arms and rocked forward and back staring past his feet. Though the old man watched him curiously, activity in the market continued as though Firas were not there. After about five minutes, Firas lifted himself up and brushed off the sores on his knees and back that he had not felt earlier. A bit of blood was coming from the palm of his scraped left hand. He tucked in his shirt and ran his hand through his hair. Drops of sweat showered on his shoulders. Steadying himself, he got to his feet and began to slowly reenter the aisle of this outdoor market. The old man just sat and watched him go, never saying word.

CHAPTER *34*

The bullet shattered his arm, but Cross's gunshot wound was not as serious as the wound to his pride. While lying in a hospital bed in the Green Zone the following day, yet another member of the hospital staff walked into his shared room.

"Major Thomas Cross?" she asked looking at her clipboard as she positioned a plastic chair next to his bed.

He looked up and nodded, then he asked the lieutenant, "How is Colonel Newborne doing?"

"He is in ICU. The doctor kept talking about how lucky he was that the bullet only grazed him. I am Lieutenant Foley, a Combat Stress Counselor," she answered, sitting down.

Cross nodded.

"How are you feeling, sir?" she asked.

He looked at her and exhaled heavily. Then he shrugged.

"Can you tell me what happened?" she continued.

After a pause, Cross dove in, "Hell, I got shot in the arm. I had Newborne's blood all over me. It was all over everywhere. Some bastard was out there waiting to shoot again. I just know he was. I tried to get out of the vehicle, but if I could have opened my damn seat belt, I probably would have gotten out and been popped. I thought for sure the colonel was gone. I couldn't believe it when he moved."

She nodded and said quietly, "Major, please go on."

"Had Newborne not miraculously regained consciousness, we both would be dead. No, we all would be dead."

"I understand. What I also understand is that you were the one who shifted the car out of park."

"I panicked. I panicked and almost got us all killed," he said turning his head so she wouldn't see his eyes.

"No, you were scared, anyone would have been, and you took the action necessary to get everyone out of the kill zone. No one was killed. You did what you had to do."

Cross shook his head and disagreed, "Oh no." He was having a hard time talking.

"It's okay. It's okay," she consoled him and changed the subject. "How are you feeling today?"

"I feel like I'm floating. My arm feels like it has a damn knot in it. A throbbing knot."

"Does it feel good to float?"

"Yeah, but I don't want to feel good. I just need to get out of here and do something. Anything but lie here like this."

"I'm told that tomorrow you will be evacuated to Landstuhl, and then back to CONUS."

Cross nodded. He figured he would be flown to the army hospital in Germany on his way back to the States.

"Are you in pain?"

"Oh no. I'm all jacked-up."

The lieutenant smiled. "Sir, you do know that everyone is fine. The colonel will recover as well. Chief Thamer, that is his name, isn't it?"

Cross nodded.

"Chief Thamer reassured me that the two security guards and the translator, Firas, are also alive."

He smiled a bit, "Yeah." Then his face contorted, "I don't want to be comfortable. I panicked and Newborne didn't."

"Look, you are going to be okay. And you might want to think about this, not to take anything away from Colonel Newborne, but he was unconscious. What he did was involuntary. We don't know how he would have reacted, but your reaction was normal. You were scared, but then you found the courage to do the right thing. So, sir, there is no reason for you to be so hard on yourself saying that you panicked, and Newborne didn't. That isn't what happened."

"I feel like I'm going to throw up," he said.

"I'll get the nurse," she said.

Elsewhere in the US Army's 28th Combat Support Hospital as Cross fretted Newborne saw something. The colors were too vivid, the shadows in the lively room were too dark. The images collided. They were fuzzy and blurry. The ringing in his ears was intermittently interrupted by beeps and buzzes of various monitors. Voices. He tried to look around. The light shining in his eyes was annoying. His throat was dry, and he had something hooked up to his arm.

Tubes.

Disoriented, he became alarmed. He tried to speak and he tried to move. He could do neither.

"Major, the colonel's awake," the medic announced to the Officer-In-Charge of the Intensive Care Unit as he tended to a younger soldier who had just been flown in from another part of town. The *OIC* who was writing on her clipboard near bed five looked up and bit her lower lip. She inhaled to compose herself before she put her clipboard down and walked over to Newborne.

She looked down at him with her gentle smile. She held his hand.

"Don," said the army nurse. "Don…" she coaxed gently testing his responsiveness.

Although it hurt him to do so, Colonel Newborne tried to focus his eyes and pay attention. The room was spinning. He felt her soft and firm hands on his hand. Though out of focus, he saw her beautiful wide, moist eyes and the smooth brown skin of her face.

He shuddered. She widened her smile.

The colonel tried to speak, "Where am I?" But his voice was barely audible, raspy and incomprehensible.

The nurse checked her watch and noted the time. His responsiveness was a good sign of healthy brain activity. That was all she needed, he needed more rest.

"Shhhh, no need to speak now Don," she cooed. "You are very lucky, but you are also badly wounded. Don't worry; we will be here for you. We'll take care of you."

She squeezed his hand and patted his forearm. The colonel's head sank back and his shoulders relaxed. She could not understand what he tried to say as he drifted back into his drug-induced sleep.

She watched him as he fell asleep. Rubbing his arm and holding his hand she quietly shook her head.

The colonel was lucky. As she understood it, the metal frame supporting the Suburban's door split the bullet in two and deflected its trajectory. Because of the deflection, the portion that hit Newborne skimmed the left and forward side of his head instead of violently smashing into and through his brain. The other half of the bullet tore up the car seat an inch behind him.

After taking his pulse, she gently placed the colonel's arm at his side. She checked his IV drips then she turned to help the medic attending the Private First Class in the bed adjacent to his. The colonel would be fine, but the same was not true for

Jorge. The twenty-year-old in the bed next to him also had a gunshot wound to the head but his skull had taken the full force of the round. He was not going to make it. They were trying to keep him alive long enough for his unit's chaplain and his combat buddy to get to the hospital. *They'd better hurry.*

She patted the young medic on the back. Then she turned her attention to the man who had shot Jorge. The Iraqi man in the bed against the wall had received two gunshot wounds in his leg and one in his chest right after he pulled the trigger on the dying soldier. He, too, was in pain and he, too, was frightened. The nurse walked over and held his hand. She felt her patient squeeze back lightly. *Soon he would be well enough to transfer to the ward.* Looking at the five patients in her unit, she held back her tears. She would have plenty of time to cry as she tried to sleep once her seemingly endless shift was over.

CHAPTER 35

Newborne's skin was pale and enflamed. Half of his face was bruised and swollen to a puffy grotesque shape. He couldn't close his left eye all the way, and his mouth was locked in a disfigured position. A swath of his ultra-black hair had been shaved off during surgery leaving a contrast that accentuated the stitched scar, like black laces on a waxy white football. His big arms moved slowly and clumsily, his voice was determined, but his words were confused.

Sahar, who was taking notes as the ninth-floor manager, tried not to stare at him. Four days after he was almost killed, Colonel Newborne stood in his regularly scheduled meeting in the minister's conference room, overcrowded with the directors general or their representatives and the dozen floor managers.

"No sir, I did not do it yet. I will do it today, *Insha'Allah*," answered the DG of Finance trying to project her voice only as loudly as absolutely necessary.

"No *Insha'Allah*. This needs to get done and you need to freakin' do it," slurred the colonel, pausing unnaturally between words as though they were echoing in his head. A string of drool seeped from his lips.

All the Iraqis glanced at one another.

"I will do it. It will get done, *Insha'Allah*," repeated the rattled Executive.

"Look, don't you think that just because I go and get myself freakin' shot you don't have to do your work. Do it, no *Insha'Allah*."

"Colonel," the DG of Medicine spoke up, "You need rest, why are you having this meeting? We can't even understand what you are saying."

Newborne glanced at the chalk scribbles that he had earlier tried to draw on the board behind him before he turned to glare at the ministry's senior doctor, but he addressed the wrong person, "I'm fine."

Many of the attendees looked down at their notepads in silence.

Sahar, looked away. Sattar sat with his hands clasped together and looked reassuringly at his colleague from the fourth-floor who seemed to not know whether to take the colonel's tongue lashing seriously or not.

For a long moment, the colonel just stared at the space in front of him. Then he mumbled, "God Damn it. My fucking head *hurst*."

The senior doctor looked up and said, "We are really sorry you were shot, we are glad you are alive. But you must rest."

The colonel looked directly at him, "Who are you? My mother? I can take care of myself."

"Mister Newborne, as a physician I am telling you that you should not be here today," the DG of Medicine said authoritatively. Then he looked across the staff, "Everyone, please go; I am calling this meeting."

Newborne looked at the doctor, "Right," then he looked at the people as they quietly began to back away from the table, "Everyone, go and do your damn work," Newborne said as he slid into his empty chair and rested his elbows on the table, closed his eyes and steadied his head with both of his hands.

The chief of medicine nodded prompting the attendees to depart. As the room emptied he slid over and sat down next to the colonel.

Until the path before him cleared Zaid stood in the corner scowling. He held his hard eyes on Newborne, his fists clenched at his sides, then he too shuffled into the hallway.

CHAPTER 36

Zaid shook his head, and then he stood up and walked around his desk. He kicked the floor where the shooter had stood not two weeks before; then he spat. He stomped back around his desk and placed his hands on its empty, smooth surface and pushed down against it feeling his biceps tighten. He kicked his chair out so he could plop down in the seat, which he did before he began to sit staring blankly across the room. A knock on his door awakened him.

"Enter."

Reem came in, and pausing just inside the door, flashed him a shy smile before she moved the brown folder that contained a report she was delivering up to her face. He faintly smiled.

"Well, are you going to give it to me?" He asked in a rough voice as he extended his hand.

She stepped forward holding the folder out to him. Taking it from her, he dropped it with a flop, then immediately aligned it to be parallel to the desk's front edge. Flipping it open, he leaned forward and began scanning the document. After reading the first page, he looked up to see Reem watching him intently.

Discovered, she quickly dropped her gaze to his neatly trimmed finer nails as his large hand held the report. The contrast between his strength and the menial task of holding the delicate sheets of paper was an awkward match—like a king making his own bed. Her glance flowed back up his arm, his chest, his neck, she immediately looked away when she looked directly into his penetrating eyes.

"Take a seat," Zaid ordered.

She scooted around the small puddle of water on the floor and daintily sat down at a chair directly in front of his desk. She was silent, and he returned to the report.

When he finished reading the last page he closed the folder. He slid open the desk's file drawer, flipped through the hanging files until he found the one he wanted and dropped the report into its proper place. As he tapped the drawer shut he returned his hands to the desk in front of him.

Looking at her, he noticed that her clear forehead was wrinkled in concern. This made him smile.

"What do you think of the Americans?" His voice was as direct as the question. He watched her fingers pull on one another as he addressed her.

She bit her lip. After a thoughtful moment, she said, "I think they are dogs." She answered quite slowly, her inflection rose as her sentence progressed.

"Yes," he replied looking at her, waiting for her to continue.

"I think that they have no reason for coming here. We would be better off without them. They should have never come."

"But, yet, here they are." Zaid offered, watching her growing discomfort.

"Yes," she said clumsily, like a schoolgirl answering a question about football to the team's star. "I wish they would go." She stopped talking and closed her mouth tightly and looked towards the cheerless, blank wall behind him.

"You wish the Americans would go away?

"Yes."

Zaid stood up. His chair slid against the floor disturbing the silence. Reem looked down and placed her hands together and pressed them between her knees.

He grinned as he leaned forward over the desk supporting his weight with his fists. Wearing a short-sleeve shirt, his veins in his forearms popped out, adding to his carefully choreographed image of power.

"Would you consider doing something to help encourage them to go away?" He asked very slowly articulating each word, intentionally breathing directly into her face.

Her pulse quickened and her features reddened. Looking directly into his eyes she answered as boldly as she could, "Yes. I would do my part." Her voice cracked as she answered.

Zaid sat back and silently watched her for a moment. Her nostrils flared and he could hear her hyperventilate. He softened his glare, and then he nodded, but he remained silent.

She continued staring at him. Her hands were now pinned beneath her thighs as she sat upright, her eyes wide open, like a gerbil in the presence of a cobra. He turned away from her and stepped back. She let her shoulders drop a bit, but she remained tense.

"Well then," he said as he turned toward her, looking directly at her and said, "Then we shall face these dogs together."

He smiled and his eyebrows rose just a bit, chasing away the last remnants of his earlier tormenting glare. Reem's spine lost its rigidity and she dipped a bit in her chair. She exhaled a bit too loudly. She smiled—threatened gerbil turned schoolgirl. She looked down and took a deep breath.

"Now go back to the ministry and collect the next set of bids," he directed.

She nodded and rose from her seat. She was suddenly very aware that his eyes were traveling over her. As she inhaled she felt the fabric of her blouse tight around her. An involuntary, embarrassed, childish smile crossed her lips adding to the awkward silence. She turned toward the door and in a self-conscious manner, she stepped out into the hallway.

CHAPTER 37
Baghdad: 27 October 2003

"Joe?" Sahar asked quietly.

"Yes, Doctor Sahar."

"I'm sorry your hotel was attacked."

"Thank you. We were lucky. Only one person was killed."

"Yes, I'm sorry. And I'm sorry that Colonel James is in the hospital."

Colonel George James was one of the MOH CPA members who was brought in to help advise the DG of Finance. He was in his room when it was struck by one of the rockets that exploded, mostly on the ninth and eleventh floors of the Al Rashid Hotel. He was now on his way back to Walter Reed Army Medical Center, via Germany.

"Thank you. We think he will be alright."

"I'm glad that you didn't get hurt, too."

Joe looked her in the eyes, she looked away, "Thank you, Sahar. That means a lot to me."

She nodded slightly then turned and left the room.

CHAPTER *38*

A car shot full of holes,
Ten in dad, six in mom,
And four in each little one.

It was overkill,
Such a waste of lead,
I'm sure after the first six shots
All of them were dead.

Maybe daddy had a gun,
Maybe baby—a bomb,
They didn't stop the car soon enough
Now they are in a tomb.

Joe asks me,
"What else could they do?"
"The car didn't stop, they had to shoot
To protect their crew."

Shoot and kill they did.
I think they learned their lesson well
They won't not stop again, Joe,
As far as I can tell.

Joe says it was just a tragedy,
A terrible part of war.
"Americans do not kill for fun
Their hearts in two it tore."

I think they did and I think they do
I think again they will.
Soldiers will kill for fun
Until they've had their fill.

Sahar sat frowning, her shoulders pulled forward. She listened to the conversation but she glared at the table. Sattar looked at her, but did not ask. Hamid sat quietly next to her.

"Okay. As you know, the World Health Organization and the World Bank adopted the MOH requirements in Amman and with their endorsement, the International Committee agreed to them at the International Donor's Conference in Madrid. So, the world community agreed to support a $1.6 billion investment to buy new equipment and repair critical infrastructure in the Iraqi healthcare system. That's great, that should fund about a four-year program but we still need to develop the construction program before we can start design or construction."

Joe looked up at Sattar as Hamid translated for him.

Sattar sat there smiling, nodding his head, "Yes, good."

"But we messed up. When our engineers went out to assess all the hospitals, most of them failed to fill out the questionnaires properly. They all say, 'need more beds.' And therefore, we still don't not know which projects are the most urgent. I propose we send them all out again, we have no choice, but this time we'll conduct a week-long training class on how to fill out the surveys before they depart."

Hamid nodded his head in agreement.

Sattar watched him and then nodded too, "Yes, I like the plan."

Sahar didn't look up.

Sattar grinned, his grandfatherly face forcing a smile out of Joe. Sahar continued staring at the desk. The two men glanced at each other, then Sattar stood up. "Excuse me, Joe, Doctor Sahar. I must go now."

Hamid also stood up and nodded towards Joe.

"Thank you *Sayid* Sattar, Hamid" Joe responded, standing up.

Sahar didn't move.

After they left, Joe looked directly at her.

"What say you?" Joe asked. "We think the plan is good."

She did not answer.

Joe prodded her, "What's bothering you today?"

"Nothing," she lied.

"Hogwash. Something is bothering you, what is it?"

"Hogwash?" Sahar stood up and looked toward the door.

Joe watched her as she looked down at the floor for a moment. The energy in her body seemed to visibly drain out, and she turned back toward Joe.

With hints of tears in her eyes Sahar asked, her voice choked-up, "What are you doing here? Why does the colonel stay here even after he was shot? And those Americans killed that family. Everything is terrible."

Joe paused a moment and straightened his back before he answered slowly and thoughtfully. "Look, I honestly don't know why we are here. But I know that regardless of the reason we came, the war is now about freedom. It is about bringing democracy to you and all the other Iraqis."

Sahar stared at Joe. "I—"

She turned her head away fighting uncontrollable crying. Standing stiffly erect, her chin up, she looked back toward the door as though she were a deer in the desert ready to take flight at the first sound of a predator. But she did not hear that sound, so she stood, silent, immobile, listening. After glancing toward the door, she glared suspiciously at Joe.

Joe continued, speaking softly, "Look, Doctor Sahar. The president says we are here because of weapons of mass destruction and others claim we are here for oil. Still others say we are here because the president is trying to finish the war that his father started. I don't know the real reason why we, the United States, are here. But I know why I am here and I know why Colonel Newborne stays even though his head is still swollen and painful and undoubtedly pounding. I come to this ministry every day and work nights back at the palace because we have a chance to bring freedom to twenty-five million people who have known nothing but oppression."

"I think it's oil. You invaded to steal our oil. It's all about oil, about oil and money." She hissed her words.

"Maybe." He paused until she looked him in the eye, "Maybe we are here for the oil, but not to steal it."

She looked away.

"Maybe we are here to get rid of a tyrannical dictator of a country with lots of oil reserves to form a democracy that will then trade with other Democracies. Maybe we are here for the oil, but maybe it is just to ensure that we have a reliable oil market that we can buy it from. But I don't think we are here to steal it."

Sahar looked back at Joe. She was no longer poised to run out of the room. She looked at this army officer wearing khaki pants and a blue polo shirt stretched over his body armor. Then she shook her head.

"You don't care about the people of Iraq, all you care about is oil. If we were all dead, you wouldn't shed a tear."

"No, Doctor Sahar, that isn't true. I do care. Most of us care. Do you think Colonel Newborne doesn't care? He took a bullet to the head, and yet he stays. Do you think he would do that for oil?"

After a pause Joe continued, "Sahar you probably don't understand the colonel. I'm sure you understand men who speak strong words, men who treat others cruelly, but maybe you don't know many men who act on conviction, people who follow-up their beliefs with their actions, even when real danger is involved.

"I'm not saying that Americans are better than Iraqis, I'm not saying that at all. But many men, people, of conviction, were either killed or imprisoned by Saddam because they posed a threat. Or some may have been seduced into Saddam's court where they were castrated of their integrity, or others were pushed underground where they learned to hide in-order-to survive, meekly turning the other cheek rather than standing up for their rights and pride."

"Ghosts, villains or sheep," she said stiffly.

"What?" asked Joe.

"You are saying that Iraqi men are either ghosts, villains or sheep."

"No," then Joe stopped and thought about his words. "I didn't mean that, I was just saying that Saddam considered anyone who stood up to him to be a threat, discouraging the type of integrity—"

She cut him off. "Joe, at least under Saddam we knew what the risks were, but now, what path leads to survival? Tell me. Do you know?"

Joe stood quietly, listening.

"I'm asking why you are here. And you are answering that integrity is why you are here, as if Iraqis no longer understand the concept of integrity. You are wrong. At the end of the Kuwait War, America encouraged the *Shi'a* to revolt against Saddam, and then you Americans stood back and watched as Saddam sent what was left of his army in to kill the people and their families that trusted you Americans. Also, your sanctions, all sorts of restrictions, destroyed our economy so that even to get healthcare for a child with a curable illness, a man had to swear allegiance to Saddam and beg for the medicine that was readily available in Jordan, Syria or Turkey. And then you judge that man to be 'weak.' Americans act like they own integrity. But I don't think Americans know what it is."

She drilled him with her eyes. "You always talk about democracy. Why do you think it is so wonderful and why do you think we want it? Why do you think we want anything from you?"

Joe paused a moment before answering her, "Sahar, I'm sorry, I never thought of what you just said."

"Well, what I said is true. Americans have no idea how the world is. They sit back and think everyone wants to be like them. Well, not everyone does. So, tell me, Joe, why democracy?"

"Well," Joe started slowly, but then spoke more smoothly, "Democracies provide the highest standard of living for their people. With Iraq's natural resources and its educated and industrious people, a democracy here could create the foothold for a much more stable Middle East. You are an intelligent woman, why wouldn't you want to be involved with your country's future?"

Sahar continued to boldly look at his eyes, an act that would be unthinkable to an Iraqi man of his stature. Joe seemed not to even notice her presumptuousness. She nodded.

"I believe that you believe that. But just how long do you think it will take, to make Iraq a democracy? People will fight it. People are always afraid of change."

Joe paused to consider Sahar's words and then continued. "I think it'll be for your children. They'll have the opportunity to live in freedom. They'll have opportunities to pursue and accomplish the goals that they themselves set, not be forced into lives they don't desire. They'll have the freedom to succeed or to fail. That is what freedom is."

Sahar turned away but still listened closely.

"You know this war will not go on forever," said Joe. "Fortunately, wars never do. Someday, based on what Iraqis like you decide and what actions you take today, Iraq could be free.

"That can happen. It has happened. Look at Japan. Look at Germany. Look at South Korea. In all these places, the United States fought wars, and in each of these places, the United States invested heavily in their reconstruction, just like we are doing here in Iraq right now. Look at these countries now. Germany is now peaceful and is the economic powerhouse of Europe. Japan is the second largest economy on earth, and, ironically, the United States' top industrial and technological competitor. And look at South Korea. People say we lost that war, but all one needs to do to counter that argument is to look at North Korea. Had the United States and the rest of the UN not intervened, the North Koreans or Chinese would have won that war. Had that happened, South Korea could be as backward and oppressed a nation as North Korea. But it isn't. Instead, the country that fifty years ago was completely destroyed by war is now one of the economic tigers of Asia."

Sahar didn't move, nor did she respond.

"Look, Sahar. I work all day, every day and risk my life traveling around Baghdad because I believe that we have a great opportunity that we can't afford to waste. Iraq can be free. You can be free. Your children can be free. And I believe that what we are doing here is changing the world for the better. We can rebuild the Iraqi healthcare system, you and me, right here and right now."

Sahar turned back towards Joe.

Joe continued earnestly. "I don't think my country is here to enslave yours or to take its oil. I believe that regardless of why we invaded in the first place, right now the reason we are here is to establish a democracy in the Middle East. Iraq can become a government that can shine as an example for the kingdoms and dictatorships that surround you. Iraq can be a bastion of freedom in this region that has known so much oppression and sorrow. Don't you want to be part of this?"

Sahar tightened her lips.

Joe pressed on. "The way I see it, Sahar, you already are a part of it. Whether you want it or not, this situation has been thrust upon you. And how you act, what you do, will help determine whether Iraq will become a democracy, or return to being enslaved to another totalitarian regime or sink into a fundamentalist Islamic republic, like Saudi Arabia or Iran or worse, like Afghanistan under the Taliban."

Sahar shuddered and stared straight ahead.

"Any of these things could happen. I believe that what we do here is important and will make a difference. Colonel Newborne stays, even though he would be received back home as a hero, because he, too, sees this unique opportunity. But we Americans will not be the ones who make all this happen."

Joe shifted his weight as if transferring it over to his reluctant audience, "People like you, Sahar, will be the decision makers. Right now, you are voting with your actions. But I don't believe your fear of American imperialism is justified. Germany, Japan, South Korea are independent democracies now, often acting in ways that infuriate the United States."

Joe smiled, "And knowing you, Sahar, if there are other Iraqis like you, I am sure Iraq won't make a very good puppet, either."

CHAPTER 39

Soldiers break down doors
take men wearing pajamas,
shamed in his own home.

German Shepherd dogs,
inches from bound prisoners
barking and growling.

Stacks of naked men
prodded near laughing women
taking photographs.

Shocks and broken bones,
US hospitality
inside Saddam's jails.

Will this win our trust?
Do you respect us at all?
our trust worth earning?

You came to help us?
If this is helping I'm glad
you didn't come to harm.

When Mister Banks walked into Sattar's office, Sattar, Hamid, Wasan, and Joe stood up. Max and Sahar who were standing around the assembly of chairs in front of Sattar's desk, stepped back and out of the way. The minister coming to the ninth-floor was very unusual and never good.

Looking Joe in the eye, his eyebrows tilted downward, Mister Banks announced, "I need the list on Tuesday."

Joe, caught off guard responded, "Sir, should we go into the other room to discuss this?"

"No, I don't think there is anything to discuss. I know your opinions, but the reconstruction cannot wait until it is convenient for you to leisurely catch up."

Joe looked away, his cheeks reddening. Mister Banks looked across the faces of the others in the room. Max nodded to him, the others all looked toward the ground, hardly breathing.

Joe inhaled deeply, "Sir, I know that politics is your main concern, and I respect that. I also know that I can be a bit idealistic at times, but I also recognize reality. The success or failure of major construction programs are based on math. Engineering and politics must be in balance for major undertakings to succeed."

Joe paused for a moment, and then continued, "Sir, I understand the urgency. But I guarantee that the shortest path to success is not to jump ahead of ourselves. If we neglect to spend adequate time planning now, we will waste months, or even years in delays and millions of dollars in changes and cost overruns as we try to make the corrections during construction that we could have avoided completely by just figuring out what we need to do before we start randomly acting."

"We need to move out. We need to show commitment, like all the other ministries."

"Yes, sir, we do. But in the next few years we will need to show progress, successful results, not incompetence."

Joe paused again and took a quick breath and closed his eyes a moment apparently looking inward. Banks waited impatiently. "Sir, the divisions are having local and immediate impact solving minor issues in clinics and hospitals with the CERP money. But long-term success will require capital investment and long-term resourcing, we need to synchronize requirements with resources before we go too far down the road."

Joe glanced around. Max was the only person in the room who looked directly at him.

Joe turned and invited Mister Banks to look out the window, the minister grudgingly accommodated him. Below them spread the ruins of the Ministry of Defense.

"Sir, imagine that we submit the projects that on their own merit we deem most urgent or important." Pointing at the rubble below he continued, "It might seem reasonable to submit

140

a project to replace the roof of that building that no longer has one," he said pointing to a warehouse-looking building two hundred meters away.

"And we might say that that building needs a renovation because its walls have been blown out. We might fix the electrical system in that building, and the mechanical system in that other one. Finally, just to show that we are thinking, we would fix the road coming in, pave that parking lot, and maybe build a sidewalk between that cluster of buildings and the parking lot."

Mister Banks was listening, but seemed disinterested. He looked up impatiently.

"So, what have we got?" Joe continued. "We have a project list. We could spend two million dollars doing the work I just mentioned, and we would fix what we consider our most significant problems. But in the end, we have nothing. We have not fixed a single building system, not a single building works and nobody can use any of those buildings for anything more than what they can use them for now."

Joe looked around. Only Max and the minister were looking at him.

"Had we taken that same two million and fixed all the components of that building and that building and reconstructed that parking lot and those sidewalks, we would have systematically provided some space that could be used by someone to perform some necessary function. And if that function were a critical function in its process, we would have added value. But the work would only be value added if, and only if, we took the time to identify what we need before we started construction."

"Have the project list on my desk by the new deadline," Banks stated flatly.

Hamid shifted and shook his head slightly. Sahar looked at him and Hamid returned her glance, then he quickly looked away.

Mister Banks also shook his head, "Everyone else has managed to meet the deadline."

Undeterred, Joe continued. "Sir, their success is hollow. No one has met the deadline. The truth is that they just skipped the planning process and rattled off a list of things. Time will show their failure as problem after problem will prevent their list from being built and those that are built will fail to solve problems. Don't be surprised if they build power plants but not the electrical distribution network connecting them to their consumers, or roads that lead to unsafe bridges, or bridges without roads leading to them. Besides, the ridiculously short deadline they want us to meet is arbitrary and meaningless. The CPA doesn't have the capacity nor the capability to instantly develop all these lists of projects into a construction program. They have no idea how they are going to manage this amount of construction. If we submit something now it will just sit on their shelf until they figure this out anyway. The fastest way to show results is to think before we act. To plan."

"That is why the Project Management Office is being expanded."

"Sir, regardless of how badly we want it, or how badly we need it, the PMO will not become productive overnight. The legacy of the United States in this effort will be doing the wrong thing poorly, to nobody's benefit. A terrible wasted opportunity to make the positive impact that we all want."

Mister Banks stood back on his heels and crossed his arms, glaring at Joe. Joe stood at a modified position of attention but he did not flinch as he looked back at Mister Banks.

After a deep exhale, Mister Banks shook his head. "Get it done."

"Yes sir." Joe and Max said in unison. The Iraqis looked up.

"We," Mister Banks said emphasizing the first word as he glanced across the array of faces in the room, "We have work to do," he said as he walked out.

The minister's footsteps had faded down the hallway before Joe turned away and looked back out the window. The room remained silent. Joe looked across the city, his face was red and tense. The Iraqis in the room glanced around, but didn't say anything.

Finally, Max suggested, "Why don't we create a list for Mister Banks to meet the deadline, and resend the engineers out to conduct the assessments as planned so they could develop the real program?"

"You know that once the list is made, it will be very hard to change," Joe replied as he turned around to face everyone.

"But I don't think we have a choice," Max replied.

Joe nodded and looked to Sattar. The older man looked back at the two Americans and calmly said, "As you like."

"Can you do it? Are you able to come up with a reasonable 'false' list with what data we have?" Joe asked intently.

"Hamid has most of this information," Sahar interjected.

Joe looked over at Hamid.

"Joe," offered Hamid, "Of course we can do it. We know these buildings."

"You may end up stuck with the list, even after your assessment teams get the information demonstrating that the projects we submit would not be a good investment."

"Joe, I don't understand how you create and organize your program, and I'm sure I don't always agree with it, but we all want to fix our buildings. We all want the healthcare system to succeed."

Sattar nodded.

Joe looked over to Sahar.

Sahar looked back at him and then realized that he was waiting for her to say something, "Yes. We can do it, *Insha'Allah*. But with your permission, you cannot talk to a minister like that. I'm surprised that he didn't fire you, or worse."

Joe and Max started to laugh. They stopped though when all the Iraqis just looked at them with straight faces.

"Uh, yeah. I guess. Maybe, I'll probably get my ass kicked when we get back to the palace," joked Joe.

The audience still didn't respond. Joe reassured them, "Look, it'll be okay, as-long-as we do what he told us to do, we'll all be fine."

After glancing at all the serious faces surrounding him, Joe changed his tone, "Okay, Sattar. Hamid, please save my ass and make the list. Max, you make sure it gets in the format the PMO wants."

"Yes, sir," responded the captain.

Then Joe exhaled deeply and forced a smile. Everyone in the room returned the smile and exhaled relief. Sattar silently nodded to Hamid. Joe sat down in a folding chair next to Sattar's desk and leaned back a bit, his shirt riding up to expose the bottom of his body armor. "Oh, Max, I think at this stage it would be better to underestimate the costs than to leave requirements out, one thing that may save us is that every program will have mission creep, later it will probably be easier to add money than scope."

Max nodded, "Roger."

Sattar sat perched on the corner of the desk next to Joe.

"Okay then, what else?" Joe asked no one specifically.

No one answered.

Looking at Sattar, Joe asked, "The schedule for the engineer assessments, have you decided on the teams yet?"

Sahar translated for him.

"Yes, Joe. Four teams."

Joe turned his head to look at Sahar, "Sahar, please notify finance of the upcoming expense."

She nodded then paused to watch Joe smile at Sattar as the other people in the room began to break up to work on their newly assigned tasks.

"We are going to be alright," Joe said cheerfully.

CHAPTER 40

Colonel Newborne walked quickly down the hall, past the three marble staircases, past the eight crystal chandeliers, past the overly-decorated, gold-colored ornamentation. He did not see any of it. Upon entering S-200, the MOH Operations office at the CPA Headquarters, he strode over to his desk, placed his MP-5 and his Beretta onto his chair, then let his backpack and a couple books plop down on his desktop as he began to take off his shirt so that his body armor could follow. His fingers busy with his buttons, he looked around for Joe. Seeing him he gave a quick grunt and loudly stated, "Joe, you dumb-shit."

Joe and the dozen other MOHers looked up from their laptops that were attached to electrical conduit taped over the white plaster walls.

The tone of the colonel's voice tipped off that he was more amused than annoyed. Joe pointed at himself with his thumb in a fake gesture of surprise, "Who me, Sir?"

"Oh, fuck you. Why the hell do you keep pissing off Banks?"

"Sir, he wants us..."

"Spare me, dip shit. I know what he wants. Just fucking do what he says and get the job done."

Joe glanced over at Max who was suppressing laughter.

"Which job? Turning in a project list or reconstructing the healthcare system? If I do what he wants, the reconstruction will never get done."

"Spare me. You don't know that. You're just following some idealistic, academic process. This is the real world, things aren't perfect."

"Actually, sir, no, I'm not. For example, the Panama Canal, for the first several years—"

"Panama? When the hell were you ever in Panama? I've been to Panama. This isn't Panama. Does this look like fucking Panama to you? Tony, go get me a fucking banana, but leave your damn monkey alone this time."

Lieutenant Colonel Tony Weeks, his hair out of place and his razor stubble a bit darker than normal, grinned as he spun around in his seat to face the colonel.

"Yes sir," continued Joe, "Reconstructing Iraq is a huge engineering project, like the canal, and we are heading for spectacular failure just like the canal was until—"

"Enough. You're pissing Mister Banks off and now you're pissing me off. You are making him look bad to his peers and to the ambassador. Give him a fucking project list so he can beat his chest and hold his head up."

"At the cost of reconstruction?"

"Who the hell do you think you are? Do you think you can do it without them? Give them what they need and then do what you need to do. You are no fucking hero. You are just a piece of the damn machine. Do your part, and in this case your part is to do what he tells you."

Joe paused long enough to look at Max. "Yes, sir," he said mechanically.

"Now you see? That wasn't so hard," he announced patronizingly.

"Now get your ass downstairs. At 16:00 the head of the PMO will be talking about the Congressional Supplemental and answering all those damn questions you have about how to do this, and all that bullshit."

Max was red, his face a huge smile.

"Roger."

"Roger my ass. Just get the fucking job done."

Joe didn't respond. There was no way to get the last word in if Newborne wanted to have it. Everyone in the room was grinning, including Newborne.

"Tony, where's my fucking banana?"

Tony replied smiling, "Sir, have you checked your pants?"

Having changed his t-shirt, Newborne wiped the sweat off his face with the worn one and was on his way toward the door.

"Fuck you all," he said, tossing the damp shirt to Tony as he stepped out of the room.

"Well, at least his head seems to be better," Joe quietly told Tony as Tony tossed the smelly shirt onto Joe's desk.

146

"Yeah, he's good as new," Tony agreed.

CHAPTER *41*

When the head of the Program Management Office walked in, the thirty CPA people representing the various ministries and the Corps of Engineers stood up from their seats surrounding the big table in conference room S-100 and became silent. The retired military officer, wearing a business suit, smiled.

He stepped forward to the fancy, rather gaudy Victorian style chair at the end of the table and stood behind it. A moment passed before he asked for everyone to be seated, and then a moment longer as he looked each of the thirty-people facing him in the eye.

"Good afternoon, gentlemen. And ladies. I would like to start by telling you all how happy I am to be here."

And so, he did. Then he picked up a folder that lay in front of him, one labeled, "Supplemental," containing the Congressional Supplemental legislation.

"Ladies and Gentlemen, we have a unique opportunity that carries with it a very solemn responsibility. We are here to ensure that the $18.6 billion that the U.S. Congress has dedicated to reconstructing Iraq's infrastructure results in a functional Iraq. I am sure each of you are aware of your ministry's share of that pot."

Many nodded and a few people murmured.

"Good. I trust all of you are aware of the corruption problem here in Iraq. I am here to make sure that the money is not stolen or wasted." He went on to describe how he saw the current situation. He introduced three people he had designated as his assistants. They, in-turn, spoke about themselves. Joe noted with alarm that, except the PMO chief himself, not one of them had a construction management background. Joe shifted in his seat and held his hands steady on the table. The chief's words indicated that he was more interested in stopping things from going wrong than making things go right.

As the end of the presentation approached, instead of any of his questions being answered, a whole host of new questions and concerns collected in Joe's mind. The reality of Iraq was that travel was dangerous, internet access was unreliable and a growing number of people were actively trying to hinder progress by ambushing convoys, killing the labor force and destroying their work. Expertise for all types of facilities was required to manage the design and construction of highly technical projects including oil refineries, bridges, hospitals, and manufacturing plants. Most American engineers and architects didn't speak Arabic, and they certainly didn't know much about Iraqi culture and Iraqi construction techniques and standards. Additionally, the average PMO's project manager would remain on the job for less than a year which was too short a time to complete any projects; this would create significant continuity problems. Also, setting up a centralized system in Baghdad would imitate the Hussein regime's methods—continuing the distrust held by the seventeen governorates that were tired of being neglected by and for Baghdad. These variables taken together predestined the CPA's concept of a hundred Americans in Baghdad overseeing $18.6 billion of construction spread out over an area the size of Texas to be very ineffective at best, with the most likely outcome being complete failure.

When the speaker opened the floor for questions, Joe decided that most of his questions could wait for another time and place. Since today was Saturday and the PMO's deadline to provide "the final" program for the supplemental money was Tuesday, he asked the question that just could not wait. He needed to know the cost factors that the PMO wanted everyone to use.

"Sir, what S&A rates, overhead rates and area cost factors do you recommend we add on to our Iraqi construction methods estimates to account for the additional expenses that will be incurred for construction and management of such a robust program in this environment?"

The man in charge stood silently for a moment. Then he glanced at his three assistants to see if any of them appeared ready to launch into an answer. Seeing no movement from any of them, he cleared his throat and answered. His loud confident voice boomed, "Had you read the Supplemental, you would know that of the $18.6 billion, $50 million is dedicated to ensuring that proper accounting procedures and progress reports are regularly made."

Joe had read the supplemental so he listened intently for the answer to his question. The rest of the room remained silent as well. The chief looked around a bit and seeing that all eyes were still on him, continued talking.

"Therefore, none. Don't add anything for overhead to the cost estimates because overhead is already accounted for."

Joe glanced back at Captain Maxwell. Max shrugged his shoulders in return. Joe turned back and looked down at the table. On his note pad Joe quickly calculated that $50 million is less than 0.3% of $18.6 billion. On military managed medical construction jobs in the states, the US Army Corps of Engineers routinely charged 6% for *S&A* alone. Even this would be dreadfully inadequate in Iraq because of additional costs that all projects would incur since Iraq was at war and that the magnitude of all the work simultaneously taking place would increase the price of management as well as both labor and materials. Additionally, there was little infrastructure to use to support construction efforts in Iraq; it would have to be created or shipped in from other countries in the region—at additional expense. As someone at the far end of the room asked the next question, the list of factors that would result in additional costs continued to grow on Joe's notepad.

Joe put his mechanical pencil down. None of this made sense. The CPA Reconstruction team could not be this clueless. They must have instructions to show progress, even hollow progress, immediately—long-term ramifications be damned. For the rest of the meeting, Joe sat there staring at the notepad in front of him.

CHAPTER *42*

"Why do you all drive crazy?"

Joe looked up from his laptop in their office on the ninth-floor to find Sahar's piercing eyes looking down at him from across the table. Leaning forward, her *hijab* hung down around her shoulders, she looked like an owl staring down a mouse deciding whether she was going to kill it or not.

Before Joe could answer, she continued, "I was at a market yesterday, and a row of cars came by driving the wrong way and turned at an intersection when other cars were trying to drive. They act like Iraqis are not important, only them."

Joe nodded. "I know."

"They point their guns at all of us."

"The soldiers?"

"No, I'm not talking about the soldiers. I am talking about the ones like you, or like the minister's bodyguards. They wear normal clothes, wear sunglasses, and they point guns at everyone."

Joe didn't answer.

"So, why do you do it?"

"Sahar, I really don't like it, but I think it started because people don't want to get stuck in traffic. When we are stuck in traffic, we are most vulnerable. When we get ambushed, it is bad for everyone—Iraqis too."

Sahar looked at him, "We are always vulnerable, you know, and we must live here. We cannot leave," she said.

Joe nodded again, "I know."

"So, what will you do about it?"

"About the driving?"

"No, about everything."

"I don't know."

"What will happen if you don't win? What will happen to us? Have you thought about that?"

Joe paused for a long time before he spoke. His lips pressed tightly together, "I don't know." Joe finally answered. "But that is why I am doing all I can to help us both win."

CHAPTER *43*

Baghdad: Early November 2003

A couple of weeks before Thanksgiving, after breakfast, just as Major Bradley Watts, Major Cross's replacement—an operations officer, and Sergeant Marty were giving the rest of the CPA MOH team the daily threat briefing, Carson walked into Room S-200 and announced to the group, "No one is going to the ministry this morning. The ambassador is calling all CPA staffers to the dining hall for a meeting at 9:30."

The dining hall was already crowded as several members of the MOH team walked in together. Some people were sitting on tables that along with stacks of chairs had been pushed to the periphery, but most just stood somewhere in the quickly-filling center of the vast, square room. There were no windows, but three of the four sides each had two sets of twelve-foot-high double doors separated by dark-colored, inset columns and inlaid display cases outlined in shiny white ceramic tile. Staff notices were tacked up on the bulletin boards inside these cases. Huge, ornate chandeliers hung throughout the space from a very decorative geometric pattern on the high ceiling that enclosed the visually over-stimulating space. The wall without exit doors held the recently installed cafeteria serving line that fed the Coalition Provisional Authority personnel breakfast, lunch and dinner.

Shaking the hands of a few of the staff who positioned themselves to meet him, the ambassador walked casually to the mobile podium that displayed the round, gold CPA logo. The ambassador was thin, medium height and dressed in his now famous suit jacket—adorned with a pin displaying both the American and Iraqi flags—tie and combat boots. His hair was freshly combed and he looked comfortable, even delighted, to be in front of his team. And that was how he began as he stepped up to the microphone.

"I am delighted to be here, in Iraq, in Baghdad, and here in this room with you."

From his position in the crowd to the left of the podium, Mister Banks beamed. He excitedly whispered to Eileen Chong who stood next to her boss holding her clipboard in one hand and his camera in the other, "He just calmed four hundred people with one sentence. Right now, few people on earth have the power or attention of the world that this man does, yet here he is standing there smiling, making people love him."

Mister Banks quieted as Bremmer continued, "I am so proud of the work you all have done, and I am so appreciative for the hardship that you all have endured for your country and for the country of Iraq. I want to personally thank each-and-every one of you for your efforts, your sacrifices and your senses of duty."

The room was silent. Only the ambassador's voice and an occasional muffled cough were heard. "Today in Iraq there are more operational hospital beds than at any time since 1990."

Mister Banks now radiated, he gave a quick nod to a well-wisher who congratulated him with a pat on his back.

The ambassador rattled off a list of about twenty of the CPA's accomplishments, or, rather the accomplishments of the people in that room, who represented the CPA.

"But we cannot do it alone. We should not do it alone. And we are not doing it alone. We need to continue to involve the Iraqi workers of the Ministries."

Banks nodded in agreement.

"Please reach out to your Iraqi peers. Get to know them. Do what you can to help them to believe in their futures. Earn their trust. Work with them. Empower them. And tell them, that we, the United States of America and the other member nations of the coalition, will be here for them. The president is committed to the long haul. The United States military and we, the Coalition Provisional Authority, will remain until we are no longer needed. We will be here to support the Interim Iraqi

Government, and the people of Iraq, until they are ready to stand up on their own two feet."

His words brought smiles and applause from the four hundred people in the room. The ambassador's confidence and dedication was infectious. It felt good to be a part of something so important.

"As most of you know, I was in Washington, D.C. last week. The president and I were discussing this very important point. He asked me how long it would take. We discussed the seven accomplishments that we need to see before we can go home. And I told him that I think it will take us a little longer than we he had hoped. I told him that I think it will be three or four years."

The crowd erupted with minor conversations. Mister Banks spoke again to Major Chong, "This is much longer than what Rumsfeld and Rice are publicly stating."

"And the president told me, 'The United States is committed to this cause, that if my appointed envoy on the ground thinks we must remain until elections for a democratically agreed upon government takes place, then he, the president, is personally committed to keeping the CPA in Iraq, doing the great work that needs to be done, until the mission is accomplished.'"

Everyone glanced at each other. The ambassador's conditions for turning the role of governing over to the Interim Iraqi Government were well known. The still unwritten constitution must be approved and virtually all the governmental organizations must be rebuilt. And the country's infrastructure must be made functional. Considering most large construction projects take eighteen months to two years or more to build after the designs are completed, four years was not a long time. Although most pragmatists knew from the start that the estimate of months that was initially stated was preposterous, to those who live by public opinion, elections and headlines, three or four years sounded like a political eternity. For some reason, few seemed to realize that rebuilding postwar Japan, Germany and Korea, all took decades.

Joe smiled and quietly told Max, "Perhaps reason is finally creeping into the process."

The ambassador's voice became even more earnest. "But at the same time, we must train the Iraqis to run a democracy. Coach them. Guide them. But do not do the work for them. The United States does not want to be here indefinitely, and the Iraqi people will not want us here forever. But we cannot leave until they are running their country. So, I ask each of you to help them do it, but don't do it for them."

Although few people in the auditorium routinely consulted with their Iraqi counterparts, and even fewer considered them as peers, most heads nodded in agreement.

"Please reach out to the Iraqis you interact with. Tell them that they can count on us. Convince them to work with us. Reassure them that the President of the United States and the leaders from all the coalition partners understand the great risks we are asking them to take. Tell them that they have the word of the United States that we will never abandon them."

After restating the level of American resolve to be there for the Iraqis for as-long-as it would take, a quick review of how much had been accomplished already, and a few more statements expressing the American people's gratitude, the president's gratitude, the Iraqis' gratitude and the ambassador's personal gratitude, the twenty-minute speech was over.

As the microphone was switched off, the noise level grew. Carson, along with a throng of other young political appointees crowded the podium to shake the ambassador's hand and get a photo taken with him as the rest of the crowd shuffled off down the noisy, echoing corridors. As they headed back to their respective offices, Mister Banks beamed and Joe smiled.

CHAPTER *44*

Joe was in the conference room standing against the column in the corner looking out the ninth-floor window trying to see what was going on outside when Sahar ran in looking for him.

Seeing her energized and smiling, a combination he hadn't seen for quite some time Joe asked, "Well, what's gotten into you?"

"I heard that Saddam was captured. Is it true?"

Gunfire was a common sound in the streets of Baghdad, but in this instance, its volume had been increasing for several minutes. Joe looked out the window again. The firing was all around them and didn't appear to be aimed at any specific target.

"This is what they do in Iraq when they are happy, they shoot guns. Just like when Uday and Qusay were caught."

Joe nodded, "Wouldn't that be something? I haven't heard; I don't know if it's true or not."

"That's why all the shooting."

Just then his cell phone rang, "Lieutenant Colonel Brown."

"Joe, get down here. We're heading out," Tony relayed.

"Got it. On our way."

Sahar continued to smile as Joe folded the phone and put it in his pocket, "So it's true then."

"I don't know."

"It is true. Everyone knows."

"Do you know where Max is? We need to go."

"Go? It is only 12:30, why are you leaving so early?"

"Probably for the same reason there is so much shooting."

"Max is in with Wasan."

"Thanks. Have a nice day, and stay safe," Joe said smiling.

"This is a great day. The nicest ever!" Sahar beamed.

"I'm glad you're so happy. *Ma'salama*," he said heading toward the door.

"*Ma'salama*. You will see. They caught Saddam."

CHAPTER 45

His fists tightly clenched, the shooter sat as still as a statue in his chair, his back straight, his legs to the front, and his feet flat on the floor. Curtains blocking outside light from entering his small apartment, the image of his once great leader repeated itself on the small TV screen: his clothes wrinkled and soiled, dirty and shivering out of fear, being pulled out of a hole like a rodent. Over and over the shooter watched, the room illuminated only by the vision of his once great leader, groveling, begging for his life.

"Iraq is not Saddam; Saddam is not Iraq," he said indignantly.

The shooter leaped up as though willing himself out of the chair and out of his state of pity. He picked up the TV then without even unplugging it, he threw it to the floor. The screen cracked and fell out of its casing upon impact. Then he turned and tore the curtains open allowing a flood of light to enter. His deep breathing allowed his blood to flow into his arms strengthening him.

"He's a coward," he shouted. "I will not be fooled again," he swore out loud, "and I am tired of waiting." Looking at the now silent broken box, he let off one last vow, "And I will not fail again."

CHAPTER 46

"*Sayid* Sattar, I have bad news." Sahar looked up from her notes that she was reviewing as she sat in one of the chairs along with Hamid, Wasan, Joe and Max in front of Sattar's desk. Joe's tone was tormented.

It was about 9:20 in the morning and the group had just gathered. Joe did not even engage in the small talk that normally preceded business.

"Oh? What, Joe?" asked Sattar.

Both Sahar and Hamid leaned in closer. Max kept his distance.

"We have to cut the number of projects or the scope of each one. The Project Management Office has realized that they cannot fund the overhead of the $18 billion with $50 million."

"That's no problem, we knew that. We increased each estimate by 25%. Remember? Before we submitted the list," answered Hamid.

"It is a problem. They are starting with a different base cost than we did."

"Why? We used our costs. That is how much it costs us to build."

Joe looked down. The pause was far longer than they were accustomed to when speaking with Joe. "*Sayid* Hamid, I am sorry. But the Project Management Office changed our base costs, because—because they don't want to build the way that you build."

The Iraqis all looked at each other. Their faces grew hard.

"They insist on using 'International standards.'"

Sattar, Wasan and Hamid had a quick discussion in Arabic, Hamid then asked, "We don't know what you mean. What are these 'International standards?'"

"I don't know. They don't know. But they are determined to contract all the design out to firms in the U.S. and the U.K. instead of using the Iraqi models."

"That makes no sense. What do Americans or British know about our healthcare and our customs? And what do our construction workers know about building American or British hospitals?"

Joe shook his head. "Hamid, Sattar, I don't know what to tell you."

Sattar's face turned red. He looked away a moment until he regained control of his breathing.

"*Sayid* Sattar, it gets worse than that," Joe added.

Sahar tensed up.

"How?" The senior gentleman asked.

"They won't allow Iraqis to serve as Assistant Contracting Officer Representatives or Technical Representatives. The PMO thinks they can manage all the job sites from their offices in the palace here in Baghdad."

Everyone in the room was motionless.

After a minute, Hamid spoke with Sattar, then asked, his voice habitually calm, "Joe, what is our role in this process?"

Joe swallowed hard. "You have no role in the US Congressional batch of money. The PMO insists that they must manage everything to ensure quality and to ensure that the US Congressional money is spent efficiently."

Sattar stood up and turned toward the window. Then he looked back at Hamid and he spoke animatedly in Arabic, his arms moving up and down. Hamid then calmly told Joe, "You are saying we will have nothing to do with the first $750 million, the first two hundred clinics and twenty hospital renovations?"

Joe closed his eyes and forced himself to reply. "One hundred fifty clinics and seventeen renovations. The cost increases will reduce what can be built."

The room was silent.

"But you told us that the ambassador wanted our involvement. You always tell us that you want us to work with you. But now, you turn us away, stopping us from being part of the rebuilding of our own healthcare system." Hamid's said louder than normal, the dimple in his chin, looked deeper than Joe had ever seen it before.

"Yes." Joe's voice was barely audible.

Hamid spoke to Sattar, Wasan chimed in at times. Sahar wrote frantically. Then after Sattar waved his hand toward Hamid and nodded, they all turned their heads toward Joe.

"Tell me Joe, we think you are sincere, and we think you truly want to help, but you must tell us, why," said Hamid, articulating his pronunciation but controlling his emotion and volume.

Joe cleared his throat. "I'm afraid that the PMO's primary concern appears to be accounting for the money, not building the buildings."

"But the PMO was created to make sure the money is spent on developing infrastructure, no?"

"Yes."

"But now they are ignoring Iraqi and Muslim customs. They think they can manage projects from the Green Zone without our involvement?"

Joe nodded.

"Don't you understand they cannot succeed?"

Joe nodded, then he looked down at his feet.

Sattar's jaw was bulging and his eyes were sharp as he looked at Hamid. Hamid exhaled heavily, then said, "We believe you. Have you talked to them?"

"Yes."

He nodded. "Joe, you realize that this will actually lead to corruption and poor quality. This will cause the reconstruction effort to be a failure."

Joe nodded.

"I see," said Hamid.

"I'm sorry, *Sayid* Sattar. I truly am." Joe said, "But there's more."

Sattar turned and faced Joe while Hamid looked on closely. "The PMO also decided to follow the Federal Acquisition Regulation on all the purchases. At the meetings, the PMO repeatedly said that they needed to drop the contracts in two weeks, so they could show progress immediately, but then at the same time, they adopted a process that requires performance specifications, multiple estimates, and lead time for bidding on every purchase. To us that means that the pending request for the first $283 million in medical equipment will take much longer to arrive, as we cannot write that many specs and acquire that many estimates from Baghdad. If we were to focus all our efforts on the purchase order paperwork to buy just that equipment, it would take months to process and we would not make any progress on the construction program. For the PMO, this magnitude is even more demanding and even more impossible to handle."

Once again, the room was silent.

"Hamid, Sattar, I am deeply sorry for this bad news. But remember, this is only $750 million, the United States' portion of $1.6 billion that the world pledged at the International Donor's Conference. Perhaps your staff can concentrate on the other $800 million that the supplemental did not cover until the PMO realizes that they cannot succeed the way they are currently headed."

Hamid explained everything to Sattar and then Sattar gave his response.

"Yes, Joe. We shall do that, *Insha'Allah*," translated Hamid, once again smiling.

Sahar looked down and frowned.

CHAPTER *47*

Zaid stood at the entrance of one of the larger structures at *Kimadia's* Al Dabbash warehouse complex watching his men unload several crates and a dozen boxes off a dirty yellow truck. The warehouse's light brown painted steel walls towered nearly ten meters high, allowing the industrial shelving inside to stack pallets four high. He glanced at the clipboard he was holding, then at a few of the shipping labels. After verifying that they matched, he turned and walked down the gravel road between the buildings back toward his office. As he was passing the remnants of the warehouse that "accidentally" caught fire just before the Americans arrived, Zaid involuntarily stopped when he saw the shooter leaning against the doorway to the office building. Stepping forward, he nodded silently before he led the man inside.

CHAPTER *48*

As Joe and Max emerged from the stairwell onto the ninth-floor of the MOH, they glanced into the conference room where Sahar, along with a group of other workers somberly sat around the table. Each holding tissues, several did little to hide their streams of tears, while a few had no expression on their faces at all.

As the two Americans stepped into the room Sahar answered the unasked question, "This morning Semar was shot. She is dead."

Semar had served as Lieutenant Colonel Tony Weeks's translator. But she was also his Iraq coach and unofficial sounding board. She would inform him of what was going on, and advise him. When Tony would tell her something he was considering doing, if his approach or words might have offended the Iraqis, she would tell him and help him find a more appropriate way to get the point across. Through this exchange, as familiarity grew, they each learned about the other's culture and became friends in the process. Semar was unmarried. She was only twenty-five years old.

Sahar stood up and approached Joe and Max. "She was killed because she worked with the Americans, like I do."

She faced Joe.

"Shot thirty times by an AK-47 from no more than seven meters away, in front of her house, right in front of her parents as she was leaving to come to work."

Joe turned white. Max looked down.

Sahar stared at Joe a moment, then she walked past him out of the room.

CHAPTER *49*

I look in the mirror
at the fear in my eyes.
I try to hide it
because when others see fear
they see a weakness.
They see opportunity
and transform into a tiger
and prepare to pounce.
I hope they don't see my fear.

"Reem, that man. That's him." Sahar squealed as she pulled Reem by the shoulder out of the middle of the crowded sidewalk and into the shelter between two of the many vendor carts selling everything from shoes, to produce, to hot food. Many shoppers strode both ways around them as traffic buzzed down the major road beside them.

Reem looked around, "Who?"

"The *amin* who used to work out of the Ministry of Defense. I can tell by his walk. I know it's him."

"Oh, so you know this man," smiled Reem, completely misunderstanding the panic in her friend's voice and eyes.

"No. Don't you remember that *amin* who would always be smoking, leaning against that wall?"

"No, it can't be. You're imagining things," said Reem.

Sahar crouched down behind a bus stop sign, a large man looked down at her. Reem looked around uncomfortably.

"Sahar, are you OK?"

Sahar, still crouching leaned back on her heels a bit, "Follow me," Sahar said, "and be quiet."

Sahar looked across the street and located the *amin* who was walking with a firm and confident stride along the opposing sidewalk. Then, she rose-up to a bent forward position, as if she were hunting, and she began rushing from hiding place to hiding place keeping her eye on him on the other side of the street.

Reem followed her, though not in spirited fashion. She caught up to her while Sahar was peering around a newspaper vendor.

"Sahar, what are you doing?"

"Shhhh," answered Sahar, holding her index finger up to her lips.

"Sahar, even if I were to yell, no one would hear me over the sound of the traffic," Reem shouted.

Sahar took off again. Walking slowly but upright, Reem followed her friend down the sidewalk, looking at the people who were curiously watching Sahar hunch over sneaking down the busy sidewalk.

"I'm not crazy," Reem told a woman about her age selling shirts, "My friend, though. Ehhhh," she said wavering her hand.

Sahar watched the *amin* walk into a rug store on the corner of a busy intersection. She gasped as a rapid sequence of gunfire erupted from inside the store only seconds later. People on the street ducked, taking cover from the shots, not knowing from where they were coming. Sahar and Reem ducked too, terror replaced the amusement on Reem's face.

As quickly and as smoothly as he had walked in, the *amin* walked out. He was tucking something into his jacket as he calmly looked to his left and stepped off the curb. A silver Toyota Avalon, drove up.

Sahar looked at the driver and quickly glanced back at Reem. Reem looked at the driver and was shocked to see Zaid's familiar scowl as the *super* slowed down and stopped just long enough for the *amin* to casually open the door, glance around and slip into the passenger seat.

Sahar looked back at Reem again. Reem's face was ghostly white. Her mouth gaped open, her eyes were wide with fear. Sahar quickly looked both ways and dashed into the street toward the store.

Before she got half way across, Mohammad, the security guard from the ministry, barged out of the store, his hands and shirt were bloody and he was holding an AK-47. Mohammad looked toward the getaway car as it made a turn a block down the road.

Sahar stopped in the middle of the street and froze until Mohammad looked directly at her. Then without gesture, he turned and darted back into the store. Sahar ran after him. Reem quickly glanced barely long enough to make sure she could cross without being hit by a car, before she ran to follow Sahar.

On the floor lay two people. Mohammad knelt between them straddling an arm of one of Mister Banks's translators. The translator was bleeding from multiple wounds. Mohammad was shouting at him.

"God will help you, you help God. You're going to make it!"

The man opened his eyes and babbled a weak response.

"Don't talk, I've got you. I won't leave you," reassured Mohammad.

The second man, obviously dead, was a tall, white man with long, bloodied, blonde hair. A large section of his head was missing, and a rifle lay next to him.

Sahar stood a few feet away, out of breath, unable to move. Arriving behind her, Reem saw the two shooting victims. One glance was enough. Reem backed toward the door, turned around and threw up.

Later, while an ambulance crew was preparing to take the wounded man to a local hospital, Sahar and Reem huddled together on a pile of rugs only a meter away. The dead man was now covered, but the cloth was saturated with blood. The magazine still in it, his weapon was leaning against his leg where Mohammad had placed it.

Mohammad approached the women, "You'd better go. It may not be safe for you here."

The two once again weakly nodded, but didn't move. Mohammad reached out and gingerly assisted them to their feet one at a time. "Please go. I'll stay here until—" Mohammad let his sentence trail-off.

The women nodded again. With tear-streaked faces, they got up slowly and made their way to the door. Mohammad watched them go, and then sat down on a stack of rugs, supporting his head with his hands.

Mohammad remained next to his dead friend's side until two policemen entered the shop. A third stood in the doorway guarding the entrance and their vehicle. Mohammad nodded at the officers as they entered. The police did not nod back. They looked around the scene from several angles before making eye contact with Mohammad.

"*Salam Alekum.*"

Mohammad did not answer.

The policeman softened his voice as he began asking questions. "Who are you?"

"Mohammad Jawad. I am a member of the Facility Protection Services Security Forces for the Ministry of Health."

The detective listened while his assistant took notes on a small notepad he had withdrawn from his pocket.

The detective nodded toward the body, "Did you know this man?"

"Yes."

"Who was he?"

"His name was Pieterse. He was a bodyguard for the minister of health. A South African."

"I see. Why were you in this store?"

"We were here to buy a rug. The Americans have a tradition of buying small rugs for their team members as they finished their tours—as a going away gift."

"What happened?"

"I was in the back room when a man came in and shot Pieterse and Yosef. Yosef is a translator. He is still alive; an ambulance just took him to the hospital. I didn't shoot because by the time I got to the front room, the killer was already on his way out the door."

"Why were you in the back room?"

"I was talking to the store owner and looking at the rugs back there."

"Who shot your friends?"

"I don't know. A man I've never seen before. He had a pistol. He emptied a magazine into them."

The policemen listened, one continued to take notes.

"I had to step over my friends to get to the door, but I couldn't do it. First I checked to see if they were alive before I chased the killer. I made it to the window as he was getting into a car. By the time I got outside, they were too far away."

"Who drove the getaway car?"

"I don't know. I didn't get a good look at him."

"What kind of car was it?"

"I'm not sure. It was silver. I think it was a *super*, Toyota probably."

"License plate number?"

"I didn't see it."

After asking for details, the detective asked his final question, "Did anyone else see anything?"

"No, I don't know if anyone else saw anything." Mohammad looked at the ground while he said this.

The police took the South African and his rifle to the police station morgue. Mohammad left the store. He walked slowly and at first without purpose. Then he sped up as he walked towards his home; he needed to be with his family.

After Mohammad worked the key into the front door, about forty minutes after he left the rug store, he removed the magazine and emptied the chamber of his rifle before he turned the nob and pushed the door open. Bushra was there to meet him.

One look at his distraught face she asked, "What happened?"

Then she saw the blood on his shirt and on his hands.

"*Habibti*, what happened?"

Mohammad's shoulders begin to shake and he melted into her arms. She took his rifle from him and leaned it in the corner behind the door.

"*Habibti*, you're home now, it'll be alright." She held him tightly as she rubbed his neck and the back of his head.

After a moment, he told her, "They hit us when we were in the rug store. They killed Pieterse. Yosef is in the hospital."

She pulled him towards her and held his head tightly so his ear was near her mouth.

"I was in the back room. God is protecting me."

She rocked him reassuringly as he spoke.

After a few moments, Mohammad pulled himself away. Bushra let him go. He went down the hallway and into the bedroom and picked up his sleeping baby girl. After holding her, he gently kissed her on her forehead and carefully placed her back on the mattress. His younger boy, Heider, was napping next to Amel. He gave him a gentle kiss as well. Bushra went into the bathroom to prepare some water for him to wash the dried blood off his skin and for her to wash the stains out of his shirt.

Frantic pounding on the door interrupted them. Rushing forward, they bumped into each other in the narrow hallway. Mohammad cracked the door slightly, and then flung it open.

"Come quick!" shouted his neighbor, tears pouring down her face as she turned and ran off the porch.

His wife ran to get the children and Mohammad reached over and grabbed his rifle and ammunition. They bolted out the door to chase the woman up the street. A block away Mohammad pushed through a crowd that had already gathered around his older son. Marwan lay disfigured in the middle of the road.

Mohammad cried out in anguish as he dropped the rifle in the street and knelt next to Marwan, looking for signs of life. Finding none, he scooped up his seven-year-old child and shrieked toward the heavens. His cry was so guttural—so piercing—that all the men silently looked away.

His wife, with Amel in her arms and Heider in tow, heard Mohammad's wail and began to scream even before she arrived at the cluster of onlookers. Holding Amel, Bushra fell to her knees sobbing beside her husband at her first child's feet. The couple wept as he held their dead son in his arms, Amel cried in her mom's arms, and their confused four-year old screamed for mom to cuddle him—in the middle of the dusty street.

Onlookers crowded around, the women openly trying to share the parent's grief as the couple buckled from the weight of their despair. Tears formed in all sets of eyes present, except one. The shooter stood in the open across the street, stoic and dry-eyed.

As the women howled high-pitched, eerie shrieks— pleading with God to accept this young child—the crowd began to reposition itself behind him. A neighbor took the boy's body from Mohammad leaving the grief-stricken father gripping his head. Sobbing, his arms fell to his side. Still facing away, through his tears, he saw the outline of the hard-eyed stranger. Mohammad knew instantly that he was looking at his son's killer; he tried to stand to face him but his knees buckled and he fell to the dirt. Two men pulled him from the road and tried to turn him to join the forming procession but Mohammad twisted back around—but by the time he looked again—the stranger was gone. A woman picked up Heider and a couple women helped Bushra to her feet. Directly in front of them, the men holding the dead boy stepped forward to lead them back to their house. Surrounded by scores of mourning neighbors, the family staggered home. The sound of their sorrowful howling spreading news of the tragedy.

CHAPTER 50

Sahar sat on the porch in the dark. The girls and her husband were asleep. She stared towards the street. The only thing she saw was a clear definition of the predicament that she was in.

The amin is alive and he is a killer. Zaid now works with the amin. And Reem is in grave danger.

Sahar continued to stare into the darkness.

Reem must run away, she concluded, *but she has nowhere else to go.*

"Mohammad knows the situation, perhaps he can help," she told herself.

CHAPTER *51*

Every time Reem closed her eyes she saw the dead South African laid out in the dark puddle of red, sticky, drying blood and she saw Zaid, driving the car that had carried the killer. The two were now distinctly connected in her mind. She stared into the mirror in the bathroom of her small apartment, her dark eyes drilling back towards her. She rehearsed to herself, "I didn't see anything."

I'm sure you would never kill anyone, she imagined herself saying to Zaid.

I hate the Americans, why do you ask?

I support the insurgency. I would kill for Iraq.

She put her face into her hands and cried.

"What can I do? I'll never be able to hide what I saw from him. He'll know what I saw the very first instant he sees me. And then what will he do?" she wondered.

Looking back up to the reflection she sniffled, "He probably killed Semar. I already declared my loyalty to him, if I don't live up to it, he'll kill me too."

Watching her mouth move in the mirror she said, "I can't even convince myself."

Her bedding twisted, balled-up and damp from her sweat, Reem gave up on sleeping and got dressed an hour earlier than normal.

She washed her face again and then put on her shoes. *He will kill me if I don't tell him everything. He'd find out anyway. To gain his trust I must not wait to be asked.* As she headed toward the front door, the torment from her soul forced her to turn around and run into the bathroom, again. *The first time I see Zaid he will know that I was at the rug store—I must warn Mohammad first.*

CHAPTER *52*

Sahar looked for Mohammad as she walked through the security point at the ministry. Not seeing him, she walked through the door that had come to serve as the employee entrance to the ministry, and she proceeded through the narrow corridor toward the security office. She asked the lady at the reception desk, "May I speak with Mohammad."

"Which Mohammad?" She replied, tapping a pencil eraser against her desk.

"*Abu* Marwan."

"I'm sorry, but he is not here today. Not yet anyway, may I help you in some way?"

"Uh, no. *Shukren,*" she answered politely and turned around to go through the door. On her way-out she bumped into Major Watts, who was entering as she was exiting.

"Pardon me, ma'am," he apologized.

"It's alright," Sahar responded distantly.

Quickly studying her face, Major Watts asked, "Are you okay? Do you need something?"

She looked up and forced a smile. She felt as though she was seeing everything through a fog. "No, really, I'm fine."

Watts moved aside and gestured her through. As she stepped out of the room and into the hall he refocused his attention on his own inquiry into the whereabouts of Mohammad.

"Everyone is asking about Mohammad. This is the first day he's ever been late. You'd think people would give him a break," the receptionist said.

"Everyone?" inquired Watts.

"Well, first there was a young lady from *Kimadia*, and then the lady you just passed in the doorway, and now you. You would think the whole of MOH revolves around Mohammad."

Watts spun around and darted out the door. He caught up with Doctor Sahar in the elevator lobby as she and about forty others were competing for a spot on an elevator designed to carry six.

To be heard above the noise of the greetings and conversations which echoed off the interior granite and concrete surroundings, he shouted, "Excuse me."

He waved his hand above his head to get Sahar's attention.

Sahar saw him and began to wriggle her way back through the crowded elevator lobby toward him.

"Yes?" she asked keeping her head down as she made her way closer before she looked at him. She held her arms tightly against her chest forming a barrier between her and the American.

"You were looking for Mohammad right now?"

Her eyes darted away. Suddenly a lump seemed to form in the pit of her stomach and her throat suddenly seemed dry, she stammered, "Yes. Why do you ask?"

Looking around the major asked, "Would you mind coming with me so I can ask you a few questions?"

She hesitated, and then she answered as casually as she could, "As you like."

Sahar gave him a three-step lead as he began to weave his way back through the crowd. When she saw that he was headed towards the Facility Protection Services office she surged forward to catch him. She reached out and touched his arm with nothing more than her fingertips, saying, "Not there."

Seeing her fear Watts fretted that there was much more going on than the considerable problem he was only vaguely aware. Colonel Newborne and he had received word that the South African security guard had been shot and killed and a translator was in the hospital. After Pieterse and the translator did not return from rug shopping the leader of Mister Banks's contracted bodyguards attempted to find his man. Baffled, the South African security team went to the Iraqi Police. The police showed them their dead friend and directed them to the hospital to find the translator, but the policeman they spoke to did not bother to tell them about Mohammad.

"Of course. I understand. Where then?" He asked.

"I work in engineering, with Joe. Can you come see me on the ninth-floor?"

Watts nodded. "Okay, I'll go up there after you have had a chance to settle in, say fifteen minutes?"

"Yes. Thank you," she said speaking softly.

She backed up a step and melted into the mob in the elevator lobby.

Sahar was sitting alone staring out of the window when Watts and Brown entered the office and shut the door behind them.

"Doctor Sahar," Joe quietly spoke her name as he and Watts slowly stepped into the room.

Sahar continued to stare at the hazy blue sky out the window. The aroma of hot *chai* steamed from the neglected cup in her hand and mixed with the smell of dust. The sun shone in, reflecting off the tabletops toward the ceiling.

"Sahar," Joe said, pausing until she slowly rotated in her chair to look at them. "Are you doing alright?" he asked tentatively.

She peered at them, her face straining to stop herself from bursting into tears.

Watts and Joe shuddered then they glanced at each other. Then Joe nodded his head gently yet firmly toward Sahar.

After another moment, her eyes welled up and tears ran down both her cheeks. She sniffled and placed the cup of *chai* on the table. She put her hands up hiding her face. The two men again glanced at each other, and then Watts looked around for a chair. Joe did the same. When all three were seated, Joe stretched over to pull tissues from a box on a nearby table and placed them in front of Sahar.

Sahar took one and in a determined effort she commanded herself to stop crying. The two men waited.

"I was looking for Mohammad, because I saw him yesterday," she said quietly.

"And…" Joe gently probed.

"I saw him at a rug store, where the two men were shot."

Sahar saw the two men pale. Watts's jaw dropped, "Mohammad was there?" A moment later he added, "And you were there?"

Sahar looked down. "Yes." She answered.

"What happened?" Watts inquired.

"I saw the Ami—I saw a man enter the store, then I heard the shots, then Mohammad ran out of the store just after the other man escaped. We ran in and saw them, on the floor."

Watts sat stunned. Sahar blew her nose, still not looking up.

"Doctor Sahar, you said, 'we' ran in and saw them.' Who was with you?"

Sahar tensed. She sat perfectly still for a moment before she raised her eyes to them. "Nobody. Just me and Mohammad."

Watts and Joe looked at each other.

Sahar shook her head and looked down.

"Okay," said Watts. Another pause. Then he added, "Is Mohammad okay?"

Sahar looked at him drearily, "Yes, he was not harmed."

Major Watts nodded, "Do you know who the shooter was?"

Sahar looked up, her face was twisted and stained with tears. "I don't know him," she said, hiding her eyes with her hand.

"Would you recognize him if you were to see him again?"

Sahar hesitated. She looked away as she answered, "I don't know."

Watts and Joe watched her intently.

"I'm sorry." Watts told her, nodding gently. "But I need to ask you one more thing. The police reported that there was a get-away car. Did you see it?"

She looked over at Watts, "No." She answered, shaking her head slowly.

"I see," answered Watts, closing the notebook in his lap although he had not made a single entry. Watts looked at Joe, shook his head and slowly exhaled. Then he addressed him, "Sir, Mohammad has not come in yet today. I'm going to go to his house to see if he's there."

Sahar immediately blurted, "Take me with you."

Watts looked over at Joe as he considered her request. Joe nodded yes. "Okay. Let's go," Watts told her.

Joe stood up and took a long look at Sahar. His face looked heavy, his eyes listless. He tugged on the bottom of his body armor then shifted it underneath his shirt, all the while watching Sahar.

Sahar saw this and reassured him, "Don't worry. I'm alright."

Joe looked at Watts. "Who all is going?"

"I suppose the colonel will want to go, you know how close he and Mohammad are. We probably don't want to involve too many Iraqis until we know what is going on though. We need two vehicles. Sir, do you want to go?" asked Major Watts.

"Yes," Joe answered, "I'll get Max as another gun."

"Okay. Twenty minutes at the front entrance, unless I call you?"

"We'll be there," said Joe.

"Thank you, Doctor Sahar," Major Watts gave a short bow as the two Americans started walking towards the door. Sahar nodded and then turned back towards the window.

Outside the two men walked down the hallway.

"Oh, sir, one more thing," Watts said lowering his voice. "We didn't know that Mohammad was at the rug store. And, I think Doctor Sahar knows more than she said. I don't think she is telling us the whole story," said Watts.

"I don't think so either. Let me try to talk to her later alone," replied Joe.

174

Newborne and Watts led the way in the colonel's permanently blood-stained Suburban. Joe, Max and Sahar followed in a dusty white *Pajero*. When they departed the parking lot, as a precaution, only Tony Weeks knew their destination.

CHAPTER 53

Outside Zaid's office doorway, Reem stood holding a brown folder against her chest. She stood as she did every week, right on time, waiting for Zaid to acknowledge her. After his usual delay, Zaid looked up from the neat piles of papers on his desk and nodded at her to come in. As she entered the windowless office, Zaid noticed that instead of her normal school-girl smile, today she wore a blank expression. He looked her in the face a bit longer than usual, then he leaned back in his chair.

"Reem, you look like you've seen a ghost."

She recoiled, her face flushed dark. Zaid continued to watch her closely, unconcerned about the discomfort such an examination created. "Sit down."

Reem sat down, clutching the folder tightly, her eyes peering over it.

Zaid chuckled. "May I see the report?"

She extended her arms holding it with both hands. Zaid pretended to ignore her unusual behavior.

He quietly began to scan the folder's contents, giving no indication that he noticed the determined stare from his young subordinate. He flipped through the pages for five minutes, and then he looked up and shut the folder, aligning it so its bottom edge was parallel to his desk. "Okay then. Anything else?"

Reem's forehead was darkened by wrinkles, her hands were visibly tense. She looked as though she was about to implode.

"A lot has happened since you were here last week. Do you remember our last conversation?" he asked coldly. "I believe you told me that you were ready to fight with me for Iraq."

Reem looked up shyly, she nodded weakly, her arms crossed in front of her.

"Our leader was captured by the Americans, but this has not seemed to help them, in fact, it seems to have inspired greater hardships for them, and for those of our countrymen who have been foolish enough to side with them."

He looked at Reem intently, noticing her begin to quiver. "You still are with me? Aren't you?"

Reem mumbled.

"Speak louder, I can't hear you," said Zaid.

"I saw you yesterday," she said loudly, awkwardly glancing up at him. Then she quickly looked down again.

Zaid's eyes flickered and he took a deep breath. Gradually, he exhaled and then he smiled. He leaned back in his chair and put his arms behind his head as if symbolically exposing himself to her. "And?" He coaxed.

Reem stood in front of him, she dropped her arms to her side. "I think you have struck a stinging blow to our enemy."

After speaking she again looked down at the desk top.

Zaid leaned forward placing his elbows on the desk and supported his chin in his hands. He grinned widely.

"What did you see?" He asked coldly, as though he were a snake questioning a mouse.

"I saw the shooter, I heard the shots, I saw the shooter, I saw you, and then I saw…" she paused, then she looked him in the eyes and said, "Mohammad."

Zaid stood up and took a few short steps around his desk to Reem's left. "Mohammad? *Abu* Marwan?"

She replied, "Yes, *Abu* Marwan."

He grinned. "I was not entirely sure that it was Mohammad Jawad, formerly, *Abu* Marwan, that came running out of the shop. And I was not fully sure that he saw me."

Reem froze, "Formerly? Is Mohammad dead?"

Feigning sincerity, Zaid said, "Oh, you haven't heard? You didn't know? Yesterday evening there was a little car accident," he said as he stepped forward and sat casually on a corner of his desk.

"My God!" shrieked Reem. "You killed him, too?"

"Him? Killed who?" Zaid asked.

"You killed Mohammad, too?"

"Oh no, Mohammad is alive and well. Well, at least alive. At least for the moment."

Reem stood stunned, her face was losing its color and her arms were shaking.

"But the little boy, poor Marwan, what was he six— maybe seven-years-old?" Zaid shook his head pretending to be sad. "He was hit by a car that happened to be driving through his neighborhood. I hear that he—" Zaid paused as he stood up, looking down on the front corner of his desk he had been perched, he slid his finger across the desk as if there had been a speck of dust that needed removing, "—did not make it."

Reem collapsed back into the chair behind her.

Zaid moved forward to stand between Reem and his desk. Then he reached back putting his fists on the desk he shifted his weight to his arms and lifted himself up from the floor. His feet swung out nearly touching Reem's legs as he adjusted his balance. Then he leaned forward, his face only a half-meter from Reem's. "What's wrong, my dear?" he asked, mockingly soothingly.

Reem moved her lips but could not speak.

"It is okay my dear. Perhaps I should get you some water?"

"No, no," she murmured.

After a moment of watching the pretty young woman disintegrate in front of him, Zaid decided to torment her even more. "I was not sure that the man who ran after us was Mohammad, but my associate, he was quite sure that he knew where that particular traitor lived. It seems he had been to his house—before."

Zaid smiled and stood up to pace, circling around his immobile audience.

"But to be honest, when we took the precaution of driving through his neighborhood, I was only guessing that it was *Abu* Marwan." He chuckled. "I am pleased that you came to me to confirm that we took the correct action."

From behind her he leaned into her ear and said, "After all, the caring gentleman that I am, I would hate to harm an innocent boy by accident."

Reem's eyes were wide, but she did not speak or move. Zaid chuckled as he envisioned her bound and gagged by invisible rope. "Tell me, my new partner, and my most loyal comrade, did Mohammad see my face? Does he know that I am involved with this latest incident?"

Reem slowly shook her head from side to side. Seeing her slight movement, Zaid stood up and stepped around her until he was in front of her. Once there, he planted his feet shoulder-width apart, almost touching her legs as he placed his big hands on his knees. He leaned forward so far that his breath moved her *hijab* when he spoke, "Reem, my dear, you know it isn't safe or proper for young women to be roaming the streets of Baghdad alone, even on a pleasant winter evening. So, tell me, how did you happen to find yourself at the rug store at that precise moment? And who, do tell me, who were you with?"

Reem's face turned ghostly white.

CHAPTER 54

Pulling up to Mohammad's house, the Suburban parked in the same location that it did the day the colonel was nearly killed. Stepping out of his Suburban, Newborne looked in every direction. Pointing at a second-floor window he said, "I bet that fucker was in that Goddamned window." The others, aware of the circumstances surrounding his statement also looked around.

"Joe and David, you two stay out here and keep an eye out. If I get shot again when I come back out, I'll fucking kick your asses." To Watts and Sahar, he said, "Let's go."

As Joe and Max, each with their pistols drawn, pointing them down their legs and out of sight behind them, positioned themselves between and behind the vehicles so they could each scan 180 degrees around them, the three walked across the rocks and onto the porch of Mohammad's small house and knocked on the door.

Sahar, standing at the side, was surprised by Mohammad's swollen eyes and exhausted look. Newborne hugged his friend, "Mohammad, we were worried about you. We are so sorry to hear about the shooting yesterday."

Mohammad did not answer.

"What is it my friend?" Newborne asked quietly.

Sahar followed Mohammad's eyes as he looked back across the room. Pictures of his son Marwan covered a table in front of the couch. A few candles were burning.

At first, Sahar, Newborne, and Watts didn't understand what the home-made shrine meant. *What did photos of Marwan have to do with Pieterse or Yosef?*

Then Sahar gasped, "Oh, my God."

Newborne heard Sahar and then the color drained from his face, "Your son," he said looking over at Mohammad.

Mohammad did not say anything but his face disintegrated. Newborne grabbed him and pulled him close in a big bear hug. They cried together near the door. Watts shook his head and awkwardly stood looking at the shrine the dead boy's parents had made. Crying herself, Sahar went into the bedroom seeking out the grieving mother.

Finding her lying on her side, awake on the bed, Heider and Amel sleeping in front of her, Sahar sat down behind her and placed her hand on her shoulder. She didn't look up, but after a short time, Bushra reached up to hold her hand. They didn't say anything, they just stared, the only sounds in the room was the whirl of the ceiling fan, the muffled voices from the other room, and an occasional sniffle.

As a conversation started in the other room, Sahar and Bushra joined the men, who now sat at the same table where Mohamad and Bushra hosted dinner almost three months before.

Mohammad was talking, "The same man who killed Pieterse and shot Yosef killed Marwan."

Sahar moved to an empty chair and sat down. She gripped the table's edge and watched Mohammad as he spoke.

Watts repeatedly glanced between Mohammad and Sahar as the story was being told. When Mohammad stopped speaking, Watts began. "Forgive me Mohammad, but I must ask you some questions,"

"Yes, I understand," he stammered.

"Do you know the shooter?"

"No, I don't. He does not work at the ministry."

Watts nodded. Colonel Newborne, uncharacteristically quiet, listened.

"Would you recognize him if you saw him again?"

"Yes, I see him constantly in my mind. I would know him instantly."

"Did you see the driver of the car outside the rug store?"

"No." He answered, looking down. But suddenly he looked up and over at Sahar. Switching to Arabic, he said excitedly, "But Doctor Sahar, you must have seen him; you saw the driver, didn't you?"

Sahar looked at Mohammad and then down at the table, but she didn't answer.

"Doctor Sahar, you were coming across the street. If you saw the shooter, you must have seen the driver," Mohammad exclaimed.

Bushra moved closer and silently stood behind her husband, taking his hand.

"I know you saw him. Please. Please help me know who has done this to my family," pleaded Mohammad.

Sahar, her voice cracking, hesitantly said, also in Arabic, "Yes, my friend, I saw him."

Mohammad looked at her a moment, then glanced at the Americans in the room. Then looking at Sahar again, inquired slowly, still in Arabic, "You know him and he is a dangerous man. That is why you are afraid."

Sahar nodded and looked down again.

"Please tell me. I promise not to reveal his name or that you told me. I will protect you," he said, then he added, "as best I can and with the help of God."

Sahar thought of her daughters. She could not bear the tragedy that he was experiencing. Even though she knew that each word could take her a step closer to the fire that she feared would one day consume her, Sahar knew she must help Mohammad. She almost said, "Zaid," but realized that the Americans, who were silently witnessing the conversation, would understand the name, so she looked at Mohammad and in Arabic said, "I cannot say."

She flicked her eyes ever so slightly toward the Americans. Mohammad's eyes darted in their direction, then back. He nodded and she continued in Arabic.

"The shooter is a former *amin* who used to work at the Ministry of Defense." Mohammad listened without breathing, "The driver was the one who used to be the assistant of the Director General on the sixth-floor before the Americans came."

He probed for clarification, "Does the driver work at warehouse number thirteen?"

"Yes," she whispered. Her eyes dropped to the table as soon as she finished speaking.

Mohammad nodded. For a moment, a gleam as bright as the moonlight flashing off the eye of a hunting tiger dominated Mohammad's tense face. It receded as quickly as it came. "*Shukren.*" He quietly whispered to Sahar.

Sahar still looking down, began to cry again.

Newborne eagerly asked, "Okay, what?"

Neither Sahar nor Mohammad answered him. Mohammad's wife turned around and walked slowly back into the bedroom and shut the door behind her.

The interview was over. The colonel stood up and extended his hand to Mohammad. Mohammad took it and shook it, and when he emerged from behind the table, the colonel hugged him. Watts and Sahar stood up and moved toward the door. Newborne broke the hug and in a soft voice told Mohammad, "Take care of your wife, she needs you."

"Yes."

"Please come see me as soon as you feel able. We are going to catch those bastards," promised the colonel as he held his right hand over his heart.

Mohammad returned the gesture, "You are my good friend, sir. I am forever grateful."

The three visitors walked back to the vehicles. Without a word, they got in and drove down the road. The mood was heavy as they headed back to the Ministry of Health as Sahar tearfully told Joe and Max of Mohammad's son's death.

CHAPTER 55

The afternoon sun shone in through the windows on the ninth-floor as Joe and Max watched a helicopter dart over the buildings of the war-torn city like a dragonfly over a pond. They were discussing the Program Management Office's decision to bundle all $18.6 billion of the reconstruction contracts into five packages to be awarded to five prime contractors.

Shaking his head, Joe said, "And now, all the medical expenditures are grouped with education and public buildings in one huge contract. If you were the prime contractor who got this contract, what would be the first thing you would do?"

Thinking a moment, Max answered, "Subcontract. If it were me, I would probably decide to manage the paperwork and deal with the PMO's contracting officers, but I would probably hire three subcontractors, one for medical, one for education and one for public buildings and provide logistical and general contracting support to each. And I would charge at least seven to 10% of the contract amount plus placement to do so."

"Maybe more since this is a high-risk environment, such a risky venture," agreed Joe. "And then, if you were the medical sub, tasked to the prime to build the one hundred fifty outpatient clinics, renovate seventeen hospitals specializing in women's and children's health, and buy medical equipment to install in hospitals that are not part of this slice of the program, and another procurement to furnish and equip the clinics and hospitals that are being built or renovated, what would you do?"

"I would subcontract," answered Max.

"Me too. That's another seven to 15% spent on management before the work even starts."

The two continued to watch the helicopter as it dipped low trying to land, but the rotor blast created a large, thick cloud of dust, making any landing hazardous. They watched it buzz around looking for a more suitable landing zone.

Joe continued thinking out loud to Max. "Maybe I would contract out a design-build team for the clinics, a more specialized healthcare firm for the hospitals, and a firm to do the equipment planning and procurement. That would be another $50 million taken out of the $570 million program."

Joe continued, his frustration building. "The single decision to follow the FAR requirements guaranteed that it would be nearly impossible for any equipment purchased by the Congressional Supplemental legislation money to arrive for at least six months; though, I think most of it will be delayed indefinitely. And since the PMO is only awarding these mega-contracts to contractors from one of the major coalition partner countries, that means that between 24% to 32% of the pie will be eaten back in the States or in London before any actual work is performed on the ground. That means that a fourth to a third of the money must be carved out of the scopes of work, tens of millions of dollars that won't do a damn bit of good to develop the infrastructure here in Iraq."

David shook his head.

Joe said, "Unwittingly, the CPA has in effect, guaranteed that there will be no real progress in Iraq for months, for years—perhaps forever. Regardless of how this goes down in history, this 'Reconstruction effort' is a tragic example of a missed opportunity."

The helicopter, apparently unable to find a safe landing zone in an area near its destination gave up and buzzed away across the city. The two men sighed in unison.

"Damn it. They have no idea what they've done. One thing for sure, they will claim success and find someone else to blame," Joe said stiffly.

Sahar quietly entered the room as Max and Joe completed their discussion. They turned around to greet her, but Sahar did not acknowledge them. She just stood and stared at the table.

Joe closed his eyes a moment and loosened his shoulders. Then he said quietly, "Sahar, if you feel up to it, I would like to talk to you."

Max announced, "Sir, I need to go talk to Wasan." He nodded toward his boss and gave an empathetic smile to Sahar as he passed her on his way out of the room.

"As you like," she said, dropping lifelessly into the nearest seat.

"Actually, it would be better if you were to come here while we talk," he swept his arm outwards, indicating that he wanted her to come to the window.

She reluctantly complied.

"Tell me what you see when you look out the window."

She rolled her eyes, "Really, Joe—" she started but she was interrupted.

"Really." Joe said firmly.

She looked out the window.

"What are you looking at?" inquired Joe.

"I am looking at Baghdad, the sky, the trees, the buildings, the people, the ruins."

"And what do you see?" he asked.

She looked at him, "I just told you. I see the sky, buildings, people, cars. Just like I always see."

"So, nothing has changed then?"

She looked half-heartedly out the window yet again, "No, nothing has changed. It is still the same." She sighed.

Joe nodded. "If nothing has changed, what has gotten into you?"

She glared at him. "What do you mean? Semar is dead. I saw two men shot, and Mohammad's son was murdered. The world is falling apart."

184

Joe took a deep breath, then he asked, "So what are you going to do about it?"

Sahar's eyes darted into Joe. "Me? What am I going to do?" She barked back at him, "Look, you created this problem. You start a fire and then stand back and demand that we put it out. Why did you Americans really come anyway? There's all this killing, and for what?"

"So, Americans shot the men you saw at the rug store? Did an American kill Semar or Marwan?"

She stepped back a little. "No," she said quietly.

"But you know who did."

Sahar looked at him, her eyes were hard.

"I ask again, Sahar, what are you going to do about it?"

"What do you think I should do?" she demanded. "I don't know."

Joe shook his head. "I don't know either," he replied quietly, "but it is not me who needs to decide. I don't know what you should do, but I do know what I will do."

Her face distorted, she looked up. "What?"

"I will keep trying. I will keep trying to establish a reconstruction program that is not guaranteed to fail. I will keep trying to convince you that your future is now in your hands. What you decide to do today will determine your children's future."

She glared at him.

He continued. "The President of the United States has given his word that the United States will stand by the Interim Iraqi Government for as-long-as it takes to write a constitution and establish themselves. Not a day less and not a day more. And the president himself promises to stand by the Iraqis who stick their necks out to rebuild this country. He cannot guarantee your safety, but he promises to do all he can to protect you. We are here to help you build something wonderful. We are here to help you turn your oppression into freedom. Why are we doing it? We are doing it because it is good for you and it is good for us."

Sahar faced Joe. "Why do you think you can do that? What makes you think you know what we want or need?"

"You do, Sahar. The way you love your children, the way you cried for Semar and the way you are sad for the men who were shot in the rug store. The way you mourn for Mohammad's son as if he were your own. Your actions tell me that, Sahar. The fact that you are angered and embarrassed by the violence that Iraqis are inflicting on other Iraqis tells me that you want nothing more than for it to stop. You know that Saddam was a thug. You know that if we fail to establish a democracy, a new thug will soon step forward to rule you."

Sahar looked down.

"You know that this new thug will be just like the old one, and your children will live under the same structure of terror and abuse that you have. And you don't want that. That is why you are struggling right now to decide."

She froze. "Decide what?" she asked.

"I know you are struggling with the decision to tell us who murdered these people." He paused a moment.

Glaring at Joe, Sahar said nothing.

"Or to tell us who was driving the car."

Sahar glanced toward the floor.

"You know him, don't you?"

She continued to look down, her lips pressed tightly together.

Joe nodded his head, "He works here, doesn't he?"

She jerked, as though to strike back, but then stopped. She forced herself not to look up.

"I thought so." Joe said.

Sahar looked out over the city, "You don't know what it's like," she said quietly.

"You're right, I don't. That's why I don't know what you should do."

"You don't know what he is capable of," she continued.

"You may be right," he replied.

"Why should I trust you?"

"Because at this stage, for better or for worse, we are your best hope. More importantly, we are Hadeel's and Dalia's best hope."

She looked up, her eyes intense. "I wish to leave now," she said in a harsh voice.

Joe took a deep breath but did not say anything.

As she began to turn away, Joe stepped forward and in a soft, quiet voice he told her, "Sahar, I want you to know that whatever you decide to do, I will understand. You are in an awful situation, and I helped put you there. I promise, I will do all I can to help you."

"Thank you," she whispered, then after a moment she stepped toward the door. She paused as if considering a parting word, but then without glancing back, she walked out.

Joe stood with his back against the window watching the empty doorway, hoping—but Sahar did not return.

CHAPTER 56

In 1974, five years before Saddam Hussein became the Supreme Ruler of Iraq, Doctor Hassan fled his homeland to avoid execution at the hands of the *Ba'athists*. From London, he kept a watchful eye on the ruthless manner the *Ba'athists*, especially under Saddam, suppressed every organization that they deemed a potential threat. In January of 2003, when war loomed on the horizon, Doctor Hassan sensed the winds in the Iraqi desert were about to change. He wrote a letter to a long-time friend who was an Iraqi expat in the United States. His friend suggested that Doctor Hassan write a letter of Introduction requesting a position during reconstruction and send it to him. Once received, his friend would hand-carry it to his more influential acquaintance, Ahmed Chalabi, who had connections with the Bush Administration.

Despite never having held a management position in a healthcare system or even a hospital, the SECDEF's office deemed Doctor Hassan qualified for consideration to be the first

Iraqi minister of health in the post Saddam era. The secretary of defense deemed him qualified to run the beleaguered healthcare system serving twenty-five million people based on his declared loyalties to democracy and to the conservative parties of England, his adopted country, and to the United States; the fact that he was not, nor had ever been a *Ba'ath* party member, and that he was a physician born in Iraq.

The CPA offered the same level of vetting over Hassan's personal selections for his inner circle of advisors and assistants, as the Bush Administration did for the new minister himself. Throughout the process the doctor didn't flaunt his philosophy to the Americans, but he didn't hide it either. He selected his staff specifically to support his objective: to work with the numerous other *Da'wa*s who had been appointed or elected to various levels and positions in the fledgling government to continue the work the Ba'athists had so violently interrupted so long before.

In December of 2003, Doctor Hassan confidently strolled into his new position determined to be a strong, decisive leader, the type that every Iraqi would immediately recognize, and use his power to bring proper morality back to the people of Iraq. In the office labeled "*Minister of Health*" Hassan's three-week-old, grey whiskers stubbed out the coarse shape of his future beard as he leaned forward addressing his already grey American counterpart, "Mister Banks, I think it is imperative that I immediately be given full authority on all issues regarding security and justice within the ministry. This is a necessary action to ensure that I can quickly establish myself while simultaneously dispelling fears that we ministers are only puppets of the CPA."

Mister Banks sat back and pulled a handkerchief from his pocket. He looked down as he cleaned his glasses. Doctor Hassan continued in his half-Arabic, half-English accent, "We both know that Ambassador Bremmer is struggling with a growing insurgency and early reports of failures in delivering the promised progress regarding infrastructure reconstruction."

He paused to see if the American would protest. Banks didn't. With rising confidence, he continued. "Likewise, we both know that the American public is carefully watching and evaluating President Bush on the administration's exit strategy from Iraq. Don't you agree that the United States would be better served if the CPA were more sensitive to the image of creating a 'puppet government?' Such an image is bad for everyone, you, me, the United States, and Iraq."

Mister Banks nodded, "Doctor. Hassan, as you know, we are here to support you. I'll discuss your requests with the ambassador and let you know as soon as I can."

Doctor Hassan's lips curled up slightly on both ends below his naturally-wild, grey head of hair and the brown plastic frames of his glasses. He sat back in his chair and cupped his chin, stroking his new growth as he nodded, looking at his adversary.

Mister Banks looked away when their eyes met.

CHAPTER 57

"Danny, why would he request this so quickly?" asked Ambassador Bremmer late that evening, as he sat across from Mr. Banks in one of the chairs in front of his desk.

Sitting across from Bremmer, in the luxurious office that was furnished with the same type of overly-ornate furniture found throughout the palace, Banks answered, "His concern is that we avoid the appearance of establishing a puppet regime. He is insistent that we show that we are really genuinely helping establish an Iraqi Government."

"Are you concerned that it will derail the transition?" inquired Bremmer thoughtfully.

"Not particularly. I think the staff is able to provide him counsel on the technical aspects of the mission."

"Well, you know how Washington wants Iraqis driving all the ministries as quickly as possible. You also know that health was the last ministry to name an Iraqi minister. Unless you have a good reason not to, I recommend you give Doctor Hassan what he wants."

CHAPTER 58

"Doctor Hassan, I am pleased to inform you that Ambassador Bremmer approved your request," he announced rather grandly.

"Excellent, Danny. That will be all," responded Doctor Hassan barely looking up from his cluttered desk as Mister Banks stood in front of him.

Mister Banks jolted at Hassan's informal and dismissive tone. *I am but a servant,* he told himself as he stood there.

"Was there anything else, sir?" asked Doctor Hassan looking up from a paper he had just started writing.

It isn't about me, let it go, he commanded himself. "Uh, well, no. I guess not," he said.

Doctor Hassan smiled, then nodded slightly and returned to writing.

Mister Banks backed away and quietly left the office. He walked into his own and shut the door behind him. *This is what my country wants, don't let little things stop big things,* he instructed himself. He looked at his watch. It was only 9:30 in the morning but he suddenly had a hard time concentrating on the long list of items he had scheduled to complete that day.

CHAPTER 59

Chief Thamer was sitting at his desk, the radio was on but he was not listening to it. Four stacks of papers; the previous day's reports, that morning's status reports, employee requests, and prep for a budget meeting were loosely arranged in front of him. He looked at his watch, it was 10:30, he had to attend the budget meeting on the fourth- floor right after lunch.

At 10:31, four large, burly men wielding AK-47s walked into and through the reception area. They walked directly in to the security chief's office and before Thamer could inquire what they wanted, the leader of the small group told him, "Get out.

By order of minister, Doctor Hassan, you are no longer the chief of security."

Thamer inspected the official memorandum signed and stamped by both the new minister and the "Senior advisor to the minister of health," Daniel Simmons Banks; it looked legitimate. Without saying a word, with the four armed men standing in the room, Chief Thamer gathered his belongings and put them into a couple boxes, one of which he had to remove several reams of paper before he could use it. He turned and carried the boxes out of the room without looking at any of the minister's guys in the face.

As Chief Thamer was juggling his belongings walking down the hallway toward the parking lot he crossed paths with Major Watts. Thamer didn't even seem to recognize him.

"What do you got there?" asked Watts.

Thamer's eyes came into focus and he frowned, "The minister has replaced me."

"What?" exclaimed Watts. "Does the colonel know about this?"

"I don't think so," Thamer replied.

Escorted by a half dozen staff members eagerly showing the American all the problems they needed money to solve, Colonel Newborne was walking down a hospital corridor he was visiting in Dora, in the southern part of Baghdad. When his phone began ringing he stopped walking causing an accordion affect in the entourage. Unfolding his phone, he identified himself, "Newborne."

The strained voice of Major Watts was at the other end of the line, "Sir, you aren't going to like this, but Doctor Hassan just fired Thamer."

CHAPTER *60*

In Ambassador Bremer's outer office, a staff officer completed a chart in preparation for the next morning's meeting. The chart read, "Ministries run by Iraqis: 100%"

"Awesome," he exclaimed as he and his colleagues traded high fives.

In the southwestern end of the same building, just off the south wing, people passing through the hallway quieted and eyed the door to the MOH front office as they passed.

"I can't believe that you're allowing this," Newborne was not in the mood to celebrate.

"I am, because it is the best action for us in this situation," Banks responded.

"How the fuck do you figure? You know that that bastard will undo everything we established. He will use the Facility Protection Services force as his own personal militia."

"You don't know that, and you are exceeding your bounds, colonel."

Newborne was standing rigid. Rage had reddened his face. He shook his head, his anger failing to pierce the outer armor of the thick skin that Mister Banks assumed in moments like this.

"By supporting this, you are betraying the Iraqis who have entrusted us with their lives and the lives of their families. You are supporting the establishment of a new regime of terror and intolerance just as we are beginning to make some progress in cleaning up the last one."

"I am doing neither of those things. I am giving the new minister some control. Control he needs to establish himself. Now back-down, colonel."

Newborne inhaled deeply and exhaled slowly and noisily. "And what's going to happen to Thamer? Now that he's out, where will he go?"

"That's not our call, but I will put in a good word for him if you like."

Newborne bit his lip. Then he quietly added, "You have no idea how much that man has risked helping us get to where we are. You don't. Without him and his influence over the Iraqis here, we couldn't have accomplished a God-damned thing. Now you just toss him aside as though he were a used condom. Everything will go to hell as soon as Hassan replaces the good men we've trained—men who risk their lives for the idea of democracy in Iraq—with his fucking cronies."

"Yes. I know that we all have worked very hard to turn this ship around. I assure you I am aware and very appreciative."

"You are neither," the colonel said, his voice raspy and choked. "You—" Newborne's body shook as he held his mouth. He stood silently concentrating on listening to the buzz of the lights and the rhythmic whomp, whomp, whomp of the ceiling fan. He took the time to control his breath and slow his heart rate. Colonel Newborne turned away but stood still, not advancing toward the door.

After silently watching the colonel regain his composure Banks spoke to the back of the colonel's head, "So it's settled, then."

Newborne tightened his throat and face, and with his entire might he resisted saying what he wanted to say. He took his first step toward the exit. Momentum established, the second and third steps became easier. He was careful to not slam the door on his way out.

CHAPTER *61*

After three nights of waking up to the image of his dead son, and listening to his wife and surviving children as they, too, tossed in their sleep; Mohammad forced his exhausted eyes to open. Since the tragedy, Heider wouldn't sleep alone and Bushra refused to let Amel out of her sight. He lay there listening to his wife and children's soft breathing, and the sound of birds and traffic from outside the open window. The pain in his heart was dominated with sorrow over his oldest boy, but there was also pain and fear for his younger children—and for his wife. Another day at home would only lead to another sleepless night and greater risk to his family. He resolved to go see his boss, Chief Thamer.

He lay there touring his memories: when he and Bushra met, their wedding day, the day Marwan was born. Bushra's face was etched everywhere in his mind and in his heart. Her voice—Her touch—Her.

He watched her sleep, the little ones next to her. They inspired his life. He could never risk their safety. He could not live if she, too, were to fall victim to the assassin's blade. He did not want to leave her, not for a moment—much less for eternity.

As he silently watched his family sleep he wished ill fate had not come his way. He looked up and whispered far softer than anyone could hear, "Life should not be like this; this is not how God intended."

His love for this woman and their children dominated him. The love for his family made him strong enough to face his own fear of death. It was this love that enabled him to get out of bed on this particularly difficult day. Standing beside the bed, he looked back at the four—the pain of Marwan's absence stung him deeply—the three—most important people of his life. He vowed to submit himself to certain death if need be, if it meant that the remainder of his family would be allowed to continue to live peacefully on this earth.

As Mohammad walked into Thamer's office, the new chief of security stood up. Zaid, sitting across from him, also rose. Zaid wore a smirk on his face. Mohammad hesitated at the threshold, struggling to hide his emotions. Weakness gained no sympathy with people as cruel as these.

Though they had never met, Thamer's replacement gave him his hand then hugged him, giving him a gentle kiss on the cheek. "My poor brother," he said softly to Mohammad while still holding him in his embrace. "We are all so sorry and we wish so much for this nightmare of yours to be gone. There is nothing worse in the entire world than for a parent to lose a child. What can I do for you? Name it and it is yours."

Mohammad was unable to answer. He involuntarily shook as his glance met with the cold eyes of a cobra, only a meter away.

But as quickly as a cobra strike, Zaid cast off his gloating and displayed a façade of concern. The new chief dropped his embrace and stepped back looking at Zaid and Mohammad, "You two know each other, yes?" he asked.

"*Seidi*, Chief," the words rolled easily out of Zaid's mouth, "if I may suggest, Mohammad is still too exhausted and mourns too heavily the passing of his eldest son. Certainly, he is not fit for duty today. He must have more time to adjust to the misfortunes of the trials he undergoes. I beg of you, spare him this moment, and send him home for another few days."

The new chief looked at Zaid and then turned to Mohammad. "I must agree with *Sayid* Zaid, Mohammad. I think you have come back to the ministry too soon. I insist that you turn around and return home at once."

Mohammad stood still, uncertain as to his next move.

Zaid, intervened, "Please let me be of some service. I will have one of my drivers return him to his home."

"I thank you for your generous offer, but it is my responsibility to care for my men."

"Well, then, allow me at least to escort him to the lot."

"As you like." The chief bowed slightly toward Zaid. "Mohammad, have the driver on duty at the guard shack bring you home. I don't expect to see you here for at least another three days. But if you need something, I will receive you with the open arms of a brother."

"*Shukren*," Mohammad stammered.

"After you," offered Zaid politely as he nodded and extended his open hand towards the door.

Mohammad stumbled through the doorway with Zaid on his heels.

"You have a very beautiful wife." Zaid whispered in Mohammad's ear.

Mohammad tried to stop, but Zaid grabbed his wrist and twisted it, pushing him into the relatively dark hallway.

"You aren't thinking of trying to kill me, are you? Zaid spoke in a low, taunting voice. "Well if you are, beware. If I die, your entire family burns. And you will be forced to watch them suffer before you join them in death."

Mohammad's answer was one strangled word. "No."

"Then I trust you have kept silent."

"Yes."

"Good. Because if we find that you haven't, you will not have died a noble death."

Twisting his wrist, Zaid was skillfully guiding Mohammed in front of him down the hallway, when Colonel Newborne appeared, silhouetted against the bright exterior as the two approached the MOH parking lot exit.

"Mohammad." Newborne stepped forward and embraced Mohammad.

As he hugged him, tears were building in Mohammad's eyes.

Newborne spotted Zaid and pulled away from his friend. "What the hell are you doing here?" he demanded. "And why the hell are you with Mohammad?"

"I am only escorting him to the lot; the chief of security's suggestion."

"Bull shit. Get the fuck out of here."

"As you like."

Newborne watched Zaid as he walked back down the corridor past the security office toward the elevators. The colonel did not stop glaring until the elevator to the sixth-floor closed its door with Zaid in it, then he turned back to Mohammad.

"Are you alright? What's going on here?"

"I'm alright," Mohammad weakly stammered. "I must go. I cannot stay here today," he said looking away.

Newborne looked questioningly into his face.

"Really, sir, I must go home." Mohammad insisted. "I mustn't stay here."

"Promise me that you're alright."

"I promise," Mohammad lied. "With all my heart."

Slowly the colonel stepped back from his defeated security guard.

"I will drive you home."

"No, I thank you, but that isn't necessary."

"I insist."

"No, please I am fine," he said, but seeing Newborne's set expression he reluctantly accepted.

Ten minutes later, the two-car convoy, Newborne, Sergeant Marty and Mohammad in the Suburban followed by a security detail in a white SUV, pulled out of the eastern entrance and headed toward and around the traffic circle marking the entrance to Medical City. As they negotiated the circle, a third car, an old, small, blue, two-door *brazili*—a first generation Volkswagen Apollo—pulled out behind them following at a distance.

As the Americans dropped Mohammad outside his home at the very spot where the colonel's life nearly ended, the shooter parked a block away and began to stroll up the road. He spat on the ground as he looked up at the window from which he narrowly missed killing the colonel. He leaned against the wall in the shadow next to the entrance of a little convenience shop down the street the translator had fled, and watched the tall, lanky American hug Mohammad before the two cars sped away in the direction passing the spot he and Zaid ran down Marwan.

Perhaps one day I will get another chance to kill him, but today, I will hurt the American in another way.

The shooter stepped out of the shadow and stood silently in the open where Mohammad would see him. He waited as Mohammad watched the Americans disappear down the street and then he watched Mohammed glance around until Mohammad froze as their eyes met.

The shooter stood motionless, feet shoulder width apart, hands on his hips.

Mohammad nodded. Then he paused, his eyes still locked with the shooter's, he nodded towards his house.

The shooter granted his victim's last request. He placed his right hand on a pole that supported the awning marking the entrance to the shop, expressing his willingness to wait a little while for Mohammad.

Inside, Mohammad greeted Bushra and told her he was leaving again to buy food. Attempting to appear casual, he hugged and kissed Bushra, holding on a bit longer than he meant to, but far shorter a time than he wanted. He hugged Heider and picked up Amel. As he kissed his baby, his nose against her soft cheek he inhaled her sweet scent and whispered a prayer that only she could hear. "May God protect you, my daughter. Obey your mother."

Then he stepped outside. Fifteen minutes had passed. He lit a cigarette and looked over to where the shooter had been standing. He was not there. He stepped into the street between two parked cars. Immediately the old blue Apollo pulled up and stopped.

"Get in."

Mohammad opened the door and slid in.

Without another word, they drove off.

Mohammad's body was found the next day floating in the Tigris. His hands were still bound behind his back. The police determined that the cause of death was the bullet that entered the back of his skull. Judging by the dislocated bones, bruises, burns and cuts over much of his body, the police detective surmised that his last few hours were most likely extremely unpleasant.

CHAPTER *62*

Sahar looked at her young friend's face. She raised her right hand and gently guided a dark curl that had fallen from under Reem's *hijab* back into place.

They sat side by side on the couch in Sahar's living room, her daughters were not home from school yet, the TV off, and empty tea cups sat on the short table in front of them.

Reem's eyes were on the cups. "What are you thinking?" Reem asked, softly.

"Nothing, my dear. I'm just thinking."

Reem looked up at her friend, "I know you too well, you know."

"I can't go on like this," Sahar said reluctantly.

"No," Reem replied, "None of us can. But what can we do?"

"Mohammad was murdered. He—" Sahar could not finish her thought.

"Yes." Reem whispered.

"He loved his son so much. I could see the pain in his eyes. He didn't cry for himself, he cried for his wife and for the hole left in his heart by Marwan's death."

Reem turned her face away from Sahar.

"He must have known what they were going to do to him. Why didn't he tell Colonel Newborne? He could have saved him."

Reem's insides jumped. She stood up and moved away from her friend.

Sahar's puzzlement showed itself as a small crease in her forehead. "Reem?"

Reem's shoulders began to shake.

"Reem, are you alright?"

"You think the Americans could have saved Mohammad? Reem asked loudly.

Slowly, but with conviction Sahar replied, "Yes. Don't you think so?"

"Well no. It's the Americans who killed him."

Sahar flinched, "You can't mean that. The Americans didn't kill him. You know as well as I do who killed him."

Reem swallowed, "But it's because of the Americans that he's dead."

Sahar frantically searched Reem's familiar face.

Reem turned toward the window and blindly walked forward a few steps.

"What're you saying Reem?" Sahar asked watching her pace.

"I'm saying that you cannot trust the Americans. They aren't our friends," she spoke confidently, clearly.

"They're here for their own purposes, not ours. Mohammad is dead because he foolishly believed in them. We could all be dead, and they would consider their Iraqi problem solved. They don't care about us."

Sahar's head and shoulders drooped as her friend's words came towards her.

Reem raised her hand as if addressing God. "What have the Americans ever done for you? For any of us? Do you think they care about you? About your daughters? Why'd they come here and kill our soldiers, kill us? Why'd they overthrow Saddam? Do you think they're doing this for our good? For our benefit?"

Reem spoke loudly and rapidly, her hand in a tight fist high in the air.

In contrast, Sahar's hands lay crumpled loosely on the table. Sahar brought them up to cover her face. Her shoulders shook as she began to weep.

Reem caught herself mid swing. She stopped talking and she brought her arm down looking at her fist. She loosened her hands intently looking at her small fingers, her thin wrist and her skinny arm. Her cheeks regained their softness as she deflated and stood silently for a moment listening to her friend crying.

"Sahar. Sahar, I wish Mohammad were not dead." She said softly and quietly. "I feel sad for his son too. I truly do. And for his wife."

She paused, watching the back of Sahar's head and listening to her sobs. She stepped forward and placed her hand over Sahar's shoulder. "But what can we do?"

Sahar continued to cry.

"But President Bush said it first," Reem said, her voice growing in volume, "'You are either with us or against us.' We all must choose a side. We are Iraqi, we are Muslim."

Looking up again Reem uttered, "Why did Mohammad have to side with the Americans? Because of the Americans, our world is hell. Those who side with them turn against their own people. They choose their own path."

Sahar continued to sob without looking up. Reem softly kissed the top of Sahar's head and then turned, silently closing the front door as she left.

CHAPTER 63

Joe sat at his desk, his laptop open to his email awaiting the impromptu meeting to begin. Around him the entire CPA MOH staff were assembled, sitting at, next to or on one of the dozen work stations that ringed the room. Standing next to a shabby Christmas tree atop a cluttered desk near the center of room S-200, Mister Banks stood beaming. "I have some great news," he announced before he stopped to clear his throat.

"Partially because of our success and the competence, spirit and ability of the Iraqi Interim Government, the CPA will be turning over the responsibility to govern the country of Iraq to the Interim Iraqi Government earlier than expected. The transfer of authority will take place in March."

Joe sat motionlessly in his chair.

"That means that we should all be home by April. And you will know that you have done the American people, the Iraqi people and the world a great service."

Carson began to cheer, but stopped when he noticed that most of the staff sat motionlessly.

Barely a month earlier, the ambassador had announced that the CPA would remain and maintain its presence in the ministries until the ambassador's seven-step plan was accomplished. The Interim Government was barely identified, it still had no charter, and four of Bremmer's seven steps had not been completed. Purple stains still marked the fingers of those Iraqis who dared to vote in the first real election in Iraq for decades. It was the president's word, his personal commitment to the active longevity of American involvement that inspired many of the Iraqis to put themselves and their families' lives into danger by publicly committing to the Americans. Now, without warning, President Bush's Administration was saying that the CPA would disband and leave Iraq in self-proclaimed victory as soon as it could.

Joe's face contorted. He and many of his colleagues surrounding him understood this reversal in policy was going to have a horrendous price, a price that would be paid in Iraqi and American blood for years to come.

Joe sat absently staring at his electronic screen.

"They do," said Joe quietly, as Mister Banks was talking.

Mister Banks who had begun to stroll down the center aisle of the room looked down at Joe, "Excuse me?" he asked.

Joe looked up, a frown creased Bank's forehead as he addressed Joe directly, "Do you have anything you want to say?"

Joe's eyes darted around the room. "I said, 'they do.' They do know, we all know what this means. Sir."

"Of course. It means we won."

"No, Sir. This means we are quitting."

"Good God. Why do you always have to find something tragic to say? Can't you ever just believe in what we are doing?"

Carson shook his head disapprovingly.

"Sir, this is a death sentence." Joe spoke the words as a dull statement of fact. Though some of the faces still smiled from the thought of success, most shared Joe's look of gloom.

"It has always been our intent and our goal to return Iraq back to the hands of the Iraqis," replied Banks, his face turning deep red.

Joe continued, "Sir, every one of the Iraqis who cooperated with us will soon be an unprotected target. They trusted us with their lives."

"Joe, come off it. There isn't going to be a blood bath. There's no evidence that this will happen. What will happen is that the Interim Government will step up and take ownership of their country. And if they feel they need it, the Army will still be here to provide protection."

Joe shook his head. "No, sir. Just last month the ambassador said that the Interim Government was still too weak to stand on its own. He was right. You know that, I know that, we all know that. That hasn't changed in the last few weeks. Semar and Marwan, and Mohammad were killed by Iraqis who are willing to kill and die for what they want; they won't be deterred by the Iraqi Interim Government. Not only does this endanger our strongest allies in Iraq, and their families, this will extend the war, and kill more American soldiers as well. And if the Iraqis who need to be focused on maintaining an environment for successful construction are busy fighting each other for power, the mission—the reconstruction effort—will fail too."

Mister Banks looked down sternly. "That's enough of that. We are here at the president's discretion and the president has determined that it's in the best interest of the United States for the CPA to disband and transition power to the Iraqi Interim Government. He always wanted to quickly hand power to the Iraqis. This is what we have worked towards."

Banks turned around and took a couple steps. Then speaking to everyone in the room, he said, "We don't need anyone here if they don't believe in what we're doing. If any of you feel that we are quitting you should go home now."

Banks paused to turn and glare at Joe.

Joe thought of Sahar. She will be a target, especially if she reveals the identity of the killer or the driver. Joe opened his mouth but then closed it. Again, Joe's eyes darted around the room. Nobody looked back at him. Colonel Newborne sat in his chair facing the center of the room with his back against his desk, his eyes glued to the floor. He was silent but he looked like he was burning up from the inside.

Joe followed suit. Insubordination is a crime for a military officer. Just as importantly, he would not be able to warn Sahar to not trust the Americans if he were on a plane heading back to the states.

"No, sir," Joe answered Mister Bank's silent question.

Banks took a deep breath. "Look," he said addressing the room. "Nobody likes this business, but this is the way it is. It's called life. It's how it always has been and always will be. I believe some of you are making things out to be worse than they really are. Joe, Minister Hassan and the Iraqis in the Interim Government are accomplished people who want to make Iraq a better place. Yes, there may be some who are not loyal to democracy, but it's up to the Iraqis who are loyal, to stand up and fight for themselves. These good people will not allow the few to destroy their country. And as far as those who helped us, well, most will be fine, but they all knew what they were getting in to, they all understood better than we did, that there are casualties in war."

Banks looked around, "You soldiers should know this. You all should know this. We try to minimize the numbers, but we all must play our role. Continue to hang in there and do your parts. You've done them well up to now. Your sacrifice and your courage are paying off. Let's finish up strong."

Nobody moved. Looking at Mister Banks Joe thought, *it's not a sacrifice if you don't lose anything of value; and it is not courage, if there isn't any real chance you'll even lose it.*

"I thought you would all be happy," Mister Banks said disappointedly, "You've all served your countries well." Banks turned and left the room, the members of the front office group quietly rose to follow him down the ornate hallway back toward their office.

Joe looked at the colonel. Newborne looked right through him, his face was ashen and his dark eyes reflected nothing.

CHAPTER *64*

"Gentlemen, I am the minister now. I will not be as tolerant for failure and disloyalty as you have recently become accustomed," Hassan said in Arabic.

"Gentlemen, I am the minister now—" the translator started saying in English but she was cut off by Doctor Hassan's next sentence. From her podium in the corner of the room, her black hair falling just past her shoulders, she glanced over at Mister Banks.

Banks sat to Hassan's left, who for the first time, occupied the chair at the head of the table at the morning meeting. Around the rest of the table the Iraqis shifted in their chairs, already reshaping their faces to reflect the new attitude. Everyone except the minister's imported cronies, who arrogantly looked at the other staff members with suspicion, held their lips tightly closed, hiding their expressions.

"By tomorrow I want a list of everyone in your directorate, to include position, age, faith, and how long they have been at the ministry."

"I want..." started the translator.

Glancing in her direction, his eyelids only partially raised, the minister continued, intentionally speaking over the translator, "All women should be properly attired," his lips snarled slightly, "and after tomorrow there will be no women in DG positions."

The translator did not even attempt to speak this time, instead she leaned forward and furiously wrote his words into her notebook.

Banks glanced over at the DG of Finance, her face was solemn as she held her palms down flat on the table staring at her unpainted fingernails. Then he looked towards Newborne.

Newborne was glaring at him. The intensity of Newborne's eyes made it clear that he wanted him to take this last opportunity to interrupt and re-establish himself—while it was still possible. *But this is what the president wants, he wants us out.*

Instead, Banks put his hand to his chin, determined to keep his face empty. He sat there as if everything were going according to plan. Banks refused to shift in his chair as he tried to hide the discomfort churning inside him. He avoided Colonel Newborne's eyes. Banks also avoided looking directly at his former director generals, ignoring the fear and panic on their faces, and their silent pleas for help. He stared straight ahead, no longer listening to the words he did not understand, no longer pretending that he did not understand their meaning.

After sitting in the meeting for about ten minutes, Colonel Newborne, glaring at the new minister, said, "Excuse me, I hate to break up this charade, but I'm leaving. Since I am no longer welcome, I will attend to other business."

Hassan's lips curled, and his eyes flared, but he held his words. He and Banks were the only people in the room who did not silently watch the colonel stride across the short distance to the door and open it. As the door closed behind him the translator put her pen down and let her eyes glaze over. The room became as uncomfortable as it would have become, had it run out of oxygen.

In the hallway Newborne pulled out his cell phone and called Watts. "We're going somewhere. Grab Firas and a of couple guards and meet me at the Suburban."

Hanging up, he set off down the hall and down the stairwell to the parking garage in the ministry's basement.

"Where are we going, Sir?" asked Major Watts as he approached the colonel who was pacing near the vehicle waiting for them.

"The Police Station."

"Sir?" The major questioned whether he heard correctly, but the blaze in the colonel's eyes confirmed it. Watts informed the guards who hopped into another vehicle and prepared to follow them. Then he got in the passenger seat as Firas climbed in the back and fastened his helmet strap and seatbelt.

As they drove out the narrow ramp and then out the gate onto the street, the major studied the colonel. He determined that this was not a good time for light conversation.

Pulling up to the Police station, they double-parked. Newborne hopped out and nodded to Firas to go with him. "You stay here," he ordered Watts.

"Yes, Sir," Watts replied watching the translator jog to keep a step behind the colonel until they entered the Iraqi police station.

CHAPTER 65

"Good afternoon, I'm here to see Minister Hassan, is he available?" a thin man with a straight face firmly asked the minister's secretary.

"No, I'm afraid that isn't possible," the secretary began to explain continuing to look at his computer screen.

The visitor didn't move. The secretary glanced up and found the visitor holding out to him a badge identifying himself as a detective from the Iraqi police force and a memorandum bearing the stamp of the minister of interior.

The secretary shot upright in his seat and changed his response, "Detective, please allow me a moment to inquire as to when the minister will be able to see you." The secretary knocked on the minister's door, entered and closed it behind him. He emerged several minutes later.

"You are in luck sir, his last appointment finished early and he doesn't have another visitor for thirty minutes," said the secretary holding the door open for the detective.

"*Shukren*," the visitor replied as he passed through the doorway.

The minister met him halfway across the room and instead of returning to his desk he led the way to a small, knee-high coffee table, surrounded by a couch on one side, and three chairs on the others. The room was spacious and lavishly decorated in a gilded, rococo style. The heavy curtains prevented the entrance of even a single ray of sunshine.

"Please have a seat, Mister…" The minister paused, awaiting introduction.

"I am Officer Laith. I am a detective with the Ministry of Interior. I am here to inquire as to the whereabouts of one of your people," the man said as he sat down.

"Yes, of course. I am here to help however I can. But please, enlighten me as to the circumstances of your inquiry."

"This morning," he looked down at an open notebook to recall the name, "a Colonel Newborne, filed a sworn statement with a few accusations, some of violence, some of corruption, against a man named Zaid Mohsen. He allegedly works at one of your *Kimadia* warehouses."

"Zaid Mohsen," parroted the minister, rubbing his chin as he too finally took a seat. "Yes, I do know him. Unfortunately, I have just sent him to Basra to investigate the medical warehouse situation down there. You do know that we suffer from a terrible shortage of supplies. Zaid is gathering information for me so we can begin to solve this problem."

"I see." The detective responded, writing a short note onto his note pad.

"I'm sorry that he isn't here now. Would you like for me to assist you in any manner?"

"No, I will alert the Police in Basra to keep an eye out for him." Shutting his notebook, he stood. "Thank you for your time, minister."

"Would you like some *chai*?" he asked in a voice not encouraging the investigator to accept as he slowly rose to his feet.

"No. Thank you. I have many on-going cases to attend."

The two walked toward the door; the minister stopped near his desk. As soon as the detective had time to depart the outer office, Doctor Hassan picked up a ceramic cup and heaved it at the wall. He stormed past the splintered shards on his way out of his office and into the adjacent one.

Mister Banks looked up from the papers on his desk.

"Your colonel has gone too far. Against our orders, he has reported one of my managers to the Iraqi police. Now they are looking for him. I know how to deal with my people. Any interaction by the police will only make fixing the *Kimadia* problem harder. Control your meddling staff or remove them from my ministry."

He left Mister Banks sitting motionless at his desk.

Doctor Hassan walked into the room where his bodyguards waited. "Come with me."

They immediately obeyed.

CHAPTER *66*

Colonel Newborne, Major Watts and Firas were sitting at a small table looking at the daily security reports. The minister's chief, was there too, he was reading papers at his new desk. There was no interaction between them.

The sound of chairs skidding and surprised voices in the next room served as a warning just before the door swung open. Although everyone in the room involuntarily looked up, only the new security chief leapt to his feet. Firas hesitated a moment, then he too stood up. Colonel Newborne didn't budge. Major Watts followed the lead of his senior.

"*Siadat Al-Wazeer*," the security chief exclaimed bowing to avoid looking directly into the minister's eyes.

The minister's scowl was a well-rehearsed look of anger and annoyance. Ignoring the two Americans, he barked at his newly appointed security chief. The chief stiffened up and braced: his chin in, neck straining, eyes straight forward, as he received the loud, one-sided communication.

Minister Hassan looked at the translator, who stood silently. Frowning, the minister inspected the translator from his well-groomed hair to his recently shined shoes. Then he glared at his security chief again and exited the room.

The security chief grabbed his hat and raced after Minister Hassan, slamming the door. The minister headed straight for the garage, his heavily armed men in tow.

"We are going to Al Dabbash," he announced. And without another word, they headed out of the ministry walls in their new, shiny blue, armored SUV.

Back in the Protection Services office, Firas, Newborne and Watts looked at each other.

"What the fuck?" inquired the colonel.

Firas glanced over at Newborne and said quietly, "He is not happy."

"No shit. What did he say?"

"I have not heard that salutation since before the war; he addressed the minister, 'Your excellence,' then Doctor Hassan said he doesn't want Zaid Mohsen arrested."

"I don't give a fuck what he wants. Who the hell does he think he is?"

"He told his security chief he does not want Zaid or anyone arrested without his approval."

"Damn it! There's no fucking way we're going to give the ministry to a dictator and let that murderous piece of shit go free."

Newborne looked at Watts. "God-damn it! Banks better not fucking support this shit or I might fucking shoot his ass."

Newborne angrily pushed himself up and strode to the door. Watts leaning forward sighed, "We can't win. These shit heads undo everything we do. We fought the war for nothing."

Newborne stopped mid-stride, turned toward Watts and said, "If you quit now you're a worthless pussy." Then he continued out the door, leaving Firas and Watts looking at each other in the suddenly silent office.

Newborne didn't notice anyone as he cut his way through the crowded hallway to Banks's office. Everyone who was in the hallway cleared the path for him and stood back until after he passed. Since surviving the AK-47 round to the head, the colonel had become somewhat of a legend. The Iraqis in the ministry trusted Newborne; although he was not always a friendly man, they knew he fought for them.

Instead of hailing him with a normal greeting, or asking him to wait a moment before entering the office, Banks's secretary looked down as Newborne crossed through the outer office. Newborne flung the door open and abruptly moved front and center before Banks's desk.

Banks sat there, his face void of emotion. "Sit down," he said authoritatively, shifting his weight back in his chair. He had a small white spot on his right cheek that was likely made by the eraser on the pencil that he held in his right hand.

"What the fuck?" Newborne asked standing in front of him.

"We are turning operations over to the Iraqi minister. We must grant him some authority," replied the man in charge.

"This place will be a fucking dictatorship with that asshole running it like he is fucking Saddam Hussein."

"He is going to do what he sees fit."

"And you aren't going to do a God-damn thing to stop him."

"Not unless I need to."

"What the hell? Don't you give a damn about the mission? About these people? We come here to fight a war, the Army wins it, and then fucks like you come in and give the victory back to the killers."

"The president has determined that it is time for the Iraqi Government to take over. The Army will stay."

"To do what? What can the Army do if every time they take a hill, fucks like you give it back? We'll be stuck here tending to this sucking chest wound forever. What is it that you think you're getting out of this? For what are you sacrificing the lives of our troops and our Iraqi allies? Why are we here if all you're going to do is quit on the mission?"

Shaking, the colonel paused, awaiting an answer. The only response from the political appointee was a defensive glare.

In a quieter, yet more menacing voice the colonel continued, "All you give a shit about are headlines and fucking photo ops. Every step of the way you sacrificed the long-term objective for a short-cut to nowhere. You God-damned son of a bitch."

"Get out. You're through." Bank's words were calm and measured.

The colonel turned to leave, not muttering another word.

Just before the colonel reached the door though, Mister Banks took a parting shot, "How dare you question my integrity and motives? We are here for the same reason, to keep America safe. Headlines are important, you naïve imbecile. Without the support of the American people, the Iraqis would still be enslaved by Saddam. And there is no comparison between Saddam Hussein and Doctor Hassan. You may be angry because Doctor Hassan does not agree with your taking it upon yourself to go to the Iraqi Police to arrest your man Zaid this morning—"

The colonel turned around like a lightning flash, his eye brows pressing in on his face, "My man Zaid?" he echoed, his teeth grinding together, hardly opening his mouth.

In a raising tone of voice, "That cock sucker is a killer. He probably had his hand in every murder at this ministry since we got here. Look at this."

Newborne tilted his head forward to reveal the scar on his head and a bump that would now remind the colonel of Zaid every day for the rest of his life. "I wouldn't be surprised if that donkey's ass was involved in the ambush that almost killed me. Don't you fucking call him, 'my man.'"

Mister Banks shifted in his chair and glanced down at the table.

"Hassan just barged into the Security office and right in front of the world he shouted that he is taking the law into his own hands. And I am supposed to just sit here and smile."

"In nation building, you must accept imperfections along the way to improvement."

"Nation building? What the fuck do you know about nation building? You and your peers rejected the advice of the technical experts, and took self-serving, shortsighted actions dooming the mission to failure. All you political fuckers seem concerned about are soundbites and headlines. Has this just been a ruse? Do enough to get headlines to satisfy the public, then find someone else to dump on, and leave. Blame them for our failure?

"First you fired the top levels of the *Ba'ath* party, preventing them from participating in their country's Government, then you disbanded the Iraqi Army. In two actions you provided the leadership, the manpower and the motive for the insurgency! Meanwhile, you incompetently set up the reconstruction effort so it was guaranteed to fail. Now you place all the Ministries under the care of terrorists who each want nothing more than to replace Saddam as the tyrant or turn Iraq into a Fundamentalist Islamic State. I don't see how any of this keeps America safe."

"War has casualties—" Banks started, but was interrupted by the irate officer.

"And you are willing to sacrifice them all, anything and anyone as-long-as you or your fucking political career aren't harmed. You sacrifice our country for your own personal benefit; you fucking disgust me."

"Colonel Newborne," the senior advisor to the minister of health stated formally, "The time I knew was inevitable has finally arrived. You've let that bullet to your skull get to your head. You've gone too far. Start packing."

"Right. What fucking difference does that make now? We won. We can all go home and while the Middle East burns in the fire that you started, feeling proud of how we saved the fucking world."

This time Banks replied, "And don't you go thinking that you have this all figured out. Spare me your righteousness and self-pity. I feel for these people every bit as much as you do, but I can't afford the luxury of letting circumstances of individual cases stop the progress of nations. And that, colonel, is something that I thought you would know something about by now. So, stop sounding like a pathetic liberal whining about injustice and how evil our country is."

Banks was beet red; he breathed heavily and his lips trembled, "Now go. Get out!"

Newborne turned without any attempt to have the last word. He strode back through the door and went back to the security office to collect his things.

CHAPTER 67

After having just delivered her weekly report to Zaid at Al Dabbash, Reem stepped out of Zaid's office and was beginning her walk through the corridor of the Warehouse complex's administration wing, toward the shuttle van, when the minister and his entourage walked toward her. Reem pressed herself against the wall and looked down as two armed men and the minister passed her. She looked back and watched them enter Zaid's office. Her heart raced, Reem saw the guards step back into the hallway. She immediately ducked into the closest doorway, which led into an adjacent warehouse.

Zaid heard the rifle slings slapping against muzzles and wood stocks approach in the hall. Standing up to investigate he was met just inside his door by Minister Hassan.

"Minister, so nice of you to visit us, I wish you would have notified me you were coming, I would have received you properly."

Looking back at his associates, the minister nodded and waved his hand slightly. His bodyguards stepped back out of the office giving them the privacy he desired.

The minister walked forward, forcing Zaid to back up. Shutting the door, Doctor Hassan instructed Zaid, "Sit down."

After the minister sat down himself, Zaid complied.

"I was just visited by a police detective. It appears that you have been named in the connection with a few, how should we say it? Murders and crimes of corruption."

Zaid's face stayed a determined calm, his pulse however, quickened.

"Personally, I don't give a shit about that. Some people deserve to die, the more painfully, the better." The minister smiled. "But what I do care about is the Ministry of Interior, who as I am sure you are quite aware, runs the police forces. I don't want Minister Ahmed in my business. Ahmed is not loyal to true Iraqis like you and me. He acts like one of the ambassador's, how should I say it?" selecting a phrase he heard some American soldiers use, "—Butt boys. But as you probably know, behind the ambassador's back, Ahmed is an *asad*, a lion, preparing to rip the heart out of anyone who challenges his power or tries to claim some for himself. He wants to be the next dictator, and he is not good for Iraq."

Zaid relaxed a bit, but not yet ready to commit to anything, he continued listening.

"And so, I am forced to come here. I told the police you were in Basra, but I am certain they are not so trusting to take my word on it." The minister looked around. "I have wanted to come to speak to you anyway. It seems you and I see the world through similar eyes. We can work well together I suspect, that is, if I can keep you out of jail."

Zaid smiled. "*Siadat Al-Wazeer*, how may I be of assistance?"

"Let us take a walk. I am an old man and I have distinct memories of how bad things can happen if one has private conversations near walls that have ears." He stood up.

Zaid stood up also and stepped past him to open the door and escort him out of the office. They began to take a leisurely stroll. "The warehouses should not be busy today."

The sunlight penetrating the holes in the roof transformed the stagnant, dusty air into streams of sparkles gently floating from the rafters to the ground as Reem hid behind a forgotten motor still in its shipping crate. A pigeon watched her from its roost sheltered from the sun and the rain.

Looking around her for a better place to hide, she surveyed the fans, pumps, and compressors that should have replaced broken components throughout the country's 240 hospitals and 1,200 clinics.

A brownish hue covered all other colors. The clear and black plastic showed a month's build-up of dust since the last time someone wiped away the earlier layer to read the number under the UN Oil for Food symbol.

Unsuccessfully struggling to hold her tears, she was determined to stay still, though her mind was active. *They must be arresting Zaid. Why else would the minister be here? And I am Zaid's accomplice. They probably bugged his office, they heard our conversations.*

She heard something. She silenced herself by holding her breath. From her hiding place, Reem saw Zaid escorting the minister, talking as they walked, the two body guards trailing by a few meters. She heard them laugh.

She stared. Though she still did not dare to move, she allowed herself to breathe again—quietly. As she continued to lean into the dirty crate she closed her eyes and quietly said, "Thank you, God."

After a few minutes, the men strolled out of the warehouse and onto the small road behind it. Reem stood up straight. She grimaced slightly, and then wiped the dust off her hip and down her skirt. She could feel that her face had become filthy. Hoping to avoid others, she snuck back into the corridor and toward a bathroom to wash.

CHAPTER *68*

Muraad and her girls were asleep. Sahar sat up writing a letter. She wrote quickly as her resolve helped the words flow freely. Almost done, she stopped writing a moment to re-convince herself that this was her best option. *I cannot let Mohammad's murderer go free, and I must also avoid Zaid—I could never hide from him what I know.*

She looked up for a moment before she continued.

Joe was right, the Americans were their best chance. If the Americans failed, beasts like Zaid and the amin would be the future of Iraq. *My life does not matter, but my girls… I have no choice but to trust Joe.*

She signed it. Then, she read the entire letter one last time:

> *In the name of God and all that is good, I swear that the following is true. I Sahar Ameer know that Zaid Mohsen, the manager of the Kimadia Warehouse at Al Dabbash, has been the leader of a cell of insurgents since the arrival of the CPA to the Ministry of Health. He has an associate, whose name I don't know, but I know he was an amin working out of the Ministry of Defense before the latest invasion. I know they are responsible for shooting the South African security guard and the MOH translator in the rug store. I know this because I saw Zaid driving the car that helped the amin escape. I also suspect and have reason to believe that they are also responsible for the deaths of Semar, Mohammad and his son Marwan. Because of boasts he made I also believe they are responsible for shooting Colonel Newborne and Major Cross.*
>
> *Although I do not know the name of his associate I know his face and I would be able to identify him anytime and anywhere.*
>
> *In the hope for freedom for all Iraqis I provide you with this information. In the name of God, please protect me and my daughters from the wrath of beasts such as these.*
> *–Sahar Ameer.*

She prayed, "God and the Americans, please protect my girls." Then she folded it neatly before she sealed it in an envelope.

CHAPTER *69*

A solitary woman dressed in the common black chador, covered completely except for her eyes, slowly paced in the quiet neighborhood outside Reem's house. As Reem rushed out of the front door, later than usual on her way to work, the lady in black intercepted her and held out an envelope.

"No, thank you," Reem automatically responded, "There is nothing I need from you and I haven't money to spare."

The unknown woman was persistent, "Take it," she nearly shouted.

"Sahar?" Reem asked hesitatingly.

"Yes, just take this," Sahar said, again extending her hand.

"Why are you dressed like that? What's going on?" her thoroughly confused friend inquired.

"I don't have time to explain. But I think that I shouldn't go back to the ministry. And we should not be seen together until it's safer. I need you to bring this to Joe."

Reem stood there motionlessly, "Sahar, you're scaring me."

"Please Reem, just take it. And promise me you'll give it to Joe."

Reem reluctantly reached out her hand and took the envelope.

"Thank you, Reem. Thank you, my friend, with all my heart."

"Sahar, please tell me what's going on."

"No. Not now. Please promise me you will give this to Joe."

Reem hesitated, "Sahar…"

"Reem. Do it. For the sake of God, please promise me."

"Alright. I promise."

"*Shukren.*"

"When will I see you again?"

"After you give that to Joe."

Sahar turned and scurried away. Holding the envelope in her hand, Reem watched her go. Then she folded it and put it into her pocket before she started walking to the shuttlebus stop.

CHAPTER 70

"*Sayid* Sattar, *Sayid* Hamid, I need to speak with Doctor Sahar, but she isn't here today. Have either of you heard from her?"

"No," answered Hamid as he and Joe looked to Sattar.

Sattar shook his head, "No."

"Do you know why she didn't come in?"

"No. But Joe, it happens. I am sure she will show up soon," answered Hamid.

"Can we call her?"

"Joe, you know she doesn't have a phone. What's so important?"

Joe looked away.

"Joe," said Hamid as the two other men watched the concern weigh down the American's face, "Doctor Sahar is a smart woman, she can take care of herself."

"Yes, I suppose. *Shukren.*"

Joe slipped quietly out of the office and weaved his way through the hallway towards the stairs.

CHAPTER 71

All morning at the ministry every few minutes Reem ensured the message was in her pocket by touching it with her fingers. In the early afternoon, she resolved to go upstairs to the ninth-floor to fulfill her promise, but on her way, as she was stepping towards the stairwell she nearly collided with one of the new minister's body guards.

"How convenient, I was just on my way to find you," the short, thin and unshaven man informed her.

"Me? I don't even know you."

"You are *Sayida* Reem, are you not?"

"Yes. But who are you?"

"What difference does that make? What is important is who sent me. I am here to bring you to *Seidi* Zaid."

"If Zaid wants me, I'll just take the shuttle to Al Dabbash like I always do."

"I will bring you to Zaid. Are you ready to go?"

Reem glanced at the stairway entrance behind the man, then she looked at his determined eyes, then looking down she said, "I have work to do."

"The work can wait. We go now."

With no options, Reem followed the man down the six flights of stairs and out into the parking lot. Carrying only her small pocket purse and the envelope containing a message that she had not read, Reem was on her way to see Zaid, under very unusual circumstances.

She was surprised to pull up to a hotel.

"Why are we here?" she asked her driver.

"Because this is where Zaid is."

"What's he doing here?"

"You're beginning to ask too many questions."

She stopped talking and got out of the van. Surprisingly, the driver pulled out, leaving her standing by herself at a hotel entrance several kilometers from the ministry. A few men were sitting on benches, one with his face obscured by a newspaper. She pivoted, carefully scanning her surroundings for someone she knew.

As she completed her circle she was startled by Zaid's grinning face standing near her, newspaper in hand. His habitual sneer was replaced by a playful smile.

"What's going on?" she asked.

"I need you to deliver a message for me." He replied, his face darkening to its normal shade of discontent.

Reem privately acknowledged the irony by fingering the paper in her pocket. "Why are you here?" she asked.

Zaid smiled, "I'm in hiding."

"You?" she said with genuine surprise, "People normally hide from you. From whom are you hiding?"

"The police."

"Oh," she replied automatically. "Is everything good?" she winced as she asked.

"Yes. Things are going very well."

She nodded slowly, then asked, "Well, I should take the message then, who do you want me to give it to?"

"Not so fast. The message is in my room. And we have some business to attend to first."

His room was more lavish than the exterior of the building suggested. Reem went to the window to peer out from his room three floors above the street. Zaid moved behind her.

As she felt him lightly press against her, she froze momentarily, and then slowly moved away. He moved in closer, and placed his hands on her slender shoulders. She was careful not to jolt. Instead she turned around, leaning back and away from him a bit before pretending to want to inspect the rest of the room.

He allowed her to maneuver away. Then as she toured past him he stepped back and sat down on the bed.

"I saw you with the minister the other day. I didn't know you two were friends."

"It's never bad to be friends with a minister," he said slyly.

She looked at him, looking for another way to delay the inevitable. "What did he want?"

Zaid smiled but ignored her question as he leaned back propping himself with his hands. "I want you to bring a message to my associate."

Thinking she may have dropped the envelope she was already carrying, her hand darted into her pocket.

Zaid saw her movement. "What is it? Do you have something for me?"

Reem turned away from him to hide her eyes. Although she was facing the door, she knew there was no escape. Reem suddenly had difficulty breathing. She swallowed hard. She didn't know what Sahar's message said, but since it was for an American, she was certain Sahar wouldn't want Zaid to see it. She could think of only one way she might be able to avoid having to keep from handing it to him.

"Maybe," she said, with a rising pitch, letting the word hang in the air in a seductive manner.

She turned around as if to present herself to him. But her hand was still in her pocket.

Zaid looked her up and down and he leaned back exposing himself to her. He looked at her face and smiled, but then he looked down again at her pocket. "Let me see it."

She smiled; her face was a mask of joy hiding a core of regret. Hips swaying, hoping her disgust was well hidden, she moved toward him, "I have something for you."

Zaid sat up, patting the space next to him inviting her to sit down.

She pulled the envelope out of her pocket and held it out to him. Her arm shook, and her pasted-on smile began to fade from the inside as she presented Sahar's message and her body to the man who already controlled her soul.

Zaid reached forward and took the envelope but instead of opening it, he tossed Sahar's letter onto the nightstand behind him. Reem's heart fluttered. "This can wait, my dear, but this cannot," he said as he pulled her into him. His lips attacked hers in a frenzy that she could not escape.

Reem thought of Sahar. Sahar had warned her that this day would someday come—and now that it was here, Sahar had somehow become a part of it. The irony was disturbing, Sahar stood as much to lose, maybe more, by this encounter than she did. Reem accepted his rough kisses for her friend. If she were to have a chance to get her friend's message away from this beast, she had to please him.

She looked up at him as he stood up straight, he pulled his shoulders and chest high forming a grand image of himself as he took off his shirt. He posed as if he were a genie being released from a bottle. He smiled down at her, commanding her.

222

His rough hands glided along her smooth small hands, coaxing her to caress his hairy chest with her soft, feminine touch.

Reem caught Zaid glancing into the mirror looking at himself straddling her. Her legs were tense, and when his face was away from hers, exploring her graceful form she looked at the ceiling and tried to breath normally. She watched the ceiling fan spin above her, trying to see the blades as they sped around out of focus.

He pulled her up off the bed closer and guided her hands around his waist as he worked his hands inside her clothing, sliding it off. After the buttons, snaps and zippers opened, he extended his fingers along her naked back. He grinned broadly as he spread his hands over her, across the smooth skin of her feminine curves.

The breathing and moaning gasps were too much for each of them. Retreating to his advances, pressing at his withdrawal, she endured being the conquest in a battle she had hoped to never fight. After countless turns of the ceiling fan, he grunted and rolled off her. This was what she was hoping for—the alpha male was satisfied. He napped, and as he did, Reem looked over and plotted how she could destroy Sahar's message. She slowly pulled her arm out from under him and rolled over on her side pushing her head further up on the pillow. She picked up her head and looked over him at the envelope. It was so close, almost within reach, but what then? What could she say to him if she took it back now? *What would Sahar write to Joe? Maybe it was not so bad.* Reem tried, but she could not think of anything that Sahar would write and send to Joe that would not result in Zaid growing angry. Reem sighed. *Grabbing the letter and running away, would just be impossible.* She held her breath as she looked at the envelope, her heart pounding wildly, almost visibly, in her naked chest.

She started pushing herself up, *I'll tell him it was a silly note from her saying that she wanted him.* But before she acted, Zaid began to stir. Reem quickly slid back down and put her head on the pillow, closed her eyes and pretended she was asleep.

She felt him rub her along her legs, over her hips, along her waist, and up to her breasts. Then he reached in and softly kissed her cheek before he carefully moved away. She could tell when he shifted around and when he was sitting on the edge of the bed facing the other way. Reem opened her eyes just enough to see between her eyelashes. Zaid reached over to the night table and picked up the envelope. He tore open the envelope and pulled out the message and read it.

Reem didn't dare move. When he finished reading Zaid turned his head and looked at the woman pretending to sleep at his side. Then he looked back at the letter.

He got up and walked to the chair that held an untidy pile of clothing that had been tossed over the backrest less than an hour before. From a pocket, he fished out a cigarette and a book of matches. He balanced a cigarette on an ashtray and he placed the letter beside it. First, he struck the match and then picked up the letter and set it aflame. Using the paper as a torch, he lit his cigarette. Then he watched Sahar's letter disintegrate into ash as he leisurely smoked.

Reem's heart pounded so hard she could feel it in her head—*What have I done?*

CHAPTER 72

After seeing her last patient of the afternoon, Sahar locked the door of her one-chair private practice dental clinic, on the second floor above a furniture store, and walked down the dirty stairwell. Just as the sun was beginning to set, she stepped out onto the sidewalk and began imagining how Joe reacted to her letter as she trudged homeward along the familiar sidewalk. It had been two days since she gave it to Reem, she wondered how she should inquire. The business district behind her she approached the last traffic light along her route, without thought or expectation, she looked up. The sight of her worst nightmare abruptly snapped her out of her daydream.

The *amin* stood casually leaning against an old, two-door, blue brazili, a cigarette in his right hand. His sunglasses on, he looked as if he were a model at a photo shoot. She stopped suddenly, her eyes on his face, he looked up and brought the cigarette to his side. *Too late*, she realized that she had just let the *amin* know that she knew who he was. No longer any possibility of pretending she didn't know him, Sahar turned around and ran.

Zaid hadn't told him that she knew who he was. Nevertheless, the amin scolded himself for not assuming it. Walking as quickly as he could without looking like he was chasing her, he kept an eye on the fleeing woman in front of him. *No more amateurish mistakes*, he cursed silently to himself.

Sahar turned the corner and nearly tripped over a dog that was sniffing around near the corner of the building. The stray yelped and darted between the closest two cars. Instead of running down the sidewalk, Sahar followed the dog into the street and crawled as far as she could under the second vehicle— a white, Datsun pick-up truck—parked in a long row. Gravel imprinting on her cheek and palms, she held her breath. A few moments after she saw his shoes pass her, Sahar slowly and silently crawled out from under the truck into the street.

As she emerged, a passing driver honked his horn and yelled, "Get out of the road!"

Sahar's heart pounded. She closed her eyes tightly as she crouched low and pressed herself against the driver's door of the pick-up under which she had been hiding.

The *amin* responded to the honking and shouting by instinctively looking toward the car that continued down the road. He stepped toward the street to investigate. As he approached the row of cars, three or four cars from the intersection, another car was slowing in the same area from where he heard the horn sound. Just then a stray dog ran out of the street and onto the sidewalk in front of him.

The dog looked at him with its tongue hanging out as it trotted past him in the direction he had been heading before he was distracted from his chase. *Just a dog.* He stepped away from the street and back onto the sidewalk to continue his hunt. A short distance ahead on his left he approached a rather large house with a wall surrounding it. Silently pushing the unlocked gate open, he entered the yard to search the possible hiding place.

Sahar finally found the courage to raise her head and peer behind the cab compartment down the sidewalk. She saw the *amin* walking away from her. She scooted around the front of the truck and as the *amin* entered a walled yard she darted back around the corner and ran back up the street. She ran past the old blue *brazili* the *amin* had been leaning against, crossed the street and then turned another corner. She continued her hurried pace to retrieve Dalia from the high school.

The *amin* crept around the yard of the walled house. Then he looked for an open door as he listened intently for movement in the small garden or from inside. Watching the windows, he saw no indication at all that anyone was there. He stood still for a long moment before returning to the gate. Before passing through it, he scanned the busy street, but seeing no signs of his target, he walked back to the corner and then up to his car that waited for him near the intersection with the traffic light.

Glancing into the rearview mirror he took a moment to frown and take a deep breath before he turned the ignition key of his *Apollo* and pulled into the road. After a short drive, he parallel parked in a crowded neighborhood and turned off the engine. Grabbing a clipboard that was on the seat beside him he went around to the trunk and pulled out a gym bag that sat next to a guitar case. After looking carefully around, he shut his trunk and stepped onto the lightly graveled dirt that flanked the road. He stepped up to the door of a nondescript house where two water barrels partially obstructed the view from the street. He glanced around and then he stood a moment as if he were reading his clipboard. Not hearing anything from inside the house, he opened his gym bag and took out a small tool. He quickly and decisively jammed the metal pin into the lock, wiggled it until he heard a faint click. Hearing it, he turned the doorknob as he pushed open the door with his left shoulder. A second later, the man and his gym bag were inside.

Inside, beside the second hand of a clock that hung in the living room, the only sound the intruder heard was a radio playing in one of the bedrooms down the short hallway to his right. He took a moment to let his eyes adjust to the relative darkness, then he quietly stepped to his left and opened the curtains only enough to allow a band of light to illuminate a streak across the living room over the couch to the wall of photos on the other side of the TV. Then he slithered along the hallway wall to the bedroom door. Taking a moment to listen, he slowly opened the door slightly to see Sahar's husband napping on the bed. Reaching into one of the bag's pockets, he retrieved a knife. Pushing a small button, the blade silently sprang from harmless to lethal. He followed the six inches of steel into the room and toward his sleeping host.

CHAPTER 73

As twilight approached, an old woman sitting on her front porch noticed a handsome stranger, still wearing sunglasses, enter her neighbor's yard. She scowled as she witnessed him push open the door and enter Sahar's house. Muttering to herself, the elderly woman waddled, dragging her well-worn folding director's chair out beside the road. She placed the chair under a tree from where she could watch for the man leaving and watch for Sahar and her delightful girls returning home, which they usually did at about this time.

"People in Iraq have no respect anymore," she complained aloud. "I will do my part," the old woman vowed, "That young man will not bring harm to my dear neighbors."

Muraad was not at the café. Walking quickly up the street Sahar towed Hadeel as Dalia trotted behind. "Mom, what's going on? Why're we running?" Dalia asked yet again.

Not answering, Sahar continued her way, searching the growing darkness, keeping her senses sharp, half expecting to see something she was afraid to name.

As she approached her home, the old woman who lived across the street raised her hand at her and got up from her seat. She began to wobble across the road towards her.

"Not today," Sahar muttered to herself, but outwardly she smiled at the old woman. Sahar stopped and waited for the woman to intersect her. She kept her hand around Hadeel's wrist. Standing beside her mother, Dalia wiped her brow and slumped her shoulders.

"Dear, I must warn you," the old woman said as she moved closer to Sahar so she could speak quietly, "A man broke into your house."

Sahar's heart leapt again. "What did he look like?" She asked.

"Well, he has black hair; he is wearing dark slacks and a blue shirt, with buttons. He looks very strong, and he was wearing sun glasses."

"Oh," Sahar gasped. Tightening her grip on Hadeel's wrist, she took a step backward already beginning to retreat away from their home.

"Mom, someone's in our house? What's going on?" Dalia asked as she moved closer to her mother and sister.

"No questions," Sahar commanded turning back to the old woman.

"What about my husband?" she asked the old woman.

"Oh dear, is he home?" she gasped, "No one has come or gone since the stranger arrived. I saw the stranger come. He came from that direction," she said pointing past Sahar's house. He came about twenty minutes ago."

Sahar looked at her watch. It had been only about forty minutes since she last saw the *amin*. "He must have come straight here," she said in a daze.

She looked at the old woman, visibly shaking and her eyes tearing up, "Thank you. I cannot tell you my gratitude."

"Dear, it is a terrible thing for your house to be robbed, perhaps you would like to come into my home until you have had time to figure this out."

Grabbing Dalia's hand, Sahar turned back the way they had come.

"Dear, your husband—where are you going?"

Sahar stopped and looked back at her house. "Muraad," she said, but then turned away.

"My dear." The old woman called. "My dears."

The old woman watched as Sahar pulled her girls back down the road. Then she looked over at Sahar's house. It was dark and quiet. She took a step towards her own house, but then she stopped and again looked towards Sahar and her daughters as they swiftly walked away. The old woman turned and started to hobble the opposite direction—towards the police station.

CHAPTER *74*

The shooter sat with his legs casually crossed in a chair positioned to see the porch through the opening in the curtains and down the hallway, which was on the other side of the couch from where he sat. The loudest sound was the ticking of a clock that hung on the wall near the couch. The only light in the living room entered through the narrow gap in the curtains which was to the left of the kitchen which was to his right. Following the incoming beam from the streetlight with his eyes he glanced to his left. A family portrait hung on the wall behind the TV. A family portrait hung on the wall behind the TV; a father, a mother, and two daughters. But standing off to the side there was another man also in the photo. The shooter stood up and walked over for a closer look. His face resembled Sahar's and was about the same age—a few years younger. *Probably a brother*. He reached up, removed the photo and returned to the darkness where he put the picture into his bag which he had placed behind him on the dining table. Then he sat back down and continued to wait.

About an hour after he arrived, the shooter moved up to the window and peered out. *If she were coming, she would be here by now.* Carrying his bag, the shooter walked down the short, dark hallway and entered the room. Muraad was on the bed wearing only his boxer shorts, his arms were tied behind his back and under him, his neck was held down by a tight rope that went around the mattress. His heels were tied to the bed posts. Muraad was unable to move. The shooter listened to his heavy breathing—only from his nose—as a bandana was tied around his head and stuffed in his mouth. Peering into his captive's wide-eyes, his stale, tobacco-tainted breath washed over the terrified face looking back up at him. "They are not coming," the shooter told him.

"In a moment," he said in a calm voice, "I am going to free your mouth. When I do, you are going to tell me where your little wife is."

Not moving his face from its position inches away from the muffled whimpers of the man of the house, the shooter reached down with his right hand and with vice grip power, he squeezed the defenseless man's testicles.

Monitoring the effect of his action, the shooter watched his victim attempt to curl up in the fetal position, but the restraints made him unable to do so. Muraad's face, at least the area visible above his gagged mouth, twisted with pain. Then, as he saw the all too familiar pleading in his victim's eyes, along with his attempts to catch his breath so he wouldn't suffocate, the shooter gave the man a reassuring smile as he reached down and squeezed again.

"About now, you probably would prefer death over our continuing this little game," he said in a friendly tone.

"No worries. All you need to do is tell me what I need to know and your wish will be granted."

230

While staring directly into Muraad's eyes once again he continued, "So, do you understand what I am saying?"

Moving to the limited extent he was able, the bound man frantically nodded his head yes.

"And you are going to answer all the questions that I am going to ask you?"

His captive desperately attempted to communicate his intent of total compliance.

"Very well, but even the slightest hesitation in telling me the truth, and you will force me to persuade you to cooperate."

Displaying the switchblade, the shooter sliced the air, the blade's light reflected across the ceiling and the tormented face. Then he flicked the gag, intentionally nicking Muraad's cheek. He smiled lovingly as the salt of the man's tears and sweat mixed with the fresh dab of his blood as Muraad ejected the gag from his mouth and gasped for air.

"My dear friend, please tell me where I might find your virtuous wife. I would like to give her my love."

CHAPTER 75

Approaching from the opposite direction of the police station, the old woman instructed the driver, "Here, this house," she pointed, "that one."

A few streetlights provided uneven light, but the house she pointed at was dark. The driver passed it and then stopped the SUV while two policemen armed with AK-47s hopped out and then quietly closed the doors. The old woman remained in the car with the driver as they rolled silently about half a block before stopping.

"That's his car, that blue one right there," she told him as she pointed across the street.

The driver turned off the headlights and the engine, gathered his weapon and prepared to join his colleagues in her neighbor's house. As he departed, he said, "*Hijia*, please stay in vehicle. We will be back soon."

A few minutes later, the shooter strolled up the sidewalk from behind her. As he passed her, the old woman shuddered. Their eyes met and she grew rigid. The man stepped toward the vehicle, smiled, and with his right hand formed the shape of a pistol. He pointed his finger at his own chin, looking directly at her, he brought his thumb into his hand mimicking the hammer dropping.

"Boom," his lips silently taunted as the poor lighting cast a broad shadow across his face. Then he smiled, winked and turned away.

Unable to move, she stared at him. He stepped in front of the unmarked police van, and crossed the street while he fished a set of keys from his pocket. Opening the trunk to his car, he put his bag into it, shut the trunk and paused. As he stepped forward, with a very cold expression on his face, he looked the woman directly in the eyes. She shivered. As she watched, he opened his car door, got in and started the engine. Closing the door, he turned on his headlights and guided his car out of the parking spot and into the road. Looking over her shoulder, the old woman watched the red taillights disappear behind her. Her heart pounded as she sat terrified in the police van in the silent neighborhood. Overcoming her fear, she slid over on the bench seat toward the door, opened it and stumbled her way out and across the street to her house.

The police found the front door of the house unlocked. A strangled man lay dead in a bed. The police determined that the killer had escaped out the main bedroom's window, an impact mark in the dirt in the back yard where he stepped was their only clue as to his identity.

CHAPTER 76

It was just past nine o'clock at night when her brother answered his door. Mahmood, who looked like he returned home from work only minutes before, quickly ushered his older sister and his two nieces into the front room and then immediately pulled the window blinds closed. Then he turned around and looked at them wondering what would bring them here in this condition. Sahar's eyes were red, the circles around them were dark. She was nervous and tense. The two girls, Dalia, still in her school uniform and still holding her book bag, held Hadeel's hand as they both watched their mom hyperventilate.

Taking Dalia's bag Mohammad began to offer, "Let me get you some dinner."

"We can't stay here, and I think it isn't safe for you either," interrupted Sahar.

Mahmood looked at them a moment then nodded his head as he accepted the unknown situation, "Okay, I'll pack my bag."

Her brother, a bachelor, was quick to load what he thought he would need for an unknown amount of time into the only two suitcases he owned and a couple small cardboard boxes. After loading his car, as he inspected the items he would leave behind, he wondered when he'd be back, if ever, even if just to pick up the rest. He touched a favorite sweater that hung in his closet and sighed as he turned his back on it. Stepping out of his apartment with Sahar and her daughters he paused on the porch only long enough to lock the door behind them.

CHAPTER 77

In a cheap hotel room Sahar sat with her heels up on the chair cushion hugging her knees. Her girls were curled together on the small bed; Mahmood snored on the couch. By the light provided by the single bulb attached to the bathroom ceiling, Sahar watched her daughters sleep.

She focused on Dee Dee's smooth skin and little nose. *She has her father's nose.* Sahar shuddered, certain the *amin* killed her husband as he waited for them. *Had the old woman not warned me, we would all be dead now.* She kept looking at her girls. "Muraad—they will try again." *But now I must live— to protect them.* Looking up at the ceiling she whispered, "Are you still alive? I wonder, *Habibti*, which one of us is less fortunate? Is it harder to die for someone? Or harder to live for someone?"

She pushed herself up, crept into the bathroom and shut the door behind her. She looked at the woman in the mirror and with the aid of a towel, she cried as quietly as she could.

CHAPTER 78

"Yes, *Sayid* Sattar, Hamid said you wanted to talk to me," as Hamid and Joe walked into Sattar's office.

"Joe, yes," he said his face wrinkled and the skin around his eyes dark. "Joe, Sahar's husband dead," he said in his broken English.

Hamid's eye brows seemed darker than before. He touched Joe's shoulder, "Sahar is not dead."

Joe stared at the wall—at first it was too bright to see, but soon it was covered in dark spots. He sat down. Sattar and Hamid sat with him.

CHAPTER 79

As was his custom when talking to people he wanted to woo, the minister met the shooter in the middle of his office and led him toward the informal sitting area.

"May I get you some *chai* or Turkish coffee?" He asked as he held out his hand.

"No, thank you," the shooter replied, as he sat down, uninvited, his back straight, in one of the chairs across the table from the couch.

The minister reached for the polished silver pitcher and poured himself a small cup of steaming *chai* on a counter across the room from his desk. Then he moved toward his guest and stood in front of the couch. He bent forward to add a couple heaping spoons of sugar from the service tray that sat on the table between them. As he did, he stated, "You look to be a very powerful man."

The shooter made no movement. His face registered nothing.

"And you look as though you are very skilled as well," the minister said standing up right stirring his drink.

Again, no reaction; the minister took a sip, noisily sucking in the hot liquid. "Has our mutual acquaintance, Zaid, been paying you well?"

The shooter raised a hand drawing the minister's attention to the elegant room surrounding them, "I do not live a lavish lifestyle. I am God's soldier. I am motivated by cause."

The minister nodded and took another sip of tea before he sat down to face his guest across the table. "In that case, I think you are not overly impressed by Zaid," he said smiling. "Certainly, you know the basis of his motives."

The shooter nodded in agreement, "I work with him because of his hatred of the invaders, not because of his motive for hating them."

The minister leaned forward, resting his elbows on his knees. "True. But, times are changing. It is time for us to begin to establish our destiny for when the Americans have been defeated. Don't you agree?"

The shooter remained motionless as he calmly looked at his host.

"Zaid is motivated by pleasure and power for Zaid. He has no morality. He has no higher purpose than to be the master holding the whip," explained the minister.

Doctor Hassan put his cup down and stood up to pace behind the sofa, "I, on the other hand, returned to Iraq to place Iraq back on the path we were on thirty years ago, before a man like Zaid, though much more competent, claimed Iraq and its people as his own."

Hassan knew that the shooter would have only been a child during the 1974 revolutionary court tribunals regarding the *Da'was,* but the minister had been encouraging his staff to spread news of his own role as a revolutionary, about how he escaped execution after the *Ba'ath* party began cracking down on the *Shi'a* fundamentalists for pushing a separate political agenda. Certainly, the shooter would have heard this.

"I wonder, my friend, what principle you fight for. Certainly, your days following Saddam have come to an end, haven't they?" asked Doctor Hassan.

"Saddam has shown the world his true character. He isn't a man; he's a rodent, hiding in fear, afraid to fight, begging for mercy like a distraught woman when the Americans pulled him out of his hole." The shooter said, his voice raspy with disgust.

The minister smiled and he asked directly, "So do you intend to continue to work for Zaid?"

"I believe the time for me has come to work for a greater cause."

The minister's smile broadened.

He leaned over and picked up his *chai.* He lifted his cup in the air in a gesture of a toast to the shooter, "To the glory of God. May we serve him with honor."

236

CHAPTER *80*

"Hamid, it's been three days since Doctor Sahar has come to work. Have you seen her?" asked Joe as he approached Hamid's desk.

"No. Joe, not since—" he let the sentence unfinished. Hamid put his hand on Joe's shoulder, and patted it a few times.

"She needs time."

Joe nodded as he stood gazing out the window for a few moments. "Has anyone heard from her?"

"I don't know. I'll find out for you."

"*Shukren.*"

CHAPTER *81*

Reem took a taxi to the *Sha'ab District of Baghdad.* She got out along a major road and walked three blocks to a market where she rendezvoused with of a friend of Sahar's brother. When she stood at the bus stop an old, white Toyota pick-up truck pulled up and a man about Reem's age, with black hair and a thin goatee yelled out the window.

"Sister, over here."

Reem saw the driver was wearing a red t-shirt and had a yellow towel on the dashboard, per Sahar's description. Although he was not her brother, Reem got in. A meandering twenty-minute drive and the truck stopped. Getting out, he motioned to Reem and said, "Follow me."

As they approached an old, four-story apartment building, barefooted kids ran about shouting and laughing and an old dog looked up at her as Reem walked past. She waved her hand in front of her face to help dilute an unpleasant odor and to chase an annoying fly away as she passed an indoor-outdoor kitchen area that numerous families appeared to share.

"Through there. I'll wait out here," her mysterious driver told her.

Reem ducked through a couple strings of beads that hung down and made a pleasant sound as she entered a dark hallway.

"Reem," said Sahar before Reem's eyes has had a chance to adjust. "I'm glad to see you."

"I'll be glad to see you too, once I can."

"My brother insists on this," she said chuckling. "His friend serves as a contact point for us. Nobody knows where we actually live and he goes to the market for us, too."

"You mean you never leave here?"

"Not since we arrived," she said opening a door that allowed some light to filter into the hall, Sahar led Reem into a room. She found herself standing in a small, run-down apartment; the doors on the cupboards didn't close completely, and the lighting was dull—barely reflecting off the worn, dirty walls.

Mahmood stood next to Sahar holding an AK-47.

"I guess anyone can get one of those things these days," Reem said.

Sahar's brother nodded and grinned. "Makes me look vicious, doesn't it?"

"I've seen worse," she answered quite honestly. "There they are," exclaimed Reem as Hadeel ran up to her, leaving Dalia standing in a doorway to what appeared to be a bedroom.

"Hi *Khala*," exclaimed the young girl.

"Hi Dee Dee, I missed you."

She hugged the little girl and tickled her a bit before looking up and seeing Sahar watching them.

"Okay Dee Dee, time for you to go back in the room with Dalia. I need to talk to your auntie," instructed Sahar.

After a prolonged hug, Hadeel disappeared into the back room and Dalia shut the door behind them.

"Thanks for coming. May I get you some *chai*?"

"That would be nice. And *Sahar*, my dear friend, I'm really sorry to hear about Muraad."

Sahar halted where she stood, her eyes darted down to the floor pulling her face with it. She stood there a silent moment then she said, "I'll be right back, please sit down," as she left the room.

Reem sat nearly motionless on the sofa near a small coffee table. After staring down she lifted her head to look at the room around her. The place was dreary.

Sahar returned with a tray holding a steaming pitcher of *chai*, sugar and cups. Sahar placed it on the table and knelt next to it opposite her friend. She paid attention to her own hands as she poured and presented a cup to Reem.

"I'm so sorry," Reem said as her friend placed the tea on the table.

Sahar held out her hand to silence her. Then looking up at her she asked, "What did Joe say when you handed him the note that I wrote?"

"Sahar, I am so sorry," started Reem, then she paused. "But I have bad news for you. The Americans are leaving. Minister Hassan announced it and none of the Americans denied it. They may be gone within a month, two at the most."

Sahar was stunned. "But Joe said they would stay for at least three years." Then she weakly smiled, "No, you must be mistaken," she stammered. "Or perhaps you are joking, just to see my reaction."

"Oh no," Reem said, her voice dropping, "I'm not. It's the truth."

Sahar stood up and turned away and began pacing in the small living room.

Reem continued but she kept her eyes on her cup. "Sahar, Joe read your note and then threw it away. He said he was sorry, but there was nothing he can do to help you."

Sahar stopped moving and stared at Reem.

Reem raised her eyes to Sahar. "Sahar, I don't know what to say." Then she glanced away, "But there is one ray of hope. Zaid never saw the letter. He will probably never know you sent it."

"But Reem, Zaid is after me—he sent the *amin*. He killed Muraad. He wasn't looking for him; he was after me," Sahar said looking directly at Reem. "We aren't safe."

Reem put her tea down. "Oh, I—." Reem's mouth twisted, as though she intended to say something, but didn't know what.

Sahar looked around, her eyes wide and her face taut, "What can we do? Eventually they will find us." She paced around the room again, staring at the walls she approached, "We must go. We must go as soon as possible. Baghdad isn't safe for us anymore. Iraq isn't safe for us anymore."

Sahar stopped pacing and looked at Reem but clearly did not see her. "We talked about it. Yesterday Mahmood went to the police station. They escorted him back to our house and his apartment. He got our passports, our money. He was also able to carry a couple bags of clothes and a few of the girls' toys and books. He asked one of our neighbors to watch the place for us while we are away."

Slowly, Reem asked, "Where will you go?"

"I don't know," she said looking and sounding frazzled again.

Sahar lowered herself into a chair across the small room. "Jordan is so expensive, probably Syria. From there we will decide."

Reem stayed quiet watching Sahar's face. "Promise me, that we will meet at least one more time before you go."

Nodding, Sahar asked, "Oh Reem, what has become of us?"

"I must see you again, one more time; I must give you a gift to remember me by." Reem's eyes were wide as she insisted.

Sahar looked her in the eyes, "Your friendship is the only gift I need, my friend. But I promise. But Reem, you mustn't just worry about me, you must be careful; promise me you will take care of yourself."

CHAPTER *82*

"Joe, Sattar spoke with *Sayida* Reem. She said that Sahar is tending to her husband's affairs. And comforting her mother-in-law."

Hamid and Joe stood in the hallway outside the conference room.

"Oh. But she didn't tell you or anyone here? Isn't that unusual?" inquired Joe.

"Yes, I'm surprised she didn't tell Sattar. She would normally tell him that she wouldn't be here. But Joe, this is a very unusual crisis."

"But there is something I must tell her, for her own safety," responded Joe.

"But Joe, it has only been a week since her husband was killed. These are not normal times."

"I know, Hamid. That is why I'm so worried."

Hamid nodded his head.

"Hamid, do you think you could help me find her?"

CHAPTER *83*

That same day, beckoned to his hideout in the hotel again, Reem stood in front of Zaid.

"So, Sahar seems to have disappeared. My associate does not know where to find her," he told her.

Reem nodded, but did not bother to try to deceive him with a smile.

"You don't look happy. Is it that you miss your friend?"

"War is not a time for friendships," she answered coldly.

Zaid kept his eyes on her face as he replied, "Yes, I suppose war is not a happy time for a young woman. Especially if she discovers her best friend is a traitor."

Reem looked away and down.

"Have you heard from my associate?" he asked sternly.

"No. Not since I gave him your message," she answered, sounding distant.

"I see." He said studying her face, "Have you seen Sahar?"

Reem looked up, but was slow to answer, "I don't know where she lives."

Zaid stared at her. She looked away as he spoke. "You know that the struggle for our country will not be easy. Everyone must make sacrifices. You do wish to do all you can for Iraq, no?" He asked.

Reem answered slowly, "Yes. You know my commitment to our country."

"But sometimes a person's resolve may be jeopardized by lesser important things," he suggested.

Reem nodded.

"Good. I'm glad you understand, because as you know, I value our fight against the Americans more than I value my life. And of course, I value my own life far more than anyone else's."

Reem breathed heavily as she was looking down again.

He picked up a cup that sat on his dresser then set it back down carefully positioning it so its handle was parallel to the edge. Not looking at her he continued, "One must always make adjustments to keep things in line," he explained. "I think that you have seen Sahar. What did she have to say?"

She glanced at him, "What makes you think that?"

"Certainly, you don't suppose that you are my only informant?" He stated.

She glanced down and then confessed, "Yes, I saw her and I have news for you."

"Really?" he asked, exaggerating the inflection.

"Forgive me for my weakness," she started, "But I'm heartbroken by the news I have for you."

Zaid narrowed his eyes.

"But my dear friend…my former friend," she corrected herself, "is leaving Iraq and I don't think I'll ever see her again."

"Really," he said.

"Yes. She is in hiding, relying on friends of her brother. But she told me that there is nothing left for her in Iraq. She will soon be gone forever."

"Well then, our problem will soon be solved. Won't it?"

"What do you mean?" She asked, hopeful that there might be a chance that Sahar's death may not be imminent.

"Once she's gone, what do I care? As-long-as she never comes back."

Reem's face involuntarily brightened.

Zaid leaned back and grinded his teeth against each other as he watched Reem's spirit return.

CHAPTER 84

Aboard a commercial airline from Kuwait City to London, Joe walked down the narrow aisle looking for Colonel Newborne. Finding him in the middle aisle seat with a couple empty seats beside him, he asked, "Sir, may I?"

Newborne pushed his tray up, holding the book that had been resting on it. He stood up and moved into the aisle allowing Joe to slide in toward the middle of the plane. Then both men sat down and looked at the back of the seats in front of them for a long moment before Joe broke the silence.

"Sir, what do you think is going to happen?"

Newborne hesitated, but then he answered in a tight voice, "I think this war will go on and on and on, until we finally realize that we lost."

Joe frowned, and then he sighed deeply. He reached forward to release his tray, which fell into position with a thump.

Newborne looked over at the younger man. "Look Joe, you did all you could. The world will work itself out."

"Sir, but we screwed them. Some of them will die because we told them we would stay and protect them."

The colonel sat motionlessly until after a flight attendant passed down the aisle on his left. "Yes, they will."

Joe looked over at his tall companion. Even in the plane seat he towered over him. "And that doesn't bother you?"

Newborne turned his head and Joe was struck with the painful intensity on his face. But after a few moments, Newborne simply blinked and asked, "Have you ever heard of Vietnam?"

Joe didn't answer.

"Do you remember what happened to the Montagnards after we left?"

"Yes sir. I read about it. But that doesn't make it right."

"Right? What the fuck does that mean? Look, it's not your job to do right things. It is your job to do your job. And you did it. Now you are going home. It is time to move on."

"Move on? What does that mean?" Joe asked.

"Look, you are going to have problems if you try to save the world because you'll fail. You may never forget this. But moving on means adjusting—perhaps pretending—that meaningful things have no meaning and that terrible things are necessary. Some people can do this easily. I think it will be hard for you."

Joe listened intently.

"And by the way, that was a pretty fucking stupid thing you did, driving around Baghdad trying to find Doctor Sahar. I know what you hoped to accomplish, but Banks was right to send you home. If I were still in my position, I would have fried you. You are lucky to be alive."

"Yes sir," replied Joe quietly.

"Anyway," Newborne continued, "The world doesn't need fucking Joe Brown racing to its rescue. And if you try to reconcile all your actions you will drive yourself crazy. You can't. Nobody can."

Newborne thought for a moment then continued, "I should have warned you. You think too much. You believe too much and you get too personally involved. If you don't get a grip on this, you'll never get over it."

A knot swelled in Joe's chest, he turned his head away.

"That being said, do you know what I'm going to do when I get back?" Newborne asked.

"No sir," Joe responded.

"I'm going to save as many of our friends as I can."

"How?"

"Any way that I can."

Joe nodded, but remained silent.

"I never forgave myself for what I didn't do to help the Montagnards." Newborne said quietly. "I spent a year in the Central Highlands, I knew some of them like we know the Iraqis in the MOH. I can't change what my nation will do, but I won't let that happen to me again."

"No sir," replied Joe, cocking his head.

"Don't be a pussy. Don't just sit on your ass and cry on my shoulder because the world is not perfect. Do something."

Joe nodded. "Sir, what about Banks and all the rest?"

Newborne asked, "What about them?"

"Well, they caused this mess. They don't give a damn about the Iraqis, in fact, they don't give a damn about the Americans. All they care about is themselves."

Newborne thought for a moment, and then asked, "Okay, so what's your point?"

"Why do we let them get away with it?"

"Get away with what?"

Joe paused before answering, "I think that what Banks and the ambassador did was criminal. They tell us to recruit the Iraqis promising that we won't abandon them and then a couple months later, after we promise them our support, we abandon them. They used us to deceive them."

Newborne nodded. "That pisses me off too."

"But now you act as though it's okay."

"It's not okay. Some of those sorry sons of bitches would sell their mothers to a whore house if it would help their careers."

"So why don't you do anything about that?"

"Do what?" the colonel asked.

"I don't know, expose them."

"There is nothing to expose. Everyone already knows about them. Nobody cares."

Shocked, Joe looked at him, "What do you mean nobody cares? They would care if they knew."

"Goddamn, you are an idealistic fuck. No Joe. They do know, and they don't care. Don't you understand a damn thing about how the world works?"

"Sir, are you telling me that the American people wouldn't care about their government lying to them about the war, then lying to the Iraqi people, using them and abandoning them, condemning them to death, once they were no longer useful to their short-term use?"

"Yes. That's exactly what I'm saying."

Joe stared at him.

"Think about it. When was the last time the US Government did something that the American public didn't go along with?"

Joe was silent as he tried to answer.

"Let me help you. Did the American people complain when the U.S. Government claimed the entire Western Hemisphere to be off limits to Europeans so we alone could exploit it?

"No sir."

"And did the people complain when the U.S. robbed Latin America of their natural resources and exported them to the US under the muzzle of rifles held by US marines?"

Joe shook his head.

"Did the American public complain when the US Government committed genocide against millions of Indians and locked the survivors onto reservations?"

"Did the American people tolerate oppression of blacks after the Civil War even though Lincoln abolished slavery and guarantee freedom?"

"Yes, Sir," Joe said quietly.

"Do you know why?"

Joe thought for a moment, "Because these actions made their lives easier."

The colonel nodded. "Not a bad answer.

Joe shrugged.

Newborne continued, "You seem to always want to talk about Panama. How about when we staged a coup to free Panama from Colombia so we could then trade control of the Canal Zone away from the Panamanians, effectively stealing the land from the Columbians to build the Canal? We did it on a 100-year lease. And then at the end of the lease, many congressmen criticized President Carter for returning the Canal Zone to the Panamanians. They didn't even want to honor a sham treaty."

The colonel paused a moment staring at the back of the seat in front of him, "Honor," he said in disgust. "Or when we annexed Hawaii against the wishes of the Hawaiians?

"The only time the people of the United States don't go along with the Government is when it makes the ruling class's life harder—like Prohibition. And as soon as the American public complained in a meaningful manner, the politicians rushed to give the people what they wanted."

Newborne was watching Joe's face contort. "Are you getting the picture? For too many people, honor means very little. Americans, but not just Americans, this applies to all people. Some people in every society, it doesn't matter where they're from, will sacrifice anyone and everything if it means more power, more unearned money in their pocket and an easier, more luxurious lifestyle for themselves."

"But I don't understand why this all wouldn't bother you."

Newborne shook his head. "What makes you think this doesn't?"

"Well, Sir, you've been in the Army more than thirty years. You were even extended on active duty to be here, and you stayed after getting shot in the head."

"I stayed because at the same time we were abusing our weaker neighbors to become the big dog in the West, Europe held colonies all over the fucking world and the Japanese conquered half of Asia. Some dumb-ass named Hitler decided the world should be Aryan. Mao exterminated the concept of family in China. Stalin ruled Russia and their satellites with cruelty you cannot even imagine, and more recently, fucking Saddam Hussein was oppressing the people you are now crying over.

"The answer to your question is that it is human nature to dominate. The alpha male mentality is what made people what they are today, for better and for worse. Believe it or not, the United States is more restrained than most of them. The US Government is a better master than fucking Saddam or the fucking Taliban."

Joe looked at his hands and then asked, "Tell me sir, why are we fighting this war?"

"Because we are soldiers."

"But why is our country fighting the war?"

"Why did we fight in Korea, or in Vietnam?" countered Newborne.

"Well, we've been told it was to stop the communist dominos."

"And what the hell does that mean Joe?"

"To stop the spread of communism—proxy wars between the American sphere, capitalism; and Soviet sphere, communism."

"And do you think those wars were worth it?"

"I don't know."

"Do you think we lost those wars?"

"Vietnam, maybe, but not the Korean War."

"How do you figure?"

"Well, we stopped Kim Il Sung and the Chinese from taking over South Korea. But we had to flee Vietnam."

"Did we stop the spread of communism?"

"In South Korea we did and now it is an industrial giant, but in Vietnam we didn't. We couldn't stop Ho Chi Minh from spreading communism to the South."

"I asked you if the wars were worth it and you were able to answer the question because you based the answer on whether we achieved the strategic objective for the wars in defining their success."

The colonel looked up at the low vibrating ceiling of the plane, "But here in Iraq, we cannot answer the question because we don't know what the strategic objective was. When our elected officials or the senior commanders can't, or don't clearly define the reason for the war, you know that the war cannot be won. For World War II we had clear objectives—defeat the Germans and the Japanese. Everyone knew what we were doing and why. Since then, the objectives have not been so clearly defined.

"Why are we fighting this war in Iraq?" Newborne continued, "Will it be worth it? We won't know whether this war was worth it until we know whether we accomplished our strategic objective. If the strategic objective was to end a weapons of mass destruction program, well, it's quite apparent they didn't have one to begin with. I don't see it as winning when you fight a war to get rid of something that doesn't exist. If it was to establish a democracy, we won't know whether we succeeded until after we see what sticks to the wall after we finally leave. If it was to stop the spread of terrorism, well, if we fail to put a democracy in place during this war, we may be helping the terrorist bastards by providing them an oil-wealthy country in the center of the Middle East to use as a home-base.

"We've come a long way since George Washington," Newborne added shaking his head, "He lost almost all the battles but he still won the war, because the strategic objective was clear for the colonists, not as clear for the crown. All Washington had to do was stop the British from winning. Outlast them until it was no longer worth it for the British to keep fighting."

"Here, militarily we won every battle, but politically, we are failing miserably. We don't have a clear objective so we don't know what victory looks like. Here, the politicians are more concerned about headlines back in the states than progress on the ground. That is why they can't stomach even the mildest setback—that is why they lie to the people. For all I know, the administration's strategic objective may merely be to win the next election. The goal of the fighting and the farce of a rebuilding program, may be to run President Bush's numbers up so he will be re-elected."

Newborne stared at the seat in front of him, "That is what I think is happening. That is what I think will happen."

Joe sat silently. The flight attendant walked by carrying a tray of water. The colonel reached out for two and handed one to Joe.

"Look. When I left Vietnam in 1972, I was twenty fucking years old. I didn't believe for a minute that we could beat communism. And while I was in Vietnam I didn't give a shit about that anyway. Inside, I was crushed about my buddies who were killed and the locals who supported us: the ones we left behind for Ho Chi Minh and the Khmer Rouge to butcher. As far as I was concerned, Vietnam was a complete loss. Lost by well groomed, chicken-assed, fuckers like Banks, telling us we could not shoot back without permission, by the body count, by politicians picking targets for bombing runs from their offices in Washington DC—basing their decisions on public opinion. Goddamn, in these ways, Iraq is just like Vietnam was.

"But then, as time went on things began to settle. Don't get me wrong, not without a horrific price, hundreds of thousands, millions, of innocent Vietnamese and Cambodians were killed who might have lived had we not left in 1972 or had we gone back in after the North violated the treaty. But we didn't. Sometimes I guess Americans believe that it just isn't worth the effort to stand up for our principles.

"But who represents the Americans? You and me? Fuck no. The politicians do, and by extension, political appointees like Rumsfeld, Bremmer, Banks and even fucking Carson Prance. All they care about is knowing what the people want and how to twist reality into soundbites that the people will support. They are lying to the people because it makes themselves look good and that is what the people want. The American public wants it easy. They want it to sound and look clean and fair so they can pretend to be righteous. But they don't care about what's right or what's wrong. What they really want is for the US to control things because that power makes their lives easier."

After a short silence, he continued, "The other thing politicians care about is getting the credit for making everyone's life so easy. They know that Americans won't complain about things, not even wars, not if they are living large. They know the Americans will ignore reality and believe the biggest lies and excitedly support the most offensive rubbish, as-long-as the economy is strong, even if the rich are the only ones benefitting."

Newborne's voice was low and raw, "And that's why both the politicians and the people are willing to sacrifice soldiers like us and Iraqis like Mohammad, Semar or Sahar, or even kids like Marwan. The people of the United States would rather have cheap gasoline than life for our allies who risked absolutely everything to support us."

Colonel Newborne turned and looked directly at Joe, "The average American doesn't give a fuck about the liberty of twenty-five million Iraqis. And people like Banks know it."

PART III: POST CPA
CHAPTER 85

"Sahar, my friend visited the MOH yesterday. He told me that Joe and the colonel are gone—they flew out a few days ago. The rest of the Americans are still there, but Minister Hassan is completely in charge. The women are either being demoted or fired, more of them are now wearing an *abaia* with *hijab* or a *chador*. Even the Christians—those who are still there, anyway."

Mahmood paused for a moment until Sahar looked at him. "And Zaid, he is back on the sixth-floor and *Kimadia* 13."

Sahar's eyes flashed and her shoulders dropped.

"People are saying that Dr. Hassan made some kind of deal with the minister of interior so Zaid could return. And," he said looking at her face as she looked down, "Everyone knows that Zaid is looking for you."

Immediately, Sahar said, "We must go to Syria, now."

Sahar stood up in the small living room and paced. It was almost evening, and Mahmood's car was not in good condition. One of its problems was that the headlights did not work. A car without headlights driving on the long stretches of desert highway would be a target for everyone, most lethally, the US military, who, unlike the CPA, had no plans of leaving.

"We'll go in the morning. It would be too dangerous driving without headlights at night."

"I'll fill the gas tank today though." Mahmood stated.

It was just after 7:00 in the morning when Mahmood popped open the trunk of the beat up grey *brazili*. His loose-fitting, long-sleeve shirt was un-tucked above his off-brand blue jeans as he and a couple of his friends carried out four suitcases, some blankets, water, and a few plastic bags of food. They chatted as they helped him squeeze as much of the luggage they could into the trunk before cramming most of the rest into the backseat; saving only enough room for the girls to fit. There wasn't space for the last small, but bulging, suitcase. Mahmood opened it and pulled out two pairs of his own shoes and handed them to one of his friends. The brown, though scuffed, ankle-high boots he was wearing would be the only shoes he would be bringing. Now, no longer excessively overfilled, he crammed it in the leg area in the front passenger seat. Then, he walked back inside to inform Sahar and the girls that it was time to go.

Mahmood bid farewell to his friends, giving special thanks to the one who owned the house they had been staying, as the girls, wearing pants, sneakers, and t-shirts, Sahar, a light, long sleeve shirt and a *hijab*, squeezed into their places.

"Good luck, Mahmood. We'll tell the others that you've gone," his host said extending out to him a new red baseball cap with "Baghdad" written in white letters on the front, "I want you to have this."

"Thank you, my friend," he said looking down at the cap in his hands.

"Don't forget where you're from," his friend told him as he embraced Mahmood and kissed his cheek.

Mahmood put the cap on his head and held his right hand over his heart before he got into the car.

From the backseat, Dalia watched the good bye, "What's going on?" she asked, "Mom, where are we going today?"

"Dalia, do you remember when we talked about moving out of Baghdad?"

Dalia sat up and leaned forward in the backseat of the car. "Really? Today? Right now?"

Sahar looked over at her brother, as he got in and started the car. "Yes."

Dalia fell back against the seat, "I thought we were just switching houses."

Dalia looked over at Hadeel, who was looking back at her with a question mark on her face. "We're leaving, Dee Dee."

Hadeel stirred, tears began to form in her eyes.

"What is it, dear?" asked her mother, "Dee Dee, look at me."

Hadeel looked up, her face forming the shape of crying, but no sound came out.

"Tell me why you're crying, sweet-heart," Sahar said gently.

"I miss daddy," she said as the tears began to flow.

Sahar bit her lower lip and closed her eyes tightly. The pain was made worse by her nightmares of imagining the terrible way he died. She never saw his body and they did not even attend his funeral. Instead she and the girls, along with her brother had their own private ceremony, but without the deceased being present. This was a terrible affront to her husband and his family and the law of Islam, which required significantly more from a grieving widow, none of which she could afford to honor while they were in hiding.

Sahar looked at her brother and nodded. He began to drive away from their home, most of their belongings, and their lives. Departing suddenly made the finality of this move come into clear focus.

Sahar looked straight ahead. "Why'd I ever trust them in the first place?" she asked aloud as the girls cried in the backseat.

"Who?" Mahmood asked.

Sahar looked at her girls. Hadeel stared out the window with tears openly running down her round cheeks. Dalia covered her face with her hands, and sobbed.

"I've heard stories about American soldiers in the desert putting two camel spiders in a small box, and cheering as the they dismembered one another," Sahar frowned. "What kind of person is fascinated by staging a battle and then watching others die? Is war a sport to them? Do Americans think we are camel spiders?"

She shook her head and repositioned herself to see out the window as the dirty buildings, ancient cars and old women sweeping dirt with foot-long brooms passed her field of vision. She noticed the glances her brother gave her whenever traffic allowed.

"I need to say good bye to Reem." Sahar announced.

Her brother looked over at her, "I think that's a very bad idea."

"Only for a minute. She's my friend."

"But it would be dangerous. How can you find her without being seen?"

"Nobody will be expecting us. We can do it."

Her brother bit his lip. The girls in the backseat remained quiet, except for occasional sniffles.

"It's 8:00. At 8:30 she will be leaving her house. We can catch her there."

Mahmood shook his head, "We really shouldn't."

"We need to. It will help us all adjust to this abrupt move. It'll be good for the girls, and for me."

"Well, if anyone is there, anyone at all, we drive past without stopping—agreed?"

"Alright," Sahar reluctantly answered.

Pulling over in front of Reem's house, Sahar grasped the car door handle, but Mahmood reached over and grabbed his sister's other hand, "Oh no, you're not getting out of this car."

Sahar glared at him.

"I'll go and bring her here. You three hide your faces. I'll give her five minutes. If she doesn't come out, we leave without seeing her."

He looked at Sahar, "Agreed?"

"As you like," she replied quietly.

Standing outside of Reem's house, Mahmood scanned the street. After a few minutes, he started to return to the car, but Reem came busting out her front door, turned to lock it and took five steps before noticing him.

"Oh, Mahmood," she exclaimed, stopping the moment she saw him.

"Reem," he explained, "We are leaving. Sahar wants to say goodbye."

"Oh, but I must go to work," she said uncertain of herself. Then after a hesitation she agreed, "Where is she?"

"She is in that grey brazili," he said pointing. "You go see her and I'll keep watch."

She stepped forward nervously. As she approached she strained to see inside the windows.

Staying low in the car seat, Sahar saw her friend in the side view mirror as she came up from behind. Sahar popped up with a smile. "Here she is," she told her two girls, who also popped up.

Sahar lowered her window, "*Salam Alekum.*" She put her hands out and Reem took them into her own.

"*Alekum Salam,*" her friend replied.

"We're going now," Sahar said, her smile disappearing.

"Sahar, I am so sorry."

"We shall meet again, *Insha'Allah.*"

Reem forced a smile. Then she looked at Hadeel who was tapping at the window for attention, Dalia barely visible behind a suitcase and a couple bags.

Reem touched the glass greeting her, "Dee Dee, grow up to be a great woman like your mother. You, too, Dalia."

Hadeel, her eyes still moist, was making a silly face. Dalia looked stern, but managed a stoic smile.

Sahar looked up at her friend. "Reem, please be careful. Today the world is upside down; you mustn't be too trusting. Promise me you'll do whatever it takes to survive."

Reem cringed at her friend's words before replying, "Yes. I promise I will."

"I'm afraid it's time to go, already the traffic will be bad. I'm sorry." Mahmood had moved forward unnoticed.

"Oh, no please don't go. I'll miss you." Reem said.

"I'm sorry, but we must. Be safe, always be careful."

"Where are you going?" asked Reem.

"We're going to Syria. We have a long drive in front of us."

"Please get word to me when you arrive."

"*Ma'salama* my *chalawi.*"

"Yes, *ma'salama, chalawi.*" Both women had tears in their eyes as the dirty, beat-up *brazili* chugged out of its space alongside the curb.

CHAPTER *86*

Coming through the pedestrian gate, just before Reem walked into the ministry, she saw the shooter standing near the employees' entrance. He turned away as if he did not know her. After climbing the stairs, she was surprised to see Zaid standing in the hallway on the sixth floor, waiting to speak to the new DG of *Kimadia*.

She greeted him, "*Salam Alekum.*"

"*Alekum Salam,*" he returned. "You're late."

"Yes, I—" she paused a moment, "—I missed the shuttle."

He nodded, not very interested.

"How does it feel to be back?" She asked.

He shrugged his shoulders. "Hiding was not all that bad," he grinned, looking her over.

She blushed, and then murmured, "The problem is solved."

He shifted in his position, turning more towards her, "Oh, which problem is that?"

"Sahar. They are leaving. She stopped by my house this morning on their way out."

Zaid flinched and quickly recovered. "That was nice of them. Is that why you're late?"

"Yes. But only by a few minutes, I was lucky a bus came right away."

He nodded slowly, looking down at his notepad to avoid her eyes. "What time did they leave?"

"They stopped by just as I was leaving my house. Her brother was waiting outside."

He nodded again, "Did she say where she was going?"

"Yes, Syria. I'll miss her so much."

"Well, it's good she's leaving. With the Americans and their patsies out of the way, Iraq can become great again."

"Yes," Reem said looking at another group of workers as they passed in the hallway.

"I doubt her brother's car makes it across the desert. What is it, an old *brazili* isn't it?" asked Zaid.

"Yes, that old thing is older than Dalia, but if they drive slowly, they might make it."

"I heard that he painted it, is that true?"

"Oh no, why would anyone waste the money? It is still that ugly grey, except where the paint had worn off."

"You better get to work; I need to see the DG."

Her face glowed as she excused herself and walked down the hall.

As soon as she turned into her office, Zaid tucked his notepad under his arm and quickly strode toward the stairway.

CHAPTER *87*

When Zaid found him, the shooter was leaning against the wall outside the employee entrance smoking a cigarette. "About a half hour ago, Sahar and her brother left Shorjah, heading to Syria."

The shooter absorbed the words and then considered whether that mattered to him. He looked at his watch. He had a

258

meeting with the minister, but not until that afternoon. Then he slowly exhaled a long drag of smoke. "Alright," he said.

"They are in a mid-to-late '80's grey *brazili* with badly worn paint," Zaid added as they walked over to the shooter's car. The blue Apollo was parked in the lot with the ministry's vans. He pulled a notebook full of photos and papers and a map from the glove box and opened it across the hood of the car. Opening the road map, he put his finger on Shorjah, the neighborhood that Reem lived. He assumed they would likely be traveling slowly and carefully. The shortest way to Syria was west to Al Fallujah, to Al Ramadi and then north along the Euphrates River to Abu Kamal, at the border.

Tracing a few possible options with his finger, he figured that Sahar and her brother would take the road through central Baghdad towards Anbar province. Studying the map, he realized that although they were most likely across the Tigris already, if traffic in the city center was slow, he could save at least thirty minutes by crossing the river further north and avoiding the more congested part of Baghdad. That meant, he calculated, that if he didn't have any delays and if he drove fast, he could easily arrive at an intersection twenty kilometers west of the city before they would.

He selected a place where two freeways merged west of Baghdad to watch for them. This job would take two people though, if he wanted to be sure to find them.

"I think they will be driving along this road, by now they are probably somewhere around here." He pointed at an intersection near Al Zawra Park, near the Green Zone, about six kilometers south of the ministry.

"I suspect they will be following this road and will get onto the Al Ghraib highway here" he said pointing to the Allqaa Skyway.

Zaid nodded.

"I will cross the river in Khadimiah, take the northern route, pass over the Al Ghraib Freeway and turn west in Khadra here, and beat them to this intersection where I'll watch for them," he said pointing to an intersection just east of Abu Ghraib.

"Why don't you just take the Freeway? Wouldn't that be faster?"

The shooter shook his head. "No, the Americans have a checkpoint on the freeway coming out of Baghdad. I'll go around it. You need to drive along their route though, to make sure that they haven't stopped along the road. If you see them, make sure you don't let them see you."

Zaid nodded again.

The shooter then opened the notebook. He glanced through a few photos until he came across a family portrait. "This is her brother?" he half asked, half stated.

Zaid leaned in to look, "Yes, that's him. Where did you get that picture?"

The shooter held a glance at him before exhaling a long drag of smoke. Zaid pulled away. Then the shooter shut the notebook and folded the map and got into the driver's seat as Zaid ran over to his car. Less than a minute later, the blue *brazili* followed by the silver Toyota *super* pulled out of the Ministry of Health.

The shooter made great time. When he had passed over the freeway, the traffic on the main road was exceptionally slow, especially going west. He was confident that he beat them there, though he wouldn't be sure until Zaid arrived—the longer it took Zaid, the more unlikely it was that Sahar and her family had already passed.

Parked on the side of the main highway heading west out of Baghdad, the shooter knew that if he remained there too long, one of the American soldiers or Iraqi Policemen would stop and question him. He got out of the car and opened the hood, opened the radiator cap, disconnected the battery and took out his air filter, all the while watching the traffic pass. He smudged a bit of grease on his hands and cheek and leaned into his engine compartment holding a wrench that he pulled out of his toolbox that he placed at his feet. After forty-five minutes Zaid drove up.

As Zaid pulled over and stopped, the shooter looked at his watch and made a few calculations in his head.

Zaid got out of his *super* and walked toward him, but before Zaid could ask, the shooter announced, "They either didn't come this way or you passed them on your way here."

Zaid looked puzzled, "This is the most obvious way to Syria."

"Yes." The shooter looked across the highway. The steady stream of cars and trucks headed both directions. Then the shooter looked at Zaid and smirked as he added, "I don't suppose you drove right past them on your way here? Did you?"

"No, of course not. I kept a careful eye out for them."

"Very well." The shooter turned away from Zaid and reached into his engine compartment. He re-connected and replaced the displaced parts. Then he let the hood drop in a heavy clunk.

Surprised by this action, Zaid asked, "What are you doing?"

"Our welcome here will soon be over."

"What about Sahar?"

"Either they are stranded behind us, they took a different route or perhaps she is hiding in one of these trucks."

"How do you know?"

"I don't know. But I suspect. I don't think they would race out of town but I doubt think they would stop for *chai* either. They would probably pre-plan their escape well enough to have a tank of gas. Since you didn't see them, and they probably didn't beat me here, either they took a different route— possible—but not likely, a different car—which they probably don't have, or their car is broken down on a side road since it is probably as unreliable as most of these heaps. If they did break down, they're either with the car trying to fix it, or they may have flagged down an empty truck, bribed one of these Bulgarian drivers with a Dinar note and climbed in the back."

Zaid stood stunned. He kicked the dirt and swore. Then he regained his composure, "So, what are you going to do?"

"I'll backtrack and see if they're stranded just off the road. Maybe they are spending their valuable time trying to fix the car. If so, I'll take them out. If I don't find them, you either let them go free or you meet them at the border."

"You aren't going to help me?"

"The way I see it, I already have. But I have an appointment with the minister this afternoon."

Zaid shook his head and scowled, "What do you think I should do?"

"How badly do you want to kill them? Do you know which border crossing they plan to take into Syria?"

Zaid looked down and shook his head, "No."

The shooter shook his head also, "Well, hopefully you can find them before you get too far west of Ramadi, otherwise you might go to the wrong border crossing."

Turning away, the shooter added, "But now if she is in one of these trucks, especially one escorted by the Americans, she probably won't be headed to Syria anymore, anyway."

"Why not?"

"Because she must go where the truck goes. The Americans prefer doing business with Jordan and Turkey more than with Syria. I suggest that if you don't see them in their car, pick the longest convoy you see and go where it goes."

"How will I know if you find them first?"

"You'll know I found them first if they never arrive to either of the three border crossings. But since you can't be at all three places at the same time, I guess you won't."

The shooter grinned as he got into his vehicle and pulled into traffic. Zaid watched him go and then eyed a couple passing trucks.

Walking slowly toward his car, he watched a gunner on a Humvee protecting the rear of the passing convoy. Zaid cleared his throat noisily as he reached for his car door. He spat on the ground, got in and drifted into traffic.

CHAPTER 88

Crossing the Tigris, Sahar looked down at the dark, slow current thinking of all the cold cruelty that has gone far beyond even the loosest standards of human decency. The wickedness that now divided Baghdad would poison Iraq, and the entire Middle East, for years to come. Zaid and the MOH on one side of the Tigris, the Americans—the CPA in Saddam's Republican Palace—on the other, she was a pawn in their struggle. The atrocities of such dreadful brutality and heartlessness have stained the banks of this great river, and in her mind, has fouled the life-giving water. The same water that gave birth to and sustained human civilization from its first teetering steps, has been tainted and made toxic by inhumanity.

With the Tigris behind them, she looked away. The girls sat quietly in their seats, looking out the window. Sahar closed her eyes and drifted off to sleep.

Barely aware of the irregular thumping of the tires bounding over the uneven tar joints connecting sections of the freeway as they sped up and slowed down in the heavy traffic, Sahar rested—until the engine sputtered. Then her eyes popped open.

Mahmood tightened his grip on the steering wheel and leaned forward, "Water in the gas?" he guessed.

Sahar sat up and looked at him, her eyes wide.

The line at the gas station was at least an hour long and would have closed before he could make it to the pump, so the evening before, Mahmood bought gas from a man sitting on the side of the road selling it out of clear plastic containers. Because everyone was forced to resort to desperate acts to survive, the gas vendor stretched his profits by thinning his product with water. In this batch, apparently, he stretched it a little too much.

"Get the car off the road! There, Al Zaytoon Exit," Sahar stressed pointing to the next exit.

Mahmood swerved into the right lane in between two large trucks, and then turned off the main road sputtering up the exit ramp. At the top of the incline, they turned right onto a smaller, local road then onto the dirt shoulder next to a tree and a few scraggly bushes behind another car that was already there. Right when they stopped, the engine died.

They flung the doors open and scrambled out, immediately Mahmood popped open the hood to peer at the engine. He disconnected and reconnected some parts and attempted to restart it. Then he kicked his car, cursed, and repeated his futile actions. Twenty minutes later, the girls were sitting on a rock near the tree. Sahar's brother still fiddled with belts and hoses.

"This fuel is piss! That man sold me piss as gas."

"Mahmood, I hope you're better at fixing cars than swearing," his sister said calmly.

He looked up frowning, his hands and face marked with engine grease. "No," he shook his head and lamented, "I can't fix this. I'm better at cursing than fixing cars."

Sahar rolled her eyes and looked over at the highway and watched as a very long convoy of tractor-trailers, escorted by American soldiers slowed to a stop. Sahar looked down the convoy and could not see the end. The front was more than 100 meters in front of the closest trucks which were only about 100 meters away from them. She looked back at her family. Her girls were quietly sitting in the meager shade of the scraggly tree. Then she looked over to see Mahmood drop his wrench and then hit his head on the bumper as he reached down to pick it up.

"This, this stupid thing," he grumbled.

Sahar shook her head and watched him kick the dirt, a spray of gravel dinked against the front of the car.

She stepped forward, "Mahmood, girls, grab the bags. We're going to get on one of those trucks."

"Good, because this thing isn't going anywhere. Ever." Mahmood dropped the hood. As Sahar and the girls unloaded their belongings from the car, he approached two men who were

264

napping next to the road in the shade of the car parked in front of them.

"*Hajji*, would you like to buy a car?"

Carrying and dragging their loads, the four of them walked back along the road and down the entrance ramp to the highway. They slowed as they approached the first cluster of drivers who were sitting in a circle laughing and chatting in Bulgarian.

Stopping a respectable distance away Sahar asked, "How much did you get for the car?"

"15,000 dinar," the equivalent of about $10.

"Maybe you shouldn't have shouted what a lousy car it was when you were cursing it," said Sahar as she reached into her pocket.

She handed $40 to her brother, more than half a month's pay from the MOH. "Get us in one of those trucks as quickly as you can."

The girls sat down on a suitcase looking down and away from the mid-morning sun and Sahar stood watching Mahmood approach the circle of drivers with a ten-dollar bill visible in his hand. The drivers had lit a small fire and were pouring water into a teapot. He waved his arm and held out the money. Several of the drivers engaged him in Arabic, sometimes gesturing with their arms and hands. The others sat back and laughed. After a couple minutes, one of the drivers pushed himself up from his sitting position and he left the group with Mahmood. He and Mahmood walked to a truck behind the impromptu gathering.

"Come on girls, take what you can and follow me," Sahar said as she grabbed the two largest suitcases.

Sahar and the girls waddled with what luggage they could carry and arrived at the back of the truck as the driver opened the rolling door of the forty-foot trailer.

Mahmood explained, "This convoy is on its way to a staging area in Al Bukamal, Syria to pick up supplies and construction material to be brought back to the airport. Most of the trucks are riding empty. He can bring us to the Iraqi side of the border, but we can't cross in the truck. I'm sorry, but you three must stay out of sight. I'll ride with the driver to make sure we go where we're supposed to go. I'll check on you when I can."

Mahmood and Sahar hurried back to collect the rest of their things and then Mahmood helped Sahar into the back of the truck. Then he assisted the girls before he handed the bags up to his sister. The truck driver pointed to an old mattress, a dusty blanket, a couple open boxes of MREs—the prepackaged food the US Army eats in the field—and a few boxes of bottled water, that along with a stack of empty pallets, were already inside the truck.

"Use, eat, drink," the driver said in broken Arabic bringing his hands up to his mouth.

"*Shukren*," responded Sahar.

"Will you be alright back here?" inquired Mahmood.

"We'll be fine," Sahar said pushing the mattress towards the front of the truck. Mahmood apologetically nodded at the girls. The two girls nodded back.

"Dalia and Dee Dee, grab those waters and put them over there," Sahar said pointing to the front left corner.

After the girls moved to the front of the nearly empty trailer, the driver pulled the door closed leaving the stowaways in darkness.

Mahmood and the driver went back to join the men drinking tea around the smoldering fire. Right after Mahmood sat down, a Humvee with its .50-caliber gun pointing outward, drove by them on the shoulder of the freeway.

CHAPTER 89

Driving east on the freeway, back towards Baghdad, the shooter saw the stopped convoy and the backed-up traffic on the other side of the median. He exited and turned left on Al Zaytoon. Looking down from the overpass as he crossed the

266

main road he saw that the convoy had been there long enough for the drivers to get comfortable, light fires and serve tea. When he looked straight ahead again, up on the right, the shooter saw the old, grey car he sought. When he pulled up next to it he slowed down; two men had the hood up and were pulling out parts. He did not recognize them so he braked and inquired as his engine continued to idle, "*Salam Alekum.*"

"*Alekum Salam,*" the one who stood up to look at him replied.

"Pardon me *hajji*, but this car belongs to a friend of mine; do you know where he's gone?"

The man tensed and he looked down at his friend, who stood up holding a screwdriver in his right hand.

"No, no, no, no. You misunderstand me. I know his car is junk. I know my friend is desperate to travel. I'm not accusing you of anything. I'm only looking for my friend and his family. Do you know where they are?"

The two men looked at each other, then one explained, "We bought this car from him. It broke down—Bad gas."

The shooter nodded his head, "Yes, always rushing, he is."

The men quickly looked at each other then shifted their weight and smiled.

"Where did the family go without a car?" the shooter asked.

The man pointed toward the road. "They went toward the highway. I think they want to go west."

The shooter looked back at the convoy. "Yes, *Shukren. Ma'salama.*"

"*Ma'salama.*"

The shooter swung the car around, crossed a dirt median and parked his car off the other side of the road, directly across from the tree. He was careful to keep plenty of distance between his car and a short but steep incline that led down to a small irrigation canal that paralleled the road on the north side of the road.

When he got out of his car he shouted to the other men, "*Hajji*, I'll be back for this car, I would greatly appreciate it if you didn't disassemble it."

They both laughed.

He crossed the road as he walked toward the freeway. Standing in the dirt median between the freeway exit ramp, behind him, and the entrance ramp, in front of him, and the local road to his right, the shooter scanned the convoy. In the closest group of drivers, the shooter recognized Mahmood immediately. *The bright red hat makes it easier*, he thought.

As the shooter looked for a clue as to which truck his primary target was hiding, a large explosion about two hundred meters up the road indicated the IED had been detonated. Without being told, the drivers kicked out the fire and began to head for their trucks. The shooter watched to see which truck Mahmood would enter. But as he was observing, a Humvee approached him coming the wrong direction up the "U-shaped" entrance ramp. With a quick glance, he noticed that the gunner had him in his sights.

"Shit."

The shooter turned away from the highway to properly address the approaching threat.

The Humvee stopped about twenty meters from him and a loudspeaker instructed him in Arabic to put his hands above his head. The shooter did so, looking directly into the M-60 gunner's sunglasses who sat in the turret above. Two men, one, a soldier and the other an Iraqi translator, stepped out from the desert tan vehicle. The soldier was carrying his M-16 in the ready position.

"What are you doing here on this highway?" asked the translator.

"My car broke down over there." He nodded his head indicating behind him and to his left. "I was going to see if one of the drivers of this convoy has any tools I might use."

The translator and the soldier conferred for a moment. Then the translator told him, "Step forward."

The shooter, heard the engines of the convoy rev. He stepped forward, pretending to be afraid, as an innocent man would be.

"Lie down on the road, face down, your arms and legs spread out."

He moved forward and to his right a little more to get onto the pavement of the highway entrance ramp and complied.

The driver of the Humvee exited the vehicle leaving it idling and came forward to cover his buddy while he searched him. The gunner stayed in the turret pointing his machine gun at the shooter.

The soldiers moved away and conferred out of earshot.

"Get up."

He got up.

"Where's your broken car?"

"On the side of the road behind me near that tree on your right. It is an old, grey *brazili*. A couple of men are helping me fix it."

"What men?"

"I don't know them, I just met them after my car broke down."

Another conference.

"Let's go," the translator told him.

Walking in front of the translator and one of the soldiers, the Humvee followed about ten meters back. The gunner waved a passing car to proceed on the other side of the pavement.

Watching the unexpected procession approach, the men stripping the damaged car stood up and stepped out from behind the car. The shooter made eye contact with them and tried to make them understand that he needed them to follow his lead. A quick glance between them seemed to seal an agreement to work together to rid themselves of this group of Americans.

"Is this your car?" The translator asked the two men.

The older of them responded, his voice shaking, "No, we are only helping to fix it. It isn't our car. That one's our car," he said nodding to another old *brazili* behind them.

"Whose car is it?" Asked the translator.

The men looked at each other.

"It's my car," stated the shooter.

"Please remain silent." The translator warned him.

"I'm sorry," said the shooter in a high-pitched voice.

"It's his car." The two men answered in unison.

"What are you doing to his car?"

The men looked at each other again. Then they looked at the shooter. The shooter smiled and gave a very slight nod as his eyebrows rose above his sunglasses. His hands extended up and out just enough to indicate helplessness.

"Uh, we were helping him fix it."

The shooter smiled encouragingly at the two men before quickly erasing it.

As one of the soldiers began poking around, under the protection of the Humvee's big gun, the translator looked at the men then at the shooter. Then back again. Then in English he spoke to the soldiers, "Their story holds, I don't think they know each other, their story doesn't seem rehearsed."

"Roger," said the staff sergeant who was in charge, as he nodded and looked around. "Whose car is that?" he added pointing at the blue Volkswagen Apollo.

Translation.

"I don't know, it was there when I got here," answered the shooter.

"Do you know?" The translator asked the two men.

"We don't know," stated one of the men. "It was there when we got here."

The translator told the sergeant.

"Check it out, Clay."

The soldier who was poking around trotted across the dirt median and approached the car. He got down on his belly and checked the undercarriage looking for wires or explosives. Seeing none, he checked the doors, windows and body of the car.

"Preparing to open."

All the soldiers took on a stance that indicated they half expected an explosion, although such a stance clearly would not have provided much protection had there been one.

PFC Clay broke the window on the driver's side door with the handle of a big knife he carried on his belt. Then he reached in and unlocked the driver's side door. He inspected the front, then the back. Then he popped open the trunk.

The men watched. The shooter watched the soldiers.

The radio cackled.

"What's your status? Over."

Staff Sergeant Hook walked over to the Humvee and picked up the handset. "Checking out a dismount. There seems to be an extra vehicle. Could belong to the bastard who planted the IED. Over."

"Negative. A remote device didn't activate this IED. This one needed contact. Do you have any reason to suspect hostile? Over."

"Negative. Story checked out. Over."

"Copy. Rejoin convoy. Take the six. Over."

"Roger. Out."

As Hook placed the radio handset next to the receiver, he shouted, "Clay, leave a card on the dash. We're moving out."

Clay let the trunk drop and dug a card from his cargo pocket that he placed on the dashboard before jogging toward the Humvee.

"Thank you for your time, and I'm sorry for the inconvenience," the translator told the shooter and the two men. "And good luck with the car," he said over his shoulder as he started walking back toward the waiting Hummer.

Halfway there he stopped, turned and shouted towards the shooter, "Hey, what's wrong with your car anyway?"

"Bad gas, watered down." Answered the real owner of the grey car.

The translator looked from the shooter over to the man who answered him, but he only hesitated slightly before answering to the group in general, "Oh. Too bad it doesn't run on diesel. If it did, we could hook you up."

As the last soldier stepped into the Humvee, the soldiers turned around and drove down the entrance ramp and on to the highway. The M-60 pointing up, the gunner spun in his turret settling in facing the rear as he prepared to guard the convoy's six o'clock position.

The two men looked at the shooter as the shooter watched the Humvee drive off. The shooter sighed as he wiped the sweat away from his eyes. He looked at his two cohorts and smiled.

"Thank you, my friends. How much did you pay for this car anyway?"

"15,000 dinars."

The shooter smiled. He walked across the road and popped the trunk open. He rolled up the carpet and reached in to a hidden latch, pried off the cover to a compartment, and retrieved several bills. Then he closed the compartment, replaced the carpet and closed the trunk. Walking back to the eager men, he reached out and handed each of them 30,000 dinars.

"This is your lucky day. You have a car, and four times your money back."

The man looked at the money in his hand, "*Allah Wiyaak*," God be with you, he said in a soft voice then he held his hand, with the money in it, over his heart, "*Shukren*."

With that, the shooter nodded, then turned around and headed back across the road.

He watched the Humvee wait on the entrance ramp as dozens of trucks slowly re-started their trek west. Finally, as the last truck drove past them, the Humvee slid in and took its position at the rear. As the convoy faded into the distance, he glanced at the card left by the soldiers.

"Your car has been searched by American soldiers. We apologize for the damage. To file a claim to fix these damages, please report to—"

He brushed the broken glass off the car seat and was about to toss the card to the ground, but caught himself. "*Hajji*," he shouted to his new friends across the road.

The closer of them jogged over to him.

"For you, this day keeps getting better."

He handed him the card.

As he read it, the shooter said, "By the look of what they did to your car, they must have been searching for something pretty small."

Looking back at his newly purchased, half-disassembled *brazili* he grinned, "Yes, it will cost quite a bit to rebuild, won't it?"

The shooter glanced at his watch and started his engine. He had an appointment with the minister. Sahar's fate now depended on Zaid.

CHAPTER *90*

As Zaid drove west the traffic and the vegetation thinned. The higher the sun rose in the sky; the lower his confidence level fell. *I don't even have a plan. I'm just driving. I don't even know where I'm going.*

As he drove the stretch from Baghdad to Fallujah, he carefully looked at every car parked off the road, just in case Sahar and her brother had beaten them to the ambush site. *How am I supposed to find them?*

After a while he laughed at himself, *If I'm lucky enough to see them, what am I going to do? Am I going to just walk up to Sahar and her family at the border, pull out my pistol and shoot them?*

He tapped on his steering wheel and shook his head. *I have no problem with killing them, but I'd rather not get caught.*

Zaid clenched his teeth and repeatedly hit the steering wheel with the palms of his hands. *The shooter should be here helping me. He should have killed the colonel when he had a chance. How did he screw that up?*

He drove in silence. Glaring at the world from behind his sunglasses he passed through Fallujah. *If I were to fail, everyone would know. I must succeed.*

As he began to get into the rhythm of the long road trip, the kilometers began to tick by. His face was now calm but his mind was aggravated. *My best chance would be to get her before they get to the border. But I don't even know if they are in a car, a truck... for all I know, they could be traveling by boat.*

He glanced at himself in the rearview mirror and said, "Get ahold of yourself. Syria or Jordan?" he asked out loud.

Zaid began looking for a place to stop, a gas station. *If they are in a truck inside a convoy, what should I do? The Americans won't let me join or tail the convoy, my .45 against their machine guns and their many M-16s? That would be a suicide mission. Suicide attacks are for the manipulated, not the manipulators.*

Zaid pulled off the highway and into the next gas station. It was almost noon, and he was approaching Al Ramadi. Though, across the freeway he could see the irrigated fields hugging the Euphrates River, this would be the last town of any size before the long stretch of desert. It was also the last city before the first Syria turn-off—west for Jordan—north for Syria. As he stepped out of his car he felt the stifling heat of the mid-day sun. *Syria or Jordan?*

Like most public gas stations, the line was long, even ninety kilometers west of Baghdad. He would refill his tank and keep the gas can as a reserve. After more than twenty minutes he finally reached the pump and topped off. He then parked and went in to the little store to use the bathroom and get some coffee.

As he stepped out towards his car, he watched a long convoy pass. "Well, now."

Standing next to his car he began to count. He counted six Humvees escorting it. After missing the lead part of the convoy, he still counted twenty-four trucks. He estimated that at least a dozen passed before he began to count. That meant there were somewhere between thirty-six and forty-five trucks in that convoy, spread out more than two kilometers.

Zaid opened the door and climbed back in. He turned the key, pulled out and reentered the freeway.

As he drove, the last trucks in sight but well ahead of him, Zaid reasoned. *That's by far the longest convoy I've seen today.* If Sahar and her family were stranded, certainly it would have taken them some time to catch a ride. And if it took them too long, the shooter would probably have gotten them. This could be the first convoy they reasonably might have caught, and maybe their last. *If they are still alive, they are probably in one of those trucks.*

Zaid smiled as he rubbed his chin and glanced at himself in the rearview mirror. *I no longer must decide. I'll follow this convoy to Syria or to Jordan.*

Sahar sat on a short stack of empty pallets that were pushed against the front wall of the trailer as the truck vibrated its way into the barren desert. Sun beams that illuminated the dust hanging in the still air entered through numerous small holes that penetrated the steel hull around them. However, most of the light that allowed Sahar to see Hadeel as she lay on her back with her arms and legs out to keep balance on the mattress, came up from the gasket-less gap between the doors and the carriage floor. With the light came wheel noise. Dalia lay on her side next to her younger sister holding her head up and countering the continuous vibration with her arms. Other than her brother and a few foreign truck drivers, nobody knew where she and her girls were. That thought made Sahar feel safer that she had since before the Americans arrived. Though it was hot, loud and dirty in the back of the truck, Sahar slept better than she had in weeks.

Mahmood, in the front seat did his best to look casual, though his darting eyes and constant fidgeting worked against his best effort. *So much could still go wrong.*

About an hour after crossing the Euphrates River just outside of Ramadi, the convoy took the exit heading north. Zaid grinned as he followed, "Syria."

Hours later, Mahmood wished that Sahar and girls could enjoy the sunset as the dust in the cloudless sky transformed the blue into an intense shade of orange, the trucks slowed to a near stop. Mahmood stuck his head out the window to enjoy the sounds of the breeze, the trucks and generators that wafted out into the peaceful desert evening. Remaining in their column, the lead truck followed the lead Humvee to a fuel point the US Army set up for military vehicles and the trucks they escorted, six hundred meters off the main road. There were no plants to hide the sentry posts—bulldozed berms with sandbags arranged to support firing positions and reinforced roofs—that popped up from the dirt every couple hundred meters apart, protecting the fuel point. Along with fuel, a makeshift rest area, complete with an air-conditioned tent, provided a respite among the flat desert scene.

As the first trucks fueled, the long line came to a halt. Admiring the beauty of the sun's last rays, Mahmood got out of the truck and stretched his legs and shoulders as he walked to the back and opened the door.

"How is everyone doing?" he asked.

The transition from the buzz of rubber on asphalt to the bumpy ride of the gravel road woke the three stowaways. They blinked in the light that greeted them as Mahmood pulled the door open.

"Where are we?" Sahar asked.

"We are driving along the Euphrates River probably about a third of the way between Al Ramadi and the Syria border."

"What time is it?"

"7:40; The sun is setting."

"Any problems?" Sahar inquired.

"None. And this convoy is expecting to drive tonight. At day break we should be at the crossing, *Insha'Allah*."

"Mommy, I have to go bathroom," Dee Dee said.

"Can she?" Sahar asked.

"I don't think that's wise. Nobody is expecting to see young girls here. I'll go find a bucket."

"Shut the door. I like the fresh air, but I want to take no chances. Oh, and can you see if the driver has a flashlight, it is completely dark back here."

276

"I'll be back as soon as I can with the bucket and hopefully a light."

With Sahar and the girls confined to the darkness but on their way to safety, the truck lurched forward.

Not yet dark, Zaid was cruising along the highway. The convoy was beginning to slow. He saw the military fuel point and watched up ahead as the first of the long line of trucks followed the lead Humvee off the pavement and onto a gravel road leading off into the desert to their fuel pumps. He changed lanes and began looking at his passenger side mirror at the cab of each truck as he passed them. He noticed that each truck had a single occupant, the driver. They all looked foreign to him. Then he remembered the shooter's words, "Bulgarian drivers."

He continued driving and glancing, making his way up toward the middle of the convoy. Another dozen and he would be past them, as the first dozen had already left the highway. Then with three trucks left before he would have the road to himself he saw a truck with two drivers. He looked in his mirror again, this time focusing on the passenger. The passenger was wearing a hat. *Could it be?*

Up ahead in the right lane a Humvee was stopped, directing the trucks off the road. As Zaid passed he looked back at his target truck and counted the trucks in front of it. "Truck fourteen," he said aloud.

The convoy off the freeway behind him, he rubbed his face and drove down the road. He smiled and his heart beat rapidly. "I think that was Mahmood." *Now what?* "What would the shooter do?" he asked himself.

The truck lurched forward a few feet at a time as the convoy passed through the hot fuel operation. Even though the drivers didn't leave the vehicle or shut down their engines, even with six pumps, it still took a while to fill so many large tanks.

Sahar heard their truck accept the nozzle, the sound of the fuel shoot into the tank, and then the clanking of the metal as they were disconnected. The truck lurched forward again. This time it moved a couple hundred meters before it came to another stop. A moment later, the back opened. The earlier pale light had turned into the dark of night. Mahmood lifted a plastic bucket into the back of the truck. The bucket was about a third full of water and the sloshing from the bucket's motion sent a small cascade over the side and onto the wood floor. Then Mahmood turned a flashlight on and shined it. "Here you go," he said as he handed it to Dalia who had moved forward to reach it.

Mahmood could see an American soldier heading their way down the line of idling trucks, shining a light into the cab of each as a new unit was assuming the escort duty.

"I've got to hurry; the convoy will start again soon."

Mahmood closed the back of the truck, and quickly took his place in the cab. The soldiers, one on each side of the truck approached and the one on the driver's side asked, "Why two drivers?"

The driver did not understand, but Mahmood did. Mahmood answered in broken English, "I drove in, but my truck destroyed," Mahmood said in his broken English as he illustrated an explosion with his hands. "I ride to bring new one."

The American nodded and tapped on the driver's door, "Have a good night, gentlemen," as they continued their way down the line.

Twenty minutes later a new lead Humvee pulled out followed by the long line of trucks.

Zaid was sipping coffee from a paper cup looking up at the stars and listening to the lonely whip of the breeze when a helicopter passed over him. Thirty kilometers up the road he sat on the edge of the parking lot leaning back against the bumper of his sedan waiting for the convoy.

Night convoys were like day convoys, except the darkness gave the Americans a clear advantage. Zaid knew that the pilots were peering down wearing night vision goggles and infrared sensors, the flight crew may not spot the IEDs that were already in place, but he knew that they caught many insurgents as they used the night hours to plant them. The helicopter headed up the road.

An hour later, a long column of headlights appearing from the vanishing point on the flat horizon approached. The sound muted by distance, it trailed the action by several seconds. As they passed in front of him, Zaid counted the Humvees and the trucks.

There were six Humvees and thirty-eight trucks. *This must be the right convoy.* He smiled. "There's my truck," he said out loud as he counted the fourteenth one. "That meant that from the rear, my target would be the twenty-fifth truck."

He climbed back into his car. A moment later he was heading onto the highway, the tail of the convoy in sight, but a half-kilometer away.

CHAPTER 91

Mahmood stretched and yawned as the rising sun revealed the traffic congestion along the last dozen kilometers of road leading to the border crossing. The driver looked over at him and grinned. The crossing, between the towns of Al Qa'im, Iraq and Al Bukamal, Syria had recently reopened after decades of distrust between the two countries—the road was not yet even paved where it crossed the border itself. Only about a kilometer west of the Euphrates River, it was not nearly as busy as the border crossing two hundred kilometers to the west which was a more direct route between Baghdad and Damascus. However, it's resources were nevertheless overwhelmed by the slow but steady stream of refugees that flowed from Iraq to Syria and the modest quantity of supplies and the stealthy Islamic freedom fighters that traversed from Syria into Iraq.

The convoy glided to a complete stop, then it began a long series of starts and stops, jolting unevenly like a millipede walking on a sticky surface. The trucks crept through the town of small masonry or concrete buildings surrounded by walls enclosing yards adorned with scattered clumps of untidy bushes.

The grid of dirt and gravel roads of the neighborhoods gave way to farms, groves and underbrush that hugged the last half-kilometer to the river. A few starts and stops past a masonry double-arch that spanned the road marking the southern entrance to Al Qa'im, the wall behind a house was only a few meters from the road. Mahmood nodded to the driver, as he handed him a twenty-dollar bill.

"*Shukren*," Mahmood thanked the driver as he began to open the passenger door.

"*Ma'salama*," replied the driver, gripping the welcome windfall.

Mahmood glanced at his watch, it was almost 6:00 a.m., as he hopped down, closed the door, and took a couple steps, the back of the truck moved forward to meet him. When the truck stopped again, he opened it.

"Let's go. And bring everything with us," Mahmood instructed.

"Some water?" Sahar asked.

"Yes, but leave some for the driver."

They hurried out, first the girls, then the suitcases and the bucket, then Sahar.

Dalia dumped the bucket into a ditch beside the road before handing it to Mahmood who tossed it back in the truck and pulled the door shut. Picking up their belongings, they moved quickly toward the edge of town, only a dozen steps away.

Zaid inched forward. Directly behind a Humvee he moved to the far right and during the frequent stops he leaned way over attempting to see if anything was happening up ahead that he would want to know about. From his turret, the gunner intently watched him.

Sahar and her family walked a block into the sleepy neighborhood of small houses spaced on large lots. The town was cluttered with litter, old vehicles and parts of farm equipment. Nobody was out, but underfed dogs with flies around their eyes sat in the first sunrays lazily waiting for the day to come to them. Most of the dogs showed no interest in the trespassers, though a young one barked enthusiastically.

Sahar and Mahmood carried the four bags, Dalia carried the bags of food and a partial box of water bottles while Hadeel carried two more water bottles. Hadeel smiled at her mom while trying to point at the barking puppy.

Sahar reassured her with a smile.

The weight of their loads slowed the group down. They began traveling in a pattern: walk twenty-five paces, rest. Walk twenty-five paces, rest.

"Let's go that way," Sahar suggested nodding down a road heading northwest, parallel to the highway.

As Zaid reached the edge of town, he glanced down the first side road. The main road was backed up with vehicles intending to cross the border. He had no intention of crossing into Syria, so he turned right and negotiated his way across a rutted, neglected path across a ditch to a better-defined side road. He wanted to get in front of the fourteenth truck.

The gunner watched the silver Avalon turn off the road and away from the convoy. *He must be a local. It must suck to live here—kind of a nice car though.* Without looking down, he picked up his water bottle that was hanging near his swivel seat and chugged a few gulps. Zaid gone and forgotten, he turned his attention to the driver of the next car that was now directly behind him.

CHAPTER *92*

After about twenty minutes, they were a few blocks from the road and now fully into the town. Sahar told her brother, "Mahmood, I don't think we should be carrying all this stuff everywhere."

She stopped and readjusted her load. The others did the same. "How about if the girls and I stop here and watch the bags? You can run up ahead and see where we need to go."

He looked around, "Okay. But let's get you out of the middle of the road first."

Sahar nodded, looking around.

"Over there," suggested Mahmood, pointing to what appeared to be a vacant lot in the middle of the block ahead of them on the other side of the gravel road. It had a house to the left, one to the right and one behind it, with concrete block walls that stood just under two meters tall separating the lots.

"That'll do. Come on girls."

Crossing the road into the morning shadows, they passed the first house and as they got to the wall they were pleased to see a tree stood providing some shade in the corner along the south and east walls. Dirt, weeds and scrubby bushes were scattered around the wheel tracks, which made it look like people often used the space to turn around. A few steps into the lot they decided that the best place to wait was in the shade provided by the south wall and the tree. The house to the north stood just beyond the wall enclosing that yard about fifteen meters away. Sahar spread out the bags, and took the box of bottles from Dalia. Hadeel dropped her bottles as she took a seat on one of the suitcases. "We'll be fine here. Please don't get lost."

"Don't worry, I won't." Mahmood said over his shoulder as he crossed the street again and continued north, the direction they all had been walking. He turned left at the first intersection, two houses down.

Rounding the corner of the first street, Zaid turned north. *Doesn't anyone live in this town?* he wondered. He drove along slowly scanning the distance ahead of him until he saw a man walking alone. The man was wearing a bright red hat. *Could that be Mahmood?* He watched him until the man turned a corner two blocks in front of him. Zaid's heart raced. Not taking his eyes off the location he turned, Zaid drove forward.

The two girls were leaning against the south wall with Sahar kneeling facing them wiping Dee Dee's face with a damp cloth when they heard the hum of a car engine and the sound of the wheels crushing pebbles against the dirt as it glided along the gravel-covered road.

Sahar looked over and saw the familiar silver Toyota appear from behind the wall. As it passed them she could see the side of Zaid's face as he stared straight ahead. Sahar's heart leapt to her throat.

"Shhhh!" Sahar quietly instructed.

The girls froze.

"God please don't let him see us," she whispered to herself. "Mahmood," she silently swallowed.

Looking at their mother's face, the girls didn't move a muscle, not even to divert their eyes. The three remained statues until the car's rear bumper disappeared down the road behind the house in front of the girls.

"Mom, who is that?" Dalia asked, trembling.

"Dalia, that's a very dangerous man. We must find a safer place to hide."

"What about Uncle Mahmood?" asked Dee Dee.

"Your uncle can take care of himself." She assured the frightened girl, but biting her lip she silently prayed, *Mahmood, look behind you.* She stood up and ran to the house on the north side of the vacant lot.

Mahmood walked deeper into the town through the quiet neighborhood. Houses on both sides of the street, he walked in the general direction the convoy drove—toward the border crossing—he hoped. The main road, still backed-up by the long convoy, curved toward the left, so it was now a couple blocks away. Mahmood could hear the trucks lumbering along, and sometimes, between the houses and walls, he could even see them. After a block, he looked back and saw a car's front bumper emerge from around the corner from where he had come.

Zaid was driving slowly, rounding the corner. Without a doubt, the man in front of him was wearing a hat like the one that the passenger had on in the truck. *That's him.*

He continued to coast on the power of his idling engine.

Sahar, ran to the wall in front of her and poked her head around to look down the street to see the car turn left. As soon as it disappeared she frantically ran to the suitcase with their passports in it and pulled them out, pulling up her pant leg and tucking them into sock. Then she glanced over at another suitcase and tore into it. She pulled out another envelope that was hidden in a shoe. She handed it to Dalia, "Dalia, put this in your sock."

"Mom?" responded Dalia.

"Put it in your sock, wrap it around your ankle and then pull up your sock."

"What is it?"

"Dalia. Do as I tell you and do it now. It's our money."

Dalia grabbed the envelope and did as her mother requested.

"Now help me with the bags."

Sahar grabbed the two largest and dragged them toward the east wall, placing one up against the wall she stood on it to look over. The top of the wall was covered with broken glass embedded into the concrete.

She looked down and saw a section of pipe lying in a small trash heap to her left. "Dalia, hand me that pipe."

Dalia complied.

Sahar took the pipe, "Now girls, stand back."

Balancing on the suitcase Sahar began to hit the larger pieces of glass that broke off and went flying. She flattened an area as best as she quickly could, dropped the pipe and said, "Dalia, hand me that small suitcase."

Dalia handed her the large briefcase that served as a suitcase. Sahar grabbed it and balanced it on the wall. She held herself up with her arms on the small suitcase and scanned the yard in front of her. There were lots of bushes and tall, dry grass along with two big trees between her and the house that was centered on the lot at least twenty meters away. To her right was a barbed wire fence with many bushes on both sides separating one yard from the next, and another wall separating the yard from the one on her left. The place looked very neglected, if not abandoned.

"Now hand me Dee Dee." Surprised, but obedient, Dalia picked up her younger sister under the armpits and held her up to her mother who was balancing as she twisted around to receive her. As Sahar tried to lift Hadeel high enough to put her on the briefcase, it fell into the yard on the other side of the wall.

Holding her daughter as she balanced on a suitcase, Sahar held Hadeel and told her, "Dee Dee, I am going to put you up on the wall. Watch where you place your feet; avoid the long sharp glass. Okay darling?"

"Yes, mommy."

Sahar gathered her strength, and she lifted her daughter until her arms were fully extended. Hadeel placed her feet on the wall and began to support her own weight. "Good girl," her mom praised her.

Standing on her toes, looking past her daughter's ankles Sahar said, "Now, do you see that pile of dirt?"

"Mom, that's cow poop."

"Jump on it."

Hadeel took a deep breath and a leap of faith. She landed on it and fell forward rolling to the ground.

"Good girl. Are you okay?"

"Yes, mommy," Dee Dee answered in a small, frightened voice.

Sahar turned around, "Dalia, hand me the other two bags." Dalia did so, one at a time.

Sahar dropped them over the wall.

"Now the water."

When everything was on the other side of the wall except the suitcase she was standing on and Dalia, Sahar looked at her daughter and said, "Now you."

On her side of the wall, Hadeel collected the water bottles that had slid out of the box and moved them out of the way.

Sahar got down off the suitcase and allowed Dalia to climb up.

"Be careful not to cut yourself on the glass," her mom instructed. Sahar stood by and held up her hand to catch her if she fell as Dalia got one knee up on the wall, and while carefully balancing, got her other foot up beside it.

"Good girl. Now jump."

Dalia hesitated before she bent her knees and hopped down to the other side.

"I'm Okay, mom," Dalia quietly said as she got up and wiped herself off.

Sahar looked around and found an old rope half buried in the ground. Pushing away some old, dirt-filled tin cans and some other trash she managed to dislodge it and she quickly tied one end of the rope to the large suitcase's handle, then she tossed the free end over the wall.

Sahar re-positioned the suitcase against the wall and stood on it, again looking over at her daughters.

"Dalia grab the biggest suitcase over there and lean it against the wall below me. Then stand on it. When I get on top of the wall, we'll pull the last suitcase over. Understand?"

"Yes, mom," then she pushed a suitcase against the wall and stepped up onto it.

"Okay, grab the end of the rope I just tossed over and don't let go of it," Sahar ordered her older daughter.

Gripping it as if holding on meant life and dropping it meant death, Dalia held on.

Sahar pulled herself up onto the wall, cutting her arm as she did so. Once on top she stood up. Dalia helped her mother keep her balance as she turned around and as she leaned down to grab the rope. Together they pulled the suitcase up the wall, Sahar grabbing the handle and placing it on the wall between her feet when it was close enough.

"Okay, Dalia, now move out of the way."

Sahar dropped the bag onto the ground next to the suitcase where Dalia had stood. Then she jumped down onto the dry manure pile. The predominant sound was the high-pitched tone of insects beating their wings to keep cool. They didn't see or hear anyone from the neglected garden behind the large house.

Sahar turned toward Dalia and Hadeel and said, "I'm so proud of you two."

Mahmood looked back over his shoulder and confirmed that he was being followed. Fighting the urge to look again he continued to walk towards a dry creek bed that at the end of the road ahead of him. *That ditch may be an opportunity for me to get some ground between me and that car.*

Zaid saw the man's face and smiled broadly as he determined that the man in the red hat was, without a doubt, Sahar's brother.

Sitting together facing the wall they had scaled, Hadeel gently touched her mom on the hand, seeing her arm she said, "Mommy, you're bleeding."

Sahar looked down and nodded. "Dalia, can you look for a clean t-shirt we can use as a bandage?" Then she looked back at Hadeel, "It's alright, my little sweetie. I'll be alright."

Dalia pulled one of Mahmood's t-shirts out of a suitcase, "Here mom, will this work?"

Sahar nodded. "That'll work. Dee Dee darling, please hand mommy that open bottle of water. Thank you, honey."

Mahmood strode down the small hill and across the sandy creek bed and up the other side. When he reached the top of the rise on the other side of the ditch, he saw a man approaching a few blocks ahead on a road that curved to the west. He began to head toward him.

Approaching the ditch Zaid pulled over and turned off the engine. The gravel road only paralleled the wash, the only bridge crossing it was the main high way, which was still completely occupied by trucks. Before he got out, he took inventory of items he may need: sunglasses, pistol, extra clip of ammo, knife, and money. He put on his holster and realized that although it was getting hot, he had to also wear his jacket to hide his gun. He reached into the back seat to retrieve it. Then he looked in his rearview mirror at his tired eyes, stubby-face and uncombed hair. As he was leaving the car, he flashed a smile to the man in the mirror. *In this miserable town, this is the perfect disguise.*

Mahmood saw Zaid descending the slope on the other side of the ravine. It would be more difficult to see him now that they were both on foot, but it also took Zaid's speed advantage away. Mahmood continued walking toward man.

"Mom, is that too tight?"
"No Dalia, that's good."
With a new bandage around her cut arm, she hugged her two girls. Then she poured a little water over her blouse sleeve and rubbed it with her other hand to cleanse the blood-stain before she pulled her sleeve back down over her cut to her wrist.

"Excuse me, *hajji*, can you help me?" asked Mahmood.
The man, who appeared to be a farmer by his well-worn robe and white, grey and black *keffiyeh* that he wore wrapped around his head and face, was carrying a small bag.

288

"I'm headed to the border, but the man behind me, please don't look now, is following me. His name is Zaid Mohsen, he wants to kill my sister—"

"Can you point toward the border? We need to convince Zaid that I am only asking directions."

The farmer put his bag down and pointed west, parallel with the main road, and then he swept his hand to the north towards the border crossing.

Zaid stopped. He watched Mahmood converse with a man. *He's probably asking directions.* Mahmood must have left his sister and her girls somewhere along the way and went on ahead to find the border crossing. Zaid's eyes stayed on the two men. That would mean Sahar is somewhere between where I first saw him, and where I left the highway. *I must have driven right by them.*

His eyes narrowed and he scolded himself for not realizing this earlier.

"Now keep going the direction you were headed until the road "T-s", then turn left to the highway. I'll tell the police that you will lead him toward the border and the police and I will come and pick him up along this road," the farmer said pointing down the road they were on. "The border is at least two kilometers, but we will meet you before you get there."

The two men turned to face each other, "Do you see him?" asked Mahmood as the man glanced past Mahmood in the direction he had been heading.

"Yes, I see him. I'll give a full description to the police. Be careful."

"Thank you, *hajji.* I'm in your debt forever. Please remember to tell the police that this man has already killed several people, so they should take caution."

The two men shook hands before each continued the way they had been heading. The farmer continued walking towards Zaid.

Zaid looked back down the road where Mahmood continued walking at a brisk pace. Zaid stepped forward, matching Mahmood stride for stride. As Zaid and the farmer passed each other the farmer greeted him, *"Salam Alekum."*

Zaid automatically replied, *"Alekum Salam,"* as he kept walking. Zaid followed Mahmood straight down the road.

After passing Zaid, the man turned right and ran toward the highway. Sweating and out of breath, the farmer flung open the police station door and began explaining the developing situation to the officer working the desk.

Zaid looked at his watch, 7:45. Then he focused on Mahmood walking ahead in the distance. *It was still at least a half hour walk to the border,* he guessed. He touched his hidden pistol with his finger, then fingered his car keys. After another pause, he turned around and set off retracing his path back to his car.

The police SUV with two officers and the farmer aboard pulled out from the station heading in the direction of the border.

Ten minutes later, Zaid passed the irrigation ditch. Five minutes after that he climbed into his car and made a U-turn to look for the quarry he had missed while following Mahmood.

Using a broken pallet she found as a step-ladder, Sahar peered back over the wall. The neighborhood was beginning to become more lively. She could hear a few cars driving nearby and she heard a voice from the other side of the house. *No one should find us here except Mahmood,* she assessed. She curled her lips at the thought of Zaid tailing him. "God, please take care of my brother."

If Zaid was here, the amin could be here too. With that thought, her heart raced. She looked down at her girls who were quietly sitting next to each other in the shade of the trees next to their meager pile of belongings. Then she looked toward the house.

"Girls, stay here, stay quiet and stay out of sight. I'm going around this house to look around."

She gave Hadeel a little hug and ran her hand across Dalia's face giving them both a reassuring smile. Then she walked off toward the house and around its side. The girls returned to quietly playing with a small stick and a couple rocks that were serving as make-shift dolls.

The SUV caught up to Mahmood, but the police did not see Zaid. They drove on ahead, made three right turns and came back to the road before turning left. Mahmood saw them pass, but resisted making any sign of recognition. There were only a few other people walking along the road, but as a precaution, as the police drove back up the road, the farmer carefully looked at each pedestrian's face.

Zaid made the right turn onto the road he left when he first saw Mahmood. Driving as slowly as he did the first time but coming from the opposite direction, he immediately saw the empty lot with the tree on it between houses that he did not notice before. He pulled the car over and turned off the engine.

As she silently crept her way around the house, Sahar nearly stumbled over a meter-long section of steel pipe. She picked it up and leaned it against the north side of house.

On the third pass, the police stopped and Mahmood walked up to their van. The farmer opened the door and called to him, "Get in, he isn't following you anymore."

Mahmood immediately jumped in, "My sister and nieces are in grave danger!" We need to get back to where I left my sister." The police SUV, pulled out into the road as Mahmood described where they got off the highway, and where Sahar and the girls were waiting.

Zaid crossed the street, trying to be quiet as his shoes struck the graveled road. As he entered it, he surveyed the small empty lot.

CHAPTER 93

Crouched behind a small clump of bushes at the front of the house, Sahar could not see anyone on the silent street. An ant struggled up one side of her face and thorns from the bush dug into her legs, but she dared not move. In the growing heat, she possessed an alertness she had never had before. She noticed that the sound of traffic was not a rumble, but an accumulation of individual motors, though in this case not very many, and not very close; the birds' songs were not random, but held warnings of territorial intruders; and colors held infinite shades and patterns that could be broken down to reveal objects normally hidden in shadows. Strength flooded her and words came unhindered to her mind:

> *Wild eyes and bared teeth*
> *I am a ferocious tigress.*
> *I have no more tears to shed*
> *I have no more fear of death*
> *In my mind my life is already over*
> *but I am very much alive.*
> *I will strike to protect my children*
> *and to avenge my husband's death.*

A short distance away, Zaid pulled off his sunglasses and slid them in his jacket pocket, squinting in the shade of the tree where Sahar and the girls had been sitting earlier. He quietly slithered along the east wall where he began to hear the faint voices of two young girls. His heart pounded harder. He stopped to ensure his breathing was not loud enough to alert his prey. As Zaid continued, he carefully watched where he placed his feet to avoid unnecessary noise. He noticed some recently scraped shards of glass on the ground. He quietly placed his hands on the top of the wall and slowly pulled himself up. Raising his head, he brought his feet up to begin to climb so he could peer over.

The girls looked up at the feint sound in front of them and screamed as the dark mustached face with the eyes of hatred appeared from the other side of the wall.

Dalia pulled Hadeel to her feet and towed her around the tree in the direction their mother had left. Dalia stumbled, but recovered as she heard Zaid curse.

Glass cut into Zaid' chest and arms as he vaulted over the top of the wall.

At the sound of her daughters screaming, thorns cutting across her face, the tigress leapt from her hiding place amongst the small thicket of bushes.

Rushing toward the corner of the house she nearly collided with her two girls who were racing from the back yard, "Run! Don't stop!" Sahar gasped as they flew past her.

Sahar grabbed the pipe that she had almost tripped over only a few minutes before, raised it above her head and swung it with all her might as Zaid rounded the corner. He bent over and stumbled backward bringing his hands to his head, but he did not fall. Before he could recover, Sahar raised the pipe above her head and smashed it into his head a second time. The sound was a loud thud, like a stick hitting a stone wall. Zaid yelped with pain but he staggered towards Sahar, swinging his arm to force her to step back. Instead she lunged forward this time hitting him solidly in the chest.

"Bastard, die," she shrieked.

Cursing and holding his head Zaid fell backward.

She stabbed at him as if the pipe were a bayonet, but he kicked at her and knocked it out of her hand. In a time-extended daze, she watched it roll out of reach.

Hate flashed through her as Zaid's face gathered into a vicious snarl. But unlike all the times back in the ministry, Sahar did not look away. She matched the hate in his eyes with fire of her own.

She kicked at his groin as he struggled to get up off his back. He swatted back with his large hand striking her thigh. She painfully fell to the ground. Thin and light, she sprang back up. He also tried to stand, but stumbled.

Blood streamed down his face. As he made it to his knees he reached into his jacket. Seeing the gun in his shoulder holster she remembered the *amin*. Glancing away from Zaid toward the screams of her fleeing girls her heart jumped, *Where's the amin?* Fear replaced her boldness.

The snap that had held Zaid's weapon in during the preceding fight prevented him from accessing it now. He could not move his arm enough nor grip the handle well enough to get the pistol out. He watched Sahar run away and out of his sight.

The police SUV pulled up to the lot where Mahmood last saw Sahar and the girls. "There's his car," Mahmood shouted, as he leapt out the door, the two policemen and the farmer following closely.

Sahar pursued her screaming girls down the street. Several residents stepped through their doorways or looked out the window alerted by the blood curdling sound of the terrified girls.

Zaid struggled to his feet, stumbled and fell and then got up again. He retreated, back towards the wall blood seeping from his head and through his raggedly torn shirt and jacket. As he stepped up on the palette to climb over the wall, he saw the men empty out of the police van. With desperation and fear diminishing his immobility he dropped back down and scrambled through a hole in the barbed-wire fence and into the next yard and out of sight through a thicket of bushes.

Hearing his nieces' scream, Mahmood shouted, "Over there."

He began to run down the road that he unintentionally led Zaid down, but this time he turned right instead of left. One of the two policemen ran after him.

The other policeman ran through the vacant lot toward the shard-glass topped wall, his AK-47 with a 30-round magazine pointed forward, he yelled to the farmer, "Keep an eye on that car."

Zaid crawled, clawed and dashed his way as quickly as he could through the adjacent yard, and then down a road that lead to a palm grove which he crossed into an undeveloped section of Euphrates River valley underbrush. His chest ached with the expansion of his heaving lungs; he blindly stumbled, bouncing off obstacles, each one smacking him, like a man running a gauntlet of a primitive tribe, taking blows from every direction unable to fight back.

Sprinting down the road behind them, Sahar caught her daughters at the first intersection and managed to calm them enough to stop screaming when they saw Mahmood sprinting toward them, the policeman right behind him.

Sahar spun around and looked up the road she and her girls just came down, half expecting to see the *amin* aiming a rifle at them.

Seeing her terrified gaze, the policeman immediately ran up the street in the direction she looked, searching for whoever it was that she was fleeing.

Trying to catch her breath, Sahar reached over and hugged her brother, "Thank God, you're safe."

Her brother hugged her back. Then they gathered the two girls into their arms, and they all began crying.

Zaid worked his way through the thicket and emerged onto some fields. To his left, he could see the Euphrates, only a hundred meters away. Sensing he had a considerable lead over his pursuers, Zaid slowed his pace. Finding a puddle left by a leaking irrigation pipe, he painfully removed his jacket, and his shirts and washed. Using his t-shirt as a washcloth, he soothed his aching head, the constant pain reduced to a barely tolerable hammering as he slowly gained control of his breathing. He washed away the blood, the stickers, the mud and cow manure as best he could. He tried to comb his hair with his fingers and straighten his crumpled clothes by pressing them with moist hands and tucking in his shirt. He had his wallet, pistol, extra clip of ammo, knife, and money. In addition to losing his opportunity to kill Sahar, he had lost his sunglasses—and his car.

As presentable as he was going to be able to become, he headed out of the thickets and across a fallow field in the direction of the highway. He could not stay there, if he hurried, maybe he could stow away in the back of a truck heading to Baghdad before the police could organize their search.

CHAPTER 94

Later that afternoon, Detective Laith from the Ministry of Interior again walked into Minister Hassan's office.

"It seems, minister, that your man, Zaid Mohsen has been spotted."

Hassan stood up and stepped out from behind his desk. He stopped when he stood beside it, "He never did show up in Basra as he was directed."

"No, he didn't, did he? In fact, he was spotted this morning in a very different part of the country."

"Oh?" replied the minister.

"Yes. He was in the border town of Al Qa'im."

"Al Qa'im? Near Syria?" Asked the minister, his inflection higher than normal.

"Yes. It seems that he drove there to kill a former employee of yours. A dentist."

The minister shook his head, "Is she alright?"

"Zaid apparently had to leave quite quickly. He forgot to take his car with him. He left it illegally parked."

The minister did not reply.

The detective watched the minister look down to the floor, his mouth was twisted. "Well, minister, if you will excuse me, I have work to do. I trust you will inform me if, and when you see Zaid. Won't you?"

"Why yes, of course," he replied looking up.

"I'll show myself out." Without hesitation, the detective turned and departed.

The minister stood quietly next to his desk.

Yes, 'she' is alright, the detective thought to himself, after he dropped his business card on the minister's secretary's desk and entered the hallway.

CHAPTER 95

Zaid was missing for a week. Every day Reem stared out of the sixth-floor *Kimadia* office wishing she had the courage to throw herself out the window. Yet, every day he did not show, she gained hope that he had not been successful in killing her best friend or her family.

But the day arrived that brought Zaid with it. From a coworker, Reem received instructions to go to Al Dabbash. As Reem stared at the message, she did not frown, she did not cry. Her pulse remained constant. As she boarded the shuttle that morning, Reem had no feelings at all.

CHAPTER 96

The shooter stepped through Zaid's office door without invitation as Zaid sat in his office at *Kimadia 13* at Al Dabbash. Zaid immediately understood that his status had fallen.

Standing up, he quickly waved his hand for his guest to have a seat.

"Why thank you, Zaid, you are so kind," mocked the shooter as he accepted.

Zaid sat back down. "The minister would like to know whether you are still in contact with the former DG of *Kimadia*, Doctor Jassem."

"Yes. In fact, I have been in contact with him within the last two days," he said boastfully.

"Well then, the minister wishes me to inquire about your loyalties."

The hair on the back of Zaid's neck stood up. He struggled to suppress the look of surprise. Then he tried to disguise his reaction as shifting to lean back in his seat.

"My loyalties?" Zaid stammered, completely unprepared for the inquiry.

The shooter, looking at him replied, "I don't think you understand. Perhaps a short story would make my message exceptionally clear."

The shooter leaned forward, "As you know, the Americans will soon depart the Ministry of Health and the CPA will soon disband completely shortly after that. Their departure will leave complete authority in the hands of," imitating the minister, "What do they call it? 'The Interim Iraqi Government.'"

The shooter grinned, "But who are these interim people anyway?" he asked, raising his eyebrows.

"Each of them is either a fool risking his, or her, life for the idea that Iraq will someday be another American satellite, or a power monger positioning himself and biding his time for an opportunity to cut the throats of his opposition and rule Iraq with power and fear."

The shooter paused, then pronounced each word with precision, "Power and fear that can hold a hundred different enemies peacefully together by being an enemy to them all, simply by being the most powerful, and the most feared."

The shooter stood up and then sat down on the corner of Zaid's desk. Looking down at Zaid, he continued, "An obvious observation about this little American exhibition of intervention is that the more the coalition removes itself, the less significant they become. And the more power they leave in the hands of their model government, the hungrier those vying for the real power become. It almost makes you wonder what the Americans hoped to accomplish here in Iraq in the first place. Did they really expect the Iraqi people to embrace the ideals of the satanic West?"

Zaid just stared at him.

He continued, "Sure, let the people dye their fingers purple as they cast ballots and rejoice at a new-found power. Did they really expect the men loyal to Islam to lay down their swords and acquiesce without a fight?"

The shooter smiled as he looked at his audience, who sat motionless, intently listening.

"No, of course not. We won't. And the interesting thing about all this is the irony. Thanks to the Americans, we are free. Free for each true Iraqi patriot to put his hat in the ring and place his vote for his future, but not with purple ink, but with the blood that runs through his veins.

"Free, unlike we ever could have been under the paranoid and watchful eyes of Saddam. Now we can decide where we will fight and kill and die like men. Now for the first time in decades, we are free to place our interests at the head of the Iraqi people, so Iraq will once again be great. And with the Americans soon to be out of the picture, we can influence how we will be great again.

"Saddam was a rat caught in a hole." The shooter spat on the floor as he continued. "He is not a man. He sits rotting in an American cell, blubbering like a frightened child to the sons of Satan. Yes, we owe the Americans that. They freed us from Saddam, so we can make a country great for God. Yes, God guided the Americans here for this purpose, and as he guides them away now, it is now our purpose to make Iraq a country that will sing His praise, and squash the infidels that dare desecrate our lands."

Zaid, who still thought of Saddam as the model of manhood and the icon of his homeland finally realized that the shooter was no longer a Saddam loyalist, and no longer his friend. An instant later he also realized just how precarious his own survival had become. The shooter truly was there to see, quite literally, where Zaid's loyalties lie. Until this moment, so caught up in his own game of vengeance he failed to realize that the Saddam loyalists, such as Jassem, and fundamentalists, such as the minister, were no longer coconspirators against the same evil. Zaid was amazed at how blind he had been.

Zaid swallowed hard. He had only one opportunity to show the loyalty he thought the shooter was demanding. Knowing his life depended upon how convincingly he spoke, he looked the *amin* in the eye and spoke with authority. "I am loyal to the new Iraq, the great Iraq of Mohammad; I am with you, my friend."

"Very good, my friend," the shooter said in a formal tone. He pulled an envelope from his pocket and extended it to Zaid.

"Please, on behalf of the minister, ensure that Jassem, and Jassem alone, is the next person to read this message."

Zaid stood. "I will, my brother," placing his hand over his heart.

"Until we meet again, my brother," replied the shooter, then he stood, turned and left Zaid's office.

Zaid sat back down, aware of the sweat running down from his forehead.

Looking at the envelope in his hand, he understood what had just happened. Both he and the shooter were now just messengers and instead of one insurgency there was a multi-faceted war.

There were too many sides, too many men and women pitting their armies of believers against one another. How could anyone win? It would just be blood and more blood spilling. All Iraqis could hope to do was what he had just done—choose the option that will allow survival for the moment.

But now Zaid was stuck holding an envelope, not knowing its contents. Did the minister want Jassem to join him? Was this an invitation? Or, more likely, was it a declaration that *Kimadia* is now Minister Hassan's? *With Kimadia goes the money, with the money goes the power.* If Zaid delivered this to Jassem, what would Jassem think? That he was not loyal to him? What would Jassem do? Kill him? And what if Zaid didn't deliver it? Surely then, the shooter would kill him.

There was no way out. He was trapped. And having been the cat in similar situations many times before, he knew that there was no safe exit for the mouse.

Zaid sat staring at the envelope. Finally, Reem's knock pulled his eyes from his death sentence. He quickly glanced at her closed lips and her hardened eyes. Gaining courage from the sight of the woman who so desperately feared him, he stood up and tucked the envelope into his pants pocket, "Come with me," he directed as he walked past Reem out of the office.

Zaid, with Reem trailing behind him, left the building and approached the *Kimadia* van that was parked outside the office entrance in the nearly empty parking lot. Earlier in the day, Zaid had claimed the van to replace his own *stolen* car. He pulled out his keys, unlocked the door, and got in. He reached over to unlock the passenger door, allowing Reem to climb in.

Zaid noticed that Reem's face remained oddly blank of all color and expression.

As he began to turn the key, Zaid looked through the windshield and saw the shooter standing next to the corner of the building holding an open cell phone in his hand. Not wearing his sunglasses, the shooter looked directly into Zaid's eyes. Time seemed to skip every other beat, reducing everything to slow motion. As the engine of his van came to life, Zaid watched the shooter break eye contact and look down at his cell phone. The shooter pressed a number while ducking behind the warehouse wall.

As slow as the shooter's actions seemed, Zaid had no time for any action of his own. He and Reem were instantly absorbed in an infernal blast of violence, fire and twisted metal.

After the roar of the explosion subsided and debris ceased to shower from the sky, the *shooter* stepped out from behind his shelter and walked over to the entrance to the Administration wing of the *Kimadia* Warehouse Complex 13 at Al Dabbash. He lit a cigarette and leaned against the wall, watching the black smoke waft into the clear, blue sky from the burning pile of twisted wreckage.

As the workers scrambled from the offices and the warehouses to see what had happened, the shooter stepped forward and stood on the sidewalk next to the shattered van. He casually exhaled some smoke letting it drift up before he spoke in a loud, authoritative voice, "*Kimadia* and all the people who work in it now belong to Minister Hassan. Now put out this fire."

He exhaled a long drag and flicked the butt much farther away than necessary towards Zaid's and Reem's disfigured, smoldering remains. Then he turned and as he walked, he cleaned his boots by wiping them gently over a small puddle before stomping them authoritatively on the concrete walkway leading to the entrance door. Then without looking around again, he entered the office building. The clomping of his boots echoing in the corridor announced his newly appointed authority over *Kimadia,* Iraq's Medical Logistics Company.

CHAPTER 97

Damascus, Syria; August 2004

A short distance from the two-room house on the edge of a vacant lot in the crowded immigrant neighborhood in Damascus, Sahar was scrounging the market for vegetables. Old men and women sat on blankets with baskets in front of them, most shaded by tarps that flapped in the breeze above them. Kids ran about as shoppers browsed and workers of all ages hauled baskets, boxes and arms full of anything and everything that supply and demand could provide to a destitute population.

Sahar was wearing a robe and a *hijab,* looking at beans with tired eyes when she heard a voice behind her, "Doctor Sahar?"

She turned around to find her *abaia*-wearing coworker from the ministry, "Wasan."

"I am so glad to see you," Wasan said placing her basket on the paved ground and putting her hand over her heart as she stopped in front of Sahar. "Everyone thought you were de—. I'm so glad to see you're alive."

"Wasan, what are you doing here?"

"Oh, Sahar, the ministry's a disaster. All of Baghdad is a disaster. The new minister fired all the old DG's and has replaced them all with *Da'was*. Most of the Christians have left, many of the *Sunnis* too. I received a letter that told me to leave or die and my family and I fled here to Syria. It's because of our work with the CPA." Wasan paused looking closely at Sahar's face.

"Everyone thinks Zaid killed you. How did you manage?"

Sahar just shook her head.

"Before he left, before you left, Joe was worried sick about you. We even tried to find where you were hiding, but we couldn't find you."

Sahar was stunned. "What?" she managed to ask.

"Yes, he begged *Sayid* Sattar to help him. We snuck out to find you without the other Americans even knowing about it."

"No. He didn't." Sahar said definitively.

"Yes, he did, I went with him, Hamid, Sattar and I. When we got back, Mister Banks found out Joe went. He was so angry that Joe wasn't even allowed to come back to the ministry. He sent Joe back to the United States the very next day with Newborne. They left more than a month before the other Americans."

"But Reem, she said..." Sahar couldn't say it without tearing up.

"Yes, I was so sorry to hear about your good friend," said Wasan shaking her head.

Sahar did not answer. She looked distant.

Wasan continued talking, "At least she died quickly, I'm sure she did not suffer, she probably never even knew she died."

Sahar began to tremble—almost losing her balance.

Wasan quickly put her arm around Sahar's waist. "Please Sahar, let's sit down," she said as she guided her to a chair under an umbrella.

With Sahar safely seated in the shade, Wasan rushed over to a crowded counter to get Sahar something to drink.

Sahar's mind was spinning. No clear thoughts took shape.

A few minutes later Wasan sat down across from her and placed a couple of plastic bottles of water on the table.

Looking at her distressed friend, she said, "Sahar, I can't tell you how relieved I am to find you here and safe. Joe will be so glad to hear that."

"How will he know?"

"I'll email him. He thinks you're dead. He feels responsible for your death. He's very angry at Mister Banks."

Sahar nodded, but couldn't focus on her friend's words. She looked back at the crowded market and then at Wasan. "Next week my brother will return to Baghdad."

Wasan excitedly responded, "No, he mustn't, it isn't safe."

"He must. We will be evicted from our house next month if we don't find any more money. We can't get a good job here. My dental credentials aren't respected, so Mahmood and I are just two more unskilled laborers competing with other Iraqi, Palestinian, and Lebanese refugees for whatever work we can find. He must sell my house and gather some things."

"He can't go. Others have moved into your house; you have no more things. He mustn't go, it's suicide."

"But others have gone back and I've seen them return."

"But Doctor Sahar, you and your family are not like the others. You were being hunted because they say you were a traitor. If you were to show up, they would be afraid that you'd inspire others. The minister's hit man would capture Mahmood and torture him to find you and then they'd come here and they'd kill you and your children. You are too well known to them. He can't go back. You are safe now because everyone thinks that Zaid killed you."

"Well then, what can I do?"

"I don't know. But we are going to try to get to Sweden."

"Sweden? They won't take us. I already went to their embassy."

"They won't take us as immigrants right now either, but once there, they are letting people stay."

"But how will you get there?"

Wasan leaned forward and spoke quietly, "My husband is paying a man to smuggle him in, on a boat. If he can get him there he will go and petition for asylum. Others have done it; we'll do it, too."

Sahar looked at her, she shook her head, "That's too risky. How do you know it isn't a scam? They'll steal thousands of dollars from him. Other stories are worse, they kidnap, enslave, rape or even murder. Once they have your passport and your money, they have your life. I'm a woman with two children and no husband and we don't have the money to buy passage for my brother."

"I understand. But we must try. I'll let you know when I get there. Promise me, don't go back to Iraq."

Sahar hesitated, but then agreed, "I promise. We'll try everything else first, *Insha'Allah*. Good luck, Wasan."

CHAPTER 98
Damascus, Syria; Spring 2005

Her dreams hibernate through the winter cold,
life on hold, awaiting better weather,
under the clouds, look forward not nether.
Her dreams sleep like buds waiting to unfold,
not a hint, not a whisper to behold.
Round, innocent cheeks, soft as a feather,
to restart her life, we wait together.
Risk disappointment, dream big, dream bold!
Sweet girl dream for something worthy of life,
worth the wait, something you have not yet seen,
I'll bear the burden of sadness, your pains,
let me protect you from war's dreadful strife,
when you awake, let your youthful eyes' sheen,
You my girl, enjoy the good that remains.

"Mom, I want to go home."

Hadeel had her hair in a pigtail tied by small strings, ties from bags of walnuts taken from the vegetable market where Mahmood now worked part time. Her clothes were worn thin to the point that washing them rigorously enough to clean them would disintegrate them. Hadeel herself was too thin also.

She pushed up against her mother.

Sahar looked down at her. From the clothesline in the vacant lot, Sahar glanced over at Dalia, who was lazily stretched out across the steps leading inside to their two-room house, her eyes in a book.

Sahar's hair, tightly concealed under her light green scarf, hardly acknowledged the erratic breeze. She licked her finger and wiped a few crumbs away from Hadeel's mouth before she continued to hang the meager laundry across bare metal wires. The sun beat down drying the clothes almost as quickly as she could hang them. Sahar stood so the cool moist cloth was blown against her hands, which along with her face, was her only exposed skin.

How do you tell a child that she no longer has a home?

She gently patted Hadeel on the head.

She and her brother were looking for a place to go. Job opportunities throughout the region required cash up front. Joe and the colonel were trying to help get their immigration package approved for them to enter the United States, but they had already warned her that since she was not an official translator employed by the US Government she did not qualify for any of the special refugee programs. And even if she were, a quota limited those who entered each year.

Sahar looked past her laundry, mesmerized by the sound of flapping clothes and the eerie whine of wind on wire in the crowded neighborhood on the outskirts of the Syrian capital.

The sound was lonely and it fed her sadness. Her constant worry had made her perpetually ill. The hardest part was not enduring their daily, unproductive lives; it was dealing with the uncertainty as to if or when their lives may once again begin.

She swallowed against the dryness in her throat.

"Mom..."

Sahar looked down at her daughter and smiled.

Standing in the sun she thought of Baghdad where for months on end the only clouds were of dust or smoke. She sighed and let her hands drop to her sides; she felt left out to dry, like old laundry flapping on a wire under the merciless sun.

She bent down and hugged Hadeel. The girl buried her face against her mom's neck and shoulder. Sahar held her as tightly as she could.

Leaning back against the door jamb, Dalia turned the page of her book, eager to see if her story would have a happy ending.

PART IV: EPILOGUE
CHAPTER 99
Arizona, United States; Fall 2013

Her ears still ringing, she sat just outside the front door holding the paper so her head did not cast a shadow from the porch light across the written memories; memories that have been in place only slightly longer than the scrawling black ink.

> *The bride sat lovely*
> *in her long, elegant dress,*
> *along with her groom*
> *as if forbidden to move,*
> *on display, together, one.*
>
> *Both can't help but smile*
> *glancing hugs at each other*
> *longing to embrace.*

In the late-night air, she slowly read each word before she leaned back in the white plastic lawn chair atop the red-stained concrete porch.

Nicely dressed men danced,
women sat talking in groups
some dressed in tight skirts
others hidden by burqa's
unheard above loud music.

Look at the couple.
The bride smiles at her man
he nods to the door.

The sound and the shadow of a moth fluttering clumsily around and into the porch lamp distracted her. The agile woman stood up and momentarily stared into the night.

I see his mother,
the groom's mom smiles back at me
our kids together,
want to rush away from us
and finally be alone.

But they must still wait
just a little while longer,
as is our custom.

She deliberately folded the paper thrice, her thin fingers tightly pressing the creases together making it a perfect rectangle. She listened to the small grains of sand and pebbles quietly crunch beneath the thin soles of her sandals as she peacefully strolled across a short path of embedded brick and flat stones. The scent of moisture rose from the short bushes in the small yard planted against the waist-high front wall. She slid the paper into the back pocket of her jeans before she gently caressed the smooth, cool metal of the gate. Rubbing it, she smiled and breathed in the night air. The perfect crescent moon hung just out of reach, seemingly just beyond the leafless branches of the nearest Palo Verde tree.

The buzz of a transformer hummed from its place high on the telephone pole next to the street in the peaceful neighborhood. She removed her *hijab* and shook her head to let her hair fall freely until it dangled loosely on the slender shoulders of her loose-fitting blouse. She absently wrapped the scarf around her hand. Tears came into her eyes as she remembered an emotion from a time so similar, yet so long before.

She tried to cry silently, but feelings from deep within her surfaced. For the first time in so long she could not control herself—soft sobs rose from her chest and overwhelmed her.

She had still been in high school the last time she felt this way. Her fingers lightly traced the faint scars on her face that on occasion still tingled, but always still reminded her of the bomb that exploded outside her classroom window so long ago. She winced when she identified this long forgotten feeling. Her shoulders shook as her mouth formed the Arabic word, *amel*.

For the first time in decades, Sahar was feeling *Hope*.

GLOSSARY

Abaia: common women's clothing in Iraq, a type of robe.

Abbasiin Muslim Empire: The peak development period of Ancient Iraq. Abbasiin refers to the ruling family's clan

Abu: Father of–. Men in Iraq are often referred to "Father of oldest male child's name." If he doesn't have a son, oldest daughter's name. I.e.: Muraad, may be called, "*Abu* Dalia"

Abu Ghraib: the infamous prison because of abuse by both Saddam regime and coalition troops, means, "Father of mischief."

Alfred Lord Tennyson: Poet who wrote "Charge of the Light Brigade"

AK-47: Kalashnikov rifle.

Al Dabbash: A neighborhood in Baghdad where a *Kimadia* Warehouse #13 is located. The warehouse was commonly called, "Al Dabbash."

Alekum Salam: Literally, Peace be with you. Response to "*Salam Alekum*," to return a greeting like "Hello" or "Good Morning"

Allah Ahkbar: Phrase: "God is Great"

Allah Wiyaak: Phrase: "God be with you"

AMEDD: Army Medical Department

Amel: Hope; Amel is also a Girl's name.

Amin: A security force officer or NCO who enforced political allegiance to Saddam and the Regime

Arrais: A respectful way to address a superior much higher in the pecking order, like a top Government official, like one of the Hussein's similar to "your Grace" also, means "President" in Arabic language

Aeusteth: A respectful way to address a professional man. Literally professor, used for teacher, doctor, engineer, high ranking official.

Asad: Lion

Ba'ath: The name of the political party in Iraq before the invasion

Ba'athists: Members of the *Ba'ath* party

Bayan: A formal statement issued by the Iraqi Government about the War against Iraq televised nightly. A situation report for the public.

Brazili: A slang word for common vehicles in Iraq. They are often Volkswagens imported from South America.

Biryani: a rice and lamb dish

Burqa': A gown or cloak with a cloth mask that covers a woman's body and face, except her eyes.

CERP: Command Emergency Relief Program. Funds available to US Army Brigades to quickly improve local infrastructure at the Commander's discretion.

Chador: A gown or cloak that covers entire body, but does not cover the eyes or face.

Chai: hot tea often served at meetings and in social settings, often served scalding hot in small ceramic cups.

Chador: An outfit worn by some women of the Middle East that does not cover the face.

Chalawi: kidney. Some Iraqi women may call a valued friend, their "chalawi" to indicate that the other is an important part of herself.

CONUS: An acronym meaning, Continental United States (does not include Hawaii or Alaska)

CPA: Coalition Provisional Authority was the sovereign government of Iraq after replacing ORHA and before the Interim Iraqi Government was empowered.

Da'wa Party: A religious and political organization that practices a fundamentalist *Shi'a* Islam faith

Dishdasha: traditional white colored robes worn by men in the Middle East

DG: Acronym for Director General (Responsible person for a staff in a ministry

DOD: Department of Defense.

Ent'ethree wa Shufee: Phrase: "Wait and see"

Estifaf: The morning ritual where Iraqis would declare their allegiance to the Ba'ath party.

E-5: Enlisted rank–fifth level. The first sergeant level of NCO ranks. Represented by three chevron stripes.

FAR: Acronym for Federal Acquisition Regulation. A set of rules the US Federal Government uses to reduce corruption in spending Government money. It also frustrates many users because these rules also reduce efficiency and effectiveness.

Habibati: An affectionate name for a husband to call his wife; *Dear*, or *Honey*.

Habibti: An affectionate name for a wife to call her husband; *Dear*, or *Honey*.

Hajji: A man who has completed his visit to Mecca as part of the Haj. Informally refers to a man.

Hatherat: Your Excellency, very respectful salutation. Common way for written messages or letters to begin.

HFPA: Health Facility Planning Agency. An organization within the AMEDD that performs life cycle management for the Army's medical facilities.

Hijia: A common and informal reference for an old woman. Female equivalent to Hajji.

Humvee: An army all-purpose combat vehicle, replaced the jeep.

HVAC: Heating, Ventilating and Air Conditioning.

Ibn Al Sina: Name of hospital located in Baghdad's Green zone

IED: Improvised Explosive Devise

Insha'Allah: "God willing"

Interim Iraqi Government: The first government formed by elected Iraqis tasked to transition Iraq from CPA rule to a democracy

Kababs: lamb or chicken prepared over open fire

Keffiyeh: The headscarf worn by men to help protect from the sun

Khala: Aunt. A term of endearment to informally refer to an older female.

Kimadia: The state-owned medical logistics company in Iraq.

LAN: Local Area Network (information technology)

Landstuhl: Landstuhl, Germany. The location of a US Army Medical Center used to support the Theater by receiving medical evacuees.

LZ: Landing Zone, usually for helicopters.

Maskoof: a type of fish; a fancy fish dish especially prepared for important visitors.

Ma'salama: Good bye

MOH: Ministry of Health

MRE: Meal Ready to Eat (US Army pre-prepared food intended for field consumption)

Mukhabarat: Iraqi Intelligence Agency (prior to invasion)

Muknasa: A traditional, short handled broom

Naqiset Aqil Wa Deen: Phrase: "Women deficient in mind and faith"

NCO: Non-Commissioned Officer (Corporal and sergeant ranks in the Army, Enlisted leadership ranks.)

NGO: Non-Governmental Organization

OIC: Officer in Charge. A military officer in a position of authority or responsibility over a department, or organization, but not a commander.

ORHA: Office of Reconstruction and Humanitarian Assistance. In Iraq, was replaced by the CPA.

Pajero: A Japanese SUV made by Mitsubishi.

PMO: Project Management Office, can also mean Program Management office. Part of the CPA assigned the task of managing the construction aspects of the reconstruction effort.

Qadisya Saddam: The Iraqi name for the First Persian Gulf war: Not the war the Americans call the Persian Gulf War, but the war between Iraq and Iran

ROTC: Reserve Officer Training Corps

Sadrya: School clothes worn by girls. Usually grey or blue skirt and a white Blouse without long sleeves.

Salam Alekum: Literally means, "Peace upon you." Often, the first person beginning the greeting of "Hello" or "Good morning"

Sayid: Mister. A common, respectful way to address a man. Married or unmarried.

Sayida: Misses (Mrs.), A common, respectful way to address a married woman.

SECDEF: Secretary of Defense. The appointed cabinet member who provides the civilian leadership that runs and oversees the Pentagon.

Section Five Khadimiah: A center run by the Saddam's son, Qusay Hussein's Security Forces located in the Baghdad District of *Khadimiah* where, before the invasion, high value political prisoners were brought for severe interrogation.

Seidi: A respectful way to address a superior with whom you report to like a boss within an office or organization; "Chief"

Sha'ab District of Baghdad: A densely populated neighborhood in Baghdad

Shi'a: A branch of the Islam faith. The majority of Iraqis are *Shi'a.* Saddam, was a *Sunni,* though Saddam did not seem to discriminate against Shi'a.

Shukren: "Thank you"

Siadat Al-Wazeer: Literally, Wazeer means "Minister." A respectful way to address a superior much higher in the pecking order, like a minister or one of the Hussein's. Could sound like, "Your Excellency."

Siit: A respectful way to address a professional woman, like a student to a teacher.

Sunni: A branch of the Islam faith. Saddam Hussein was *Sunni.*

Super: A slang word for high quality sedans in Iraq

Supplemental: Common name for the Congressional Supplemental of fall 2003, to fund the reconstruction effort in Iraq

S&A: Supervision and Administration: Costs added on to a Govt. managed construction project to cover the Owner project management and Quality Assurance expenses.

SUV: Suburban Utility Vehicle

Swinging-Richard: A term (perhaps outdated) used to refer to the individual soldiers in a formation.

Um: Mother of–. Women in Iraq are often referred to "Mother of oldest male child's name." If she doesn't have a son, oldest daughter's name. I.e.: Sahar, may be called, "*Um* Dalia"

Udw: A common rank in the *Ba'ath* Party

Udw Amil: A junior rank in the *Ba'ath* Party

Udw Far'a: One of the top four levels of the Baath Party

Udw Firqah: One of the top four levels of the Baath Party

Udw Qutriyya: One of the top four levels of the Baath Party

Udw Shu'bah: One of the top four levels of the Baath Party

Um Al Ma'arik: The war the Americans call the Gulf War. Iraqi party members referred to it as *Um* Al Ma'arik, whereas common Iraqis referred to it as the Kuwait War.

ABOUT THE AUTHOR

jMike Olson is a retired army officer. He was a lieutenant colonel assigned to the Coalition Provisional Authority in Baghdad to work as the senior advisor to the director general of engineering of the Iraqi Ministry of Health. While there, he worked with a staff of forty Iraqi architects, engineers and healthcare providers. Their main task was to establish the reconstruction program for the Iraqi healthcare system.

This is his first novel.

ACKNOWLEDGMENTS

I want to thank the many people who helped guide me: My wife and daughter, my mother, sisters and brother, Kathy, especially for the cover design, Charlie and Marcy. Two editors: Brenda Velasco and Mary Martha Miles, both provided me technical advice and guidance. Two authors: Mark Haskell Smith, who taught my UCLA writer's workshop group and Robert Vaughan, who coached me along with other amateur writers during a week on the Alabama coast. University of Maryland writing professor, Peter Porosky, from whom my wife and I took an introductory novel writing class together, ironically, shortly before my second deployment to Iraq.

Ravi, John and Jeannie; many of my friends: John and Susan L., and her book club in Tucson. And Marwa, Dale, Usama, Andrea and Kerry, Helen, Charse, both Mark B's., Dave G. and Dave K., and Kees, who all took the time to read my draft(s) and provide me with their opinions. Special thanks to Maysaa, who ensured that my references to the culture, the religion, and the geography were not inaccurate, incorrect or offensive. Also, Simran, for helping me with the jmikeolson pages on social media as we began to publicize.

Of course, my army peers and CPA MOH team members and the people who inspired me: the Iraqis from the MOH, who I hesitate to mention by name as I don't know what ramifications could occur since for many of them, safety is not yet at hand.

I'd also like to thank people such as Sawsan Aldawodi and her colleagues of the International Refugee Assistance Project, who help people such as Sahar negotiate the immigration system enabling them to seek a peaceful and safe place to live their lives.

Although I dedicate this book to my father, I would also like to honor the victims of the war; people of many ages, nationalities, religions and races harmed, wounded or killed in the violence, which, sadly, continues to rage and spread—and tragically probably will for many years to come—with or without US.

Made in the USA
San Bernardino, CA
12 May 2017